Praise for *Servitude*

"Another home-run by one of the best authors in the business. Costi Gurgu is a genius."

— Robert J. Sawyer, Hugo Award-winning author of *The Oppenheimer Alternative*

"Even with a recursive narrative structure that regularly flashes back to account for how this ordeal came about, the novel keeps the momentum rolling along, and readers will feel chained to what happens next."

— Kirkus Reviews

TITLES BY COSTI GURGU

RecipeArium

The Lighthouse at the End of the World (RO only)

The Glass Plague (RO only)

SERVITUDE

Costi Gurgu

Limited cover edition (October-November 2022)

Kult Books

This is a work of fiction. All of the characters, organizations, and events portrayed in this novel are either products of the author's imagination or are used fictitiously.

SERVITUDE

www.costigurgu.com

A Kult Book
Published by KULT Books
Toronto, ON, Canada

ISBN (Trade Paperback): 978-1-7386593-0-2
ISBN (e-book): 978-1-7386593-1-9

Firts edition—limited cover edition: October 2022
Second edition : Novermber 2022

Cover design by Superpixel Design
Book design by Superpixel Design
Printed in the United States of America

ACKNOWLEDGMENTS

First comes my wife, Vali, who gave greatly of herself to
see this novel come to life. That including reading, giving
advice, and giving up her husband during long stretches
of writing time.

Also, my extraordinary editors—Suzanne Church and
Marg Gilks—worked quite hard on this novel. Their help
was crucial in turning it into the novel you now hold.

As always, my beta readers have been an amazing help.
In alphabetical order: Emanuel Grigoras and Peter Halasz.

If no person releases the condemned debtor by paying the debt, the creditor can either sell him as a slave or put him to death. This is the nexum.

(ANCIENT ROMAN LAW)

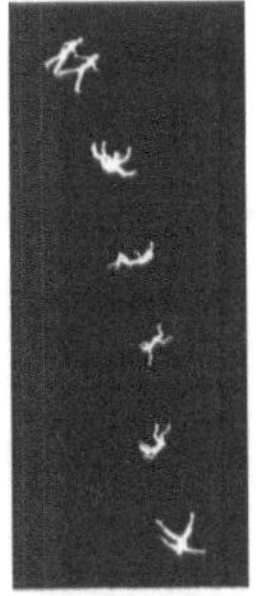

BLAKE AND THE SNAKE

Blake averted his eyes, then forced himself to look.

The man was visibly in shock. His wife, her head draped in a hijab, tightly gripped her young daughter. Silent sobs shook the girl's body.

A mercenary stood in front of them, his features concealed by a black mask. He scanned an inflamed barcode tattooed on the man's arm, checked the result against a list, and pushed the man to his left. The man stumbled in that direction and fell. The woman tried to follow, her eyes wide with fear, but the mercenary grabbed her, pulled her sleeve up, and scanned her tattoo. Then he checked the woman's barcode against the same list and signaled that she remove her hijab.

The man struggled to his feet and shuffled forward, trying to help his woman, but the mercenary Tasered him. The man fell, thrashing, to the dirt. Two other mercenaries picked up the flopping man and dragged him away like a sack of potatoes. The daughter began shrieking.

With the man safely dispatched, the mercenary yanked off the woman's hijab, checked her against the image on his list, and sent her in a different direction. She lowered her eyes, her chin trembling, and reached for the little girl. The mercenary snatched up the child and shoved her in a third direction, away from both parents. The child screamed louder and higher. When the woman tried to grab her daughter, other mercenaries forced her away.

The image pulled back, revealing a camp where mercenaries

surrounded hundreds of frightened people, scanning their tattoos and directing them in different directions. A caption on the lower right side of the screen read *LIVE, OCTOBER 17th, 2046: BRITISH SERVITUDE EXCHANGE—LONDON CAMP, BRIXTON. SECOND MONTH OF THE FREEDOM ACT PROGRAM.*

Blake Frye broke away from the huge screen in the shop window. Every day, London turned uglier. Luckily, he only had to endure this long weekend vacation, and they'd go home tomorrow. Although lately, the surety of *tomorrow* felt uncertain.

He looked up Oxford Street toward Marble Arch, involuntarily scanning every person walking up and down the street. Blake had expected more foot traffic. In the not-so-long-ago past, Oxford Street had been the most celebrated shopping artery in the world. Now misery lingered here. The scars of the war with the Second Ottoman Empire endured in just cleaned but not rebuilt devastation. That dour change represented everything he witnessed about London in the news from every source, with slave camps, disregard for human rights, demolished streets, and extreme poverty. Most of the stores on the famous commercial boulevard now sported bars on their windows and drone surveillance. Some of the stores had disappeared, leaving behind dark and deserted buildings. Other stores pumped up their appeal with colorful decorations and moving electronic facades. What survived of the street commerce now aggressively attracted the few people with money to spend. But few of the shoppers out and about wore rich garments; most appeared as poor and broken as pedestrians in New York.

Blake's guilt pressed deeply against his spirit. He felt as though he was taking advantage of their misery, surrounded by so many gaunt faces with little to eat, or a safe place to live. As a rare member of the tourist demographic, he stood out, a braggart who shone like a beacon of lost prosperity.

He turned his head to check on Isa. His wife crouched near a young homeless boy, deep in conversation. The two shared a brief laugh. His joyful wife, always finding some tiny glimmer of positivity. Blake hated this vacation. London was supposed to be a rich and cosmopolitan city, with an intense cultural and artistic community. But he felt oppressed in this new London, an odd reaction for a police officer. It was partly due to his own actions, of falsely displaying his family's wealth while 95 percent of the world's population wanted for so much. He hated that the key sentiment was *falsely*, and even worse, he hated to be forced to boast. He couldn't even tell Isa that he loathed being in London, as this trip had been his idea, his gift for their anniversary.

He sighed. He'd been embracing the word hate too frequently. Although, truth be told, he'd been thrown out of his regular lifestyle, normalizing the feeling of…not *hateful*; more like *unsettled*.

Blake turned his back on Isa and activated his wristband. He selected the DRUGS folder on its holo-display, then double-tapped on one of the names and dragged the icon of a pill being showed from the display onto his skin, where it melted and disappeared. Then he turned around and saw Isa approaching.

"Come on, HoneyB." Isa grabbed his hand and dragged him to the homeless kid. "This is Tom. He'd been on the streets for three weeks now. Came to London from Manchester to find his girlfriend. He guesses that she was taken by the Corp Police while in London with her parents, a month ago."

Blake nodded. "Hey, Tom." The kid frowned at him. Blake knew he looked tough and aggressive and supposed his expression came from his years on the police force, though Isa had a different theory.

The kid gathered a rucksack to his chest in a protective gesture and said, "You bacon." Not a question. More like a statement made in anger and disappointment.

"I'm sorry, me what?" Blake said.

"You one of them. Your lady's too good fa'you."

"No, Tom," Isa intervened. "He's not Corp Police. We're Americans."

"You think that when Corp Police gets there, in America, the pigs'll side with the population? Bacon always root for power, for money. Not for people." Tom pulled his possessions even closer and turned his back to them.

Blake watched the kid for a few seconds. What could he

say? Even if the Corp Police did come to the States—a move that Blake would fight against—the possibility had no relevance to a homeless boy in London.

With a loud sigh, Isa pulled Blake away. They crossed the road and stopped. Blake pulled out his tourist map of the city.

"That there's Oxford Circus," Isa said, pointing to a circular intersection in front of them. "Famous in the nineteenth century for having circus elephants brought from Oxford performing their dancing routine right in the center, while lions and tigers guarded them from all around, ensuring every bystander paid attention to the elephants and the acrobats."

He smiled, relieved. His wife could breeze through a war zone and still find a source of light and goodness. "You should be hired as a guide, love." He gave her a quick hug. "The cities would be much more interesting in your version of history."

They walked into Oxford Circus and slowed to get their bearings.

Isa asked, "Where to now?"

Blake checked his watch—11:36 a.m. It was getting closer to his secret meeting hour. They weren't far from the meeting place, but he didn't want to risk Isa's safety.

"I'm done with Oxford Street, Circus, and whatever other Oxford stuff they have," he said. "If we take what's-its-name… Regent Street, down that way, we're going to Piccadilly Circus. Can't wait to hear its story."

"Well, mister, it seems English people loved their circuses…"

Suddenly, dozens of men in black suits filled Oxford Circus and Oxford Street, boxing the whole area in with vans bearing the BSX (British Servitude Exchange) logo. They demanded papers from anyone with Middle Eastern features, and detained every homeless person. Many people ran or tried to hide, but agents ran after them, and violence erupted on every corner. Blake cursed under his breath, angry with himself for missing the signs before the Corp Police raid.

Isa turned, searching around, then gasped when she saw two men in black catch up with Tom and smash the kid into a wall. As they threw him to the ground and cuffed him, Blake took

Isa's hand and squeezed, ready to stop her from going after Tom. Instead, she remained motionless, apparently frozen in panic.

Like two prehistoric insects caught in amber, the two American tourists stood amidst the onslaught, useless, helpless, fearful. Blake hated his helplessness as he waited for the nightmare to finish. He scanned the area for escape routes, his body tensed and ready for action. But Isa touched Blake's chin and eased his head down. He assumed he was frowning, looking ready to pounce on the Corp Police. He met her eyes, trying to smile reassuringly.

Within five minutes, the street was almost empty, only well-dressed white people walking calmly past, as though they had witnessed similar scenes before. The Corp Police had retreated, their vans filled with potential subjects for servitude. It left a bitter taste in Blake's mouth.

He walked faster down Regent Street, Isa barely keeping up with him.

"Sweetie, it's all right. Let's—"

"Since when do they grab homeless people off the streets?"

"I don't know. It doesn't say anything in the Freedom Act with respect to the categories of people they can arrest."

"And that's the brilliance of the Act: no limitations. They can define and redefine what turns a person into property, into a slave!" Blake said loudly enough that people stared, or crossed the street to avoided them.

He took a breath. He had to remember where he was. *Oppressive London. Not home.* This city wasn't a democracy anymore. His rights, Isa's rights, could be lifted at any time and no one would ever know, or care, back home in the States. He stopped, waiting for Isa to catch up. Despite her obvious fear, she met the entire situation with a brave face. He focused on her jacket, staring at the pink buttons. She remained silent. He counted the buttons, first up, then down. Two of them were turned in the wrong direction. He twisted them, trying to align them. They simply slipped back into their rogue positions.

She placed a hand on his hands and squeezed gently.

He swallowed hard, looked at her face, and took a deep

breath. Their fear slowly lifted. The danger was gone for now. They could return home. He smiled and tried once more to rearrange the wayward buttons.

"There," he said. "I'm sorry."

"Don't be, sweetie." She kissed him lightly, and smiled. "It's not your fault."

"I wanted to come here."

"And I agreed. I mean, if we don't see London today, in a couple of years it may be too late. Now, let's go to Piccadilly Circus and see what makes it so special."

http://undergroundpress.res

A text box overlaps the player's interface:

Here at Underground Press Resistance we're happy to present a documentary smuggled from the claws of tyranny. It's been produced by a brave team, most of whom have already paid dearly for their courage and professionalism. But the truth has to be shouted to the whole world. We need to know so that we can resist.

Play.

The title popped up on the screen: *Debt Hunters. Producer: Isabella Frye.*

The screen filled with a world map from twenty-five years ago. The United States stretched from Canada's border to Mexico's border and from the Atlantic to Pacific. The European Union encompassed all of Europe minus the UK.

A voice-over narrated: *We all know when all this began and how we got from the Great Division to the Last Depression.*

A chronological bar appeared at the bottom of the map. At the starting point on the left it said *Great Division (2019)*, then it stretched to a midpoint marked *Last Depression (2044)*, and ended at a point marked with an *X (Present)*. The picture of President Donald Trump overlapped the map and then floated to the left and positioned itself above the starting point. More pictures appeared along the timeline: San Francisco's Golden Gate Bridge being blown to bits; Chinese troops taking down the American flag at the Hawaii State Legislature; dead children, skeletal from starvation, covered in snow in the shadow of the Empire State Building.

An arrow slid along the chronological bar from left to the right, the map changing alongside it, and the voice-over continuing its narration: *We've been through our second civil war, secession, reunification, Russian and Chinese invasions, dismantling of the European Union and rebirth of the Eastern Bloc, the first nuclear war at the hands of the Second Ottoman Empire, so…*

The arrow reached the X at the end of the chronological bar. The map looked completely different from what it had at the start. The USA was diminished, and the eastern half of Europe was covered in a red swath that stretched from Switzerland to Canada and over Alaska. It was labeled with the Russian insignia.

…the Last Depression was bound to happen in a world torn by wars over resources and irreconcilable differences between East and West. What followed — the total collapse of the global market, the drastic climactic changes that brought the death of billions in a span of only three years and the sudden disappearance of vast resources on a continental scale…all that forced the search for a different social and political system, for different management of the remaining resources, and a new direction in international trade. All this was expected.

The map was replaced by footage of mass graves with hundreds of corpses stacked on top of each other, followed by footage of camps with worse conditions than those in the Nazi death camps.

And yet, HOW did we get from the Last Depression to today's rotten reality? How did we solve humanity's greatest crisis by bringing back slavery?

– Extract from the documentary *Debt Hunters*. Producer: Isabella Frye

Blake's coffee was getting cold. He was a coffee man, through and through. He drank coffee in the morning to wake up, during the day to stay alert, and sometimes at night to relax and get some shut eye. Obviously, this need for java was all in his mind, but what wasn't? What wasn't in his mind was out of his control, so he didn't care about anything else.

His favorite joke with his brother had been about the two soldiers: Soldier One asked Soldier Two, "Do you know what went through our lieutenant's head?"

"No," replied Soldier Two. "What?"

"A bullet this big!" said Soldier One.

That was back when two brothers could joke about soldiers and laugh. Kids didn't know better. Later, the brave new world made them both aware of war, and of all sorts of atrocities where a bullet through one's brain was most certainly not a joke. The lesson he'd learned from that childhood joke was that nothing else mattered in life but what you had in your head and what you made of the world you lived in. People could be selfish, your health could fail, but your mind was the only thing keeping you afloat, through the good times and the bad.

Blake came back to the present, and glanced at Isa. She was absorbed in browsing through the apps on her wristband, probably downloading some new ones and trying to figure out how they worked. He returned his attention to the news he was watching on the display floating above their tabletop. He took a sip from his coffee, then placed the cup back on the table in the exact spot it had been, turning it so that its handle was on his right-hand side.

The same caption that had appeared in the morning was again superimposed over the horrific images: *BRITISH SER-VITUDE EXCHANGE: LONDON CAMP, BRIXTON, LIVE. England's first slave camp.* There was talk of building a few more camps around London, as the capital was the biggest slave re-source in the country. Most of the immigrants and refugees had arrived here in the last decades. Seventy-five percent of the po-tential servitude subjects were concentrated in London. Some of them were now trying to flee, to escape back to their homelands. But it was already too late for them.

The image pulled back even farther, revealing more of the servitude camp. Tall, electrified fences with guard towers every fifty yards surrounded dozens of long metal structures with small windows.

The demonstration snaked along for several miles. Most of the protesters looked Middle Eastern or Central Asian, and held cardboard signs and banners stretched between metal poles. The slogans repeated, again and again, *NO TO SLAVERY! NO MORE CORP POLICE!*

The protesters marched and shouted on Charing Cross, passing three important targets on their way down to White-hall: the prime minister's residence at 10 Downing Street, the Metropolitan Police headquarters nearby, and the Corp Police headquarters. Corp HQ had been established right next to the Metropolitan Police, probably in an effort to give the force more legitimacy. One head of the protest snake crawled down Charing Cross and another one wound down Regent Street, both moving toward the same targets.

At the Cranbourn intersection, several police cars blocked Charing Cross. One police officer stood behind a car, shouting into a megaphone, "Your protest is illegal. Please stop and go home! Your protest is illegal!"

The snake wavered for a few seconds. The people at the front paused before they turned left and poured down Cran-bourn Street, toward Leicester Square. The energy of the crowd, as those from the back pushed ahead, would not be contained by a barricade.

"Now, that's what I call an anniversary trip," said Isa. "Bad news and an absent-minded husband."

Blake snorted and spilled some coffee. Grinning, he gestured to Isa to give him a minute with the news. She chuckled and grinned in reply. He dabbed at the coffee on his shirt with a napkin, then tucked the used napkin under the edge of his plate. The best choice would be to stop watching the news and enjoy the few moments of false vacation he still had left with his wife. But relaxation and joy seemed unattainable when the entire world was profoundly changing.

And yet, in Leicester Square, one of the few places un-touched by war, life seemed to go on as if nothing had changed.

Blake had heard that London in October could be particularly wet and miserable. Not cold; more like grim and moody. But that Sunday the weather mimicked a late summer day—warm, sunny, and lazy. In Leicester Square, usually bustling with people noises and an entire mélange of aromas wafted past, all slow and pleasant. The sidewalk was perfumed with the scents of hot pies with gravy sauce, and dark ale.

The tranquility felt surreal. Beyond the surface calm, one could see that more than half of the shops had closed down. Fewer people strolled past, and most of those were poorly dressed and grim. The last world economic crisis, the Black Crisis, had left poverty and despair in its wake like no other catastrophe had. It had rightfully been compared to the Black Death that long ago decimated the European continent.

Blake registered a droning sound, almost imperceptible to his ear. Something was coming. Noticing crumbs on the tabletop, he brushed them to the end of the table, swept them into his palm, and poured them onto his empty plate. The faint noise wasn't another anxiety attack. It was more likely his police instincts clicking in, his detective nose warning him that something was wrong.

A jolly shout startled Blake, and he turned to study its source at the next table. He concentrated on keeping his expression calm and friendly. Isa had told him that her friends often considered him brooding and too intense. He'd laughed, but knew she spoke the truth. He'd always looked somewhere between angry and severe, and his black hair and black eyes didn't soften the harshness. How he'd managed to convince sweet, cheerful Isa to date him, let alone marry him, remained a mystery.

At the next table on the quiet patio, an American family eating their breakfast was the only element of chaos. The father wore a colorful shirt and ate hurriedly from a large plate of fried eggs, bacon, fries, and beans. His wife struggled to make the two children sit still and eat. The little girl seemed incapable of sitting still, and her brother clearly enjoyed contributing to the mischief.

Blake noticed his wife grinning at the little girl's antics. A deep sadness pressed down on his chest, a familiar emotion whenever thoughts of Isa and children occurred in the same moment.

Oblivious to his sadness, Isa returned her attention to browsing through the holo-display that floated above her wristband. Eventually she selected the Lipgloss app. Her face appeared on the display as if it were in a mirror. She looked younger than her thirty-seven years. Her curly walnut hair and her olive complexion helped, but most of all it was her eyes. Blake brushed away a curl that was falling again and again across her eyes. She smiled, and that warmed him. Isa's appetite for life and her joyful nature shone in her eyes, keeping her appearance young. She zoomed in on her mouth and chose a pink tone from the color palette sidebar. She spread it on the image of her lips, smoothing it with her fingers. The pink appeared on her real lips.

The anchorman continued his report, grabbing Blake's attention once more. *"The clashes around a 'rampant refugee crisis' have turned more and more violent, threatening the peace on the streets of an already battered and impoverished London."*

Blake sighed and tugged at his shirt to straighten it. He then checked every button to ensure they were all dutifully aligned. Order kept him sane and functional. Order and patterns of behavior. He noticed that Isa had left some food on her plate. Several green peas, shreds of dark orange carrots, and some crust crumbles had tried to escape her chicken pie but were stuck in the leaked white sauce. He pulled her plate near him and arranged the remnants on her plate into order by color. Between adjustments, he glanced at the screen, listening to the bleak news.

"Really, HoneyB, you find the news more attractive than your gorgeous, pregnant missus?"

Blake looked up, surprised. "Missus" was a term she'd picked up while in London, finding it so wonderfully antiquated that she couldn't stop herself from slipping it into every conversation. Blake hesitated. He pushed back her organized plate of food. "What was that word, after gorgeous?"

Isa slid an open pregnancy test app across the table's display. Studying the numbers next to colors, Blake couldn't hide his surprise at his wife's initiative. What had gotten into her? "Missus?" She grinned, her eyes wide and filled with pleasure.

Blake picked up the pregnancy test and transferred it to his wristband.

The demonstration flowed uninterrupted down Cranbourn Street, avoiding the police cars. The officers looked frustrated at the new route. Some of them spoke frantically into their wristbands, probably trying to coordinate their efforts with colleagues.

A few people wearing black masks and leather jackets suddenly emerged onto Cranbourn Street. They were all white, their forearms covered in tattoos. Almost in unison, they yelled, "Go home! Go home!" Then they threw stones at the protesters.

Like a muscle reflex, the mass of protesters swelled and swallowed whole the masked men, like a hungry beast feeding as it snaked toward the final kill. There were no more stones, no more counterprotest shouts to weaken the demonstration's own chants.

In front of them, at the intersection with Coventry Street, new police cars announced their presence with sirens.

Again, the leaders at the head of the snake maneuvered almost instantly and the huge mass of people overflowed down Bear Street, while the rest of the mob continued toward Leicester Square.

Blake moved the pregnancy test app from the random place on his wristband's desktop to the next empty spot where he stored his apps, all neatly organized in columns. Only then did he open the test.

He sucked in a shocked breath. If the test was a prank, it was a very cruel one. Isa would never joke about something this important. It wasn't in her character. Not to mention that the whole cycle of pregnancy attempts and failures had been harder on her than on him.

"Is this for real?" he asked, unable to look at her.

After two seconds of silence, he glanced up at her. Isa gave a final touch to her digital lips and collapsed the holo-display, cheeks rosy, eyes bright, grinning with delight. Blake looked back at the pregnancy test, checked the numbers again, and then the ID. Isa's number. The results were hers.

"Oh my god! We're really going to have a baby?"

She squealed, rose from her chair like a toy on springs, and jumped into his arms. He hugged her and looked over her shoulder to hide his tears. With his upcoming meeting, tears could derail his plan. How…

"All the failed IVF…" He fought to keep his voice steady. "The doctors, they said…" *Do. Not. Cry.* "I thought you were being foolish when you insisted on trying one more time."

"I know. I couldn't believe it myself! I told you I had a feeling that we needed one last try, B."

"I love you so much!" He held her close for one more minute.

Slowly, Isa detached herself from his arms and sat back in her chair. "Can you hear that, B?"

"What, love?"

"In the air, like a constant noise, like a…"

"Like a mass of people chanting and shouting," Blake said automatically, and his face slid back into his professional expression. "Yes, I've been hearing it for some time now. I believe it's getting closer."

Leicester Square was insanely small for a demonstration, altogether the wrong shape for a mass gathering. Plus, the location had no political relevance. More likely, the thousands of noisy demonstrators were on their way to a more appropriate location, like the nearby Trafalgar Square.

She drained her lemonade. "Let's finish here and leave."

Blake had ten minutes before the meeting. "I think it's one of those protests against the Freedom Act. Maybe they'll go around." He couldn't send her back to their nearby hotel, not alone on the streets of London during massive social upheaval.

"Freedom Act." She snorted.

Blake leaned across the table, kissed her, and faltered, aware of the three men in dark gray suits and identical sunglasses approaching the café's patio. The trio looked official and somehow sinister as they walked with purpose directly toward them. Blake glimpsed a gun under a jacket. He straightened in his chair.

Isa said, "Immediately after we get back home, we…" She trailed off as the gray-suited men closed the distance.

Blake touched his wristband and pressed a number on the keypad. Almost instantly, the display showed Blake's digital police badge: *DPA – Digital Police Assistant*. The three men were close now. Blake whispered into his wristband, "Record video. Send to Captain Moore. Alert the American embassy."

Extra police cars stopped a short distance from Leicester Square and blocked the intersection of Swiss Court and Leicester Street. The additional vehicles were visibly trying to box in the demonstration and prevent the mob from reaching Downing Street. But a multi-mile snake cannot be contained.

The mass of hundreds of thousands of people wavered, undecided, when they saw the new barricade dozens of yards ahead. People pushed on, from the middle, from the sides, and even from the back. The streets were too narrow to allow the mass of people to maneuver easily, and pressure points began to overload. Individuals had to keep moving to protect themselves from being forced through shop windows. The leaders recognized the danger and immediately looked for an escape. They had to reach their destination before the action and violence erupted.

The largest portion of the snake made another left down the west part of Leicester Square. The right side of the column didn't have room to turn, and couldn't halt their forward motion, so they continued advancing, straight for the police cars.

A dense throng of people poured down the east side of Leicester Square. The shops secured their doors and windows. Patrons on patios ran, trying to stay safely ahead of the chanting mob. Tranquility turned to panic as those caught in the wrong place at the wrong time fled.

After ordering his DPA to monitor and record, Blake touched an option on the sidebar—*Invisible Display*—and the holo-display above his wrist vanished.

The three men passed Blake and Isa and stopped in front of the American family's table. The mother pulled the little girl close. She rose from her chair, turned to leave, but another trio of gray-suited men entered the patio from the adjacent hotel; now there were six.

One of them said to the parents, "Mr. and Mrs. Miller, we're the British Corp Police. Under the Freedom Act, your debt title has been transferred from the United States to Marron Investments Corporation in London, as of this morning. We're here to escort you and your family to a Center for Distribution of Work Capital to begin servitude arrangements."

"You can't," said the father. "We're American citizens. We demand to speak to our embassy." He pulled his son away, and tried to retreat into the restaurant.

The gray suits quickly shifted to fully surround the family. "Your embassy is not permitted to intervene," said the leader. "Please follow us."

"No," said the father, sounding more aggressive. He pushed his son toward his wife, and added, "We have rights. We're *Americans*."

"You forfeited your rights when you defaulted on your debts."

The droning sound turned into distinct slogans being shouted by protesters as the mob moved closer. One of the agents checked over his shoulder. He looked more worried than in control.

Two agents grabbed the father by the arms and forced them behind his back. The mother tried to move her daughter to her side so she could pick up her son with her free arm, but two agents snatched both children from her. The remaining two agents quickly pinned her arms behind her back.

"Don't touch my kids!" the mother screamed. "Don't you dare touch them—" One of the agents covered her mouth.

The father tried to break free, but an agent Tasered him. His body spasmed and collapsed. The agents holding him kept his head from hitting the pavement.

Blake pushed back from the table, preparing to stand, but Isa's fingers dug into his arm and kept him seated. Her eyes held his, imploring him to stay out of the conflict. He nodded. *Family first. Remain calm.*

The first protesters reached the market, carrying slogans on banners and signs. Isa inhaled, frightened. She lifted her cell phone and said, "I need to speak to someone from the embassy's security. Yes, I'll hold."

Blake followed the Corp Police squad with his eyes as the men carried their prisoners away. Isa kept her fingers pressed into his arm.

"I'm calling to report the kidnapping of an American family," she said into her phone. "Six thugs saying they're Corp Police forcefully removed an American family—two adults, two children—to sell them into slavery." She listened and replied, "Yes, they said they're American citizens, but the Corp Police said that didn't make a difference, because their debt has been sold from the States to Europe." She glanced at Blake, then continued. "The agents dragged the Americans into the street, toward two black vans. There's a group of protesters here now, and they must have witnessed what happened."

The agents were about halfway to their vans now. Mrs. Miller shouted, "Help! They're kidnapping us!" After catching her breath, she screamed, "Leave my children alone." She continued to fight the agents. One punched her in her ribs, and she collapsed onto the pavement.

As the agent struggled to pull her up, the little boy started screaming. His sister joined in with the ear-splitting, high-pitched shrieks of a small child. The agents had to cover the children's mouths as they dragged the small, wiggling bodies toward the second van.

"Yes," said Isa, "I promise not to interfere, but you must hurry. They're getting away. Their license plates? One moment."

The protesters pointed at the Corp Police. The mob, sensing the injustice, surged toward the men and their vans with a sudden, almost reflexive twist. Protesters flooded Leicester Square.

Blake gauged the distance and determined that the agents wouldn't reach their vans before the mob reached them. The agents carrying the children must have also calculated their predicament, because they dropped the children and sprinted.

Isa released Blake's arm. Red dents marked the places where her fingers had dug into his flesh. She used her phone to take photos of the license plates on the Corp Police vans, and then of the violent scene unfolding in the square.

The mass of protesters engulfed the scuffle with the remaining agents and the American family. Screams and shouts rose, followed by gunshots, breaking glass, and the screech of car tires. Members of the regular police force arrived at the scene, their patrol cars stopping and blocking lateral streets.

Blake exhaled noisily. He rearranged his plate, then set his fork and knife on each side, perfectly vertical, all the while observing the madness in the street, the sudden and total collapse of London's social order. The vacationing couple had landed in the middle of a war, although no one had actually named it as such yet. He looked at Isa. A dagger of guilt was ripping his guts out, punishing him for dragging her across the ocean to England, to violence and madness. Why had he guided her into harm's way? This was no vacation. He'd heard of the trouble, but had no idea the danger would be this intense. Worse, though, he'd lied to her about the purpose of the trip, a lie that now threatened her life.

After one last warning, the police launched tear gas canisters. Most of the demonstrators had anticipated this move, and donned gas masks before they charged the police, muffled screams urging them ahead.

Isa pulled him up. "Come on, honey. Time to go."

He retrieved his handkerchief from his pocket and tied it over Isa's nose and mouth. Pushing her back toward the safety of the restaurant's interior, he scanned their table to ensure they hadn't forgotten anything.

After taking a step toward the restaurant, he paused. His love for her insisted that he run for cover with her, but the entire scene in the square was hypnotic. The patio had become a sort of oasis, where he and the wait staff could safely observe the battle—a real-life skirmish, with tear gas canisters spilling into the crowd, gunshots, rocks smashing into windows, and blood. Blake opened his wristband and selected one of his work apps—nose filters. He activated it and felt the filters cover his nostrils. They were regular police-issue implants. Then he scanned the mob.

None of the Corp Police agents remained standing. He couldn't see the American family, either. "Can you see the Miller kids?" He glanced at Isa, and let go of her hand.

She said, "If they vote the law into effect in America, we'll be caught up in this." She placed a hand on her belly, already thinking of their unborn child's safety.

"Not while I live," he said. The futility of his promise made it sound foolhardy, even to his own ears. Blake was a mere speck of dust in the huge bowl of political and economic interests. His opinion and resolve didn't matter, not without the power to make a difference.

Blake spotted the little boy protecting his younger sister with his small arms. They were stuck near the patio's fence. Pointing at the ground, he firmly told Isa, "Stay here!"

He ran across the patio. The fight was already spilling into this safe zone. He avoided a cluster of people resisting the police and reached the fence. The children were crying and shaking with fear. He bent over the fence and grabbed the girl. Her crying brother wouldn't let go. When the boy looked up into Blake's face, a brief flash of recognition shone in his young eyes. He let go of his sister, and stretched his arms in the universal pick-me-up gesture.

Blake pulled the boy over and checked them both for injuries. Next he scanned the area for their parents. Their mother was lying in a pool of blood, eyes closed, unmoving. The father was nowhere to be seen. Blake herded the children away from the fence. The conflict was already swarming over the patio.

Isa waved at Blake to hurry. She even rushed forward to help him with the children. Blake noticed a man standing behind Isa, waiting. He reached Isa and she took the children away. They all entered the restaurant. The waiters shut the door behind them and locked it. The man nodded for Blake to follow him into the hotel. He was heavyset, elegantly dressed, wearing a hat and small round digital shades; he looked like a classic wealthy Englishman.

My meeting contact, thought Blake.

The restaurant was crowded, with nowhere private to chat. "Let's move to the lobby," Blake said. "It's a quieter place where we can call the embassy back." He nudged Isa and the children gently through the restaurant.

The children were crying and calling for their mother. Isa patted them on the shoulders. "You're safe now," she said.

Blake leaned close and whispered in her ear, "Love, can you take care of them?"

Isa nodded, took each child by the hand, and gently led them toward the reception desk.

The Englishman sat in a leather chair near the street windows and motioned for Blake to join him. Outside, the battle raged on. The lobby was nearly empty, with no other potential contacts in sight, so Blake took the offered chair.

"I'm Samuel Brit." The man's voice was as impressively aristocratic as his appearance. "My employers paid for your vacation in England."

Blake felt an impulse to respect the man, but immediately questioned it. *Respect must be earned.* "It's a business trip. You didn't pay me, you paid to meet me."

"Whatever suits you." Mr. Brit slid a piece of paper across the small side table. The paper was printed with the British Servitude Exchange's logo. Under that were Blake and Isa's passport photos, their personal details, and a summary of their finances. The two largest debts had been underlined: $72,000 owed to the IVF clinic and an outstanding mortgage of $255,000 with the bank. At the bottom of the page, their tagged debt was tabulated at $327,000. Blake raised his eyes to stare defiantly at Mr. Brit.

"Our report on your family," said Mr. Brit, his voice soft and sympathetic. "According to the Freedom Act, everyone owing over $100,000 with only one skipped payment is liable to be detained and forced to pay their debt in servitude."

Blake crossed his arms and waited, wishing he could imagine a solution to his increasingly gloomy predicament, but his thoughts froze on the huge number. Three hundred and twenty-seven. Thousand. Dollars. Blake had never been spontaneous. Even though his job often called for action, he felt more comfortable as the strategist. The planner. Without the time to properly plan, he tended to freeze and rely on his instincts. Unfortunately, past experience had proven the freeze-and-react response unreliable.

The Englishman said, "We are also aware that you skipped a few payments."

Blake pushed the paper back to Mr. Brit, stood, and played his height as a power move, looming over the man. "Is that why you *paid* to bring me here? Because servitude is illegal in the United States?"

A rock flew through one of the windows with a loud crack. Shards of glass sprayed inside in a dangerous, jagged volley. Blake startled at the noise and looked quickly from the window to Isa. She was unharmed, still talking on her phone. The children huddled close, as though she were the only cover in a storm. He glanced back at Mr. Brit, who hadn't flinched.

"You're the perfect candidate. A detective with unpaid debt. Please, sit and listen to my offer."

Blake lowered himself into the chair, maintaining an aggressive, police-trained posture.

"The way the world's political and economic trends are headed, you'll have servitude stateside soon enough," said Mr. Brit. "You witnessed what just happened to the Millers. They're Americans."

"Enough threats," said Blake. "I'm still waiting for your alleged offer."

"Here it is." Mr. Brit crossed his arms over his chest. "We'll erase your debt in exchange for your services."

"My services?" Blake clenched his teeth, waiting.

"You've probably heard that an American slavery organization is on the rise. Sure, it's technically illegal, but not for long, considering the progress your Congress is making in the Freedom Act debate."

"Rumors," said Blake. "The media always plays to our fears."

"Nonetheless, we have leads on who heads up this new organization. Our intelligence operatives report that he has already designed and built a servitude camp. We'd like you to find this camp." Mr. Brit produced a cigarette and lit it with a gold-plated lighter engraved with the initials S.B. in large, fancy script.

"Why me?"

The Englishman tsk-tsked, waving a finger at his exhaled smoke with a flourish. "Above your pay grade, I'm afraid."

"If that camp exists, it's probably well hidden and well protected. With a full complement of private security. If I'm to use my detective badge to dig into the facility, you need to give me a better answer." Blake studied his adversary.

Mr. Brit smirked, inhaled deeply from the cigarette, and blew the smoke up toward the ceiling. "Let's assume we dislike the fact that a single person has developed a monopoly over the entire American servitude market. In England, hundreds of corporations compete in a free and healthy market. One man, imposing prices and conditions on the biggest market on Earth, can only be described as a servitude *dictatorship*. That sort of political powerhouse could be very dangerous for the rest of the world."

Blake kept his features neutral, even though he was pleased with how the meeting had turned. Adrenaline still pumped high in his chest, but he concentrated on keeping a cool head. He'd come to London expecting a similar outcome. Had he missed an important detail, one that might endanger Isa's future? Or his unborn child?

The FBI had predicted that a British company would offer to erase his debt, in exchange for covert actions connected to the American slavers. The Bureau wanted Blake to gain access, go deep, and gather information on the American setup, before the organization, or the dictator, became unstoppable. If Mr. Brit spoke the truth, the Europeans had the same endgame, and their operatives had dug up better information. Why not take advantage?

Mr. Brit studied Blake, his expression smarmy and amused.

Blake looked away to check on Isa. She paused in caring for the Miller kids to meet Blake's eyes, her face full of suspicion as she nodded questioningly at his companion.

Turning his attention back to Mr. Brit, Blake said, "I can see how this one power-hungry American and his greedy initiatives could pose a danger to the world."

"Obviously, we'll support you every step of the way. Money, influence, and information. Let me assure you, my organization wields considerable weight."

"This man, this dictator—do you have a name?"

The Englishman nodded. "William Wilmot."

Blake furrowed his brow in recognition. What were the odds that they wanted him to go after Wilmot? Everything related to the billionaire felt like a setup. He leaned forward. "The William Wilmot? Mister Billionaire who hates my wife?"

"One and the same. The man who arranged to have your wife fired and the television station where she worked shut down, all as retaliation for her snooping into his affairs in the name of the free press. Your debt troubles were caused by his meddling in your affairs. From my position, I would think that constitutes a strong motivation for you to agree to my proposal."

Blake shook his head. "Wilmot's too dangerous, and I'm already compromised. He'd be onto me before I even started." He glanced at Isa, and added, "Onto *us*."

"My organization will provide assistance. All our intel. Whatever you need." Mr. Brit placed an orange cell phone foil on the table between them. "Think about it, then give us a call. You'll find our contact information under the BSX entry."

Blake picked up the foil, considering his options. He was already involved in the FBI mission, which included agreeing to whatever the BSX proposed. Finally he said, "My wife and I have already put the whole Wilmot thing behind us. I don't want her involved in any way."

"I promise. No involvement. Your skills, your mission, not hers."

Blake set the foil down in the exact center of the small round table. "It's easy for you to make the promise, but how can you keep it from her? You don't have jurisdiction in the US." He stood, shoved his hands in his pockets, and said, "I'm not interested."

Mr. Brit extinguished his cigarette. "Think carefully."

"I have. I'm not interested." Blake scratched his head, leaned down, and pushed the orange patch back to Mr. Brit.

The Englishman stared at it for a moment, then rose. "Keep it. The affairs of foreigners can become tricky in London, especially for those on the *wrong* side. These are not times for debtors to travel abroad. I urge you to reconsider." He left without looking back.

Blake stared at the foil, waiting, thinking. Reconsidering.

"Honey?" Isa approached, the Miller children still holding her hands.

Picking up the foil, Blake weighed it carefully.

Isa guided the kids to a sofa next to the armchairs. No one else in the lobby seemed to be paying any attention to Blake. He placed the orange foil on his skin near his wristband, and watched as the data was absorbed. The Englishman's cell phone number appeared on his display. He dragged it inside a folder, hid its icon, and collapsed the display.

Blake checked to see that Mr. Brit was out of sight before he sighed and leaned back in the armchair. He carefully checked all of his buttons, then rearranged those that had wiggled out of line.

"Who was that man you were speaking with, honey?" Isa's voice broke his fixation on the buttons. Blake took another long, deep breath and managed a vague smile. "Nobody, love. We need to focus on staying safe."

A group of bloodied people rushed in from the street. They hesitated to scan the lobby, then removed their gas masks and slipped past Isa and Blake to hide behind the couch and armchairs. Blake turned his head to the hotel door, now ajar. Everyone in the lobby stared, fixated and terrified, at the open door. Yet no one dared move closer to close it.

Blake walked over to the door and closed it. He motioned for Isa to join him. Kids in tow, she followed Blake through the lobby and up the stairs to the first floor of the hotel.

"Who was the man who just left, honey?"

Honey. Not HoneyB. Already a degree colder. He shook his head, smiling at Isa. His wife now looked stern and serious, a change Blake recognized as reporter-Isabella, the multi-award-winning investigative news producer. Her nose was as honed as his to sniffing out bullshit and lies. "Nobody, love. Let's go to the embassy." How quickly he had switched from giving her a warm, loving smile to lying to her face, dragging along all the guilt that came with his deceptions.

"Honey"—more insistent now—"who *was* that?" Isa planted herself in front of him.

Blake weighed his chances of keeping up with the lie. With every fib, he dug a deeper hole for himself, had to remember more details, had to create a more intricate façade, with more edges for her to chip away. He'd been warned not to tell anyone about his secret mission, not even his wife. He'd never lied to her in their marriage. Not ever. Funny how such an easy lie could bring him such pain. Decades of marriage and friendship now perverted, even if the excuse was valid. Necessary.

"Love," Blake said, meeting her prying glare, "its work, that's all. Unfortunately, I'm playing the confidentiality card. I would tell you, if I could. I promise, I'll tell you anything you *need* to know."

"I thought we were on vacation, for our anniversary."

"We are." The guilt knife twisted in his gut. *Not a lie. More like skirting the truth.*

"Our anniversary includes a guy you can't talk about?"

"I'm sorry, love. I really am."

"I think I'm getting the picture. You lied to me about the money for the trip, didn't you? You didn't cash in some kind of bonus for twenty years in the force. This is a bloody mission, isn't it?"

He looked away.

"I hope you didn't compromise us in a hostile foreign country." She placed a hand on her belly. "Not now." She looked down at the Miller son and then the daughter, and drew the little girl closer. She didn't sound angry, more matter-of-fact—probably forcing herself to remain calm to keep the children's fears in check.

"I promise, we'll be okay. Don't worry." He said the words with determination. Not a lie, more of a belief. He'd refused the offer, and now they could go home.

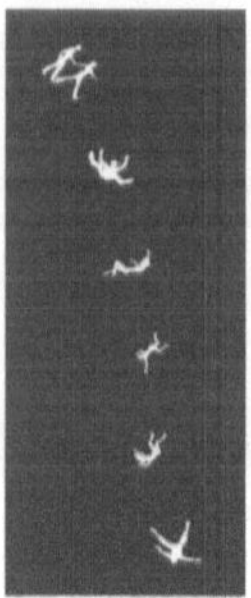

NIGEL AND THE RIPPER'S FISH

Nigel Blakesley paid for his fish and chips and waited for the order. He inhaled and grinned, hungry for the greasiest and most authentic takeout in Whitechapel. Just about any fish and chips cooked in London tasted better than the fare he'd suffered through in the States. But Jack's Fish and Chips in Whitechapel had an unparalleled, proprietary recipe.

The server called his number and offered up the package, wrapped in brown paper already sprouting grease blossoms. Jack's had jacketed their delights in the same simple manner for more than two centuries. No fuss, no pretentions. In New York, most fish and chip vendors printed their own versions of this paper blanket. Some imitated a long-dead print newspaper page, others experimented with different hues of brown paper, except for the addition of a waxed lining, to prevent the grease from soaking through. None of them understood the importance of tradition. Jack's could be neither duplicated nor matched.

Nigel ate standing at the tabletop outside the shop. He missed New York, in small ways and in large ones. The small were the most corrosive, since the only big one, *family*, would be taken care of soon enough. Until then, he would seek out small pleasures here. Things that could convince him that London was now his home. He didn't care that London was considered the entertainment and cultural capital of the world. His sense of entertainment had nothing to do with culture.

During his entire stay in New York, another so-called world

capital, he'd never visited a museum or attended a Broadway show. Why plan to start here? The pubs in London were pretty great, although not on Friday nights, when patrons were forced to drink their ale outside because all London was out getting hammered. Lately he'd discovered fish and chips. At first he'd thought that the tartar sauce in London was the finishing touch that upgraded the culinary pleasures for him, but after one visit to Jack's Fish and Chips he'd come to realize the importance of the entire experience. Jack the Ripper (the serial killer after which the shop was named) would have enjoyed precisely the same experience during his era in London. Jack's offered a satisfactory experience unchanged in centuries. Now that was an achievement worth celebrating.

Blakesley imagined what it must have felt like to hunt the Ripper. Any man with that job description would have been forced to think like Jack the Ripper. To act like Jack. To delve deep into the mind of the famous and possibly the first documented serial killer.

In his first months in London, Nigel read everything he could dig up on the Ripper. Now his life had devolved into an intellectual exercise where anytime he hit a dead end, he'd ask himself, "What would *good old Jack* do?"

He gobbed some tartar sauce onto the fish and took a big bite, chasing the mouthful with a fistful of fries. While working hard to keep the food from spilling from his mouth, he observed the street. At first the number of people in London who looked like bums spooked him; it looked as though the entire population had been replaced with homeless vagrants. Most of them hurried along the streets with their heads lowered, and they'd all scatter like roaches at the sound of a police car siren or the sight of a black suit. How had the corporations managed to turn England into a craven nation so quickly? Could they duplicate the results in the States? Of course they could, though maybe not as quickly as they'd manipulated the British population.

Nigel preferred to be on the winning side of history, if he had any say in the matter.

A dark-skinned Indian boy started to cross the street, noticed a group of punks harassing a woman in a hijab, and changed his mind. "Hey, there's yer brother," yelled one of the punks. "Running like a chicken, leaving you for us!" If the cruel remark was meant to be a joke, his tone betrayed the lie.

They wouldn't risk raping the woman in public, even with the new laws against immigrants. But they could probably beat the boy to a pulp and claim he was a terrorist, declaring themselves heroes for saving the city from another deadly rampage. With frequent suicide attacks occurring in all the major European cities, the police tended to show leniency to the "right-colored" people who beat up the "wrong-colored" ones.

Nigel watched them race to catch the Indian boy, feeling as though he had a ticket to a stadium sports match. He had to control his professional instincts, since they were not good for his health in London. In this city, no one jumped to help others in need. Not anymore. The citizens had all been castrated by the new laws, their reluctance to help exacerbated by fear. The average person feared everyone who didn't fit into the new definition of a *neighbor*. The government dished out hatred and mistrust like food rations to keep the population paralyzed and ripe for exploitation.

A chime brought him back to the moment. He activated his wristband and opened his cell to find a new message from an anonymous source. Not an ad. Probably trouble. He opened the message and read: *American spy works with British Servitude Exchange against American servitude players.*

Nigel opened the pictures attached to the message. They showed two men talking in what looked like a hotel lobby. *Wow, the plot thickens.*

He dragged the last piece of fish through the rich tartar sauce, popped it into his mouth, and picked at the small, burnt chip remnants. Finally he tossed the brown paper wrapper into the table's recycler, wiped his greasy hands on a couple of thick paper napkins, then turned his attention to his wristband.

Enlarging the first picture, he studied the two men. One wore an expensive suit and spoke with another guy dressed like a tourist. Tourist-guy had his back to the camera. After a careful examination, Nigel confirmed that he didn't recognize rich-guy. He cropped rich-guy's face and saved it as a separate jpeg. Later he'd run it through a face recognition database.

Enlarging the second picture, he had a better angle on tourist-guy's face. He froze. *Hmm, the plot is definitely thicker.* What was Detective Blake Frye doing in London, talking to some rich guy? Or, more importantly, how did Blake Frye get to London? The cop never traveled. Frye was deep in debt. He couldn't afford a trip to Queens, let alone one to an expensive London hotel.

"Are you done, mate?" The man touched Nigel's shoulder to gain his attention. The brute's eyes were bloodshot, no doubt from a drinking binge the previous night. Jack's greasy fish and chips could certainly cure a hangover.

"Not done." Nigel turned slightly, opening his jacket to expose his gun. "Not by a *long shot*, buddy."

The man withdrew in silence.

Nigel returned his attention to the photos and came to two conclusions. First, *somebody* knew who he was, otherwise they wouldn't send *him* Frye's photos. A fact that needed to be investigated. Second, Frye's presence in London was alarming. That same somebody had sent a message that labeled Frye as an American spy. Nigel needed to identify rich-guy, and uncover his connection to the BSX.

There was another matter, too, regarding Frye, and Nigel had to make a decision fast. He asked himself, *What would Jack the Ripper do? Besides portioning another hooker.*

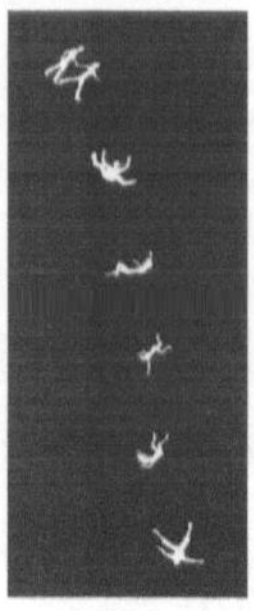

FIVE MONTHS EARLIER

Blake and Isa sat on the visitors' side of the desk, its surface filled to capacity with statues, busts, old clocks, photos in frames, mugs, and stacks of papers and files. An Elvis bust stared at Blake from the desk's corner, while an alabaster statue of a dancing Elvis prevented a pile of papers from toppling over. Framed photos faced the other side of the desk, where Dr. Weissenberg spoke into a microphone, dictating details into his computer. It appeared that the good doctor had gathered all his vacation souvenirs and personal obsessions onto one desk, a bit disconcerting for a professional's workspace. The man was either hiding secrets under the clutter, or struggled to express something buried deep in his subconscious. Either way, Blake didn't trust him. Not as a doctor, or as a man.

Isa waited while the doctor finished his report. As soon as he paused, she immediately resumed her questions. When a subject interested her, she was like a dog with a bone. *A cuddly dog,* Blake thought, smiling despite himself.

"So, in your opinion, we should try again." Not a question, exactly, but a statement in need of confirmation.

Blake's smile withered.

"Yes," said Dr. Weissenberg. "Clinically, I don't see a reason not to try another round. The tests confirm that your chances to conceive on your own are quite low, but that's what we do here."

Slowly, Blake said, "We've already tried. Five times."

"True. You must also consider the cost. Is money an issue?

Have you set a limit, based on your resources, for the number of attempts?"

"Yes," said Blake.

"No," said Isa.

The doctor looked at each in turn, then continued. "You must also take into consideration that as Mrs. Frye gets older, her conception rate decreases. As of today, she has a 27 percent chance of a successful fertilization and implantation."

Blake sat up straighter. "When we first tried this, you told us her rate was 48 percent." He kept his voice low, emphasizing his intent to fact-check, not accuse.

"I did," said the doctor. "Every year robs your wife of a few percentage points. I'd like to advise you, again, to speak with our psychologist. You should also consider all of the alternatives, including using a sperm donor, an egg donor, or adoption."

As they left the doctor's cluttered office, Blake stopped Isa before they reached reception. He rested his hands on her shoulders and squeezed gently.

She smiled, but he could tell the gesture required effort. "Please," she said, "can we just—"

"Wait until we're home?" he finished for her.

She nodded.

He sighed. Despite his instinct to give her the space she needed, he asked, "Are you sure you're up for another round, love? Not just the physical pain, but the emotional—"

"One more." A tear formed in her right eye, but didn't have the volume to spill down her cheek. "Please, HoneyB. I thought we had a deal."

"We had a conversation. One where *you* told *me* to agree to one more round. I wouldn't call that a deal. You promised we'd talk more."

Her eyes pleaded for him to agree. Her usually happy face was suddenly stark and drawn. Bitter, even. He closed his eyes, ashamed at his own shortcomings. His second-rate sperm was the main reason they couldn't conceive like a normal, healthy couple. She had some fertility issues, but none as crippling as his.

A different doctor had suggested that even with his faulty sperm, Blake could still conceive a child via IVF, at any age, because age didn't matter as much for men as for women. That doctor had suggested they use Blake's sperm to fertilize another woman's eggs. A *younger* woman's eggs. The doctor would then implant the embryos in Isa's uterus, so she could carry the pregnancy to term, making the children feel more like hers.

During the two weeks that they'd considered the option, Isa had been lost to him. When she finally came out of her distant, contemplative haze, she'd told him, "No." Insisted it was a final, *definitive* no. As she'd said the words that fateful day, she'd looked the same as she did right now, standing in Dr. Weissenberg's hallway. Resolute. Steadfast. Unflinchingly certain.

Blake lowered his head to look into her eyes. "I know it's my fault, but—"

"Fault doesn't matter. You need to let that go."

Blake closed his eyes briefly. "*I know it's my fault* we can't have children the natural way. Nothing in the entire world would make me happier than to give you a baby. Your baby. Our baby. But we *need* to talk before we commit to another IVF treatment."

She looked up, staring at the nurses and the couples passing by, on their way to the treatment rooms. They all pretended not to notice this intimate moment between husband and wife. They'd all probably faced similar choices. And yet, here they were, trying again.

He let go of her shoulders.

She smiled briefly, then moved to the lobby, where she sat in one of the chairs.

He followed a few moments later, sat next to her, and said, "Talk to me."

"What's there to talk about?"

"My father's genes are terrible. He stuck me, stuck us, with this terrible inheritance, my disorder and my fertility problem." He paused to adjust the buttons on his shirt, lining them up in a tidy row. "You shouldn't have to bear my cross. You agreed to this marriage, despite my problems. Now I'm forcing you to accept another cruel flaw. I can't describe how much that pains me."

Isa took his hands in hers. The gesture helped him find the courage to keep talking. He swallowed hard and said, "I've seen what these treatments do to you, to your *body*, but mostly to your beautiful spirit. And I don't think it's right for you to suffer any longer."

"I'm not suffering, Blake. I want—" she paused, bit her lip "—I need this child. Our baby. A boy or a girl with your kindness, and your brilliance—"

"And your beauty, and huge capacity for love and joy."

She caressed his face and smiled. "Exactly. Let's try one more time. Just one more."

After all of the failed attempts, this was probably her last, desperate shot for happiness. He kissed her, wiped the tears from his eyes, and rose. "All right. One more time."

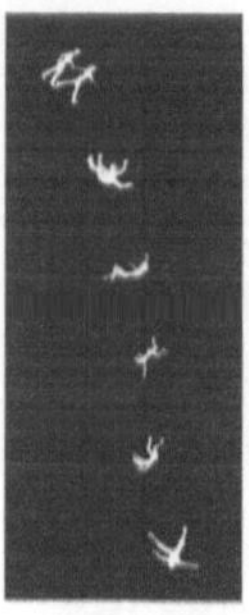

WASHINGTON DOESN'T BELIEVE IN TEARS

London's U.S. embassy was heavily guarded, as if the building were a fortress under siege. The fences and walls rose higher than Blake had expected, the tops strung with razor wire. Dozens of armed Marines stood alert and ready, dressed in full tactical gear. A few hundred people stood in line along the fence, protected from the street by cement traffic barriers. The Marines patrolled the line, ensuring that the waiting citizens weren't accosted. Black vans emblazoned with the British Servitude Exchange logo were parked across the street, surrounded by Corp Police agents, all of them waiting for anyone in the line to emerge with rejection papers from US Immigration. Most of the desperate people in the line were of Arab or Asian descent, with occasionally a white family, all of them probably so deeply in debt that they feared for their future.

Blake and Isa stopped in their tracks and gaped at the scene across the street, at the people who looked more like trapped animals than humans—scared, close to panic, and perhaps a little resigned, knowing that their chances of gaining asylum in the USA were minimal. They tried not to look over at the Corp Police agents who appeared ready and eager to drag every desperate person into a life of servitude.

Exposed in the line, there was no chance for anyone to escape their fate. The Guardian newspaper had dubbed it "The Terminal Line," stating: *If there was ever a false gate to freedom, it's the gate into the US Embassy in London. Thousands of people bound for servitude in the UK have queued at that gate, hoping against all odds to walk forward into freedom. Yet every day, we watch nine out of ten refused entrance. They're easy pickings for the Corp Police, as helpless as if they'd chosen to walk straight into the British Servitude Exchange offices to surrender.*

In front of the main gates, a young woman wearing a somber two-piece suit recognized the four of them and waved. They had called in advance, informing the embassy of their intention to drop off the Miller children.

As they waited and watched for an opening to safely cross the busy thoroughfare, a commotion started. A young man exited the embassy, carrying his rucksack. He looked wildly around him and saw the Corp Police approaching. Throwing the rucksack at a Marine, he jumped onto the pebbled wall and scrambled up the rough surface, desperate to find another way into the embassy. Ducking the rucksack, the Marine raised his Taser-gun and fired. The young man fell thrashing onto the pavement. Two soldiers hauled his convulsing body around the barricades and dropped him in the street between two markers labeling the spot as a no-park towaway zone. The Corp Police picked up the unconscious man, cuffed him, and loaded him into a van.

The woman in the two-piece suit waved again. Blake looked at the children in his care and gave them what he hoped was a reassuring smile. The four of them crossed the street and approached the woman.

"Blake and Isabella Frye?"

"Yes," they said in unison.

"Follow me, please."

They passed through three checkpoints before they were allowed inside the embassy. During the final confrontation, which was more of an intense interview, they worked hard to convince security that they had urgent business, which could not be conducted anywhere except the US embassy.

Gone were the days when the embassy served as a refuge where American citizens could seek help. Now it felt like a cross between a prison and a castle, where anyone at the door had to convince the guards of their importance. *I must convince them we're favored citizens of America,* thought Blake. Or more accurately, favored, card-carrying members of the Republican Party, an elitist organization that had managed to remain in power for the last four presidential terms. With a majority in Congress, the Senate, and the Supreme Court, they'd managed to completely transform the country. God forbid that anyone consider admitting to embassy security that they were a Democrat, or even liberal-minded. It would make more sense to climb onto the selling block and wait to see the face of the new master with the winning bid.

The woman led them to a small office containing only one table and one chair, then excused herself. Blake offered the chair to Isa, and stood behind his wife. She sat holding the little girl on her lap. The boy stood beside Blake. The children, tired and confused, glanced around the room with zombie eyes, alternating between sobs and silent trepidation.

Eventually the woman returned with a man wearing an official-looking dark gray suit and a severe expression. The man carried a file folder. Ignoring the children, he focused first on Blake. After a pause, as if the man hadn't seen what he'd been looking for, he turned his attention to Isa and smiled coldly.

"Mrs. Frye," he said. "We thank you for your kind gesture. We appreciate you taking the time and effort to bring these children to us."

Without any preamble, Isa asked, "Did you find their parents?"

"Only their mother. Unfortunately, she's not in any condition to take them home."

Isa sat back. "What does that mean, exactly?"

The man lowered his voice to a whisper. "Mrs. Miller died. She's in the morgue. We'll ship her remains stateside, along with the minors. The father's still missing."

Blake watched in silence as Isa swallowed hard and caressed the little girl's head. She asked, "Are other family members waiting for them, back home?"

"Their affairs are no longer your concern, Mrs. Frye. We cannot divulge any more details. Privacy laws, you understand."

Before Isa unleashed her reporter barrage, Blake gently placed a hand on her shoulder. "We did everything we could, love. Let's go."

We also need to fly home, he thought, but he dared not say the words in front of this severe man. Now that his mission was over, they needed to escape their vacation nightmare and face other ugly realities back home.

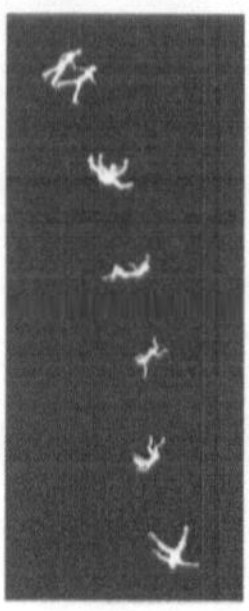

THE RIGHT HAND

Nigel slouched in the chair, rubbing his chin while he considered what he'd just learned. The facial recognition software matched rich-guy's photo with images from London's street surveillance camera database. In one, rich-guy met with several leaders in the British Servitude Exchange. In the others, he enjoyed different servitude network parties. As if to live up to his nickname, rich-guy was present at all of the recent "must-attend" events for the wealthy in London. Unfortunately Nigel still couldn't put a name to the face, or determine his place of employment. If Nigel could run the guy's face through some American surveillance databases, what would he find?

"I need your name," he said aloud. Nigel had been in London, working inside the BSX, for a couple of months now, and had never met rich-guy. There was something shady about Frye's meeting with the man.

Nigel dialed a number. A rough, severe voice on the other end answered with, "Mr. Blakesley."

Choosing his words carefully to prevent raising the suspicions of Lord Wright's right-hand man, Nigel said, "Mr. Thompson, I require information concerning the identity of a person of interest. I'm sending you the image." He pressed Send and waited.

A few moments later, Thompson said, "That's Samuel Brit. What business do you have with him?"

"He crossed my path through unusual circumstances, and I wanted to put a name to the face. What does Brit do?"

"*Mister* Brit is richer than most English lords and more influ-ential than any of them. Whatever he *does*, as you say, is none of our business."

"If he's *that* rich, he must run a business. How does he factor in the servitude market?"

"Why do you require this information, Mr. Blakesley?"

"I learned that he's arranging a scheme to spy on the Amer-ican servitude market, and wondered why he didn't contact me. If he is as influential and rich as you claim, he must have heard of me from Lord Wright. As you well know, I could be very use-ful to such a man."

"If Mr. Brit is involved in such a scheme, I'm not aware of it. You might not be on his radar, Mr. Blakesley, despite the man's connections. I'll poke around and see if anyone has any informa-tion with respect to such matters."

"Appreciate it, Mr. Thompson."

"You will find Mr. Brit's business on Sydney Street, South Kensington. I'll send along the address."

"Say, Mr. Thompson, are you up for a Guinness this coming Saturday?"

"My apologies, but I am otherwise engaged."

"No worries."

Nigel waited for Thompson to end the call.

After more than five seconds of silence, Thompson said, "You are aware, Mr. Blakesley, that I must report our conversa-tion to Lord Wright. If everything is as you mentioned, you'll require Lord Wright's approval to work for Mr. Brit."

"Sure, of course, Mr. Thompson. As I said, I appreciate your help."

Nigel ended the call and rose from his chair. *Hmm, a big BSX player arranges a personal meeting with Frye?* Finding out the British guy's identity had only added to the mystery. Samuel Brit. Seriously? The guy was trying too hard to convince people he was English. *Hey, look, I'm Sam the British Man. Sam Brit, for short.* Did he have some kind of weird fixation with the old Uncle Sam?

Oddly enough, Nigel felt as though he now knew even less

about rich-guy, aka Samuel Brit, than he'd known before. If, as Mr. Thompson had claimed, Brit was richer than most English lords, he must be rich enough to have a business location in South Kensington. That meant he'd live somewhere even higher up the food chain.

Brit had to be a broker, or something similar, for the servitude industry. Maybe even an owner. Nigel grinned. A slave owner! Frye must've hated having to interact with an owner. The righteous Frye that Nigel knew wouldn't touch an owner with a ten-foot pole.

"What's changed?" he mused aloud. "How did Frye make the jump from NYPD cop to spy? And where is Frye's Joan of Arc, the sweet and nosy Mrs. Isabella Frye?" Sacked, last he'd heard. No doubt on the run from the hunting dogs. He smiled. "Perhaps that's my missing link."

He had to dig up more on Brit, and wondered about visiting the man's business address. *What would Jack do?* Probably dissect Isabella and expose her entrails on Black Fryer Bridge—or was it Blake Frye's Bridge? Nigel giggled at his own cleverness. The Ripper's advice was to disembowel the nosy Mrs. Frye.

The more he thought, the more he wasn't sure if he was ready to finally let go of the past. Once and for all. Before such a big, important step, he must be absolutely certain.

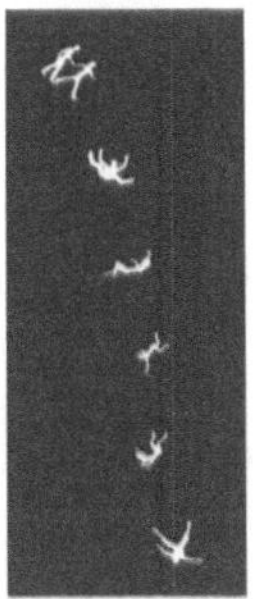

ONE YEAR EARLIER

Isa threw her bag on the couch then startled, noticing Blake seated at the dinner table, arranging his stamp collection. The assorted stamps were as impressive as they were worthless. Since his grandfather's youth, members of the Frye family had torn postage stamps from the envelopes that landed in their mailboxes. Not collectibles, or rare series. Only the cheapest, most common stamps used to send number ten envelopes filled with bills and notices. She'd often watched her husband arrange and rearrange the stamps, all mounted with care onto three-ring binder pages with glue, or tape, or old-fashioned corner holders. The task brought him comfort in times of trouble.

The last time he'd brought out the binder, he'd just been assigned the Spring Cleaning Serial Killer case. That night, he'd rearranged the stamps chronologically from newest to oldest, based on their postmarks. Before that, when he was first assigned to the Brooklyn Cannibals case, he'd arranged them by color. She hadn't exactly understood Blake's color system, but the arrangement had been pleasing to the eye. Before that, he'd sorted them based on each stamp's original price.

She equated the collection with his looming despair. Each time he retreated to this odd place of comfort, she'd managed to coax him back to the real world, *her* world, where she helped him to reason through his problems. When he first admitted to her that he suffered from obsessive compulsive disorder, OCD for short, she wondered how or even if she'd be able to cope with the symptoms. Now here she was, still his wife after fifteen years.

"HoneyB, you're home early." She took off her shoes and left them in the hallway. Settling into the chair next to him, she slowly set her hands on the table, waiting for a signal that it was safe for her to mention his collection.

He nodded, and continued sorting.

Blake had a magnificent mind. He wasn't, strictly speaking, a genius, but his thought processes were so precise, so rigorous and logical, that he solved every puzzle assigned to him. After first dissecting clues based on their consequences, he would place the facts into the right context, be it cultural, social, or historical. Only then would he allow himself to feel anything about the case. Isa had always been enchanted by the sophistication, depth, and breadth of his feelings, once he completed his cold, fact-based calculations.

She briefly scanned his progress and determined that he needed at least a couple more hours to sort through his stamps and his thoughts about whatever troubled him. Two or more hours for her to kill until he was ready for something else, like dinner and a brainstorming session over a glass of red wine for her and a beer for him. He was a beer sort of man.

Blake smiled at her and asked, "Off the record, madam reporter?"

She kissed him and grinned. "Off the record, I swear, sweetie."

"I've just been assigned to a task force concerning a case. A whopper of a case that, twenty years ago, would've been all over the press. But now we just got the orders that 'It's in the state's interest to keep it off the grid.' What's strange is that no one is curious as to *why*."

"I was about to say I feel a celebrity name coming, but then you said 'task force.' Which implies it's something more serious. Another serial killer?"

"We don't know yet, but I don't think so. Maybe worse."

"What's worse than a serial killer? Aliens?"

He burst into laughter. When his giggles subsided, he hugged her. "Thank you, love."

"I'm always here for you, HoneyB." Isa hugged him back.

He took a deep breath and said, "We found a mass grave. It's quite recent. Filled with men, women, and even children. All deceased within the last year. Some fresh enough to have been dumped over the last few weeks."

"Sounds like a serial to me."

"Not for three reasons. First, the state's interest in keeping this quiet tells me the case is likely a political crime rather than the work of a sociopath. Second, the MO doesn't match that of any serial killer's motivations. Unless we're talking about a serial *gang*."

"And third?"

"Uh, I recognized two of the corpses." His eyes clouded over.

Isa feared she was about to lose him to his thoughts again. The facts were horrifying, but any detective could handle horrifying. Blake had served in the NYPD for almost twenty years. What could affect him so much?

When he spoke again, she startled. "The two victims that I recognized are from a list of missing people. They're from all across the country. We call it the Escaping Families list. We used to joke about it."

"What are the families escaping *from*?"

"About a year ago, families began to disappear. Parents and children together. One case in LA, two in Chicago. Nobody connected the people or the motives. Over the last year, we've had six families disappear from Manhattan. No trace, no witnesses, nothing. The only connection was that every family had extensive debts, and were on the verge of losing their homes and ending up on the streets. We assumed they were on the run from their creditors."

"Hence, escaping families."

"In my gut, I know this isn't the work of a serial killer."

"What, then?"

"The department doesn't have any theories, yet."

"What do *you* think?"

"Unofficially?"

She nodded.

"I think it could be the beginning of an underground slavery movement. I think they confiscate the people rather than their possessions, work them *hard*, and when they die, dump them like garbage into a hole."

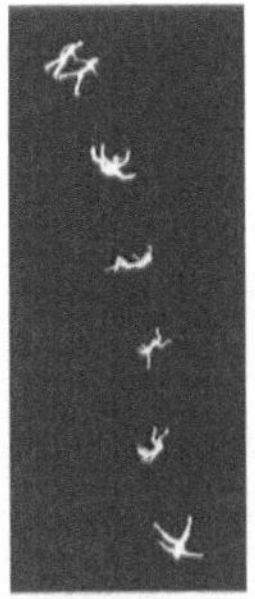

THE BORDER OF DOOM

The Border Control Office at Heathrow Airport was a new department, created to deal with the new realities of the Freedom Act. The definition of terrorism was no longer restricted to abominable acts committed by people to instill terror. The Freedom Act expanded the definition to include *financial* terrorism. People who defaulted on their debt were no longer allowed to declare bankruptcy. Instead, they were labeled as criminals—more specifically, financial terrorists, since they had the potential to sabotage the international financial system through their insolvency. Or so the new law stated.

The Border Control officer watched a screen that showed numerous families entering England. As each name was scanned from their passports, the names were automatically checked against two lists.

Red flags flashed next to each of their names on the Debt list. The Servitude Exchange inspector frowned, checking their names with the list on his tablet.

"Sir," said the Border Control officer, "the entire family of seven is flagged."

"Process them," the inspector sneered.

"I don't see how all of them, particularly the children, could've earned a red flag."

"Computers don't lie. They've all been sold to a buyer here in England. The system tracks them from the moment they purchase an airline ticket in their names, trying to flee. The flags sort them out, not us."

"Yes, sir." The officer looked down, avoiding the inspector's glare.

"Leave them to me." The inspector walked away, filling out a form on his tablet.

The Border Control officer returned to his screens. As he caught sight of Blake and Isa Frye approaching the border, he tapped on their faces and opened their files.

In deep thought, Blake dragged his cabin luggage after him. When Isa stopped suddenly, he bumped into her. "What?" he said, startled by the sudden change in rhythm.

Isa pointed to a family of seven, ahead in the line: parents, grandparents, and three children. They scanned their passports to cross, but the barrier didn't open. Border soldiers closed in on the group from several directions and took the protesting family away in a matter of seconds. The usual airport activity resumed as though nothing had happened. Border soldiers guarded the line, eyeing everyone with suspicion.

"Blake, what do we do?" Isa's voice quavered.

Blake looked around. Nobody seemed to be watching them. Then he noted all the cameras and sensors covering every angle and everyone in line. "Give me a minute, love."

"Blake?"

But he stepped back, turned his back to Isa, and activated his wristband. When he selected the orange cell number, he hesitated, hating himself for bringing this upon them. Another lie in the end, after the meeting with the English gentleman. He'd promised his wife that nothing would happen to them. Swallowing hard, he dialed and picked up the holo-cell.

Brit answered almost instantly. "Yes, Mr. Frye?"

"All right. I'm in. I'm in."

"I'm so glad to hear of your decision. Welcome aboard."

"Now make sure we can leave England."

"You're free to go, Mr. Frye."

Blake switched off the cell and returned to Isa. He tried to smile reassuringly. "Let's go. We'll be all right."

"How do you know that?"

"Trust me, love."

They approached the border, scanned their passports, and the barriers opened.

As Isa slept in the seat next to Blake, he replayed the meeting with Samuel Brit in his mind, analyzing phrases and gestures for unusual elements, for any word that had felt out of place or generated suspicion. The only thing that gave Blake pause was the name "Wilmot." It seemed as though everything in the Frye family's life had revolved around Wilmot for the past year.

Isa mumbled something in her sleep. He smiled, kissed her temple, and she quieted.

Blake activated his holo-display, selected HEARING IM-PLANTS ONLY, and tapped the orange icon that opened the folder from Brit. Inside it was a video file with the title *Debt Hunters (Selections)*. When he hovered over the file, the text *Producer Isabella Frye* appeared over the cursor. Blake paused, unsure whether to play the contents. Samuel Brit had given him a montage of his wife's reportage. The same investigation that had incriminated Wilmot and had terminated Isa's career as a TV producer. Blake knew the story by heart. Yet, he played the selections from Brit.

The first footage showed the walls of several police precincts, in different states, with hundreds of photos of people pinned to bulletin boards. The sequence was from the first part of Isa's story. A voice-over narrated:

"In the last year alone, tens of thousands of people have disappeared. Not just single subjects, but entire families. According to Chicago's chief of police, it's the first time in the history of the United States that thousands and thousands of families have vanished without a trace."

Skipping to the second segment, where two men, rough and bulky, their hands tied behind their backs, were being transported under escort into a precinct, the same voice narrated:

"Arnold Van der Hutte and Jack Macklinger are two of a new breed of bounty hunters. They're called 'debt hunters' because they capture families who are carrying debts and who have skipped one payment. In exchange for a plea bargain, Van der Hutte and Macklinger have confessed to hundreds of kidnappings of entire families, and to delivering them to modern slave traders, the so-called 'servitude brokers.'"

After another transition, financial documents flipped across Blake's screen, the images moving through dozens of detailed papers, while the narrator continued:

"The debts of most of the people on the debt hunters' list have been purchased by five companies, from whichever financial institutions originally held the loans, mortgages, or other forms of credit. The majority shareholder of all five of these companies is the billionaire, William Wilmot."

The video paused, leaving William Wilmot's frozen face staring back at Blake.

"What?" Isa's voice woke Blake from his concentration.

He switched the video off immediately.

Isa said, "What's that?"

He studied his wife as she blinked sleepily. "I'm sorry. Was the light too strong?"

"Was that my story?"

"Yes. Go back to sleep."

"How..." Isa sat up, more awake now. "Why do you have it?"

"It's nothing. Don't worry."

"Does the guy in London have something to do with this 'nothing'?"

"No. I keep your work with me for old time's sake. I'm proud of you. That's all."

She snuggled against him and sighed deeply. Another lie, another hurt.

"Your brother and Neil did most of the heavy lifting," Isa whispered and hesitated.

"Corbin and Neil," Blake agreed.

"Shame they didn't agree to be credited for the story."

"Maybe we should pay my brother a visit? See how he's doing."

"Why?" she asked, already half asleep again.

Blake exhaled, trying to hide his anger. That damned story had brought them all so much grief. But more than that, he hated lying to Isa. Better to hide the truth than to expose her to more danger. She deserved better.

"Just sleep, love." He kissed her head and took her in his arms as best he could, given the discomforts of their economy seats. The plane was full. The air was chilly yet somehow it also felt thick, making it hard to breathe.

He looked up at the red emergency exit signage, remembering the mother of the two children in London lying in a pool of her own blood, as though she was an extra in a bad movie. How had murdering people like cattle become possible in England? The country used to take care of its people, no matter their origins or beliefs. How had such a democratic society slid so far down the slope of authoritarianism?

He smiled sadly and looked out the plane's window. Why couldn't people simply stop being obtuse? The decay had been insinuating itself for decades, and yet nobody had stopped to consider building an economy for the long term. The rich got richer. Occasionally another economic crisis would strike and the global economy would decline for a while. During the subsequent recoveries, why didn't the governments and courts surgically remove the decaying, rotten parts of the economy when they had the chance? Instead, corporations were bailed out with tax dollars, over and over again. Headed by the wealthy elite, they rose again as rich, stupid, and careless as ever. And when the mother of all economic crises pushed the entire world into chaos and necrotized the system, those who could have done something about it had given away their power to the only union that shouldn't have existed—ironically called the World Prosperity Union. Corporations gained all the power. Was there any daylight at the end of this long night?

"Please fasten your seatbelts. We'll be landing at JFK shortly."

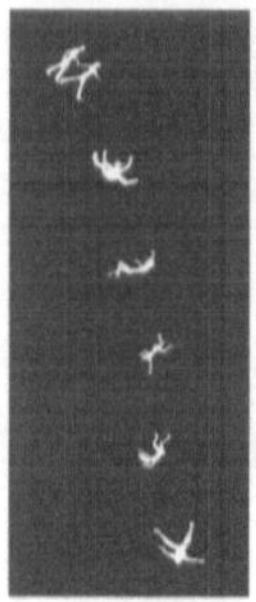

MOORE IN THE NIGHT

Moore stared at the ceiling. He'd been in bed for the last two hours and couldn't fall asleep. He'd counted sheep, ducks, and pigs, and finally he'd given up. His wife slept next to him, so he climbed out of bed as silently as possible, left the room, and closed the door behind him. The house was dark and quiet. He tiptoed to his grandchild's bedroom to check on the little one. The boy snored like a tiny mouse. Moore crept in, covered the child with a blanket, and caressed his soft hair.

Feeling less agitated, he moved downstairs to the kitchen. The digital clock in the coffee maker's display showed 3:25 a.m. Too early for the appliance to have automatically brewed the breakfast pot.

For three nights, he'd gone without sleep. He needed to crash for at least two hours if he was going to survive the day. He wasn't expecting a particularly important or hard day, only the same routine and shit.

I need a smoke, he thought. Grabbing the pack from behind the toaster, he pulled one out, tucked it behind his ear, and hid the pack once more.

Out on the back patio, rain fell in a cold drizzle. Typical October weather. He lit the smoke and sucked greedily. Lately, he couldn't sleep three out of four nights. His wife begged him to take melatonin, but he needed to deal with the source of the insomnia, not just blindly treat the symptom. Something was keeping him awake. And if he knew his mind, it meant his subconscious needed to warn him about some looming danger or urgent problem, but it didn't know how.

Sure, his daughter-in-law was dead and his son was doing time. But this tragedy had become their reality, for almost two years now. Status quo. System normal, if death and incarceration could ever be considered normal. No way would his mind start punishing him for that ugliness this late in the game. His grandson was being cared for, and that was all that truly mattered. Little George was going to grow up under better circumstances than his father Duane, and do something special with his life. Maybe become a doctor. Moore had already started to put money aside for George's college. His wife was already retired, but Moore still had a few good earning years left to build some savings.

He puffed on the cigarette and smiled. Had the craving been satiated? Could he fall asleep now?

No.

The nicotine hit hadn't defeated the unsettled beast. *Come on,* he thought. *Just figure it out, already.* He sighed and sat down on the wooden bench under the eaves, away from the drizzle. The clouds and fog hid the stars. The world was sad and overburdened, like him.

The patio door slid open and his wife approached, carrying a folded blanket. She pointed at the lit smoke and grumbled low, but didn't scold him. Unfolding the blanket, she wrapped it around her shoulders and used some of the hanging material as a cushion to sit next to him.

"Can't sleep?" she said.

He shook his head. Slowly, he lifted the cigarette to his mouth, and when she didn't yell at him to put it out, he sucked in a good lungful and blew the smoke away from her. In an apologetic tone, he said, "Tomorrow I'm taking you to chemotherapy."

"You don't have to. I know you already have a lot on your plate."

"I need to spend more time with you."

She shook her head, as if not convinced. He took another

drag. In the beginning of her chemotherapy, when their surprise and shock at discovering she had cancer was fresh, he used to drive her to the hospital for every appointment. A year later, as the chemotherapy continued relentlessly and the doctor wouldn't pronounce on a definitive verdict, he'd stopped going. It depressed him to sit in a room full of broken people, clinging to life with the last of their strength.

She asked, "Is it George?"

"I've always loved how deeply children sleep. They trust the grown-ups to take care of them and slumber without fear. You can caress them, kiss them, sit right next to them and they carry right on, sleeping without a worry in the world. It's comforting."

"I know. I jump when you touch me while I'm asleep. As though I've been burned. Not that I don't trust you. It's just..." She shrugged and blew into her palms to warm them up.

He felt guilty for waking her, knowing she was a light sleeper. Slipping out of the bedroom unnoticed was an impossible goal. He wrapped his arm over her shoulders. "We adults become increasingly worried and burdened with life, to a point where tension and fear never leave our bodies or minds."

She nodded, then watched him with a worried expression as he took another drag from the cigarette. "So, it's not George."

"Nah. It's work."

"Why don't you just retire?"

"With Duane in prison, I'm the only one saving money for George's future. I need five, maybe six more years."

"We've been over this. Don't kill yourself working. We can sell the house, if it comes to that."

Moore shook his head, too tired and disappointed to talk about it. No matter how many times they discussed his employment status, they'd never agree. On the subject of family matters, he'd always followed his wife's lead. But when it came to their son's kid's future, George trumped every other priority. Moore would not fail his grandson. Not after he'd failed Duane.

She said, "What is it, then?"

"I've lost a few good people over the years. I've cried, and I've done my share of missing the close ones. But I'm bitter over the deaths I couldn't balance with some justice. Those cases I was *forced* to close. Leaving them unfinished. Unsolved. When I was young, I used to fight for every case. I'd push back, demand irrefutable reasons before I closed a case. Over the years, I lost that spark. I'm too tired. It's…" *Hopeless*, he thought, but somehow admitting it out loud would make it worse. Lately, hopelessness had become a houseguest who'd outstayed its welcome.

She met his eyes, waiting for him to finish his sentence. "It's what?"

"Nothing."

"Go on. It'll feel good to share."

"You're too clever for your own good."

"Now you're stalling."

"Fine." He smiled weakly and cleared his throat. "It's *hopeless*. Cops can handle just about any bad situation, so long as there's hope. It's what keeps us sane, fuels us to keep marching through the gritty, bloody darkness. Without hope, who can face the killings, or the pain, or the misery of human life?"

A tear rolled down his wife's cheek while she stared straight ahead.

He dropped his butt, stepped on it, and kicked it into the yard. Overwhelmed by the bitterness in his mouth, he spat into the grass. "Frye worries me. I've worked with Agent Hansen from the FBI on many cases. I recommended him to Frye, because in the past he's always been fair and thorough. Not now. I have an ugly feeling in my gut after every conversation with Hansen. As though I just entered a secret club where I'm only allowed to wait in the foyer, glancing through the curtains to the next room, never managing the right angle to see the whole picture."

He remembered his last meeting with Hansen, in an Irish pub in midtown. Hansen kept dodging his questions. The incident flashed vivid and real, complete with the stench of beer and vomit, and the way the bottom of his glass kept sticking to the table.

"So, what is it, exactly, that you need from Frye?" Moore lifted *the beer to his lips and pretended to take a sip. "What's his mission in England?"*

"I can't say," said Hansen. "Not until he comes back with the goods."

"What're you expecting? A souvenir replica of London Bridge? Or were you thinking more along the lines of a communicable disease?"

"You're funny," Hansen growled. "I can't talk mission specifics." *He finished his beer and started to stand.*

Moore grabbed Hansen's wrist and motioned for the Fed to sit back down. "This is our mission, not yours."

"It's an FBI investigation. We're on point, not the police."

"Come on, Hansen. How about some cooperation."

"What do you want from me, Moore?"

"What kind of undercover mission is led by agents who don't know what they're after? No one would approve the budget, for starters. Not to send a cop like Frye on a fishing expedition."

Then Hanson's phone rang and the agent slipped away, like a snake on the surface of a murky river.

Moore came back from his memory.

His wife asked, "Where'd you go, just now?"

"Nowhere good." He sighed and rose, then helped his wife to stand. "I'm ready to try to sleep again."

"Sounds good to me."

He slid open the patio door and waited for his wife to enter first.

She stopped in the doorway, turned to him, and said, "What if Hansen's as powerless as you, with his strings being pulled by someone higher up the food chain with their own secret agenda?" After a pause, she stepped into the house.

Moore hesitated outside, absorbing the darkness like oxygen while he thought about her question. *Could Hansen be another tiny cog in a bigger, more powerful machine?* Not likely. He entered, and followed his wife upstairs. "I'll shut my eyes for a couple hours, and then I'll drive you, before I go to the station."

"If you insist."

"I do." He smiled, covered her with the blanket, and kissed her bald head.

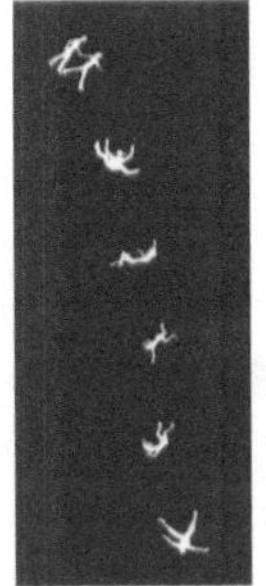

ELEVEN MONTHS EARLIER

"That's a fantastic idea, Isa," said Philip Kadesky. The man always spoke in a soft, gentle voice, as though he could single-handedly lower the energy level in the station. "But I can't authorize it."

She glared at her boss, the vice president of NWN TV, hoping her anger might add weight to her side of the argument. "Something horrible like this happens and we choose not to investigate? Why should we hide the truth from our viewers?"

"Because the people you're investigating can take everything from you. From us. If your husband's right, and politicians are implicated, then you're going to find yourself holding an angry cat by the tail, in the middle of a mine field."

"We're talking about fifty corpses in a mass grave, Phil. Children, women, the elderly. Good people who probably fell on hard times and missed a bill payment or two. Regardless of the economic mess we're facing, do you think any journalist with a shred of integrity would keep quiet about a story this horrific?"

Philip stretched, looking visibly uncomfortable. He grimaced and cracked his knuckles. "You've already said too much, Isa. What'd you call it? Oh yeah, I remember," he said sarcastically. "A *secret* task force."

"I trust you, Phil."

"What's your end game? What can you prove?"

"Even though the US hasn't adopted the Freedom Act, an underground slavery movement is operating in America. They're murderers. They kidnap entire families, force them to do God knows what kind of slave labor, and then when their bodies give out, they're dumped in mass graves. These criminals dispose of their dead slaves like they're waste. Human beings, tossed aside like garbage. I want to expose them all. And if the government is involved, the taxpaying public has a right to know."

"You'll never dig up enough corroborating evidence."

"I'll get at least half of what I need."

"You could waste years on this investigation. Let the police handle the investigation. If they don't release every fact you'd like the public to know, *then* you can open your own investigation."

"The police are tied up in red tape, and they'll never be allowed to share their evidence with the public. Even if they manage to dig to the very bottom of the truth, they'll hide it from everyone without top secret clearance, and especially from the press."

"How can you investigate, if there's a gag order in place?"

"For now, police precincts will still share details of active investigations of missing families. The gag order only pertains to our local grave. It hasn't gone national in scope. Not yet, anyway. This is my window, Philip. I bet I can sweet talk most of the police jurisdictions to cooperate. If we don't act now, that window will keep on closing, until all we can do is pound on the glass while they wave at us from the inside."

"I can't spare you any resources."

"Doesn't matter," said Isa. "Give me a month and I'll dig, solo. If I can gather enough proof, juicy enough for us to make the national feed, we'll both be in line for a promotion. Let's be *authentic journalists* again. Give me the green light, Philip. And you might just learn what it feels like to play an instrumental role in the kind of story that gets shared for generations. Think Watergate."

"All right," Philip said. "But we'll keep the investigation quiet for now. *Our* top secret mission. I'll give you two more people, for a basic team of three. Plus, my FBI contact checks your facts, to green light the subjects you can touch and ones you can't."

"Done!" Isa grinned like she'd been handed a Pulitzer. "I want John Taylor as my reporter, and Sam for research."

"You can have Sam, but not Taylor. I won't compromise his reputation."

"Come on, Phil. A subject this serious requires our *best* reporter."

Philip shook his head, clearly defeated and frustrated at the same time.

Isa sent Blake away to score some drinks, whispering to him to stay away for at least fifteen minutes, to give her time alone with her crew.

John Taylor had a face that matched his name—common, but pleasant. Beyond his simple first impression, Taylor definitely had a spark in his eyes. Maybe it was curiosity? Or could it be cunning? Maybe some viewers might even see brilliance. Isa wondered if perhaps cold calculation might be more accurate. She hadn't worked with him before, and John's producer hadn't exactly been forthcoming when he heard that his star had been loaned out to a different producer for a secret project.

On the flip side, Sam was a young woman who dressed like a rebel. Isa knew she was studious and hardworking, though she had her own strong opinions—but so did all of her peers. Isa appreciated Sam's willingness to change her opinion if proven wrong—a rare trait.

"First, thank you for signing my confidentiality agreement," she said to them. "This project covers some sensitive topics. That said, if you feel uncomfortable with the subject, you're in no way constrained to remain on this project. Everyone involved must be convinced of the utility of what we're doing. I need one hundred percent commitment."

"I'm in," said Sam, smiling. "Whatever you're working on, Isa. Your projects are ten times more important than most of the shit they're churning out at NWN. Or anywhere else, for that matter."

"Thanks for the vote of confidence, Sam. But hear me out.

Afterward, if you're still willing—"

"All right, Mrs. Frye," said Taylor. "The suspense is killing me."

"Isa, please." She rested her palms on the table and added, "I'm also hoping, with your permission of course, that I can call you John. To speed up our communication."

"Done, *Isa*."

"Great." She took a deep breath and let it out slowly. "Now, in a nutshell, my next project concerns the underground slavery movement in America."

"Hell, yeah!" Sam smacked the table. "I'm totally in."

"Sounds interesting, but…" John paused, squinting enough to form crows' feet at the corners of his eyes. "I'm not sure what you—"

"First," interrupted Isa, "this American underground slavery movement may involve some political personalities. Second, the movement may be directly linked to more than one mass murder." Isa paused to allow them to process that information.

Sam frowned.

John stared at Isa, smirked, and said in a superior tone, "Is this some sort of prank?"

"Quite the opposite." Isa pressed her palms on the table once more. "I need you to agree to work on this story. You have to be willing to attach your name, your *reputation*, to this important journalism."

"Careful, Isa. You're slipping into dangerous territory."

Isa smiled. "How so?"

"If we succeed in digging up these facts, proving your allegations, then those 'political personalities' you mentioned would also be mass murderers."

Isa's smile turned into a grin. John had said "if we succeed," which meant he was halfway convinced to remain on her team. More importantly, he could think on his feet, proving he was as sharp as his reputation. The spark in his eyes had turned out to be neither cold calculation nor cunning. He was clever and inquiring. Now, more than ever, she wanted him on her team. "You're good, John. So? Are you two willing to fight against the establishment and brave the storm that will surely rain down on us all?"

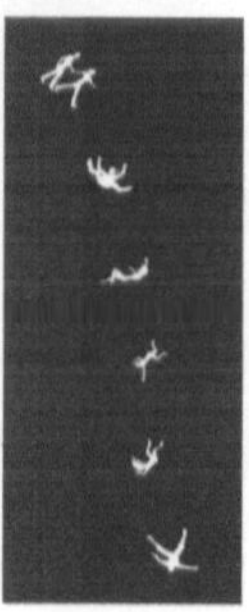

THE SECRETS THAT ROT OUR SOUL

The corridors to US Customs were overcrowded. Big screens hung from the ceiling, broadcasting the news. Thousands of people protested in front of the White House. The closed captions summarized the anchorman's words, delayed by a few seconds:

"The number of people protesting on Capitol Hill against the Freedom Act debates grows by the hour. The protesters are dubbing it the 'Slavery Act' and claiming it's a law that violates the Constitution. Already a week long, discussion on the bill's specifics continues. Several governors have expressed their willingness to create state-specific legislation as a way to save local economies and provide a respite to local businesses. These governors stipulate that their constituents should learn to be responsible for their lifestyles, and should not expect the government to bail them out of bankruptcy every time they overspend."

Blake stretched and advanced in line. They'd almost reached the front of the endless queue, where people split off into dozens of smaller lines leading to the passport scanners. On the big TV screens, coverage switched to a speech by the governor of Texas, who began his oration with great aplomb:

"Servitude is merely a form of adult education. If you have graduated from the American education system and proceeded to live your life as though there is no tomorrow and spent more money than you have earned, well beyond your fair share, then you must be re-educated with America's modernized value system. Servitude is an educational tool for the people."

Isa poked Blake. "I hate you," she said passionately, but with an air of weariness.

Blake grinned. "I hate you, too." He kissed her and gently touched her belly. "God, I'm so happy to be home."

Isa kissed him back, smiled, and extricated herself from his arms. When Blake stepped into the line in front of him, she chose a shorter line.

Blake said, "We should stay together."

"Let's make it a game," she countered. "If I cross first, I'll choose the baby's name."

"Okay. You're on."

Isa took out her passport, preparing to scan it. She turned to him with a serious face, and said, "I expect you to tell me the truth once we're home."

Surprised, Blake blinked, trying to look confused. As if her request had no context. He was happy they'd reached US soil, where he could smooth the waters and do his job without lying to his wife. But any truths had to be metered by his needs, or more specifically, those of the FBI. God, he really felt elated, now that they were back on American soil. Safer than the UK—*Go figure!*

Isa's line advanced more quickly, putting her a few steps ahead. She waved as if saying goodbye, and prepared her passport for scanning.

Blake noticed two agitated Customs officers approaching.

One of them asked, "Blake Frye?"

Blake tucked his passport into his inside pocket and carefully buttoned his jacket, ensuring every button and crease was perfect. Then he nodded in acknowledgement.

"Please come with us."

"Why?" he said, looking at Isa. "What's wrong?"

Isa stopped where she stood, observing her husband interacting with the two men.

"Sir, as an officer of the United States Customs and Border Security, I'm asking you to come with me." The two officers placed their hands on their weapons.

Blake glanced at Isa, noticing that she was holding up her line while she stared at him in confusion. The officers positioned themselves on either side of Blake. As they escorted him outside the Customs area, in the opposite direction to his wife, Blake shouted, "Isa! Go through without me, and call Moore." Then he activated his wristband, saying, "Record."

"*Recording,*" said the digital assistant.

"Sir, please switch off your phone."

"It's procedure. I'm a police officer—"

In one swift move, one of the officers grabbed Blake's arm and inserted it in an isolation cap, breaking the signal and ending the recording.

"You can't—" Blake turned to face the officer but the other man grabbed Blake's other hand and twisted it back and up, forcing him to his knees. Choosing not to resist, Blake waited for them to cuff him and pull him to his feet. They dragged him through a side door.

Isa crossed the border through the Customs screen, zippered her passport into her purse, and activated her wristband with trembling hands. She exhaled, trying to calm down, and dialed Blake's boss.

"Captain? This is Isabella Frye. Blake's been arrested at the airport, on the wrong side of Customs."

"What did he do wrong?"

"I don't know."

"I'll make a call and get back to you."

"All right. I'll wait."

She collapsed her wristband and looked around. This country, her *home,* was supposed to be safe. Not like the constant tension in London. God, how she'd hated their trip. The constant fear, the overt injustices. She didn't want to tell Blake, and tarnish his anniversary gift. Their first time in England, a place she'd dreamed of visiting for her entire life, was now ruined by the fascist actions of the authorities, in the new slavery capital of the world. She'd planned every detail, bought theater tickets and museum passes, even booked them on a starlit cruise along the Thames. Instead, they'd caught the earliest flight out, unable to enjoy the city where every life around them was in tatters.

She scanned faces as people moved through the Customs screen. Someone touched her shoulder, startling her. Behind her stood two men dressed in black, their expressions serious. They looked very much like the Corp Police. Unable to hold back her fear, she stared at them wide-eyed, and her trembling returned.

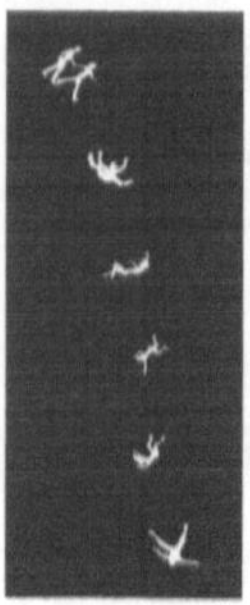

WHEN THEY WATCH US

Blake Frye sat in an uncomfortable chair, one wrist cuffed to the table. He'd been waiting for at least fifteen minutes and nobody had charged him with anything. The door finally opened and a man in his early forties stepped in. He looked like a federal agent: black suit, white shirt, black tie, and black digital shades. The eye gear made Blake frown—either the agent was trying to look dangerous, or he was full of self-importance, vanity, and arrogance.

The man collapsed his digital shades and tapped on his wristband's holo-display. He sat on the opposite side of the table, clicked through some menus on his display, then eventually acknowledged Blake. "Agent Emilio Alvarez, National Security Agency," he said in a throaty voice as he flashed his badge.

"Please, can I see your credentials once more?" Blake had employed the standard practice of hazing civilians with a badge flash whenever he didn't want the person to remember his name.

Agent Alvarez seemed out of balance for a couple of seconds, as though no one had ever asked for an ID confirmation before. Then he grinned, took out his badge, and left it open on the table for Blake to inspect.

"Thank you, Agent Alvarez. I'm a police officer."

"I know who you are, Detective Frye. Tell me about your vacation."

"Why?"

Alvarez threw images from his wristband's holo-display

onto the room's walls. Photos captured by different surveillance cameras from the hotel in Leicester Square, showing Blake's conversation with Brit, the English slaver.

What the hell! Blake suppressed his shock, keeping his gaze focused on the wall while he calmed down.

The agent pointed to Brit and said, "Who is that man?"

"I don't know."

"Come on, *Detective* Frye," Alvarez said, his tone level, angry. "Do you expect me to believe that you spoke at length with the man and never got a name?"

"I want my phone call."

"Not until you tell me what I need to know."

"You have no grounds to refuse my rights."

"And so?" Alvarez leaned back in his chair, looking more smug than ever.

"One phone call, to my captain, will clear up this misunderstanding."

The agent leaned forward, dropping his chair back to the floor, and grabbed Blake's right arm. He yanked off the isolation cap and twisted Blake's wrist to access the wristband.

"You have no right to touch my wristband."

"Traitors don't have any rights."

"I. Am. No. Traitor."

Alvarez nodded at the closest photo. "That man is a British Servitude Exchange agent. A BSX shithead. Proof you're working for slavers." Alvarez stared into Blake's eyes.

"You're way off base."

Alvarez tapped Blake's holo-display, trying to slide the contents over to one of the walls.

"Lock!" said Blake. The wristband hissed and shut down.

The agent slammed the table. "You wanna play?" Without waiting for a response, Alvarez punched Blake in the mouth with a right hook, then jumped to his feet.

Blake's mouth quickly filled with blood and he spat some onto the floor, grinning at Alvarez as the man moved around to stand behind him. Assholes like the agent would likely be first in line to sign up for the American Corp Police. "An interesting move, Agent Emilio Alvarez, NSA badge number 47S534."

Alvarez grabbed Blake's hair and pulled his head backward with one hand, and wrapped his free hand around the base of Blake's throat. "Who recruited you?"

Keeping his tone as calm as possible, Blake repeated, "Agent Emilio Alvarez, NSA badge number 47S534."

"There are only two options for you, Frye. Cooperate, and we'll go easy on you. But if you stay loyal to those scumbags, we'll shove you into a deep, dark hole and throw away the key."

"Don't vent your frustrations on me, Agent Alvarez. Please, do your job and contact my captain. To clear the air."

"*Your* captain?"

"Yes, please."

"All right. We'll head somewhere safe, where you'll share." Alvarez switched gears, becoming oddly agreeable. "We'll invite your captain to join us, too, if that's what you really want." The agent activated his wristband. "Bring the car around."

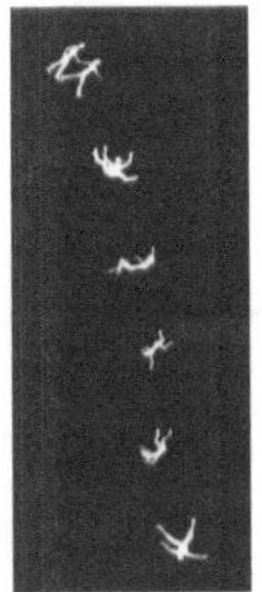

TEN MONTHS EARLIER

Blake escorted his friend, Senator Norman Chadwick, to Isa's home office, carrying a four-pack of beer and a bowl of popcorn for her team. The young senator was tall and chubby, with a jovial expression and the air of an exiled Russian aristocrat. He carried his own glass of wine while he made effortless small talk. Blake envied the politician's people skills, since casual conversation always left him exhausted. He'd rather chase a pack of armed criminals than chat with strangers at a house party.

Norman took a sip of his wine, then said, "Corbin mentioned your OCD tendencies. He was surprised you were accepted into the Academy, let alone rose through the ranks to detective." He dropped the jab casually, as though he were summarizing the plot of a movie.

Blake concentrated on playing it casual. He didn't want everyone in Isa's office to learn of his disorder. Other than his captain, no one at work knew. Not even his partner, Neil Grissom. Keeping his tone as neutral as possible, Blake said, "My brother has a big mouth."

"Fear not. I assured him that as long as you don't clean your gun every two minutes, we'd be right as rain."

Blake stopped this time and chuckled. Norman acted as though they were busting each other's balls over a beer, not Blake's political connection being called on to help Isa with her research. Corbin's lack of discretion was more upsetting. "Thanks for keeping an open mind, Norman." Pointing with the bowl of popcorn at the entrance to Isa's office, he added, "If you don't mind, though, I'd appreciate if you keep my, uh…"

"Affliction off the books?" Norman nodded. "Naturally. Your secret will stay between us." After a pause, he added, "I understand the sensitive nature of your…affliction. I won't make waves. Perhaps you aren't aware of it, but I have a great deal of respect for you and your wife. I'm proud of our friendship."

"As are we." Blake stepped into Isa's office, where his partner, Neil, was sharing a laugh with Sam.

Isa sat in the corner, quietly discussing something with her reporter. Blake found it odd to have the rising star of NWN TV, John Taylor, in his home. His wife had a small budget for her piece on homegrown servitude, so she had to assign both Sam and Taylor to perform extra legwork. To bring more hands to the job, Blake had invited his partner and their senator friend to Isa's team meeting.

"Norman!" chirped Isa. She rushed over and hugged the senator. "Such a pleasant surprise. Where's Corbin?"

"I'm by myself tonight. Blake only offered a solo invitation to your mysterious meeting. And as it happens, I'm a great fan of secret societies, so here I am. Wondering about the specifics of my initiation."

Isa grinned. "Initiated you shall be! Let me present the fine members of my team." She pointed first at her young researcher. "That's Sam, and that's John Taylor." Gesturing to the senator, she said, "Everyone, this is Senator Norman Chadwick."

"Call me Norman, please."

Raising his beer, Neil smiled warmly at the senator. "And I'm Neil, Blake's partner in crime." He took a swig, then added, "The bad guys call me Detective Grissom."

Norman sipped from his wine. "Nice to meet everyone." He shuffled back a step, trying to blend into the room.

Neil leaned forward and asked, "So, you and Corbin?"

"What?" The senator glanced at Blake.

Neil pressed. "Isa asked why you didn't bring Corbin along."

Norman glared at Neil, holding his mouth in a rigid politician's smile. The room fell silent. Sounding agitated, Norman said, "Corbin and I go way back."

Blake stepped between the men, shoved the popcorn at his partner, and said, "Neil, what the fuck?"

"Oh, sorry. I just…" Neil shrugged, keeping his eyes on Norman.

Blake nudged the senator with the beer. "Ignore him, Norman. He's a dick. But he's our dick." Blake used the beer to guide Norman toward the reporter.

Neil shoved popcorn into his mouth, chewed a few times, and with his mouth half full, said, "I've decided to help Isa with her story."

Blake turned to sneer at his partner. Then he set down the four-pack, pulled the cans from the plastic rings, and passed one to Neil, one to Sam, and one to John. Isa hated beer, saying she could never get past the bitter taste or the strong hops smell. Blake had tried to explain to her that people don't sniff gently at the aroma before they chug a beer. She would simply smile and order a sweet cocktail. Or red wine, as a last resort.

Reacting to Blake's sneer, Neil shook his head at Isa as if to say, *What did I tell you?* Then he said, "I'm serious, Blake. I'll do some investigative work for Isa."

"You can't," said Blake. "Police don't share intel with reporters."

Neil scoffed. "Isn't that *exactly* why you invited me to your little soiree?"

Blake shook his head. "Did I mention you're a dick?"

"Many times, partner. Look, I won't give them *police intel*. I'll give them casual info, on my own time. No badge involvement."

"We'd love your casual help," said Isa.

Blake looked from Neil to Isa, shrugged, and took a swig from the last beer. Then he scooped a small bowl of popcorn from the main supply. After a quick survey of the new mood in the room, he sat in the armchair behind the desk, taking a position of neutrality. "Whatever suits you, Neil. As long as you can keep a clear record of your off-duty activities, and promise to never allow an active investigation to shift into your off-duty portfolio."

"Sure can do, boss."

Blake took another big mouthful of beer, allowing the fizz to dissipate in his mouth before swallowing. Finally he asked, "So, Neil, what exactly will you be investigating?"

Neil grinned. "William Wilmot's business in the state of New York."

"That's a tall order," said Norman.

Taylor asked, "Why is that, Senator?"

"Norman, please."

"Why is that, Norman?"

The senator put his wine glass on the desk.

Blake moved the wine from the wooden surface onto a coaster, and turned the glass so that the lip mark faced Norman.

"Wilmot controls more than half the Congress. Known fact." Norman raised a finger to indicate his first point, then continued. "God knows who else he presses with his influence. He practically pulls the strings on most of the new legislative acts."

"Norman has the inside scoop," said Isa. "He's the last Democrat in the Senate."

Norman smiled as though Isa had made a joke, but there was bitterness in his eyes.

John Taylor shook his head in annoyance, and took a sip from his beer. "That's a sorry state of affairs, gentlemen." He pointed at Isa and added, "And lady. You know what they say about the next elections."

Isa laughed, raising her hand in the universal sign for stop. "Don't start with your conspiracy theories again, John."

"I want to know," said Neil. "What *do* they say?"

"We're due for the fourth Republican president in a row," said John. "And, hopefully, a one hundred percent Republican Congress."

Blake said, "Impossible, John."

Norman grunted and drank deeply from his beer. Everyone waited for his response, staring at him expectantly. As the last Democrat in the Senate, he must have inside knowledge regarding the fate of his relic party. "I hate to say it, Blake, but John's theory is very close to reality. I can't confirm one hundred percent, but any elected Democrats will only be there for show. Zero power. With no substance to counter the Republican horde. We all know what happens to a Democrat who opposes them too openly."

"So, you're saying that *all* Republicans are bad?" John sat up straight in his chair, as though he was about to anchor the evening news. "I'm a Republican, and I don't condone what some of them are doing."

"I didn't say that," said Norman. "All I'm saying is that in the absence of competition, whoever controls the jungle sits at the dictatorship table. The opposition's job is to oppose single-minded rule. The press's job is to report the truth, no matter how unpleasant it sounds. If those in power gain the ability to silence these two elements, they've built themselves the framework for a dictatorship."

"Sure," said John. "But not *all* Republicans are setting the board for a game of domination. Take me, for example. I'm a Republican and I'm risking my career to do a story on a subject that's dear to many Republicans."

Norman smiled sadly. "If only more people cared as much as you do."

Blake leaned back in the chair, which squeaked loudly. "So, Norman, what's your take on servitude? Is it a real threat to America? Should my beautiful wife tell this story?"

"Too late, HoneyB," said Isa. "I'm involved, no matter what."

"Yay to the woman who sticks to her guns," said Norman. "The Freedom Act will pass through both the House and the Senate, probably in less than a year. They would've passed it through sooner, but wanted to avoid a revolution. Instead, they're waiting for the rest of the world to align, and then they'll hop on board, as though their decision is the natural choice."

Isa held her drink high, as though giving a toast. "See? We, the journalists, must do our duty. If they're afraid of a revolution, well, we'll give it to them!"

Everyone cheered, and took a drink.

Norman waved his hands to get everyone's attention.

"You're taking a huge risk. Consider, before you take another step, the new laws on the books that restrict the freedom of the press. You could end up behind bars. Your network could be forced out of business. We're approaching the end of the era of the news industry."

"Bring it on," said Isa, fearless. "If we do this right, our numbers will skyrocket. We'll have all the eyeballs pointed at our team. The traffic will make the advertisers drool, and they'll be fighting one another for space at the trough."

Blake smiled at his wife's enthusiasm. He turned to Neil and said, "You'll be chasing an awfully big, dangerous dog in this operation."

"An important one," said Isa. "We need someone to dig up every one of Wilmot's businesses in New York State. We need the where, the who, and most importantly, the how."

"Sure," said Blake, then added quietly, "We should talk about this. In private."

"Let's go, HoneyB." Isa's tone warned Blake to be careful. Pointing at the senator, she added, "Norman, would you join us, please?"

Looking surprised, Norman gave Isa a confused look, then nodded.

Blake led the way to the kitchen. As soon as they were far enough away that the others wouldn't hear, Isa attacked first. "What's this about, Blake?"

"You should be using my brother for this investigation. Not Neil."

"Why would Corbin help us?" Isa slipped back into her reporter's skin. "We're basically his competition."

"More like soldiers on the same side," said Blake, smiling. "Your piece and his article would complement each other. Bring in Corbin."

Still not sounding convinced, Isa said, "Fine. I'll tap him. But it feels like my team's getting uncomfortably large."

"Don't say that to him," snapped Blake. "Maybe use a bit more sugar and less hot sauce."

"Sure. I'll call up your brother and ask him to pick up a

dozen donuts," said Isa with a sarcastic smile. "I'll order him to hand deliver them to Wilmot. Is that enough sugar for you, Blake?"

"Actually," interrupted Norman, "Corbin's already investigating Wilmot."

"Well shit," said Isa. "There's no way he's going to share."

"Maybe if you find a unique angle for your story that makes it different enough from his, he'd join forces." Norman crossed his arms over his chest. "Corbin's been deep in this story for at least a year. He's in possession of a mountain of data. Why waste time and alert Wilmot's people if all you get is a duplicate of the same information?"

"True." Isa brushed her hair behind her ear. "Will you talk to him for me? Put in a good word?"

"It would be my pleasure. I'll soften him for you."

"Perfect," said Blake. "I think we're done here."

The three of them gathered more drinks, then returned to Isa's office.

Addressing Norman, John said, "How is it that I only, just now, learn that Blake's brother is a reporter for the *Times*?"

Neil winked at Norman, but the senator didn't react. Blake watched the exchange, becoming more concerned about Neil's behavior. Why was he taunting Norman about his connection to Corbin? Neil had never struck him as a homophobe.

Two presidents ago, gay citizens had slipped back into illegality due to a controversial bill. After two years of arrests and their associated trials, millions of people were convicted, sent to prison, and forced into treatment. An addendum to the law had instituted a fifty dollar reward for reporting homosexual behavior. Funny how such a low incentive could modify the social structure in America.

Norman faced John head on, one polished man to another. "I wouldn't be much of a senator if I didn't establish relationships with the best reporters in town." He flashed a wide politician's smile. "Anyone strong enough to oppose the servitude law should join the fight. We all need to work together, shoulder to shoulder, and set aside any competitive tendencies. Forget prizes like the Pulitzer. Besides, I don't think many journalists in America will deserve it. Not for a long time to come."

Blake said, "He's my brother and I trust him to have our backs." He smiled at his wife.

"Trust is good," said Neil. "Getting back to our to-do list, what else should we research on Wilmot?"

Isa stepped to the center of the room, in front of Neil, and said, "There's another angle to the story worth investigating. What enticed me in the first place."

"Shoot," said Neil.

"Families are going missing. Being snatched without warning." Isa glanced at Blake and added, "They're called Escaping Families."

Neil raised a hand to stop Isa. "I thought we weren't mixing police info with civilian info."

From his seat behind the desk, Blake winked at Neil and said, "Hear her out, partner."

Sam asked, "Are you saying that entire families are disappearing?"

"Yes," said Isa. "Parents, children, sometimes even grandparents, all slipping away from their lives at once. I don't know how many total incidents exist, but they may be connected to the servitude black market in the US."

She gave the idea a chance to sink in, then continued. "We should compile a list. Then map the occurrences. Contact the associated police precincts."

"I'm on it," Sam said.

"That's my smart wife," said Blake. He waved Isa over. She moved behind the desk and settled onto his lap. He glanced at Neil, then Norman, still sensing that everyone wasn't as enthusiastic as Sam. Focusing on his wife's beautiful eyes, he asked, "Are you sure you're up for this?"

"Of course I am!"

Glancing at everyone, and wondering whether he should bring up their personal life, he decided it was best to speak his mind. "We're about to begin our sixth IVF. Our last try. You know how demanding the procedure can be. Maybe you should rest, take care of you, before you shoulder this immense story."

"This story is too important. The Escaping Families can't wait. If the Freedom Act is voted in, we'll have lost before we started." She hesitated and glanced at her belly. Blake smiled, looked down, and touched her. "Besides," said Isa, "I have a good feeling about this one. I won't bring a child into a world where she could lose her parents to slavery."

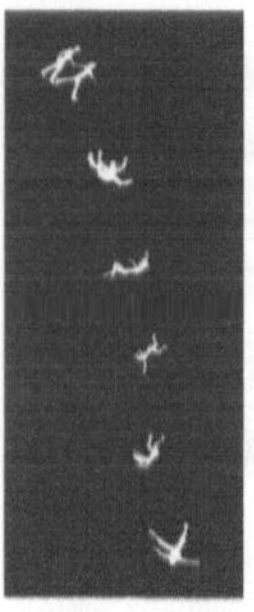

AT GUNPOINT

Agent Alvarez removed one of Blake's cuffs, unhooked it from the table link, then recuffed Blake's hands behind his back. Then he grabbed his prisoner and dragged him into the corridor. An airport security guard glanced at the two men, appraised Alvarez's black suit, and turned away as if to say, "None of my business."

Alvarez pushed Blake toward a set of metal exit doors at the end of the corridor. When Blake dug in, stopping their forward momentum, Alvarez bumped into him.

Turning back toward the guard, Blake yelled, "Hey, you! Airport security gal!"

Alvarez slammed Blake in the center of his back, forcing him forward.

"I'm a police officer!" Blake dug in again. "I'm NYPD and this is a kidnapping!"

The security guard placed her hand on her weapon and hesitated.

Alvarez shoved Blake into motion with one hand, and flashed his badge at guard with the other. "I'm NSA. This is none of your business."

The guard took one step back and raised her hands in surrender. "Right, sir. Not my business."

When Alvarez pushed Blake toward the exit, the detective heard a familiar voice behind them shout, "Stay right where you are. Don't move or we *will* shoot."

Alvarez grimaced.

"Hey, Cap," said Blake. His boss had brought along two airport police officers.

Alvarez typed a code into the door's access panel and the lock clicked open.

Blake watched Moore draw his gun and aim at the NSA agent.

Alvarez dug his fingers into Blake's arm, trying to drag him through the exit, and yelled over his shoulder, "I'm NSA! Stand down. This is a national security op. Not a problem for the local brass."

"That's my detective," said Moore. "I have a court order stating that Detective Frye is free to go."

Blake wedged his feet at the base of the door's frame, but Alvarez had too much forward momentum. He heard the sounds of squealing tires, then a car door opening. The moment of no return quickly approached.

Alvarez said, "You're free to tag along, *Captain*."

"I have a judge's order," said Moore. "Your actions are illegal, Agent. Let him go!"

"That's no judge's order," said Alvarez.

"Shoot him, Cap."

"Shut up, Frye!" Moore paused, then shouted, "*Release my man!*"

Blake twisted his shoulders, trying to escape the agent's grasp. He heard running footsteps. *Probably a second agent.*

Moore sprinted the last five steps and tackled Alvarez like a linebacker. Blake fell over them both, and looked back at the two security officers, who watched in confusion. Finally they drew their weapons and aimed past the open door.

A second dark-suited man caught up to the scuffle. "I'm NSA Agent Saunders," he yelled as he produced his badge. "Lower your weapons. You're interfering with a National Security Agency investigation."

The airport officers hesitated. But by this time, Moore had rolled clear; he pointed his gun, point blank, at Alvarez's head. Rising slowly, he helped Blake to his feet. "Uncuff him," he barked at the airport officers.

Deciding which side was the right one, the taller officer did as Moore asked, unlocking Blake's handcuffs. The shorter one trained his gun on Saunders. "Stay right where you are, agent," he said.

"Thanks for having my back, sir," said Blake.

With his Glock pointing at Alvarez the whole time, Moore covered their retreat along the corridor to a different exit. The NSA agents watched them, their faces as hard as granite.

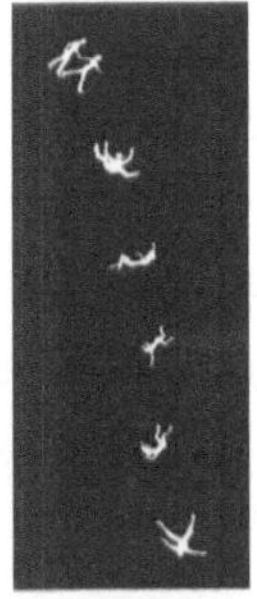

ACCESS

Simon White grinned like a schoolboy. Beside him, Gabriela Wilmot drove like a stock car racer in a Humvee, leaving a curtain of mud behind them on the dirt road through the thick forest. Pouring rain darkened the sky on the gray October morning.

They approached the big gates of an electrified fence. *Game on.* Gabriela smiled at him in her glacial way. Arrogant, but supportive. She braked dead-center in front of the tall silver gates, each bearing the giant Wilmot Conglomerate logo. To the side, a metal sign announced the facility as the Wilmot Research Center.

An armed drone hovered silently above them. A side camera sent their vehicle's details to unseen security staff. After about a minute, the gates opened. Their black military-style SUV crossed through. The gates closed behind them.

Two guards, dressed in black and wearing crowd control armor, stepped out from a fortified booth. In their military-style fatigues, dark combat glasses, and military-grade filters over their noses and mouths, they looked like mercenaries, not civilian security. *Are they expecting a chemical attack?* Simon wondered, staring at them as he stepped out of the vehicle. When Gabriela had picked him up, he'd thought the vamped-up SUV was a bit over the top, designed to impress. Now, he wasn't sure. Military-grade equipment seemed to be a requirement for access to the camp.

One of the guards scanned him. The other unloaded his bags from the back of the vehicle and slammed them down on a large stainless steel table. He searched Simon's field bag with gloved hands, without any consideration for the delicacy of its contents.

Gabriela remained in the car, waiting patiently at the wheel for the guards to finish their appraisal of Simon and his gear. *She still doesn't trust me,* he thought. *We're sharing fluids and gifts, but I'm still the outsider. If the guards find something unsavory, she'd probably turn her back while they drag me away. She's a fucking ice queen.* Funny how he was expecting arrest and torture, rather than simply being expelled from the premises. The guards were definitely dressed for serious business. The torture and murder kind of business.

Simon surveyed the camp. It looked like a deserted university campus, with modern glass buildings surrounded by neat gardens, and no human movement. Not at all what he'd expected. Drops of water made complex patterns in the puddles on the asphalt, like signals warning of the future.

"He's clean," said the first guard, sounding disappointed.

The second guard dangled Simon's state-of-the-art camera negligently and demanded, "I need to see a permit for this."

Gabriela smiled from the driver's seat and said, "I'm his permit."

Simon smiled back.

"Understood, Miss G." The guard tossed the camera back into its bag and pointed for Simon to grab his possessions.

Once he was back beside Gabriela in the vehicle, she revved the engine and put it in gear. He watched her for several seconds. She was stunningly beautiful. Just like her namesake—a glacier—he could observe her in awe from a distance, but would never build a home with her.

Gabriela parked in front of a large, dome-shaped building, got out of the vehicle, and ran to the entrance. Simon grabbed his bags and followed, catching up to her before she opened the door. He grabbed her shoulders, whirled her around to face him, and kissed her.

She detached herself from his kiss without comment. Then the doors slid open and they both walked inside.

The lobby was a huge circular space with a fountain in the

center. Three bars had been built at equidistant points around the fountain. Bartenders served the people mingling in the space around it. Simon watched, feeling more baffled than anything else. It was an oddly early hour for alcohol.

Gabriela leaned close to his ear and whispered, "Welcome to the Great Hall of Science."

"Studying the science of inebriation, are they?"

"Sure," she said. "It might seem a bit premature for alcohol to the average man on the street, but they're journalists."

"Huh," he said. "Is that why I'm here?"

"You're among the reporters covering our annual science festival. Have a libation with your colleagues."

"You know that's not my field—"

He was interrupted by a beep, and Gabriela checked her wristband. She grinned as a message floated on her holo-display. "Enjoy the opening ceremony," she said. "I'll see you later."

"Later?" He looked at her, puzzled. "Where are you going?"

"It doesn't concern you." Without another word, she left.

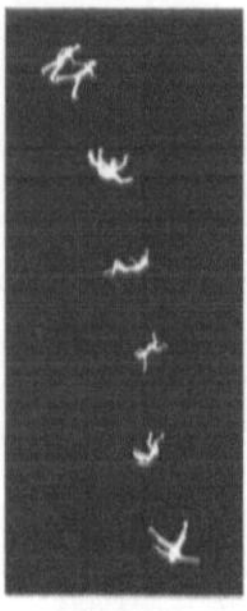

NINE MONTHS EARLIER

Norman placed his wine glass on the table, observing Corbin. The man was lost in his own mind, probably hatching plans and working overtime at his research project. Norman didn't have any right to complain. He'd acted the same, or worse, during his last election campaign, and Corbin had been respectful of both his schedule and his need to excuse himself to occasionally think things through privately.

Corbin was approaching the finish line, and soon the research phase would end. The next stage, the time for action, scared Norman the most. Action meant months apart, while Corbin worked undercover, taking risks and facing dangers.

"You wouldn't believe where I've been," Norman said with a smile in his voice.

Corbin raised his eyes and focused, returning to the present. He looked like a man waking up and trying to get his bearings. He even attempted a smile, something that had become increasingly difficult for him. Norman had wondered whether their relationship was winding down, and that's why Corbin couldn't seem to feel joy in his presence anymore. Once in a while, Corbin would surprise his partner with a grin or a kind word, making it all that much harder for Norman to step back and offer Corbin his freedom.

"Where've you been?" Corbin repeated Norman's last words and smirked. "Were you trying to hook up with a Republican, knowing full well that their dominion will be complete and absolute after the next election?"

Norman paused before reacting. He wasn't sure if Corbin's remark was deliberately boorish, designed to broadcast another message about their crumbling relationship, or angry at being pulled from his thoughts. Regardless, Norman didn't take the bait. He was here for dinner and a nice evening, not to play a role in Corbin's empty home drama.

"I'm sorry," said Corbin. "I was thinking something unpleasant and…my bad. You were saying?"

"Doesn't matter. Listen, I'm taking off. Will I see you this weekend?"

"Don't be like that, Norman. I apologized and I *meant* it." Corbin placed his hand over Norman's and produced a genuine smile.

Is that love? thought Norman. Guessing Corbin's moods and innuendoes was so damn tiring. Did he want in or out? Had his love been extinguished? Was he playing a game or were his actions fueled by something more serious?

Corbin leaned over and kissed Norman. With this one action, the tension faded as though a sunbeam had burned away a thick fog. *All right,* thought Norman. *I'll give it one more night.*

In a sexy voice, Corbin asked, "Where were you last night?"

"Well, when you put it like that…" Norman kissed him back.

"Want to tell me all about it, in the bedroom?"

"Do you think I suffer from satyriasis? That I'll spill my guts if you're really good?"

Corbin stopped, blinking in confusion. Silence lingered for a fraction of a second, then he laughed. Finally. Norman hadn't heard that sound in a week. Corbin's laugh intensified, bringing tears to his eyes. He grabbed a napkin and dabbed them. Then he gulped down half a glass of wine, killing the sexual vibe.

Norman took the half-empty wine glass, grabbed Corbin's hand, and dragged his lover to the couch. "I was invited to Isa and Blake's."

Again, Corbin looked confused, this time by the mention of this sensitive subject. He usually avoided talking about his family. They didn't visit, didn't talk on the phone, didn't even bother with the occasional social media interaction. And yet there was no feud between them. It only seemed like a sort of…coldness, Norman knew that Corbin's bigger brother was a detective with OCD, but little more.

"Blake invited me to meet Isa's team."

Corbin nodded, trying and failing to maintain his smile.

"Isa's working on a new project with that guy from NWN TV, uh, the hunk, John Taylor."

"Good for her," said Corbin.

"Yeah, it's a small team, but they have big goals."

"Sure. No doubt involving making Taylor a real star?"

"Ha, good one."

"*Blake* invited you?"

"Yeah. He called me one morning and, uh, we had a nice chat…you know…"

"You had a nice chat with Blake? My brother?"

"Why is that so hard for you to believe?"

"Long story. What did they want with you?"

Norman pulled back from Corbin, sipped at the wine, and thought fast. Should he press the brother angle, or simply move on? If he wanted to help Isa, he should probably deflect. With an air of indifference, he asked, "Are you all right?" Another sip.

"Yeah, no, I'm good."

"Isa is researching a story on American underground slavery." Norman casually smiled, observing Corbin.

"That's…interesting."

"She discovered that William Wilmot could be at the center of the controversy, and she wants to dig deeper."

"Seriously?"

"You know the saying—all roads lead to Wilmot."

"I wouldn't go that far." Corbin rose from the couch and started clearing the dinner table.

"Well, anyhow, think about it," said Norman in the same casual voice.

"What's to think about?"

"So, you want to play that game?"

"Mister Senator, have your political tools rusted that much?"

Norman moved closer, to help Corbin with the cleanup. "Life's been hard in the political arena."

"Apparently so." Corbin carried the dirty plates into the kitchen.

Norman followed with the food trays. As they busied themselves, the silence grew.

Corbin walked back to the dinner table, began wiping up the crumbs, then stopped. Turning to Norman, he scowled. "How would they know what I'm working on?"

"I may have something to do with that."

"Damn it, Norm! My work is *secret*. You can't just spill insider information to the *press*."

"Isa isn't press. She's *family*."

"She's not *your* family."

"And?"

"I decide what I tell my family, and what I don't."

Norman moved to the living room, walking around the couch to put some distance between them. "I've known Isa and Blake for three years now, and I have no reason to think Isa would do you harm. Hell, Corbin, they don't deserve your condescension. They're good people."

"It's my call. I decide." His voice sounded a little calmer as he added, "If they're good people or not."

"That's not how it works. I don't care what might've gone wrong between you and Blake years ago, if anything, but you don't get to govern how I feel about your family. I know them. They're my friends. They deserve to be included in your life. In our lives." Norman took his jacket from the hook near the entrance door. "But if you prefer to live alone, in darkness, plotting years-long plans for undercover missions that may or may not take place, then be my guest. But don't tell me what to think." He opened the door.

"You're right."

The sadness in Corbin's voice pierced Norman's resolve. He paused in the doorway, his hand on the knob.

"About *them*, you're right. They're good people."

"Then why do you continue to shut them out?"

"Because they don't deserve the darkness that invades my life. I need to protect them from the shit that follows me."

Norman stepped back into the room, closed the door, and silently strode over to embrace his lover. Wordlessly, he gripped Corbin, refusing to let go.

Dressed like beggar in dirty rags and a faded gray cap and dark shades, the man sat on a bench in the shadow of a great oak tree in Central Park. People walked or jogged by, but none gave him a second glance.

When Corbin sat next to the man, he wrinkled his nose. "Good grief," he said. "What the fuck did you rub on your skin?"

"A bit of stay away mixed with what the fuck do you want," said the man, looking away and barely moving his mouth.

"I'll never sit here again." Corbin sidled away until he ran out of bench.

"Do I look like I give a shit?"

"Tommy…"

"What?" The man still looked the other way. To an observer, he'd look as though he hadn't even noticed Corbin's presence.

"My sister-in-law's a television producer. She's working on a story about American underground slavery and William Wilmot."

"And?"

"She wants my help."

"How does she know about your research?"

"Fucking Chadwick."

"That's no way to speak of your love-dove," said the beggar.

"Fuck you!"

In response, the man picked at his nose. When he produced a sizable gob of snot, he turned to Corbin and made a show of rubbing it between his fingers. Corbin recoiled in disgust.

With a flick, the snot flew to the ground. The beggar stood, said, "I'll let you know what you can share," and left.

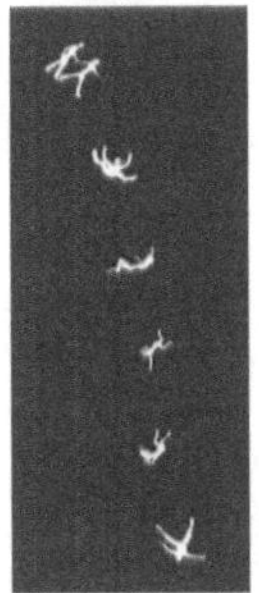

THE AIRPORT OF LOST HOPE

Blake marched through the doors into a public baggage pickup zone, Captain Moore still guarding his back. Clusters of people, in various stages of impatience, waited for their luggage to drop down onto one of the carousels. The activity felt more familiar to Blake, as he watched the Americans moving freely, still lucky enough to have money to travel and dress well, and still believing in the idea of freedom. These citizens kept their heads high, not bowed down in submission like those in London.

Where was she? Blake turned to Moore and asked, "Did you get my wife?"

"She's waiting for us here."

"So why didn't you talk to that NSA agent? Wouldn't it be easier to have them on our side?" Blake continued to scan for Isa while the events with the NSA played repeatedly in his mind. He needed to explain the situation to the NSA. He didn't need them as an enemy.

"For what it's worth, your FBI handler, Agent Cortez, asked me not to trust the NSA, or any other agency. That's what *undercover* means."

"Until the NSA learned about me and the English slaver." Blake inserted his password and unlocked his wristband.

The captain shoved him against a wall. "How did *that* happen?"

"The NSA was waiting for me as soon as I disembarked. They have images of me, on camera, with the European slaver."

"How the hell is that possible? Nobody knew about our op."

"Exactly." Blake studied his captain. "Like you said, the key word is *undercover*." If this kind of shit had gone down so quickly in the States, Blake would have assumed he'd been followed from the beginning. But the meeting with the English slaver had happened on the other side of the Atlantic. Why would anybody follow an exemplary police officer to a different continent to spy on him? Worse, why would they *pay* for an operative to spy on him? He was a nobody.

"I hate that I brought you into this mess." The captain sounded genuinely distressed. Even though Moore was tall, black, and acted tough, the old-timer had a soft side. Those who knew him—*really* knew him—had witnessed his well-guarded marshmallow core. Blake had seen him tear up at a sad movie, and knew his boss would get his hands dirty helping anyone caught in deep shit. There were plenty of rumors in the department, but Moore refused to spill the details about how he'd gotten promoted to captain. They all loved him. *Trusted* him. Every cop under his command would to stand alongside their cap and take a bullet for him, if necessary.

"Thing is," said Blake, "I rejected the Europeans' offer at first. They want Wilmot. I don't want to put Isa through that torture all over again."

"All right," said Moore. "We tried to—"

"Then the English Corp Police intervened. If I hadn't accepted their offer, we would've been arrested at the border. People with debt there…"

"I'm aware of the iniquities occurring over there."

"I had to agree. To bring Isa home."

"So, you're on-mission?"

"Yes. I'm in a lot of trouble with my wife. I hated having to lie to her about our trip. I can't keep up the illusion. I have to tell her the truth."

Blake's heart raced, and he struggled to catch his breath. He hadn't had the courage to admit the truth until this very moment. He needed to tell Isa the whole story, and then send her somewhere safe. Now that she was pregnant, and their dream would finally come true, nothing else mattered. And yet…he couldn't just watch while the whole world deteriorated around them. He had to do something to prevent the servitude plague from reaching American shores. To defend the future for his child.

"One step at a time, Frye." The captain's favorite slogan put a stop to Blake's thoughts.

They moved through baggage claim, checking all the corners and chairs. Something caught Blake's eye. He rushed to a chair and grabbed Isa's handbag. "This is hers."

Moore shook his head. "I told her to stay put."

Blake opened the zipper and found her passport. Scanning the contents, he didn't notice anything missing. *Not a theft.* Feeling even more frantic now, Blake made another thorough scan of the area. No Isa. She wouldn't abandon her purse. Blake dialed her number. It rang three times and flipped to voicemail.

At the security desk, one officer watched the baggage area. Blake approached, searching on his wristband, while Moore followed behind. When they reached the desk, Blake displayed first his police badge and then Isa's photo. "Have you seen this woman?"

"Yes," said the officer. "She was standing right there for a while." He pointed to the chair where they'd found Isa's purse.

"Well, she's not there now," said Moore.

"No, sir. Some federal agents took her away, maybe half an hour ago."

Blake turned to Moore, scowling. "She wasn't supposed to be involved."

"The NSA must have taken her," said Moore, "after they arrested you."

"This is bad. "Really bad."

"She'll be all right, Frye. We'll find the right contact in the NSA. But as far as I'm concerned, your undercover mission is complete."

"Now, more than ever, my mission is the *opposite* of complete. Those NSA bastards need to understand what's at stake. Why would they go after Isa?"

Something was off. Isa had nothing to do with him or his mission. Even if they suspected her of working with him for the British Servitude Exchange, he'd just escaped from the custody of the same agents who could easily learn the truth.

Was Isa in too deep now? Was there no safe place for his pregnant wife? Blake grabbed Captain Moore's arm and dragged him to a quieter corner. He looked around, but no one seemed to be spying on them.

"Talk to the FBI lady, Cortez. She needs to help me get Isa back. The Bureau must have some pull with the NSA. Meantime, let's see who that agent is."

Moore nodded and dialed.

Blake switched on his wristband and said, "Activate DPA."

The robotic voice answered almost instantly with, *"Active."*

"Search for agent Emilio Alvarez, NSA badge number 47S534. Collect everything you can about him. Especially present affiliations."

The DPA pulsed once to confirm, and vanished from his holo-screen.

Blake turned to Moore. The captain's face was red and sweaty. Blake knew something must be going wrong with the call.

"What do you mean I can't talk to her?" Captain Moore tried to keep his voice low. He turned his back to Blake. "I just talked to her half an hour ago. If you see her, tell her Captain Moore, NYPD, needs to talk with her, immediately." The captain switched off his cell and finally looked at Blake. The confusion in his eyes gave Blake chills. "Your handler, Agent Cortez…"

"What about her?"

"Apparently she didn't make it to the office."

"Where was she when you talked to her?"

"How the hell should I know?"

Blake rubbed his temples and exhaled, exhausted. He unbuttoned his jacket carefully. Slowly. Trying to think and hold back the tidal wave of approaching panic. "We need to find some other way inside the NSA." He stared at his captain, looking for approval—or a sign that they still had a fighting chance.

"Without Cortez, we have no way of proving you've been undercover." Moore sounded tired.

Before Blake digested the captain's words, his cell rang. The caller's name was blocked. After a deep breath, he answered, "Frye."

A young woman's voice said, "We have your wife. If you want to see her again, cooperate. Surrender yourself to Agent Alvarez and maybe we won't sell her."

The call ended.

Blake collapsed the holo-display and looked around in shock. His legs felt like jelly. He collapsed onto the nearest chair, unable to breathe.

"What?" Moore grabbed his arm. "Tell me, Frye!"

Blake's shoulders sagged, and he worked for every breath. *Isa. My beautiful, pregnant Isa.* He inhaled, exhaled, counting the seconds for each one, while he ensured that his jacket was buttoned up completely. Properly.

"Who was that?" Moore was almost shouting now.

Blake stood slowly, then began to pace in a slow circle, feeling his hands shaking. The captain blocked his path. Unable to move forward, Blake sighed, shut his eyes, and dropped into the nearest chair again. Activating his wristband, he tapped on an icon on the holo-screen and the image of a pill appeared. He dragged the medicine over his skin and waited for it to be absorbed. He whispered, "I promised her we'd be safe. That nothing bad would happen."

Moore sat next to him. "Talk to me, Frye."

"Isa's not with the NSA. She's been kidnapped. By slavers."

The airport's chief of security nodded at whatever he was hearing on the phone, and looked away for a brief second. "Yes, I understand. It's clear," he said to the person on the line.

Freshly shaven, bald head gleaming like polished chestnut in the overhead lights, dressed in a crisp uniform—everything about the older man cried former military. He spoke on the phone while he studied Blake and Moore. The office was modern and neatly kept, his desk a perfect example of organized space, with one exception: several pens scattered in a random pattern in one corner. While he waited, Blake arranged the pens so that their tips aligned. Then he raised an eyebrow at the fascinated expression on the chief's face. Even though Blake found comfort in the order and cleanliness, the chief's expression unsettled him.

The chief nodded at the phone. Definitely a military man who obeyed without question. Eventually he finished with, "Yes, I understand. It's clear," and hung up. He stared out the window at the parking lot below his office, then turned to them.

A good sign, thought Blake. *He seems to have a conscience.*

Addressing Moore, the chief said, "Sorry, Captain, no can do. Procedures are procedures."

"I don't think you understand the situation here," said Moore.

Blake cringed. He feared Moore's overconfidence might destroy his precarious and probably temporary freedom.

"I understand it perfectly," said the chief. "We have procedures in place for *exactly* this type of situation."

The chief remained calm and professional. Wanting to keep it that way, Blake spoke before Moore responded again. Keeping his own voice calm and nonconfrontational, he asked, "What's the procedure now, Chief?"

"I'll assign one of my officers to the case. They'll take a look at the security footage and investigate further. Then, we'll contact you and give you everything you need to know."

Blake nodded.

Moore pointed at the phone and demanded, "Who were you speaking with?"

Come on, Captain, thought Blake. *Enough with the pissing contest. We need to get out of here.*

Fortunately, Moore's phone rang. He read the display and raised his index finger to the chief. "One second, please." Then he stepped away to answer.

Blake exhaled slowly and quietly while he worked on the best way to exit the situation, before the NSA arrived.

The chief of security smiled awkwardly. "Actually, I'm very

busy, so could you please wait in my outer office with my assistant? I'll get back to you in a matter of minutes."

Blake looked from the captain to the chief. *I'd bet a hundred bucks that the NSA was on the other end of that phone call. And that they insisted the chief stall us here.*

The chief shouted, "Lucy, please take care of these gentlemen. Coffee, tea, whatever they want." In the smooth voice of a man in charge, he added, "I'll call you in as soon as we have something."

Lucy, plump and coiffed, arrived. She invited them to the waiting area. Blake nodded at the chief and guided Moore out of the office.

The captain turned to Blake, exhaling angrily. "Did he just throw us out?"

"We need to go," he murmured close to Moore's ear. "I'm pretty sure he was speaking to that NSA agent. We need to be long gone before they arrive."

Moore softened his stance.

Blake led Moore out of the waiting area.

Lucy followed them into the hallway, carrying two mugs. "Chief asked you to wait here, gentlemen. What do you take in your coffee?"

"Please tell the chief that we'll be back shortly," said Moore. "I need a private word with my detective, on other pressing police business."

Lucy nodded, set the mugs on a low table, and closed the door behind her, leaving them alone in the hallway.

Moore waved his cell at Blake. "That was the DA."

"Did he send the warrant?"

"No. He actually..." Moore hesitated and shook his head.

"What now?"

"He ordered you to the precinct. They want to start an internal investigation. It seems that Jeffrey Bouts wants to personally interrogate you."

"*Attorney General* Bouts? He wants to interrogate *me*, a lowly detective?"

"Unfortunately, yes."

"Shit," said Blake. *Just when I thought things couldn't get any worse.* When they were young, their father used to tell Corbin and Blake that things could *always* get worse. That they should keep a joker up their sleeve and remember to make a backup plan.

Not this time.

Blake had been caught with his pants down. His backup plan had been the FBI handler. The joker up his sleeve had been Captain Moore, his superior who was up to speed about the whole operation and usually had his back. Unfortunately, *Joker* had become an apt description. Moore's effectiveness in this particular situation was bound to generate a future "funny story," assuming Isa and Blake still had a future.

Moore sighed again and said, "Time to run."

"Definitely."

They hurried away from the chief's office and the administrative operations area. Blake wanted to reach a public area as soon as possible. If the NSA had indeed been on the phone, then they didn't have more than a handful of minutes.

Blake stopped walking when they reached the terminal's great hall. He put his hands on his head and stared at Moore.

Moore scowled, spreading his hands in confusion. "Don't say it. I know the shit-storm we're in. First the NSA, then the DA, and now the attorney general. Not to mention the ineptitude of the FBI."

Moore looked older than his sixty-plus years. He wasn't the kind of negotiator who sweetened a deal. He preferred to call it, label a raw deal as such up front, and deal with the consequences, no matter how bad, on the fly and without hesitation. Now he looked more desperate than confident.

Blake rubbed his temples and exhaled, exhausted. He hadn't slept in more than twenty-four hours, and hadn't had time to process Isa's kidnapping. Especially the fact that he couldn't simply report her abduction, knowing deep in his heart that her disappearance was the NSA's doing, and that they were probably about to charge him with treason. Isa had become collateral damage. Nobody would care about her once he was detained. Everyone else would be too busy wiping the shit off their own hands to help her. She'd disappear into the slave market, lost forever.

Blake said, "In one short hour, I became an enemy of the state." The summary, partly for Moore, but mostly for himself, didn't improve his situation, but naming the problem was a starting point. Captain Moore, Blake's last ally, needed to hear it stated so bluntly, without any sugar-coating, so he might also know how deep the hole had been dug.

"You still have our force standing with you." Moore's expression didn't convince Blake that he believed his own words.

"You know that's not exactly the whole truth." Blake didn't have the patience to placate his boss. "My wife's been kidnapped and my badge won't help me get her back. I only have hours to save her. Meanwhile, the whole system has turned against me. NSA. The G-men. Even the fucking Justice Department!"

Blake unbuttoned his jacket, straightened his shirt underneath, making sure it was absolutely perfect, and then rebuttoned his jacket with slow precision. "I need to rescue my wife."

At his temple, Blake's cell-patch vibrated. He subvocalized the acceptance. It was his DPA. Blake activated his wristband, putting the audio on speaker and the Digital Police Assistant's icon on display.

"I've downloaded a medical report and a personnel report connected to NSA Agent Alvarez to your wristband. Other than that, his file is too high-level for police to check. The access is highly classified, and I triggered some alarms when I sent the request."

"Are there any details at all concerning his current case?" Blake made an effort to keep his voice low.

"No. They're on their way back here. The NSA's security system asked for my identification, my warrant, and… didn't…" The DPA's icon vanished. Replacing it was a message in all caps, no doubt to emphasize the severity of his infraction. *DPA IN VIOLATION OF NATIONAL SECURITY PROTOCOLS. PLEASE REMAIN WHERE YOU ARE WHILE OUR AGENTS APPROACH.*

"Hell, no!" Captain Moore looked ready to have a heart attack.

Blake collapsed on a long metal bench. The captain continued cursing, practically foaming at the mouth. When Blake tried to speak, Moore interrupted. "They're not allowed to touch a DPA without a judge's order. Not NSA or any other goddamned agency."

Moore shook with fury. His holo-display buzzed and he opened it. He stared with incredulous eyes, then said, "I just received a warrant for your arrest, Frye. Seems the attorney general's directly interested in your connection with the British Servitude Exchange. They mention treason…"

Blake inhaled deeply, shook his head.

"Like you said, nothing else matters." Moore pointed a finger at Blake. "We need to find your wife."

Blake nodded. After a pause, he placed a hand on his boss's shoulder and squeezed. "They took her because of me."

"We'll get her back."

"How? I don't have any leverage."

"They want you, not her. It would help if we knew why they want to shut down your investigation."

Blake shook his head again and bent forward, leaning his elbows on his knees and holding his head in his hands.

"You know I'm with you," said Moore. "All the way."

Blake nodded, opened the medical file the DPA had retrieved, and browsed through. He found it weirdly satisfying that now he knew why Alvarez was in bed with the slavers, yet it didn't make his situation easier. It raised more questions than it answered. He leaned toward Moore. "You need to see this."

Moore stared at the point in the document where Blake had paused.

"The son of NSA Agent Alvarez is terminally ill," Blake read from the report. "He was recently admitted to hospital for a very expensive medical procedure. Way beyond what an NSA agent's salary could pay for. They enslaved Alvarez's dying son."

"Hmm." Moore's tone was cold. All business.

Following his captain's lead, Blake switched back to police investigator mode. "I'm in this undercover mission against the American slavers. Then, out of the blue, the NSA wants my hide.

At the same time, my FBI handler vanishes and the attorney general personally declares me a traitor. We must assume that Wilmot has all of them by the balls. From this report, I'd say Alvarez is definitely compromised."

Establishing a timeline was a good place to start. No investigation ever took only hours, but in this case, time was definitely in short supply. He needed answers. Needed to dig deeper, as quickly as possible, starting with the people who took Isa. Where would they take her? What could he do if he found them, especially without backup from his own police force or the FBI?

Blake needed to enlist his structured analysis routine. He needed to put his thoughts in order, study the facts, and begin to draw conclusions. He extended his holo-display and double-tapped on the Police Notepad app. A blank page appeared. He drew a circle in the middle of the page and inside the circle he wrote *FRYE*. All of the problems had begun when he'd accepted the undercover mission to London. So, within the first circle he drew bullets and filled them in with the names *Capt. Moore* (who proposed the mission); *Isa* (whom he'd brought on the "vacation" to make the trip less suspicious); *Agent Cortez* (his FBI handler, and the one who approached Moore for an operative); and *Samuel Brit* (his English target).

The British slaver, Brit, had given Blake another mission within the official one. That secondary objective was what mattered to the FBI. They didn't give a crap about the activities of the English slavers. They wanted to find out who orchestrated the slaver activity in the US. They also needed to know the methods and locations of the American slaver network. Who better to be aware of that activity than the competing European slavers? They carried out their operations in full public view, with their governments' approval. A legal servitude business model.

Blake returned his focus to the case. He needed to find a list of corporations involved in international slave trade. Within that list, he needed the names of the people pulling the strings internationally, who probably had counterparts and contacts in the States.

He drew a second circle, around and containing the first one.

Moore leaned over his shoulder. "Frye, we don't have time for your musings right now."

"This is how I investigate."

"It's not an official police investigation any longer. All that you and I can do is act. Quickly. Focus on those two key words: *act* and *quickly*."

"I can only act with the right information."

"You need to run on instincts."

"I can't. Neil was the action man, the fast one. He…" Blake stopped and swallowed hard, remembering his partner. It was the first time he'd said his name since the department abandoned the investigation. *Into my partner's disappearance. Not his fucking death, as the DA's office spun it.*

"You're underestimating yourself." Moore's voice softened. "What's your detective gut telling you to do, right now, about Isa's abduction?"

"I need her last known position." He paused, then added, "And also, her captor's escape route."

"Good." Moore smiled. "There's my detective. Write your notes and schemes later."

Blake stared at Moore, inhaled deeply, and collapsed his holo-display. With Isa's purse in his hand, he scanned the vicinity, counting one exit sign, a second, then across the huge hall, several more. The routes to every one of them looked clear. But after checking the positions of the surveillance cameras, and accounting for the number of people waiting for their luggage, he narrowed down the possibilities.

"The closest exits are on this side." He pointed them out to Moore. "They had to take her out of here as quickly as possible, avoiding any interference from security."

Moore grumbled his approval and squinted toward where Blake was pointing.

"Their call was about half an hour ago. By then, they'd already moved Isa to a secondary location, which means they must have had a car parked close and ready. Doing the math, their camp is within a one hour radius. I'll take this exit. You check the other one."

Moore strode toward his assigned exit.

Blake hurried to the first exit on his left. The automatic doors glided open. Two signs on the wall directed passengers *TO AR-RIVAL HALL* and *TO BLUE PARKING*. Blake slowed and talked into his cell. "My exit leads to blue parking."

"Same here," said Moore. "Keep going."

Blake ran down a narrow corridor, looking for other signs or doors and continuing the conversation with Moore. "How did the NSA get access to images of my London meeting in less than twenty-four hours? Especially considering my low profile."

"Maybe your handler?" Moore sounded breathless.

"Did the FBI have access to the hotel's cameras? Or were they following me?"

"They couldn't follow you abroad. It's against their mandate," said Moore. "But they could've passed you off to the CIA."

"Even harder to believe. I'm not a spy, for crying out loud. And why is the NSA involved?"

Moore kept silent. The captain was an efficient cop, but even more old-school than Blake, who was well known for his thoroughness. Blake never rushed his investigations, always calculating and re-evaluating possibilities. Everyone in the department talked about his slow, turtle-like approach. How he focused on every little detail. Blake wasn't a "chase the perp while dodging bullets" cop. Instead, he aimed to be on time, on task, and so well prepared that there'd be no need to draw his weapon.

Arriving at another exit, Blake emerged into a sprawling public space, lined with restaurants and shops. Three more exit signs were spaced around the concourse.

Speaking into his cell again, he asked, "Remember Neil?"

"The DA thinks he's dead," said Moore.

"Neil vanished. Just like Isa. And if it wasn't for the message I sent you before they cuffed me, I would've mysteriously disappeared as well."

"Your partner's case is closed."

"It shouldn't be."

"There's no body. No ransom. Even if he did run away,

which I doubt, the city of New York isn't going to spend another nickel trying to find him."

"That's not our way. Or, it didn't *used* to be the way our department took care of its own."

"Come on, Frye."

On the other side of the concourse, Moore appeared through a door, caught sight of Blake, and shook his head. Then he pointed to the other two exits. Blake nodded and moved forward.

Hanging up on his boss, he quickly dialed his brother, and heard, "This is Corbin. Leave a message."

He hung up, activated his holo-display, and said, "JFK Airport map." The wristband connected to the airport's network to fulfill the request.

By the time Blake reached his new exit door, his wristband vibrated. He quickly downloaded the airport's map and displayed it.

Outside the shopping concourse, he strode along a wide hallway that led to oversized double doors and the roadway. Side doors dotted the route. He checked his map, and learned they were entrances to various administrative offices. Blake noticed overhead cameras in fish-bowl housings, strategically located to record every movement in the corridor. He took pictures of the nametags on the doors along the way, in case that data wasn't available online or from his map. Then he called Moore again.

"Hey Cap," he said. "I remember when we used to investigate a missing person until we were so stuck that we had no other choice but to suspend the search. We never closed a file because of a budget shortage."

"The cease order came from upstairs."

"Did you push back?"

"Some orders, from certain people, must be followed. Or I could've pushed myself right off the force."

Blake hurried through the double doors to the sidewalk where cabs, buses, and hotel shuttles queued up for passengers. Moore appeared from an exit about a hundred yards west. He walked closer, while Blake made a note of every surveillance camera, recording every possible angle of the loading zone.

When Moore caught up, Blake said, "You told me there was evidence that Neil ran away."

"Those were my orders."

"I'm guessing your next no-debate order will be to release a statement to the press about a certain dishonorable detective. Something like, 'Detective Blake Frye is a traitor to his country and is now a coward on the run, along with his television producer wife.'"

Moore grimaced. "I'm sorry about Neil. I could've done more."

"Damn right, you should've done more. You taught me that we don't quit. Not until we're at the edge of a cliff with nowhere to go. And even then, we always drop a few breadcrumbs, just in case."

"The department has changed. I had two choices, evolve or retire."

Blake nodded. He hadn't intended to attack the old man, but with Isa in danger, the stakes were too high. Too personal. He needed Moore to object, or at least stall, if he received another no-debate order. He needed the old Captain Moore, the man who'd pounded every rule into Blake until he could recite them in his sleep. The seasoned officer with a backpack full of know-how, climbing a mountain peak to high moral ground.

Blake said, "I know of another case related to Neil's and Isa's."

"Which one?"

"Senator Norman Chadwick's disappearance six months ago."

"The senator's case is closed."

"Another order from above?"

Moore shrugged. "I was told that he was under investigation for homosexual behavior. He went into hiding before they could prosecute him."

"Goddamn it, Captain. There was no such witch hunt for Chadwick."

"That's the official statement from chain of command. And

we both know the senator liked men. If I'd kept his case active, it would've exposed his lover's identity. One Corbin Frye."

"My brother's not gay. He's had many public relationships with women."

"Okay, so he's bisexual, or whatever. No judgement. But from the law's perspective it's the same finish line. Corbin was in danger. Which means that, by association, so were you."

"We were investigating his disappearance, not his sexual preferences."

"If we'd kept digging, it would've blown up in our faces. Those in power won't hesitate to pay informers to rat out anyone in a homosexual relationship. Somebody sold out Chadwick. It was only a matter of time before they ruined Corbin."

Blake started pacing up and down the sidewalk, keeping his voice low to dampen his frustration. "You don't know the whole story. The senator was helping Isa with her research on servitude in America. Someone high up must've learned that he shared the wrong information. They made the senator disappear."

He pointed at his boss. "Neil was digging in the same spot, turning over the same rocks. Then *he* disappeared. Now I'm on your mission, which just happens to focus on the same industry, not to mention William Wilmot's sudden and inevitable involvement. Now I'm a traitor, and Isa's in a fucking dungeon somewhere." Blake bit his tongue, trying hard to keep his anger under control.

Moore rubbed his temples, thinking. "We need proof, Frye. Not suspicions, or circumstance-based theories."

Blake waved for them to go back inside the terminal. When he found a bench, they both looked left and right, searching the crowd for anything suspicious.

Forcing himself to sit, Blake asked, "What do we know about Bouts?"

"He's the attorney general. What else do you need to know?"

"Any small detail could make all the difference."

"As the head of the Department of Justice, he's done all the dirty jobs for the last two presidents. Implementing all of the most highly disputed policies."

"If Bouts is calling for my hide, that means servitude will be the next law on the books in America, and he's taking down anyone making an opposing argument."

"Probably," said Moore.

"He knows Congress will pass the Freedom Act, and he'll be the one to implement it. And that means I was chasing a dead horse. My mission had no meaning. Their only goal was to play with me, like a cat with a mouse, until they trapped me." Blake stood and walked in tight circles, fueled by nothing but adrenaline.

"I disagree. I think it means they're still afraid. That's why they're so hell-bent on catching you. To stop you from doing whatever it is they're afraid you'll do."

Blake stopped pacing, and as he considered Moore's words, a small smile began to form. "Okay," he said, "let's test your theory. I'll perform my first act of treason. I'll ask the English to help me rescue my wife."

Holding out his hand, Blake said, "You can't be anywhere near me, or you'll get sucked into my undertow. Leave now. Buy me some time. I'll contact you once I have something substantial."

The captain grasped Blake's hand, shook it, and then walked away.

As soon as Moore reached a safe distance, Blake activated his wristband and opened his notepad again. He added names to the second circle: Agent Alvarez; Agent Saunders; William Wilmot (with a question mark next to his name); and Attorney General Jeffrey Bouts. He studied his notes for a moment to be certain they matched his thoughts, then he called Samuel Brit.

Brit answered halfway through the first ring, as though he'd been expecting the call. "Yes, Mr. Frye."

"Hello, Mr. Brit, I require your assistance."

"How can I help you?"

"The NSA knew about our meeting. They were waiting for me and my wife at the airport. Now, the American slavers have her."

"What would you like me to do?"

"Help me to access the airport's security footage. The kidnappers had to pass by several European airlines' offices. I've sent you pictures of their nameplates."

After a brief pause, Brit said, "I have an even better solution for you, Mr. Frye."

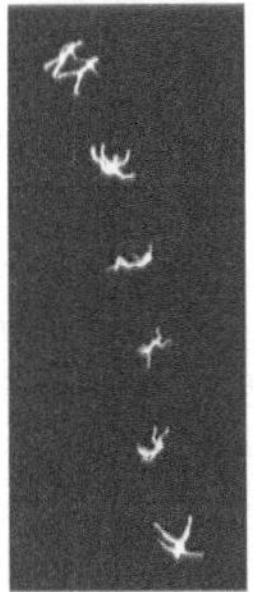

THE HIDDEN TREASURE

Simon observed the people in the Great Hall of Science. The journalists and scientists drank early morning champagne, quickly becoming drunk and ready to party. Nobody gave him a second glance, since he wasn't part of their world. He didn't know any of them, but more importantly, he didn't have a glass in his hand.

He pulled out his camera, dropped his bag on the floor, and walked to the exit. When he opened the door, he glimpsed Gabriela driving away down the long driveway. He looked left and right and didn't see any security. With a smile, he began strolling along the outside of the building, glancing at Gabriela's vehicle every now and then. It turned onto a road deep inside the Wilmot compound, which led to a line of trees away from the gate.

Simon continued around the building, checked to ensure that he wasn't being followed, then sprinted through the rain toward the tree line.

The trees were part of a small wood. Simon glimpsed light through the dense branches, so he hurried along a narrow animal track. The overhead boughs deflected most of the rain. On the other side of the wood, a wire fence bordered a vast valley with a hangar-like building at the bottom. He crouched in the tall grass and weeds growing along the fence.

Gabriela's vehicle pulled up in front of the hangar, next to a black government-type car. Nearby, two rough-looking guys wearing leather jackets and bandanas waited in a Jeep. Probably

Debt Hunters.

Simon pointed his camera, zoomed the lens, and started snapping pictures.

Gabriela got out of her vehicle and approached the black car. Two government agents clad in black suits and white shirts got out of the car and roughly pulled a woman from the back seat. Gabriela looked at the woman, consulted her holo-display, and nodded.

Without warning, the woman kicked one of the agents and tried to run. The second agent slapped her so hard, she fell to the ground. They yanked her back on her feet.

Zooming his lens in closer, Simon got a better look at the woman's face and gasped. "Isa?" The word escaped his lips before he could stop himself. "What the fuck did you do, Blake?" he whispered.

Several security guards hauled Isa inside the hangar. The agents climbed back into their black car and drove away. Simon watched, stunned, incapable of organizing his thoughts.

Next, the two rough-looking guys in the Jeep dragged a man, a woman, and three children over to Gabriela. Simon raised his camera again, zoomed in on the family, and shot a few more pictures. The family tried to resist, but not for long. Gabriela checked a list on her holo-display, made some notes, and called more security guards out of the hanger to lead the captives indoors. Simon tried to frame each person below, snapping their faces one at a time.

Gabriela nodded at the Jeep dudes, and they followed her inside.

Simon activated his wristband, opened his holo-cell, and wrote a message: *Found proof of slave camp. Pictures of two debt hunters and their vehicle follow.*

He hit Send, opened another message box, and typed: *Blake, I've just seen Isa taken into a slave camp. Where are you, bro?* Simon signed the message, *Corbin.*

A new message popped up on his display: *Message cannot be delivered at this time. Security is jamming the signal.*

Rustling leaves startled Simon. Through the trees, he made

out a security guard patrolling the perimeter. He hesitated over the Resend button, then collapsed the holo-screen and withdrew.

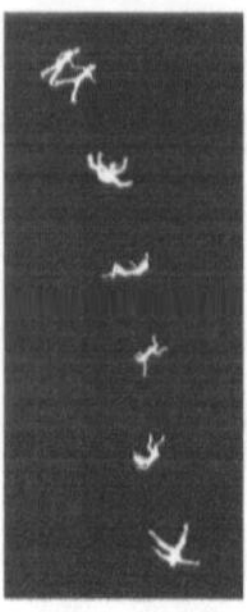

SEVEN MONTHS EARLIER

Isa had always been curious about Corbin's office. She'd been in his condo a few times before, mostly for picking up or dropping off items for Blake. Corbin wasn't a very social guy, at least not with family. Usually they'd interact once a year, twice for exceptional occasions. The main family event involved a Christmas visit to their parent's house in Florida. Other than family get-togethers, Isa didn't think Corbin had any social life. No girlfriend, no group of mates to drink beer and watch the game, and certainly no parties. He was 150 percent dedicated to his job. Isa might've found his devotion to work a positive character trait if it wasn't a little creepy to see a bright young man living his life in the shadows.

Then she found out about Senator Chadwick. Corbin had helped the young politician by covering his election campaign and helping to set up fundraisers. Somehow their working relationship became more personal, and then more intimate. Considering the social climate, they both worked hard to keep the affair clandestine. Once Isa learned Corbin's big secret, she was embarrassed about her previous assessment of her brother-in-law, and a little melancholy that he had to work so exhaustively to be happy.

Blake and Isa stood close to Corbin's front door, waiting for him to properly invite them in. Blake didn't try to hide his confusion as he stared at Norman.

"I don't think so," said Corbin. "I told Norm I don't want

to be involved in your research. Frankly, I'm surprised you two showed up at my door unannounced."

"Don't be rude, Corbin," Norman intervened. "Come on in, you two. Please, take your jackets off and I'll hang them up." After they did so, he pointed at the sofa. "Please, have a seat. Corbin, would you grab some glasses and the wine I brought over?"

Corbin stood motionless for a couple of seconds. Isa watched his face slowly change from uncomfortable, to placid, and then he tried to smile. It was a very crippled grin, but still, there it was, his first attempt at being friendly with his older brother and sister-in-law. He headed for the kitchen, an open-concept space that extended from the living room.

"Forgive him, guys," said Norman. "He's just, you know, closer to a *morose* wolf than a *lone* one."

"You know I can still hear you, right?" Corbin's smile became much more genuine than Isa had ever seen.

"I don't know," said Blake. "Growing up, I remember him as the confident and cocky one. Father was always proud of how, even when he was obviously out of his league, my brother could still manage to get through any situation. He was, in a way, a little cold-blooded."

Norman laughed and looked at Corbin with what Isa could guess was love. The two men were still in the first act of their love story, still discovering themselves and courting each other. Isa found it odd, compared to the many times she'd seen him behave the same way with women.

Corbin leaned over the coffee table and set down glasses and a bottle of red wine. He uncorked it quickly and efficiently, then carefully filled four glasses.

"Sorry, bro," he said to Blake. "I'm out of beer."

"For you, brother, I'll make an exception."

Norman laughed once more, and touched Corbin's hand. He smiled back at his partner.

Behind them, the door to Corbin's office remained closed. *As always.* Isa's temptation to sneak a peek, could save her some precious time researching slavery in the US. Time had become scarcer with each passing day. The project timeline had been in-sufficient since the beginning, but as the government shut down avenues she was permitted to officially pursue, she wondered if the story would die before it ever aired.

Isa said, "Look, Corbin. I'm aware that Norman filled you in on the story that I'm pursuing with my team. I'm not aware of the angle you're taking, but I'm sure we can find a way to pool our resources while still maintaining the exclusivity of each of our stories. You have my word that I will only cover specifics that you don't find interesting."

"I'm sorry, Isa, but I won't compromise my investigation."

"You don't have to show me your notes. But I'd appreciate anything you could share, no matter how small."

"No, Isa. There's nothing."

Norman looked reproachful. "Are you absolutely sure?"

Isa looked at her husband for support. He began arrang-ing the napkins on the table so that they were on the same side of every glass, at the same distance, in the same position, and identically folded. As his discomfort became even more obvious, Corbin reached out with his hand to stop his brother. Isa shook her head and glared at her brother-in-law, mouthing, *"Don't."*

Trying to ease the tension, Isa said, "We have a list of people who've been declared missing. From that list, we fine-tuned it to only the persons we're 90 percent sure have been forced into slavery. We could share our list with you."

"What would you need in exchange?"

"Any of your research that involves William Wilmot."

Corbin shook his head. "Too steep."

"I can add a list of missing people who we've confirmed have died as slaves."

Corbin tapped his finger against his lips.

Now satisfied with the state of the napkins, Blake sat back and stared at his brother.

Norman took a loud sip of wine, feigning interest.

"Fine," said Corbin. "We have a deal." He held out his hand. Isa gripped it firmly, to solidify the accord.

Blake sighed and rose to look out the window. He began to

nod, as if he were engaged in a separate conversation that only he could hear. When Corbin rose and approached his brother, Isa made to stand and intervene. Norman lightly touched her shoulder and smiled as if to say, "Leave them."

"Hey, bro," said Corbin. "You okay?"

Blake smiled and nodded, looking happy and somewhat anxious. "Yeah, sure."

As an only child, Isa could only guess what having a brother could bring into or take from her husband's life. Her parents had been from larger families, but they were both gone now.

"See?" Norman said to Isa. "They're fine." Norman moved from his armchair to sit next to Isa on the couch. "Sometimes you need to trust those you love. Have faith that they'll do the right thing."

"Thanks, Norman. For everything."

"Don't mention it." He took another sip of wine. "I'm just selfish."

"In what way?"

"I think your piece would do a lot of good, for so many Americans. From what Corbin's told me, I think his story's just as important and influential. I want you both to succeed. Bring us all some hope. And since I'm no reporter, but I really want to feast on all of that hope, that makes me selfish. I have to rely on you two."

Isa reached over and hugged Norman. "Thanks for the vote of confidence." She noticed Blake laughing with his brother. Actually *laughing*. He only laughed after a joke passed through his analytical filter and triggered a feeling. By the time he laughed, the joke's timing got so messed up that his response sounded awkward. A heartfelt laugh was rare for her husband. Witnessing this uncomplicated moment of joy made Isa feel happy for the first time in a long while.

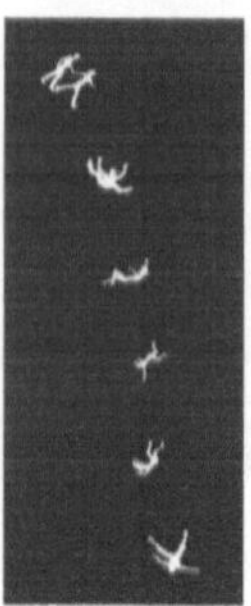

THE MAN IN THE WHITE COAT

Isa trembled, wishing she could wake up from this horrible dream. Ever since she'd landed in the United States, she'd felt as though she'd never escaped England and its horrors. *Please wake up*, she thought, even though she understood that not only was she fully awake, but she was caught like a lobster in a deep cage of madness.

Two men dressed in blue led Isa inside a building that looked like an airplane hangar. Inside, they shoved her through a labyrinth of corridors to what looked like a medical facility. Choosing a small exam room, they pushed her through the door.

"Take off your clothes," said the taller guard.

"No."

He drew a serrated hunting knife from his hip. "Last chance, or I cut them off."

"Could I have some privacy?"

He pointed at a pair of orange coveralls hanging on a wall hook. "Put on the coveralls, leave your clothes on the hook, tie back your *pretty curls* under the hairnet, and then knock."

Hating the creepy way that he'd described her hair, she decided it was safer to follow the guard's instructions. After she knocked, he confiscated her clothes, waved a device over her wristband, and locked her inside the room.

"See you," she shouted sarcastically. She immediately tried to activate her wristband, but as she suspected, the guard's unusual device had deactivated her link to the outside world.

She looked around. A large chair that looked like it belonged in a dentist's office was bolted to the floor in the center of the room. "Damn," she said. "I hate the dentist."

Without her wristband, she couldn't check the time, but it felt as though at least an hour had passed before the two guards returned with a man dressed in a doctor's white lab coat. He pushed a cart into the room. A machine with a touch-pad display and a series of ports on top was strapped onto the cart. He set the wheel brakes, then donned a pair of blue surgical gloves.

She swallowed hard and asked, "Are you a doctor?"

He didn't respond. One of the guards smirked, but didn't speak. White-coat man typed a string of seven numbers and symbols into the machine's touch-pad display.

Without warning, the two guards pushed Isa onto the chair. They cuffed her wrists to the armrests. Then they left her there with white-coat man. Isa looked around for any sign of what might happen next. The room could've been in any strip mall in America, part of a typical walk-in clinic . The combination of normalcy and foreboding confused her.

White-coat man checked the string of numbers he'd entered against his wristband's holo-display, then nodded with an air of satisfaction.

"Please, tell me. Are you a doctor? Like a certified MD?"

He remained silent. She felt as though they existed in different realities, where he did his thing, unaware of her presence. Once more, he typed a series of letters and symbols into the touch-pad. A barcode appeared above the screen, with a projection similar to a holo-display. White-coat man unclipped what looked like a stylus from the back of the machine and tapped the side of it with his thumb. A projection emerged from its tip, like a short beam of red light.

"What's that? What're you doing?"

White-coat man worked something on the stylus' body and the beam of red light widened and displayed the string of seven numbers and symbols from the machine's touch-pad. He tsked gleefully.

"My husband's a detective. Please, listen to me."

White-coat man turned with the stylus in his right hand. Then their realities merged and the nightmare became a horror show. She bit her lip so fiercely that her mouth filled with blood.

"Doctors swear an oath to do no harm. Please..."

He grabbed her arm and twisted it at a ninety-degree angle to the chair, pulling so tightly on the cuff that the metal dug into her wrist.

"Stop. Please. I'll do anything you want."

Then she screamed as the tip of the red beam touched her skin. The man aimed the beam for what felt like forever, but somewhere far away, Isa could hear him counting.

"One-one-thousand, two-one-thousand."

Then the stylus moved away, the humming ceased, and the pain lessened. White-coat man had burned a mark onto her forearm. A barcode, and a sequence of numbers. The stench of burned meat hung in the air.

That's me, she thought. *The smell of my scorched flesh.*

Putting the experience into words flipped an internal switch. The pain turned to fury. "You're fucking dead!" she screamed. "I will fucking kill you, with my bare hands." She aimed a kick at him, but he dodged out of the way. Her foot made contact with the machine, almost overturning the cart.

The doctor pressed a cloth over her mouth, with adhesive on one side. When she tried to wiggle her head away, he only pressed harder. She could feel the glue stinging her lips. He checked her eyes, one by one, keeping a brutal hold on her mouth.

When he released the cloth, it stayed on her mouth while he checked her blood pressure and pulse. Next, he drew blood in ten test tubes. He placed each tube into different slots on his machine, and flipped a series of metal switches, one by one. Once the last one was tripped, he checked the first one.

Her mind raced. *Why are they doing this to me?* She remembered the woman outside. She'd checked Isa's name against a list. The woman's face had been vaguely familiar, but Isa couldn't place her yet.

A list is methodical. Systematic. *This isn't a random abduc-*

tion. The guards, the coveralls, and the barcode tattoo all added up to a terrifying conclusion. *I'm in a slave camp.* One of many that she'd researched for her story. *I guess I'm the corroborating witness now.* If her abductors were actually slave traders, then they wouldn't keep her for long. *Except they had NSA badges,* she thought. They couldn't be debt hunters.

When she and Blake were separated, he'd been in the custody of airport security, not the NSA. *They're all on the same side,* she thought. If she was right, then did that mean that Blake was somewhere in this facility, too?

White-coat man checked the last of the blood tubes and grinned. "Oh, good," he said, his voice squeaky. He pressed a blue button pinned to his coat and the two guards returned.

"Take her to processing," he told them.

Before they could unlock her cuffs, the young woman from the camp's entrance wandered into the room, her expression cruel and cold. Isa still couldn't place the stranger.

The two guards stepped away from the chair, waiting with their hands behind their backs.

"Miss G?" said white-coat man.

G, thought Isa. *Whose name starts with a G?*

"What are her stats?" the woman's voice was as cold as her face.

"All normal, within acceptable parameters, but with one unexpected result. She's pregnant."

"I see." She leaned over so that her breath brushed against Isa's cheek. "Congratulations, Mrs. Frye. Now we'll get a much better price for you."

Isa stared in horror. *I'm property now. A commodity.* How could this happen to her, in a free and democratic country with a bill of rights to protect its citizens? Isa felt naked, exposed, helpless, and in dire peril.

White-coat man nodded and pointed at the cuffs.

"Take her to solitary," said Miss G. "And wait for my instructions."

The guards stepped up to either side of the chair and unlocked her wrists.

As soon as her hands were free, Isa's terror turned to anger. After years of fertility treatments and thousands of dollars, their wish had finally come true. No way in hell would she carry her baby to term as a slave!

She pounced on the first guard, kicking him in the groin. Letting her momentum carry her, she punched the second guard in the gut. Unfortunately he was massive, and took the punch as though it had been nothing more than a friendly tap. He raised his palm to strike her.

Miss G grabbed his arm, and insisted, "Mrs. Frye must not be harmed."

Isa turned and ran, all the while thinking, *Not harmed? You just tattooed a fucking barcode onto my arm!*

The huge guard pulled out a Taser and pressed it to her shoulder. Isa fell to the corridor floor, thrashing like a fish out of water. Through teary eyes she watched Miss G user her own Taser to stun the massive guard until he finally dropped his weapon. Isa's thrashing ceased.

"She is *not* to be *harmed*. In any way. If you two idiots can't follow orders, then you're useless. And you know what happens to useless people around here."

The second man, still groaning and cupping his groin, nodded, mumbled, "Yes, ma'am," and reached down to pull Isa to her feet.

"Since you seem incapable of processing commands, I will repeat my orders. Take her to solitary and wait for my instructions. I will closely monitor Mrs. Frye. If she's harmed again, in any way, then you two imbeciles are finished. Understood?"

"Yes, ma'am." The guard looked scared.

He's terrified of her, thought Isa. *Of the Ice Lady—aka Miss G.*

With gentle hands, the guard helped Isa down the hall to her next destination. Solitary.

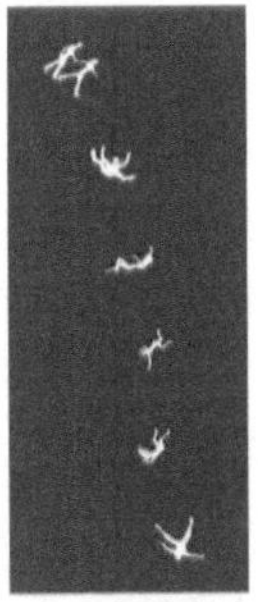

NIGEL ON SYDNEY

Nigel Blakesley parked his car right at the beginning of Sydney Street. He walked down the road, looking for the address that Mr. Thompson had given him for Samuel Brit's office. Cheeky Mr. Thompson, giving him the information he needed in exchange for future favors. *A typical racketeer.* He acted more like a rat than a man, quiet and invisible, ever present and willing to help someone in need, backed up by an army of psychos wielding torture paraphernalia whenever any shit hit the fan. One never knew if Mr. Thompson served for profit, or pleasure.

Even though the Georgian houses on Sydney Street were not spectacular, the area sweated luxury from every crevice. People with money still populated the world. Wealth had become as polarized as politics, creating those with colossal portfolios and those with barely enough to live from one day to the next. Automation had eliminated nearly all the labor jobs. The remaining positions still available for living and breathing humans had existed available since the beginning of civilization: the double Ps. *Prostitution and protection.* Two thirds of the labor market involved sex and muscle. Hookers followed straightforward procedures. On the other hand, protection had broadened to an industry with many facets, some not even imagined a few years previously.

Ah, here it is, thought Nigel. The house's dirty yellow brick façade was dotted with white sash windows, larger on the ground floor and growing smaller toward the top of the structure. No company sign or logo advertised the activities occurring within. It could be a private residence, or an empty house. *Time to test Mr. Thompson's sources.*

Nigel activated his wristband and selected an app represented by a pixelated spider. He tapped twice and the app opened a settings window. He studied the façade and then selected four spiders — one for each floor (set to *hide and record*), and one for Samuel Brit himself (set to *track and infiltrate*). He accessed the plan for a typical Georgian house and pinned the locations for the first three spiders, leaving the fourth one on *touch transfer*.

Sighing with satisfaction, Nigel climbed up the four front steps and rang the bell. His fingers lingered on the bell, pressing not for the pleasure of hearing the exaggerated ring, but to allow the spiders time to transfer from the app to the building. He didn't know where the surveillance camera was installed, but he was certain they were watching him now, so he smiled.

Samuel Brit grinned, and spoke into the cell phone. "I have a superior solution for you, Mr. Frye. Bear with me for a moment."

He typed the address of an office and a contact name, and sent the message to Blake. Then he switched his attention back to the phone. "Still there, Mr. Frye? I sent you a text." A pause. "Glad you've received it. Wonderful. Travel to the address and the contact person will help you with whatever you require." He disconnected the call before the police officer could blurt out an unnecessary response.

Next, Brit dialed another number. The person answered after one ring. Quickly he said, "Frye is on his way. Give him any information that airport security would customarily share in this type of situation. Nothing more." Again, he ended without waiting for a reply.

He switched off his cell, deleted his text message to Frye, and collapsed the holo-display. Stepping over to his desk, he activated its holo-display, settled into his leather armchair, and opened a document.

The digital assistant pinged and said, "Mr. Brit?"

"Yes."

"There's a guest to see you, sir. He claims that Mr. Thompson sent him."

Brit accessed the surveillance camera's live feed. A tall, red-haired man with the features of an Irish bully and the inquisitive air of an American cop waited by the front door. He stood with his arms crossed over his chest, confidently implying that he was a man who likely wouldn't accept "no" as an answer.

Brit considered his options. If he sent the stranger on his way, the man would no doubt unlawfully enter the property at his earliest convenience. If he interacted with the pest, Brit might expose himself to God knows what secret agency on a mission to dig up all his dirt. Regardless, the first pawn had already been moved. He couldn't hope the man would wait more than twenty-four hours for Brit's counter-play. Better to gain more data about his new opponent.

Brit searched his database for a reminder concerning "Mr. Thompson." and found a picture and file for one man with that name. Apparently, he was head of security for Lord Wright. *He's an important man,* thought Brit. *One of the main investors in the BSX.* Brit had never had the pleasure of making the lord's acquaintance. Why would Lord Wright's head of security need to meet with Brit? Sending an underling was more than a little rude. Especially a red-haired bulldozer.

To his digital assistant, he instructed, "Invite him in."

While Brit watched the monitor, the door opened and the man entered confidently. Not the slightest hesitation or pause to glance around the hallway. He quickly made his way to Brit's office, approached the guest side of the desk, leaned over, and extended his hand for a shake.

For fuck's sake! The operative had used one of the oldest tricks, knowing that Brit would have no way to avoid the pleasantry. Unless he was prepared to make a bold statement.

Brit rose from his armchair and shook the man's hand.

"Nice to meet you, Mr. Brit. My name is Nigel Blakesley."

With the simple gesture, Brit knew that a bug had passed onto his skin, and was now digging into his flesh to find a nice, safe place from which to gather information. As a countermove, Brit moved his hand under the desk, and inserted his hand into the digital burner, one of the CIA's top-rated counterespionage tools. A clink pinged in his earpiece, so quiet that Blakesley wouldn't notice. *That should fry the bug.* Brit smiled widely and sat, inviting the intruder with a wave to the oversized leather guest chair. Blakesley looked as though he'd stolen a priceless gem. *I should snap a photo,* thought Brit. *And post it, worldwide, on all the spying agencies' web-walls. For fun.*

The digital assistant pinged quietly in his ear, and then stated, "Three bugs, of the spider variety, found wandering the house. They have been destroyed."

Spiders, thought Brit. *Well played, Mr. Blakesley.* He kept his face neutral. Nobody had access to those except the CIA and the NSA in the States, and MI6 in England. This man could only be a top agent. *What, exactly, does he want with me?* He didn't even hide his American accent. It definitely sounded as though he came from New York.

"What can I do for you, Mr. Blakesley?"

Brit activated his holo-display in private mode, and tapped on the search icon. He typed *Nigel Blakesley*, comma *CIA*, comma *NSA*, comma *MI6*, comma *secret service*.

At the same time, Blakesley activated his wristband's holo-display in private mode, and said, "Mr. Thompson hinted that you're looking to hire."

"I've known Mr. Thompson for years, but never worked with him."

"I understand, Mr. Brit. I didn't approach you *for* Mr. Thompson. I'm simply *available*. For hire, if you need my skill set."

Brit nodded, and checked his display. The search found zero results. Apparently, Nigel Blakesley had no connection to any agency. The curious American finished whatever it was he'd done on his wristband, collapsed the display, and made eye contact. Brit saw Nigel's face through the one-way transparency of his display. He rendered a rectangle around the man's face and snapped a photo. Then he opened the face recognition program and ran the image through its databases.

"You're simply keen to assist, are you, Mr. Blakesley? Since I've never worked with Mr. Thompson, there's no reason why I would've spoken with him concerning my hiring needs."

The man didn't show any signs of discomfort or worry. Despite his bully face, he managed a friendly and trustful smile. *Damn, he's good!*

His tone warm, Blakesley said, "There's a rumor that you want to invest in a portion of the American market. You probably recognize my accent. I'm willing to help you gain a foothold in my country's budding market. In whatever way that I can."

Brit nodded, trying to hide his sudden surprise, when on his display, the software face search stopped, and a message appeared: *THIS IS THE MAN I USED.*

Interesting, thought Brit. The arrogant American was fishing for information on Brit's meeting with New York detective Blake Frye.

Brit rapped his fingers on his desk in a rhythmic pattern, as though he was intensely considering Blakesley's offer. After more than thirty seconds, he locked eyes with the man and stated, "I'll thoroughly consider your offer, Mr. Blakesley. If I find a task that is suitable for you and your *skill set*, as you put it, I'll contact Mr. Thompson. Is that satisfactory?"

Blakesley rose from the guest chair. "Thank you, Mr. Brit. I hope to see you soon."

As soon as the American closed the front door behind him, the digital assistant stated, *Your system has been breached by a mole group. No proper countermeasures in store. Recommend auto-destruction.*

"Delete all the hard drives," he said in his calm British voice.

System auto-destruction in five, four, three, two, one. System destroyed. The assistant's voice announced in the same polite, cold voice.

Brit rose from his armchair and paced the room. Of course he had a recent backup of his hard drives, but why would Blakesley make such an arrogant move with his spiders? He must be aware that Brit's system would be equipped with an auto-destruct plan.

Everyone in their line of work kept up-to-date backups.

The assistant pinged. *A mole has installed itself in the house surveillance system and accessed all the information regarding guests and video recordings. Recommend auto-destruction.*

"Fucking prick!" Brit allowed himself to lose his temper. Who the fuck was this Blakesley? Had he dug up Brit's true identity? He straightened his tie, cleared his throat, and shouted, "Destroy everything!"

System auto-destruction in five, four, three, two, one. System destroyed.

Brit looked around, absorbing the peaceful, quiet atmosphere of his office, despite the colossal destruction of so many digital assets. He moved to the window and drew back the curtain, just enough to peer outside. Blakesley stood in the front garden, waiting for Brit to make a move.

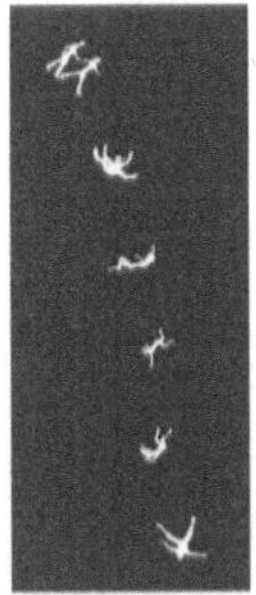

SEVEN MONTHS EARLIER

Isa cheered with satisfaction. The deal with Corbin had ended with great success. Her brother-in-law had given her more than she'd imagined. Now she could finish her story on time.

She asked, "How should I credit you, Corbin?"

He shook his head and raised his hands defensively. "I don't want my name anywhere on your story. Not even on internal documents at the station."

Norman rose from the sofa.

Blake observed the exchange with his usual somnolence. But she knew nothing escaped her husband's attention. She asked, "Why? Your information is sound and reliable."

From the doorway, Norman added, "This could be good exposure for your career."

"Stop," said Corbin. "I'm in the middle of an undercover investigation. I need anonymity. Corbin Frye must keep a low profile for now."

"Still doing your cape and sword thing, bro? Which alias is in play? Roger Black?"

Isa sensed that Blake was trying desperately to change the subject, so she decided not to press. Roger Black sounded familiar. Five years earlier, an investigative journalist with that name had exposed a huge government cover-up. Black's revelations had shaken the administration to the core, causing many heads to roll. If Corbin was Black, then she now felt a deeper respect for her brother-in-law.

"No," said Corbin, "Black's compromised. I'm Simon White now."

"Blake appreciates you protecting the family name," she said. "Cops generally prefer to fly under the radar."

Blake took the beer Norman was offering, twisted off the cap, and asked, "What's Simon White up to?"

"Playing Casanova," said Corbin, "With the daughter of an important player in the American slavery business."

Norman grimaced, emptied the last dregs of his wine, and turned his back to his partner. "I'll open another bottle." He left the room.

"Sometimes," said Corbin, "I hate what my job does to the people in my life."

"I'm sorry for asking," said Blake.

Norman threw his cigarette butt over the balcony railing. He watched it fall for twenty-seven floors, then opened the sliding door into the apartment. Corbin was tidying the office, collecting bottles and glasses from the meeting with Isa and Blake. Lingering in the open doorway, Norman cleared his thoughts, too exhausted to process the evening's specifics. Corbin remained the dark and moody writer he'd fallen in love with. To expect something more from the man was a mistake. *Norman's* mistake. Life and time moved forward.

In the polarized and toxic political climate, a public gay relationship was impossible for any man, and ten times more dangerous for a senator. He'd been around the block, and understood how to play the game. Real love was as unrealistic as a Democrat majority. But… *The but says it all*, he thought.

Norman should've set himself up with a pretend family. A smiling and waving wife and kids looked great on a campaign poster. Or at least the wife. Then again, the time for Democrats to keep their seats in either house was coming to a swift end. The next election they'd all lose, down to the last blue-clad candidate. An American dictatorship. It sounded bad in theory, but in practice it could be even worse. As a "former Democrat Senator" he'd be thrown to the curb like last week's trash. He was too far down the rabbit hole of his career to sentence any potential fake-wife to that miserable fate.

Without looking up, Corbin asked, "Hey, you all right?" He removed the bag from the garbage bin and tied it closed.

"Yeah," he answered. As he trudged through the room toward the front door, he thought. *Soon, he'll be taking me to the garbage chute.* Norman had understood, right from the beginning of their affair, the nature of Corbin's cold-blooded duplicitous journalist personality. But the man radiated charisma, and Norman had fallen hard. He'd thought a one night stand with the dark, handsome man would be worth the risk. Then it happened again. After their third night together, he'd wanted to enjoy the benefits of a relationship for a while. For a year. Maybe longer? *Too perilous.*

Corbin stopped in the front hall, looking a little bewildered at the sight of Norman donning his jacket to leave. He hurried for the door, blocking the exit and using the bag of garbage as a shield. "What're you doing?"

"Going home," said Norman.

"I thought we'd decided on a movie for tonight. Might be the last chance for you to spend the night for a couple of weeks, while I'm on assignment."

"I'm beat. I could use a shower and a good night's sleep."

"I have a big, luxurious shower. Two weeks is a long time. Plus, you often sleep better—you know, *after.*"

"I'm not in the mood."

"What happened, Norm?"

"I told you, I'm tired. I just…want to go home."

"Seriously. What did I do?"

Norman didn't want to answer. He wasn't in the mood for a lengthy argument about the ticking clock of their relationship, or Corbin's bisexual work-related affair. He was too proud to be clingy or needy. He smiled and tried to open the door, but Corbin didn't budge.

"Come on, Norm. Talk to me."

"I'd rather maintain my dignity and make a gracious exit.

Okay?"

"Gracious?"

"Have a nice trip."

"It's because of the woman, isn't it?"

"It's your job. I understand."

"Yeah," said Corbin, sounding angrier by the second. "I bet you do."

Norman cleared his throat and used his cold senator voice. "You need to move out of the way, now."

"I don't need to do a fucking thing. You want to leave? Fine. But first, you have to be honest with me."

"I *understand* this step you're taking for the investigation, I just don't *accept* it. There's a difference."

"That's what *undercover* means. I behave like Simon White. To be convincing, I must *become* Simon White. If I can connect with this woman, she'll trust me, and take me into the inner circle. I don't have feelings for her. She means nothing to me."

"If she says she loves you, will you say it back?"

"That's not fair. I love *you*, Norm."

"Or so you say. How do I know you're not role-playing with me, too?"

"Now you're being dramatic."

"I've wasted months with you. We should've kept it light. A few one night stands for fun."

"You don't mean that, Norm. I know you love me." Corbin dropped the bag and kicked it aside.

He does seem to care. To love me. But how much? "I guess I find it hard to understand that you can love me and be intimate with a woman at the same time."

"It's not promiscuity. It's business. A calculated move to advance my research."

"Do you hear yourself? How can you talk so coldly about intimacy and expect me to trust you? I love you so much, but that love puts my job at risk. I'm putting my fucking life on the line!"

"Without trust, how can you love me?"

"I don't know. And that's why I have to go home." He

moved Corbin's hand away from the doorknob and pushed him gently aside.

"Please, don't go."

"I'll see you around." Norman opened the door and left.

Corbin stood motionless for several minutes, giving Norman the chance to get in the elevator. Finally, he took the garbage to the chute, and returned to his apartment.

"Now what?" he asked the empty kitchen.

He glanced at the coffee pot, then at the half-finished bottle of wine. Neither one said "drink me." He had absolutely no desire to watch the movie by himself, not after they'd chosen the title together. *Damn it*, he thought. *I used to be so good at being alone.*

He flopped onto the couch, took a few deep breaths to ease his anger, and dialed Norman's number. It rang once, twice, thrice, and then voicemail. He repeated the pattern: call, wait through the ringing, then listen to Norman's voicemail message. Clearly he wouldn't take any calls from Corbin tonight. *Maybe ever?* That final thought became an anchor around his heart.

Corbin's father had taught him that for every problem there is a solution. That mantra had helped him to become a successful journalist.

I need to find the solution, he thought. Maybe construct a better, more romantic apology. That idea would only work if they could talk like adults, either on the phone or in person. No chance for that any time soon.

Norman was a politician. A player in the game of deceit and appearances. So why didn't he understand Corbin's false relationship with his source?

Oh shit. He fucking played me.

His pain turned to anger, boiling into a fiery rage. Without taking the time to think it through, Corbin dialed another number.

"New York Police," they answered. "Is this an emergency?"

"Not really," he said. "I'm calling to report a faggot."

"Please begin with his name, which I need you to spell. Then his address, phone number, and any other information, if available. If you would like to be eligible for the fifty dollar reward, we will need your banking details."

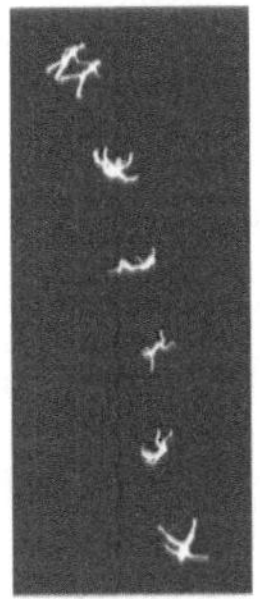

IN THE GAME

Gabriela was feeling energetic and optimistic. Managing the Wilmot Science Research Facility was a challenging job, but she'd enjoyed it from day one. She excelled in situations where she had to prove herself. Especially to her father, or to any of the powerful men who kissed her father's ass.

She entered the room with the wall-sized array of screens displaying the security feeds for the entire slave camp. Two clerks, a young woman and an older man, sat in the observation chairs. Hundreds of images showed different sections of the camp, from the large dormitories full of hundreds of bunkbeds to the small one-person cells. She glanced at the bottom left corner, displaying the coffin-like shelves housing prisoners in hibernation behind glass walls. The facility managed close to a thousand assets, and that was in a country where slavery wasn't entirely legal yet. Once the Freedom Act passed Congress and the Senate, the Wilmot Servitude enterprise would become an open, mainstream venture, the largest servitude business in the world.

Without glancing at them, Gabriela asked the clerks, "How many no-returns?"

The young woman checked her data and said, "Twenty-six, considering the latest addition."

"Isa Frye?"

"Yes."

"Remove her from the no-returns dorm and transfer her to

an isolation cell. I specifically asked those two dimwits to put her in solitary. Change her status to pending."

The woman nodded, browsed through her desktop's icons, and found Isa's picture. A quick double tap brought Isa's file onto the screen. The clerk opened it and entered the new status.

Gabriela's wristband cell buzzed. She'd received a new message, an image of Simon, sprawled naked on a bed. After a subdued giggle, she turned back to the two clerks, and returned to her ice-cold demeanor. She asked the older man, "Can you confirm, twenty-five no-returns?"

"Yes, ma'am."

"Are we expecting more?"

"We're executing two warrants. The hunters will soon make contact."

"We need thirty no-returns for Gambit Pharmaceuticals' China facility. Put it on queue as urgent."

The two clerks glanced at each other. Then the young woman looked down to her keyboard and the older man scratched his chin. Neither entered anything into their computers, completely ignoring her order.

The silence and inaction lingered, until the old man pushed his chair back and stood. "Uh, Dr. Mancini already reserved twenty no-returns. Unfortunately, Miss G, there are only five available for your order."

"Cancel his reservation, and put Mancini back into the queue, right after my order," she said, sharply enough to cut deep.

"My deepest apologies, Miss G," said the older man, his voice trembling. "Dr. Mancini has top clearance from your father. We cannot possibly alter his reservation."

Is everyone in this facility a bloody dimwit? Gabriela activated her wristband and dialed. The holo-screen popped up and displayed the image of Dr. Mancini, a middle-aged Italian vulture of a man. She couldn't stand him, but he was an old and trusted friend of her father's. They'd been through a lot together; valuable experiences that her old man refused to let go. He felt a sort of duty to his friend, the carrion-eating Italian.

"Dr. Mancini, I—"

"Ah, Miss G. What a pleasure."

"I need you to cancel your no-returns reservation."

"I'm good, thank you for asking. How are you, Miss G?"

God, he's a nuisance. One day! When he least expected it, she would finally put him in his place. She just had to wait until her father turned his back for a second, then she could dispense with this disgusting creature. Carefully, of course. Covering her tracks so that they could never lead back to her. Her father would not be forgiving.

"My request is of an urgent nature, doctor. I need thirty no-returns by the end of the week."

"And I need fifty by the end of the month. Your father ensured that I would have them by my deadline."

Dr. Mancini was the only person in the facility with the nerve to stand up to her. "I think you can appreciate that this company requires money, if we are to continue to fund your research."

"Talk to the old man. You know this is his soul-searching project."

"My father doesn't have the time to be involved in every minute detail of our day to day operations. He trusts me to run this facility."

"Well then, you have two options, Miss G. Either you speak to your father or you will have dinner with me tonight." He paused. "No, scratch tonight, I have other plans. Dinner sometime this week."

"Fine," she said. "Dinner this week. And I'm taking all of the no-return subjects for this week."

"Agreed. It was a pleasure—"

Gabriela switched off her cell. She had to accept his condition as quickly as possible. If she gave it any thought, she'd vomit right then and there. She swallowed the bitter taste in her mouth and turned her attention back to the two clerks.

"Reserve all of the no-returns for the Gambit Pharmaceuticals transaction. Let me know as soon as we have all thirty." She strolled to the door, paused, and turned back. "I want to be the first to know when Dr. Mancini makes another move for my stock. *Preferably* before he sweet talks my father into signing off."

"Yes, ma'am."

Gabriela stepped out, murmuring to herself, "One more greedy grab for my resources and you're dead, shithead."

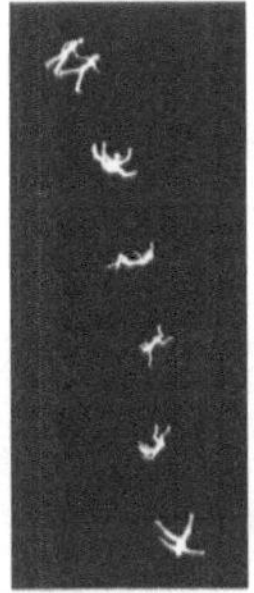

THE SLOW GUARD

The small man in blue opened the cell door and tried to push Isa in. She braced her feet against the edges of the doorframe and leaned away. He grabbed his Taser but didn't use it, his expression oscillating between fear and frustration. She lunged in the opposite direction, twisting the arm holding the Taser, and managed to slip behind him. With his body between her and the cell, she considered whether to push him into the cell or to make a run for it. He was small, but he might be fast.

"Forget the Taser," she taunted. "Miss G warned you. One more mistake and you're done."

He released the Taser and it clattered to the floor. Isa shoved him away and raced toward the end of the corridor and the closest door.

"Fucking bitch," he growled. She heard his clumsy footsteps but refused to look back.

She slammed into the door's crashbar and the door flew open. A moment later, she bumped right into William Wilmot and two of his security guards.

He grabbed her arm and shouted, "You!" He sounded shocked and angry.

Isa punched him, but it was like punching a sandbag. The force rebounded along her arm, the pain traveling all the way up to her shoulder socket.

He slammed her into the wall, forcing the breath from her lungs. The guards tried to intervene, but Wilmot snapped,

"Leave her to me."

Isa's guard stumbled through the door, out of breath. When he noticed Wilmot, he dropped to his knees. "Sir, I'm so sorry. She—"

"Shut up, you worthless idiot," Wilmot snarled.

"Please, sir. She's—"

Isa regained her breath and twisted to escape Wilmot's grasp.

A vicious slap, and the edges of her world grayed. She heard her guard say, "Sir, she's pregnant. Miss G insisted that Frye's not to be harmed!"

Wilmot tapped Isa's belly. "She's pregnant here." Then he pressed his thumb to her temple. "Not here." Without warning, he slapped her again, knocking her toward her blue-clad guard. "Lock her in a cell. I don't believe I need to remind you to *not lose her again.*"

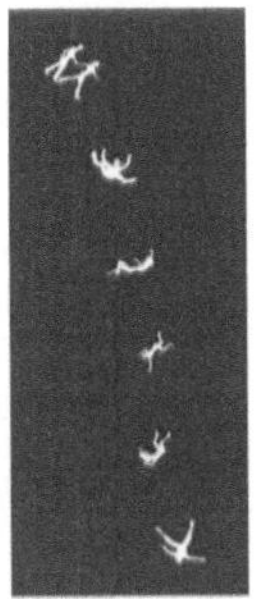

SIX MONTHS EARLIER

Three weeks after his fight with Norman, Corbin returned from his "adventure." The trip hadn't unfolded as he'd expected. Actually, it had been a waste of time.

When the elevator's doors opened, he noticed Blake standing in front of the condo door. Corbin grabbed for his suitcase but missed the handle, unnerved by his brother's presence. Until recently, they'd been fine living their own lives, separate and distant from each other. Trying to sound casual, he said, "Hey, bro."

Blake stepped aside, allowing Corbin to unlock the door and step inside. Blake hurried through the door, closed it quickly, and demanded, "Where have you been?"

"I was on a research trip. Why?"

"Didn't you hear?"

"Hear what, exactly?"

"Norman's been arrested. They charged him with homosexual behavior."

"Where are they keeping him?"

"He's out for now. Lack of evidence."

"That's good, I suppose." Corbin turned his back to Blake and hung his coat on the hook while he did an internal check on his emotions.

"You *suppose*?" Blake glared at his brother.

"It's all a shock." Corbin cared somewhere, deep down, but he wasn't ready to face his own actions. Not now, when he was getting close to some concrete results.

"And?"

"And what, Blake? What exactly do you think I should do?"

Blake didn't answer. Instead, he followed Corbin around the condo as he stashed his luggage in his office, then walked into the bedroom to change his clothes.

Blake sat at the foot of the bed. "I thought you two were partners."

"You mean *lovers*?"

"You seemed comfortable, like a couple. I thought you were together. Three weeks ago, it almost seemed perfect."

"Maybe. But that's what happens when family members stick their noses into someone else's business."

"I had no idea my question would've put you in such an awkward position. You could've lied, or obfuscated the truth. I'm sorry you got hurt."

"No, you're not. It might seem hard to believe, but the moment you and Isa insinuated yourselves into my life with Norman, our relationship turned to shit. It's probably not some- thing you can wrap your neat-freak head around, considering the charity relationship Isa has with you. I think it's better if you just leave, before you ruin something else for me."

Blake looked startled. Corbin could almost see the line of pain rising through his brother's body, as though he'd been struck by lightning. He had no time to deal with Blake's mental deficits while his research project cranked into critical mode. *Family just slows me down*, he thought.

He waved a hand and said, "Leave, Blake. Now. Before I throw you out."

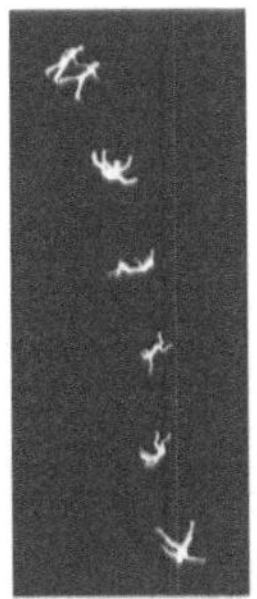

THE MEN IN GRAY

Blake checked his map of the airport. In front of him, the corridor opened in two directions. He chose right. Brit had told him the BSX had a security office in the airport, which should've triggered all sorts of alarms in Blake's mind. But right then, he couldn't care less. Instead, he was actually *grateful* for its presence.

Several doors lined the right side of the corridor, and cameras loomed at every intersection. He walked grim-faced to the first door, labeled *Office*, and knocked.

The two men on the other side of the door were expecting Blake. They sat him in front of a screen and hovered on either side of him, following his every move. They pointed to the icons for each video he'd requested, and waited as he watched each one.

On the first clip, two NSA agents picked up Isa. Blake chose the cameras in the next section of the airport, angle by angle, following the route of Isa and her escorts to an exit.

Next, Blake selected a different area of coverage from the surveillance grid. It showed Isa being led outside the airport into a parking garage. They approached a black vehicle and she was forced to climb inside. When the vehicle turned left, Blake had a great view of a face through the lowered window. He hit Pause, took a snapshot of the man, then replayed the video one frame at a time, until he could capture a good snapshot of the vehicle's plate.

Satisfied, he enlarged the man in the window's photo and downloaded it to both his wristband and his display.

The man on Blake's right tapped him on the shoulder and motioned for him to check another screen. On one of the real-time surveillance feeds, four black cars pulled into one of the airport's loading zones. A small army of NSA agents poured out of the vehicles.

"Thanks," he said to the man. Blake rose, checked around the small office, and noticed the coat hooks on the wall next to the door. One hat waited for its owner to pick it up. He pointed to the hat and asked, "May I?"

Both men nodded.

Blake grabbed the hat, opened the office door, and ran.

Blake entered a convenience store across from the train station, opened a fridge door, and chose a bottle of water. He studied the corridor through the fridge's glass door. Two NSA agents walked hurriedly by the shop. One glanced inside, but didn't stop.

Blake took the bottle, threw some cash on the counter, and headed to the exit. After checking left and right, he hurried toward the train ticket machines and purchased a ticket. He scanned it at the entrance and crossed over to the platform, keeping his head down and his face covered by the hat's brim.

Over the PA, an automated voice announced that a train would arrive in one minute.

As he strolled carefully down the platform, he noticed a commotion at the entrance. The two agents demanded their way through the crowd of travelers. They arrived at the ticket machine and one of them tapped a sequence on his wristband.

Damn, thought Blake. *How did they get a warrant so quickly, to flag my details in the train's purchasing system? My details must be hot in every database by now.*

Blake hurried down the platform while the train approached the station.

The agents entered the platform, demanding their way

through the travelers once more. As soon as they had a clear view of the length of the platform, they both drew their weapons.

The train stopped, opened its doors, and disembarking passengers flooded the platform. Blake forced his way through the throng of people into the last car. He could see the agents farther up the platform, checking car by car.

As more people boarded, the agents worked their way closer to the last car. Blake scanned for an exit route. When the first agent reached his car, Blake bent down to tie his shoelaces.

One of the agents stepped through the door, just as an automated voice announced, "Stand clear. The doors are closing."

Blake got up forcefully and bounced into a young man's backpack, knocking the youth off balance. Faking the move as an accident, Blake tried to get a grip and then pushed the young man out of the car just as the doors began to close.

Reacting to the sudden movement, the agents dove out of the car and tackled the young man. The doors finished closing and the AirTrain left the station. Blake kept his back to the platform and slowly opened the bottle of water.

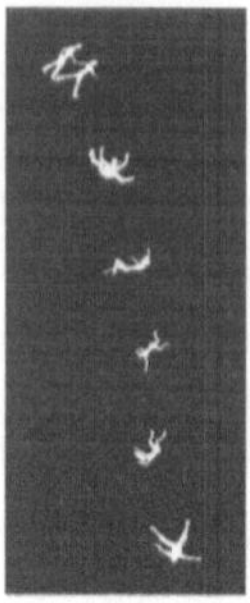

NIGEL AND THE LONDON WAY

Nigel activated his car's onboard computer and transferred the wristband data on the progress of his digital moles to the car. *All right, sucker,* he thought. *Your burner trick failed. Take this.* He watched the moles multiply on his screen. Some encountered resistance and were taken out. He selected a couple of newly born moles and re-directed them toward the house's security system. They slipped into the new, pristine system and started digging. *And take that!*

Nigel sighed with satisfaction. *Nothing like a good day's work. So, Mr. Brit, let's see who you really are, and which businesses you've stuck your fingers into.*

Why didn't a fancy guy like Brit hire any muscle for his house? Either he considered himself quite the fighter, or his business was so elite that he didn't trust anyone enough. *If that's the case,* thought Nigel, *bad day for you.*

Usually, a pack of moles could take up to twenty-four hours to transfer all the data to Nigel's wristband. Samuel Brit would eventually notice and take counter-actions. Nigel needed to be close by when that happened.

If Brit called in some muscle to take care of him, then Nigel would be in a bit of trouble. What could he say to his employer here, in London? Forget Mr. Thompson, who provided Brit's address for a totally different purpose. If Brit really did work for the Americans, either the slavers or the government, Nigel's ass would be covered. On the other hand, if Brit was a big shot in the BXS, as Thompson inferred, then Nigel had just declared war on an entire division of the BXS. If the blame fell on his English employer, he'd have time to disappear, but that would also mean that his English mission had just ended and his plans for his future with his family had just gone out the window. Where could he go after this job? Not back to the States. Unless…

A report popped up on the screen, stating *2.8% data saved and stored from targeted hard disks. Targeted hard disks destroyed at source.*

What the fuck? Nigel stared at the screen for several seconds, processing the message. Before he could make a conclusion, a second message appeared, stating *0.3% data saved and stored from targeted house surveillance system. The targeted house surveillance system destroyed at source. Mission terminated.*

Nigel looked up the street toward the house. It looked exactly the same from the outside. The neighborhood was as quiet as before. No muscle appeared, ready to deal with the intrusion, and Mr. Brit didn't seem in any hurry to leave. *Why would he destroy his entire digital system in a blink of an eye?*

Nigel got out of the car and turned onto the cross street, following the wall of the corner house on Sydney. The street sign announced it as Fulham Road. No backyards. The houses on the next street were back to back with those on Sydney. Brit couldn't escape through the back garden. Nigel returned to the corner of Sydney and Fulham Road, and stood next to his car. Why would Mr. Brit run? If he was as rich and powerful as Mr. Thompson thought, he had no reason to flee in terror from Nigel nobody fucking Blakesley.

So, what was Samuel Brit's play? He'd destroyed his own system to prevent the possibility that someone could spy on his data. He had to have a backup. But he wouldn't risk accessing it until he knew that the danger was neutralized. He also had a face and a name for the infiltrator: Nigel Blakesley.

What would Brit's next move be? He couldn't command Mr. Thompson to take care of his employee. Brit had insisted that he'd never worked with Thompson, so he wouldn't have any pull there. Any high-end player had access to muscle. But after fifteen fucking minutes, the hired thugs had yet to appear.

Nigel got back in the car and ordered his onboard computer to recover the 2.8 percent of Brit's hacked files.

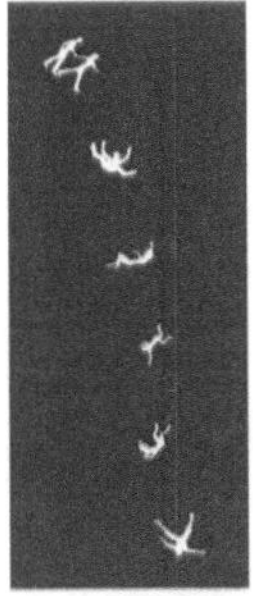

EIGHT MONTHS EARLIER

William Wilmot was a man of great taste, great ambition, and colossal accomplishments. He was regarded as royalty among the richest in wealthy America. Or so he'd been told. His advisors had confessed this to him, and he'd shared the insight with television hosts when interviewed. Everyone admired him. He topped the guest list for all of the most elite East Coast soirees, and while he would have loved to attend every event, he chose a select few, to keep everyone on their toes. If one desired his attention, one had to earn it.

Wilmot was also a powerful man. Even though money did not guarantee happiness, wealth could certainly create power, if one knew how to capitalize on its benefits. He was a master at using money to acquire power and eventually happiness. And while information was power, to a certain extent, the right relationships could create a sort of super-power. The super-natural sort, or even better, the super-hero, Superman type of super-power. Did anyone care about Superman any longer? Was the man of steel still trendy? Wilmot would have to find out.

A knock on the door interrupted his train of thought. Then came a second knock, this one more timid than the first.

"Yes?" Wilmot answered without hiding his annoyance.

The door to his office opened and Attorney General Jeffrey Bouts crept in, wearing a broad smile. Wilmot turned his snarl into a smile. *I must have a word with that idiot assistant,* he thought. He'd ordered her to call him before allowing anyone past her desk, and she was certainly not supposed to allow any uninvited guest to knock on his door.

"Mr. Wilmot." The AG saluted and stepped closer to the massive mahogany desk. Every nook and cranny of the desk was filled with Wild West carvings.

Wilmot rose and walked around his desk with his hand extended. "Mr. Attorney General, what a surprise."

They shook hands and then Wilmot invited Bouts to sit before returning to his own chestnut brown leather chair. The desk and chair sat on a dais, to give Wilmot the higher vantage, dominating whoever sat in the guest chair, no matter how tall they were. He glanced down on the AG and asked, "How can I help you, Jeff?"

Bouts transferred a file from his wristband to Wilmot's desk. "Take a look at this, Mr. Wilmot."

He accepted the AG's file and opened it on his desk display. It was a video entitled *Debt Hunters*, produced by a woman named Isabella Frye for the NWN TV affiliate. John Taylor, NWN TV's playboy, starred in the segment. *Debt Hunters? That's too close to home,* he thought.

Wilmot watched the segment in its entirety. During the fifty or so minutes, the AG kept his gaze focused on the floor, waiting in silence for the video to finish. When the credits rolled, Wilmot wanted to smash something, or perhaps hurl the AG across the room. Instead, he controlled himself, watching and memorizing the people who'd created this rubbish, building a special list of names he intended to hunt down for all eternity, while keeping his face devoid of expression. *Another mark of a great leader,* he thought. His self-aggrandizing improved his mood. People appreciated him because he understood the difference between private and official business, knowing better than to display his anger in front of a minion.

When the reportage ended, he decided who he'd chastise as public examples, like that smug reporter Taylor. Others he'd punish in private, to satisfy his burning appetite for revenge. Starting with the producer, Isabella Frye.

"Where did you get this, Jeff?"

"My people brought it to me. It hasn't been aired yet. It's scheduled for tomorrow."

"And what do you think of it?"

"I think it strikes too close to home. I'd prefer to block it from being broadcasted." The AG was all business now, his face looking severe—his official face. He acted with caution around Wilmot.

Too close to home? Is Bouts a complete moron? Wilmot straightened his back and focused on his breathing to reduce his heartrate. Once he could manage a relaxed smile, he spoke slowly, so he wouldn't be misunderstood. "The title strikes *too* close to home. The *content*, on the other hand, names *names*, and points fingers to exact *people* and *locations*. That's not close to home, Jeff. That's an inbound missile striking the *bullseye of the fucking target.*"

"Precisely my thoughts, Mr. Wilmot."

"Actions speak louder than words, Jeff, and I need to see *you* in action. This story *must not* be broadcasted. Ever. You're now personally responsible for confiscating every copy. You're to arrest *every* person named in the credits. Then *revoke* their television network license."

"You can count on me. I'll ensure that every step is carried out. I'm here simply to ensure that we're on the same page."

It was becoming harder and harder for Wilmot to remain calm. He'd made a list of demands and the stupid AG had just tried to stonewall *him*? "Jeff, please, do tell: how will you ensure that every step is carried out?"

The AG stared at Wilmot, looking genuinely surprised, for three full seconds before he remembered his place and smiled reassuringly. "I'm the attorney general. I have control of all the district attorneys and the police force. That's how I'll take care of this problem."

Wilmot's fist smashed the desk. The glass top shuddered, and cracks spread in all directions with loud squeaks and pops. The AG's eyes opened as wide as a virgin's on her wedding night.

He swallowed hard, his Adam's apple bobbing like a buoy

in rough seas. "I'll confiscate every copy and arrest everyone involved. But closing down the network will require more time and resources."

The glass on the desk began to self-heal. Each crack filled, fusing the pieces back together. In a matter of seconds, the desk's surface appeared brand new. Wilmot had purchased the gadget a couple of years previously, to impress his daughter. As an added bonus, the display made quite the impression on his minions every time. He deployed the trick, when the time was right, with almost everyone. His father, the great magnate Gregory Wilmot, *God rest his soul*, had taught Will that people liked to see their leaders demonstrate physical and moral strength from time to time, to remind them that power was rooted in more than mere inheritance. Power also required a degree of prowess. *Yes*, he thought, *prowess. That's a word I can get behind.*

"Don't worry, Jeff," Wilmot deployed his paternal voice this time. "I'll help you take down their business. As for the people you'll arrest, I'd prefer that you arrange for them to be taken out *forever*."

Once more, the AG swallowed hard. Sweat beaded his forehead. He looked very visibly distressed. "Mr. Wilmot, we're not in the business of killing people. However, let me assure you that we'll punish them to the full extent of the law. They'll rot in jail for their crimes."

"No, Jeff. You're not catching on. I'd be more comfortable when they're arrested for treason. It's a marvelous atrocity, which allows us to *disappear* people."

"I don't follow."

"You will. Tomorrow the NSA will be in contact. They'll take over some aspects of your investigation."

"Whatever you wish, Mr. Wilmot."

"Then, Jeff—" he paused for effect "—after the feast comes the reckoning."

"Uh-um…"

"Thank you for your help, Attorney General Bouts." Wilmot waved at him to leave.

The AG scrambled out of the room. Wilmot remained behind

his desk for a while, gazing at the door. To think that some people still believed that they could do whatever they wanted. The press had a duty to report only what those in power encouraged them to report. The elite few in this country knew better what was important to the country and its citizens. This type of journalistic transgression must never be repeated.

The desk buzzed. It was his assistant.

Wilmot accepted the call. "Yes?"

"Some NSA agents are here to speak with you, sir."

"Let them in." Wilmot closed all the open windows and folders on his desk display. He collapsed the display just as the door opened to allow two agents entry.

"Mr. Wilmot," said the first. "I'm Agent Alvarez, and this is my partner, Agent Saunders."

"Please, sit down, gentlemen."

Wilmot typed Alvarez's name on his computer, and searched his connected databases. Wilmot's bots mined more extensive and secret data than the storehouses in the AG's office or even inside the FBI. He needed to know more about the two agents they'd sent to him.

Alvarez maintained continuous eye contact with Wilmot, while Saunders wandered around, checking the office before he occupied one of the guest chairs. Alvarez waited before settling into the other one.

"Sir," said Alvarez, "I've been told to report here to discuss a case of a very sensitive nature. I had the chance to skim the file on our way here, and I'm not certain what, exactly, we're supposed to do for you."

"Whatever I ask."

"Huh." Alvarez adjusted his position, sitting up straighter. "Sir, the NSA doesn't generally interfere with this type of issue."

Wilmot nodded and smiled, keeping the exchange friendly. Rather than verbally respond, he opened the results from his database on Alvarez and began to read them.

"Sir?" The agent broke first, showing his hand like an amateur.

Wilmot raised his palm, the standard gesture for be quiet

and wait for your turn to speak. The file contained interesting details. Alvarez was a good agent, almost as good as Wilmot's chief of security. He needed men like Alvarez.

Turning to the other man, he said, "Agent Saunders, can I ask you to step out for a moment?"

"That's not necessary, sir," Alvarez said quickly. "My partner needs to remain here, with me. It's procedure."

Wilmot dialed his cell, waited for the person to answer, and said, "Hey, Matt. How are you?" A pause. "Good, good. Listen, thanks for the agents you sent over." Another pause. "Yes, they're quite attentive. The thing is, I need to speak to Agent Alvarez alone. Just for a moment, you understand. Would this be too much of a breach of protocol?" Quickly, Wilmot switched the call to speakerphone.

"Whatever you need," said Matt.

"Wonderful. You're on speaker, so would you be so kind as to tell Agent Saunders to step outside?"

"Do it, Saunders. Under my authority as director."

"Yes, sir," said the agent.

"Thanks so much, Matt. Until next time." Wilmot switched off his cell and smiled at the two agents. Saunders's wristband clinked. He double-checked the message with a grimace, rose from the chair, and reluctantly left the room. Alvarez watched his partner, looking more intrigued than angry.

"Now, Agent Alvarez. I need your help to infiltrate and eradicate a traitorous plot against the United States."

"Sir?"

"This blasphemy, disguised as legitimate reportage, represents a serious threat to our national security."

"I'm sorry, sir, but I don't see it that way."

"Let me explain it differently. Perhaps if your son were to be cured of his grave illness, you *would* see it that way."

Alvarez froze, as tense as a cat ready to pounce. He frowned at Wilmot and stood. "Sir, I understand that you're friendly with my director. But this tactic is bribery. And it's also a crime. I don't need anyone's permission to throw your ass in prison."

"You misunderstood me, Alvarez. I did not offer you a bribe.

I offered you a legal way to pay for your son's treatment. Call it *advice*."

Alvarez remained silent.

"I'm very familiar with our nation's many laws pertaining to its individual citizens. I'm also well versed in our corporate rules. I can advise you, based on my corporate authority, in a manner that allows you to utilize said corporate rules to gain access to the treatment your son so desperately needs. Not only the kind of treatment that reduces his pain, but the kind that would heal him."

"So, you'll *advise* me as to how to get the treatment, on my own?"

"Precisely. Didn't you ever learn that the best things in life are free?"

"If they were free, you wouldn't be asking me to see the problem 'your way.'"

"Wrong again, Alvarez. I simply need your expertise and advice on how to deal with this threat against the country's security. It's not a matter of compromise, it's a matter of professional advice from one specialist to another."

Alvarez sat down, adjusted his tie, and nodded slowly. "Okay, let me look at the file again, sir. Perhaps I need a second read to interpret it correctly."

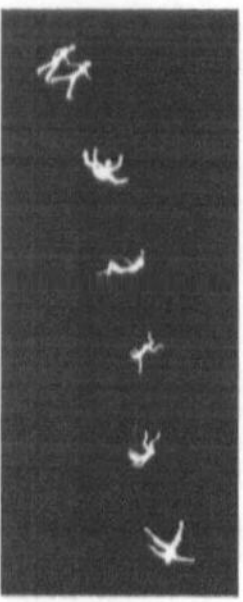

THE VEIL OF SECRETS

The room they'd given Simon was large and luxurious by any standards. He had no doubt that most of the rooms in the complex were just as opulent, ensuring the comfort of the journalists covering the events, and thus positively influencing their articles on Wilmot's business. Simon had been a little curious about the nature of Wilmot's research. To attract so many journalists, every year, this research must be off-the-scale impressive. Many of his wordsmithing colleagues probably returned solely to enjoy the Wilmot Center's extravagances. Hopefully, at least a few of them were real professionals who attended for the science, to catalogue and publish the results of Wilmot's research. And if that was true, then the Wilmot Research facility was not only a façade to hide the slave camp, but it was also a center for real scientific study.

What kind of results could they gather by studying captive human subjects? The thought made Simon shudder. Prisoners wouldn't be asked to give consent for the experiments. The Freedom Act legally considered servitude subjects to be objects for the duration of their enslavement. Legal torture, if the Freedom Act passed into law. Simon remembered the list Isa had given him, of all the corpses found in mass graves. The "escaping families."

Simon's fingers moved swiftly along the holo-display's keyboard. If he wanted to uncover their secrets, he had to dig his way through their firewalls and hack into their network. He surrounded his holo-display with a white-noise wall of protection, to prevent any onlookers from peeking at his display.

For the outside observers, assuming he was under nonstop surveillance, he maintained a focused face, free of any emotions, even when he broke through the back door of the Wilmot Center's network. *Damn, I'm good!* He almost grinned.

He searched for their communication directory. Jamming procedures. His fingers were a blur of movement. His secret lessons with the best hackers in New York were proving really useful. He moved like lightning over the holo-display, sorting objects and typing code.

Then a message popped up, filling his screen. *SECURITY JAMMING DISABLED. MESSAGE IN QUEUE SENT.*

One down, he thought.

Next, he accessed the database directory, browsing through the lists of files and folders. One folder was labeled *US Servitude Exchange*. He held his breath for a couple of seconds. Could it be that easy? He selected the folder. Inside was a list with eight column headings: name, qualifications, amount of debt, object of debt, company to which the payments are owed, credit company owning the debt, broker dealing the debt title, corporation interested in buying the debt. *Very thorough.* He scrolled down, and stopped to read a specific entry at random:

John Peterson | chemical engineer | $273,000 | house mortgage | Thor Crescent Co. | Moonlight Investments | Vehstulge Brokerage Hamburg | Phochuk Chemical Plant, Vietnam.

This John Peterson was a chemical engineer who owed $273,000 on his house's mortgage to Thor Crescent Company, which made him indebted to Moonlight Investments. Vehstulge Brokerage Hamburg brokered a deal between Moonlight Investments and Phochuk Chemical Plant in Vietnam and transferred the debt to the latter, thus turning John into a servitude subject for the Vietnamese corporation.

Simon scrolled down the list, finding hundreds of pages and hundreds of thousands of names.

Hearing movement in the hallway outside his room, he gave the command to copy the list onto his wrist-bracelet. The footsteps were getting closer. Not just his contact, Gabriela. She'd brought some friends along. At least three people, from the sound of it. He opened a random page of text, filled with words.

"So, what's with all this secrecy?" Gabriela's voice was as cold as usual, so Simon tried to remain calm, turning to smile at her. Behind her, two security guys hurried around the couch and waited for her instructions.

"You know writers," said Simon. "It's bad luck to share our work before it's finished and polished."

"Well, not in my facility. We expect journalists to offer their work for inspection at the Wilmot Research Center."

"That sounds a little heavy handed."

She signaled one of the security guards. The one with steroid-sculpted muscles approached Simon, carrying a small device in his hand. With one press of a button, the thug disrupted Simon's white noise field. The holo-display became clear and visible, filling the entire viewing area with the written page he'd opened.

Gabriela sat next to him to get a closer look at his display. She donned a smile worthy of a press photo-op. *Nothing could get close enough to touch her,* he thought. *No question or statement from any reporter, no matter how good.*

"So, what are we writing?"

"First impressions."

She bent forward and read aloud, somehow maintaining the same smile. "It's all veiled in secrecy."

Simon had often wondered if she was really a living human being, or if old Wilmot had built this daughter to his own specifications, one of the first generation of a new army of androids.

She read on. "Locked doors, passwords, facial checkpoints, security in the dozens, all armed with crowd control gear. It feels like a war..." She glanced at Simon and grimaced with displeasure.

Goodbye smile, he thought. "You don't like it?"

She continued reading aloud. "A war for the future of America. Are we going to be left behind by the new social revolution, triggered by the Corporations Union with their Freedom Act, in an effort to save the civilized world? Will we succumb to their rules and fall into barbarism, clinging to the ideals of the past, born of a crumbling democracy and built on an erroneous economic model?"

Gabriela's face lightened. As she neared the end, her voice rose, sounding just a tad surprised. "Or will we rise again," she finished, "above the other nations of the world, and join the civilization of the future?

"Well, well, Simon." She smiled at him, using the version he'd only seen during their intimate moments. She kissed his mouth, quickly, and rose. With a wave of her hand, she dismissed the security guards.

Simon held in a huge sigh of relief.

As soon as the door closed, leaving them alone, her dress fell to the floor. She was naked underneath. No panties, no bra, not even stockings.

Simon grinned like an adolescent, collapsed his holo-display, and yanked his shirt over his head. *I'm back in the game.* Gabriela acted remarkably nonchalant, considering the room was certainly bugged, and that old man Wilmot was probably watching the security feed.

A subliminal message floated in front of his eyes—a progress bar showing *63% copied.* He took her in his arms.

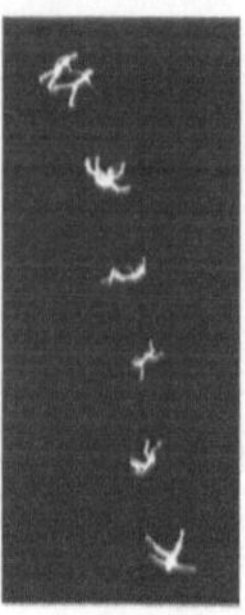

BACK IN THE HOUSE

Blake entered his precinct and his mood improved. He felt at ease. At home. He looked over his shoulder at the street and felt a sense of wonder. No black government vehicle waited for him. If the NSA agents were doing their jobs, they should've been lurking here. He shrugged and walked to his unit.

People saluted him jovially. He shook hands and tried to keep a smile on his face. As he moved through the room full of desks, he stopped next to the workstation of rookie Margaret Chung. Dressed in civilian clothes, she typed nervously on her display, head bent so all he could see was her short, dark hair. She'd replaced Neil, his former partner, after his disappearance. Even though she was certainly a bright young woman, Blake thought the pairing was less than perfect.

Neil had been younger than Blake, and far more idealistic. He'd also been nervous, and too quick to draw or react in a time of crisis. Blake's cerebral focus and cool demeanor had been the yin to Neil's yang, keeping their partnership balanced. After they'd worked together for a long time, Neil expected Blake to rationalize their actions before he dove into the moment. Neil was more like a brother to Blake than his true sibling, Corbin, who was just as cerebral as Blake, but far more daring, and downright cocky. He loved his brother, bur never felt the need to invite him over for a beer, or out to a game. Neil, on the other hand, fit like a puzzle piece, fulfilling every brotherly role. *Now he's gone.*

"Well if it isn't Detective Frye." Margaret sounded surprised. "You're back already?"

"Yep. My vacation got cut short." He sat on the corner of her desk. "Marg, I need a favor."

"Shoot."

She was always efficient, ready to help. Blake liked her enthusiasm, but at the same time it made him feel a bit awkward, as though he might be taking advantage of her inexperience. Not anymore. He needed all the help he could get.

Blake sent two photos onto Margaret's display. The first was the kidnapper's image, somewhat blurry and at a bad angle, but his face was clear enough to generate a lead. "I need you to run his face through the recognition software."

"Sure."

"And put out an APB on this license plate." Blake pointed to the second image, a good shot of the kidnap vehicle's license plate. It was likely leased by the NSA, but better to follow procedures.

"Consider them both done."

Glad to have something going his way, Blake hurried to the captain's office. Through the glass wall, he saw Moore pacing and speaking to someone on the phone, looking agitated. Moore signaled for Blake to come in.

The captain hung up and scowled at Blake before he dropped into his chair behind the desk. He tried to smile at Blake, but failed. It was almost painful to watch. "Please," he said, "tell me you've got a lead."

"I have two. A male suspect that Chung's running through recognition. And a license plate."

"Probably NSA," said Moore.

"I know, but it's worth a search." Blake wanted to lighten the mood, but he didn't have the strength.

Moore said, "I just talked with the DA and he's on his way here to talk to you."

"Unless he's going to help me, I don't have time for his bullshit."

"Come on, Blake. You know I have to follow the rules. We

can't open an official investigation without the DA on our side."

Somehow, after all that had happened, Blake wasn't sure that was the DA's intention. Sure, he was probably on his way. More likely, though, to activate the Internal Affairs rats and open a public investigation into Detective Blake Frye, suspect number one in the latest case of treason against the USA. *I'm an enemy of the state. But whose state?*

Sergeant Sebastien Vallejo burst into the office. He was one of the old guard at their precinct. To make his last years easier, he was confined to a desk, likely to save him from a work-induced heart attack caused by his addiction to cheeseburgers. His face was red and sweaty under his thick-rimmed glasses. "Captain," he said, "the NSA is here. They're really pissed off and they're demanding to see Detective Frye."

The four NSA agents were taking over the precinct. Agents Alvarez and Saunders had brought along two of their colleagues. Their "search" of the precinct looked more like a raid. No professional courtesy. In fact, no professionalism at all. More like prison guards tossing a convict's cell for contraband.

Blake followed Moore into the center of it all, cooperative on the outside and suspicious on the inside. When they saw the two approaching, the agents stopped what they were doing. Everyone in the department followed suit. To an outsider, it would've looked like a paused video feed.

A few seconds later, everyone seemed to collectively reboot, beginning with Alvarez, who had an ugly grin stretching across his face. He said, "Frye, you're under arrest."

Captain Moore stepped between Alvarez and Blake and raised his hands. "Let's all take a breath. No need to jump to conclusions. Why don't you follow me into my office, and we can discuss the situation in private."

Alvarez ignored the request. Instead, he motioned for the other agents to surround Blake.

Blake took several steps back. Like a ballet troupe, all the other detectives and police officers in the area rose from their chairs, moving toward the commotion to protect their own.

Captain Moore remained firmly planted between the agents and his detective, both palms raised.

Alvarez broke the standoff, sounding authoritative and menacing. "We are the National Security Agency, not fucking mall cops. We don't need to have a *private chat* in your cozy little office. You're interfering with my investigation, Captain Moore, and that means you're an accessory to *treason*."

"Son, you're on my turf. I'm the captain of this precinct. You won't intimidate or blindside me with your NSA bullshit."

Alvarez held up his warrant. "You've all seen the attorney general's warrant for Frye's arrest. Every goddamn institution in this country is after this *traitor*." For emphasis, he pointed at Blake.

"I haven't seen it," Sergeant Vallejo challenged from behind Alvarez, his voice betraying his age. "Captain, those two upstarts were here earlier." Sergeant Vallejo nodded at the two agents Blake didn't know.

Moore asked, "When was that, Sergeant?"

"About two hours ago, Cap."

"When we were at the airport," said Blake. "They swooped down on both locations simultaneously." Blake chose his words carefully, trying to remain calm while he processed the new information. He glanced around at the men and women in the room and wondered, *What are my chances? Anyone who helps me will be charged with treason, and I can't live with that.* He couldn't prove that Alvarez was dirty, nor Saunders and the backup they'd brought along. *I'm cornered.*

"Enough talk," said Alvarez. "Captain, you have five seconds to hand over Frye, or we call in enough backup to lock down your entire precinct, and process the lot of you for harboring a fugitive. Oh, and I'll throw in obstruction of justice as a bonus gift."

The officers looked uneasy, but didn't stand down. The captain tensed, looking as though he, like Blake, was analyzing the room while he raced to find a solution.

"Listen," said Moore. "I'll give you my detective. Okay? But first, you have to speak with me. Alone."

"Three seconds," said Alvarez.

Officer Chung slipped a piece of paper into Blake's palm.

"Two seconds."

Blake read the note, and then handed it to Moore.

Moore read it, gnashed his teeth, and took a long, loud, deep breath.

"One."

The captain commanded, "Ready Tasers."

All of the detectives drew their Tasers, and pointed them at the NSA agents.

"You're making a big mistake." Alvarez's voice was as sharp as a razor.

He's still prepared to fight us, thought Blake.

Moore held up the note for Alvarez to read, and said, "This is the plate for the vehicle that kidnapped Detective Frye's spouse. We ran it, and it came back NSA." He paused to allow the words to sink in. "And that, Agent Alvarez, proves that your agents abducted Isabella Frye."

Turning to the old sergeant, Moore added, "Vallejo, what did the NSA agents want earlier?"

"To search Detective Frye's desk."

"Did they offer a warrant?"

"No, sir. I assumed that we should cooperate. After all, we work for the good of the country, don't we?"

The question hung in the air, like the stench of a roadkill skunk.

Blake checked over his shoulder, to get a good look at his workstation. "You took my computer!" He moved closer to Alvarez and added, "You confiscated my hard drive, including digital records of open cases, and without a warrant. That's a federal offense."

Alvarez flashed an ugly grin and placed his hand on his gun. "For the last time," he said, "I'm taking Frye into custody."

Margaret handed Blake the second photo with *Martin Breckenwell, chief of security for Wilmot Enterprises* scribbled on its back.

Blake sneered. "The man who took my wife is Martin Breckenwell, the chief of security for Wilmot Enterprises. And as I said before, he's in an NSA vehicle. That's proof that your agency is directly linked to the slavery black market. You, Agent Alvarez, don't work for the NSA any longer, do you? This is proof that you're employed by Wilmot."

Moore drew his gun and pointed it at Alvarez. All four agents drew their guns in response.

Blake felt the situation deteriorating. Normally he would've been the calm head in the room, insisting that everyone stand down. But Isa was still missing, likely in the hands of the slavers.

As all the detectives readied their Tasers, closing in on the agents, the air crackled with electricity.

"Agent Alvarez," said Moore. "I'm placing you and your men under arrest for the kidnapping of Isabella Frye, and the illegal seizure of Detective Frye's computer."

Alvarez remained motionless, with his weapon at the ready. He opened his mouth to speak, then closed it. After a quick sigh, he raised his free hand in the air and holstered his weapon. Then his hand tapped his ear.

Chung said, "Did you see that?" She pointed at Alvarez. "He's listening to a live feed."

Moore stepped closer. "Who's whispering in your ear, Alvarez? Who's your boss?"

Alvarez raised both hands in the air as I sign of cooperation. "I think it's time for you and I to have that private chat, Captain Moore."

Captain Moore entered his office and walked around his desk, but didn't sit in the chair. Blake leaned on the glass wall just inside the door, staying between Alvarez and the exit. As he studied Alvarez's body language, he automatically checked his buttons and collar.

Moore said, "You're in deep with Isa Frye's kidnapping. We can talk all you want, but you're not walking out of my precinct."

"Relax, Captain Moore," said Alvarez. "In less than five

minutes your phone is going to ring. And a minute later, I'll be free to go."

Captain Moore opened his mouth to respond, but Alvarez cut him off. "And before you open your smarmy mouth, you'll see by the caller ID that it's a call you can't possibly ignore."

Blake stepped close to Alvarez, nose to nose. "Where's my wife?"

Alvarez turned away, addressing Moore. "Captain, would you wait outside, while I have a nice chit-chat with Detective Frye?"

Blake shook his head. "Moore stays."

The agent stepped toward the guest chair, undid his blazer, and sat. He looked up at the two police officers. "Bad call, Frye. You're involving this man in some dangerous shit. He'd be safer if he stayed ignorant."

"You've got one minute, asshole. Say what you came here to say."

Alvarez turned his eyes to Blake.

"Today's your lucky day, Frye. You've got an appointment to sort out your wife's fate."

Blake leaned on the desk, to get closer to Alvarez. "Let me guess. You'll take me to her."

"Wrong," said Alvarez. "You go alone. But you must hand over your gun to Moore before you leave. And if you want to see your wife again, you won't be late for this appointment."

"Don't listen to him, Frye," said Moore. "He's a lying weasel."

"Sounds like a trap," said Blake.

"If he doesn't go, then his wife will be lost." Alvarez studied his nails, then added, "Forever."

"You realize you're confessing to a crime," said Moore.

Ignoring the captain, Alvarez said, "He's so naive. I hope, Frye, for your wife's sake, that you're smarter than him."

"All right," said Blake. "Tell me what I have to do."

Alvarez rose and pointed at Moore. "Give him your gun, Detective Frye." After a pause, he added, "Now. I won't ask again."

Blake opened his jacket to show that he wasn't wearing a

holster. "I came straight from the airport, after a transatlantic flight. I'm not carrying my gun."

Alvarez glared at Blake, removed a business card from his inside pocket, and threw it on the desk near Blake's hands.

Automatically, Blake adjusted the card so that its edges were aligned with the desk's.

"Three more minutes until that phone call. You better use the time well."

Blake checked the name on the card. *William Wilmot.* He slid the card close, picked it up, and turned it over. On the back, in blue ink, was written *HQ – 10:00 a.m.* He unbuttoned his blazer and tucked the card in his own inside pocket. Then he carefully buttoned his jacket. "Cap, it's William Wilmot's card." He smirked and added, "What are the odds?" Then he made eye contact with his boss, to be sure that Moore got the message.

The captain gave a slight nod.

Blake's wristband showed 9:40.

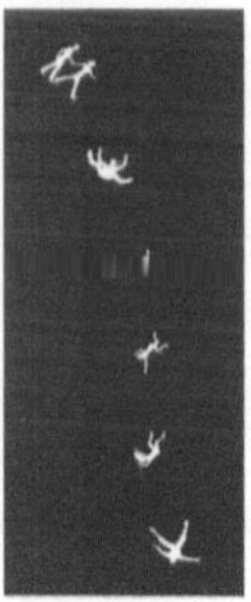

FIVE MONTHS EARLIER

The elevator door slid open, and Isa got off on the fifty-seventh floor, even though her destination was the fifty-fifth. On her way to the NWN TV building, she'd gotten a strange message from a friend of her boss's personal assistant, asking her to come straight to his office.

She was intrigued. Especially since her story was slated to air in a few hours. She laughed as she thought, *Maybe they're throwing me a surprise party?*

As she walked down the hall, she saw John Taylor leaving Kadesky's office, escorted by two men in black suits. He walked right past her without speaking, and pressed the down button for the elevator. Weird for Taylor to ignore her, but a loud "psst" from the other direction drew her attention. Philip Kadesky, her boss, waved furtively at her from the end of the hall, beyond his office.

He's hiding from the suits, she thought.

Behind her, the elevator dinged. She heard the doors open, and watched as Taylor entered the elevator and the doors closed.

Kadesky entered the men's restroom. She waited outside his office door for him to return. Then he poked his head out of the men's room door and signaled for her to come over.

That's really weird, she thought. *Guys in suits, looking like government agents, taking John Taylor away. And now my boss wants me to meet him in the toilet?* After a pause, she thought, *I'll take the bait.*

Inside the restroom, Philip was alone. As soon as Isa stepped closer, he grabbed a *Closed for cleaning* sign, hung it on the outside doorknob, then locked the two of them inside.

Looking agitated, he said, "I'm glad you're here."

"What the hell's going on, Philip?"

"They took John Taylor and…" He snapped his fingers, shrugged, and said, "What's her name, your researcher?"

"Sam."

"Right, Sam. They took her away when they confiscated all of your computers. Now they're waiting for you in your office. My lawyer is trying to stop them from hauling off my computer, as we speak."

"What? Why?"

"Somehow, they got their hands on a copy of your story. They intend to prevent it from airing, saying it's, and I'm quoting here, 'A breach of national security.' They want to investigate you on suspicion of treason, and to prosecute all of you for slander."

Isa took two steps back, leaned against the wall, and tried not to pass out. She felt dizzy, as if she'd been struck by lightning. She'd expected some pushback after the story aired, but not this much grief. She said, "Seizing our computers, and taking Sam and John away? What's next?"

He shrugged. "I have no idea."

"Who are the guys in black?"

"The NSA. We're going to need some time to prepare our defense. Our legal department—"

"Listen, Philip," she interrupted him. "They're trying to intimidate us. The material hasn't been aired yet. It's not slander or treason until the material goes public."

"Yeah, you're right."

"They have no legal basis to arrest us, or to confiscate our equipment. We should sue them."

Philip stared at her in confusion. Somebody yanked on the door a few times, and he jumped like a frightened child. "Isabella, these guys are with the NSA. When they claim something is a threat to national security, they probably don't need to get a warrant or have the legal upper hand. Agents like that do whatever they bloody well want to do."

"Philip, pull yourself together. *Please.*"

"'I'm *trying.*"

"It's a news story, not a terrorist plot. Lean on the Legal Department. They're on our side. Journalists don't bow down to bullies."

"True. But if you leave now, they won't haul you away. That'll buy us time to work on our strategy to push back. We'll keep in touch. But be aware, they could tap your phone, or show up at your house."

Isa activated her wristband and typed furiously. "I'm leaving," she said. "I'm also texting you that I can't make it in today. I booked a research trip."

"They can check stuff like that, Isa. I didn't get a text from you."

She pressed Send, and smiled as his wristband pinged. "You just did."

"Where are you going for this trip?"

"To Chicago. To meet with a source."

"Good. I'll call you."

Isa collapsed her wristband and left the men's room. The corridor was clear. She pressed the Down button for an elevator, and got off on the twenty-third floor, where there was a walkway to the next building.

She'd expected trouble, but not this soon. *I need a contingency plan,* she thought. *Treason's a bit over the top.* And how did the NSA get an advance version of the story?

Her cell rang and she jumped and gasped. The people nearby looked over in surprise. She activated her holo-display to take Blake's call. His face was so close to the cell phone that she couldn't see the top of his head.

"Hi, HoneyB," she said.

"What's wrong, Isa?"

She flashed a weak smile. "What do you mean?"

"You look and sound like you're scared shitless."

She checked over her shoulder to see if anyone was listening, and said, "Something happened. Can I come to you?"

"I could meet you for coffee, at our favorite place."

"No. It's better if I come to you at the precinct."

"All right, love. I'll be waiting."

Isa arrived in Philip Kadesky's office, closed the door behind her, and sat on the couch across from his desk, next to Sam. John Taylor leaned against the window, studying the Manhattan panorama from the fifty-seventh floor. Philip avoided making eye contact with any of them, appearing preoccupied as he tapped nervously and kept checking his watch.

Isa asked, "Are we waiting on someone?"

"Mrs. Wilson, from Legal," said John, still looking out the window.

"Okay," said Isa. The law firm the station had hired to fight the attorney general and the NSA had won the legal challenge, to a certain degree, but all the arguments had been behind closed doors. Isa and the others had been informed of the win, including being cleared of all criminal accusations, and having their computers and equipment returned. And yet, Philip behaved as though they were still in trouble.

Mrs. Wilson finally arrived, closed the door behind her, and walked behind Philip's desk to shake his hand. As the two of them stood there, on the employer side of the desk, the line was drawn, leaving the employees on their own, on the other side.

Mrs. Wilson began abruptly. "We're letting all three of you go."

Sam smiled sadly, as though she'd been expecting to be sacked.

John turned, looking surprised and a little hurt. "What do you mean, *let go*?"

"You'll receive a severance, of course," Mrs. Wilson continued, without a hint of kindness or empathy. "Your personal effects have been packed by security. They'll escort you to reception to retrieve the items on your way out."

"But we *won*," said John.

"*We* did," said the attorney.

"I know it's hard to hear," said Philip, with a degree of courtesy. "We've come to some agreements, preventing you all from doing jail time."

"That's pretty vague," said John, stepping forward. "I think I deserve a better explanation."

"They withdrew their charges against you," said Philip, "but the attorney general got a decision from the Supreme Court confirming that your story has touched on subjects that interfere with national security. The high court ruled that the station's *Reports from Around the World* division has breached the National Security Act and therefore it's been dissolved, and all its employees are terminated, including you three."

"I'm not with *Reports from Around the World*," John insisted. "I'm the lead anchor for *News at 9*."

For the first time, Philip looked John in the eye. In a comforting voice, he said, "We had to make that deal, to keep NWN TV alive. I'm sorry, all of you. For what it's worth, I think your collective efforts on this reportage were the last piece of legitimate investigative journalism we'll see in this country. Hell, in the whole world."

Isa rose, smiled to Philip, and walked away. Sam followed closely behind. John stayed behind, probably to beg for his job. *Too bad for him*, thought Isa.

They'd all discussed the risks when they began this journey. But she didn't think any of them imagined the fallout would be this severe.

We should've known, she thought. Over the last two decades, TV networks had been cut by two thirds, and the survivors were mostly submissive ghosts, not passionate journalists.

In the hallway, three security guards waited to escort them out.

Sam said, "Give me a sec," to the guards, and turned to Isa. "Wanna grab a beer?"

"Sorry, hon. I'm not in the mood. But you're always welcome at my place. Anytime. Do you want to tag along now?" She pointed at the guards, and added, "Not you guys. Just her."

Then she leaned close to Sam. "We'll drink enough beer and wine to drown a frigate."

"Maybe next time." Sam gave her a quick hug, and hurried away, escorted by her guard.

Isa looked back to see if John was done talking to Philip. *More like begging*, she thought. The former rising star of NWN TV could theoretically hustle out a second chance. *It'd be nice if one of us survived this mess.*

After a minute or so, the female security guard tapped Isa's shoulder and said, "Sorry, Mrs. Frye, but we should be going."

"Fine." Isa followed her toward the elevators, thinking *What now?* The hope for a baby was gone. They'd postponed the treatment to finish her story. Now her career was over. This black mark would follow her to every network. Thirty years earlier, scandals could turn into book deals. She could've made *The New York Times*'s bestseller list, and earned enough for two lifetimes. Not anymore. Disgraces like her toxic story were just as poisonous to publishers as networks. Most had been swallowed by huge conglomerates.

The doors opened and she walked into the elevator, shocked at how pale she looked in her reflection. *I'm finished.* The thought weighed so heavy, she lost her balance and had to lean against the elevator's back wall for support.

The guard asked, "You okay?"

"Not really." They'd already paid for their last IVF procedure. *What will it take to dig ourselves out of that hole, if I'm unemployable?*

She followed the guard out of the elevator on the main floor, and waited while she retrieved her boxes of personal effects.

"Please sign for the boxes," said the guard. "And make sure everything's there."

Isa glanced inside the top one, saw the photo of Blake she kept on her desk, and nodded. "Good enough." She signed the form, and tried not to cry as she pushed her way out the front door into the noisy street.

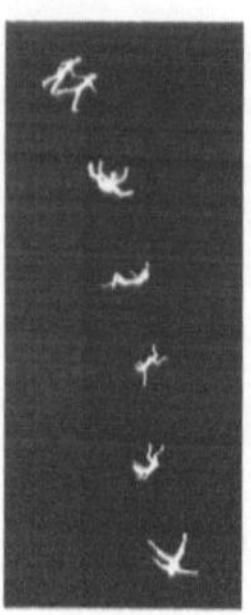

NIGEL AND THE PICKLE

Nigel bought a digital caffeine shot. He had to be in top shape. Whatever was coming, he'd get through it. The caffeine shot app's icon appeared on his holo-display. He slid it over to the edge and from there directly onto his skin. He pressed it and activated the app. The shot melted under his skin, and he could feel its pixels integrating with his own cells.

A few seconds later, he shivered, feeling as fresh as if he'd just awakened from a nap. The zing wouldn't last long, but he wasn't planning to hang around for much longer.

He checked the time, and noticed he'd been waiting for almost half an hour. Good enough. He exited the car, stretched, and checked his gun before checking the time again. A bleep from the car's onboard made him sigh with relief. He transferred everything back to his wristband. Only one meager folder. *Could be Pandora's box*, he thought. An old friend had taught him, not long ago, that nothing was as insignificant as you thought.

Before he could open the folder to scan the contents, he heard tires skidding on pavement and glanced over his shoulder.

Two cars entered the street. The first came to a stop in front of his car. The other parked right beside the car, blocking his exit.

Here we go, he thought, ready to confront Brit's muscle. When he recognized a familiar face exiting the first car, he mumbled, "Oh, shit."

Mr. Thompson and three goons stepped from the first car, and four goons from the second. Nigel felt honored that the powerful Mr. Thompson thought he deserved an eight man escort—or death squad, depending on his orders from up the ladder.

Nigel drew his gun. All eight men froze.

"What's going on here, Mr. Blakesley?" Thompson's voice sounded as polite as ever.

"I'm not sure, Mr. Thompson. You tell me. But, please, in the meantime, all of you should keep your hands where I can see them."

"There's no need for a gun, Mr. Blakesley. After all, we're colleagues, aren't we?"

"I generally use a gun when two cars flank me, especially when the street has plenty of available parking spaces."

Thompson seemed to be constructing an appropriate response.

So, thought Nigel, *Brit has enough pull to turn employer against employee. And he called on his right hand, no less.* The revelation confirmed Nigel's suspicions that Brit was actually and only a distinctive member of the BSX. *Bad play for me.*

Thompson leaned on his silver cane and said, "Even if you shoot three or four of us, we'll still get you."

"Or I could kill you first. That'd leave your men without the brains of the operation. I wonder if they'd still try to kill me?"

"Mr. Blakesley, this isn't America. English criminals crush men like you because that is their duty. Their entire lifestyle is based on fighting, drinking, and killing. They will preserve their pride."

Thompson signaled. His thugs drew their weapons in unison, and pointed them at Nigel's head. The gesture was executed flawlessly, sending shivers down Nigel's spine. Cold and beautiful.

"Mr. Blakesley, I offered my advice only to be polite. The truth is, you have no out. Let's be peaceful adults. Drop your gun, come with us, and speak with our employer."

"My original employer?" Nigel smiled, while he kept his gun trained on Thompson. "Or did you mean Mr. Brit?"

"Mr. Brit is merely the aggrieved party. Lord Wright is curious to learn how you offended Mr. Brit."

"Call Lord Wright, then," said Nigel. "He'll be interested in learning about my information concerning Mr. Brit, especially if he intends to do something he'll regret."

"Lord Wright never regrets anything," said Mr. Thompson. "His orders are ironclad. If you have any interesting research to add to our facts, then you should share it face to face with his lordship."

Nigel smirked. The situation was getting out of hand. He could take out at least four of them, as Thompson suggested, but not all of them. Worse, he was pinned to the house behind him, with no way to run or hide. He asked, "Don't you at least have some liberty to assess a situation? Isn't there room for you to improvise?"

Thompson raised his cane, caught it between his two hands, and tapped on it thoughtfully with the fingers of his left hand.

When he caught sight of the two Corp Police vans, Nigel hid the gun and smiled.

Thompson's goons hesitated, likely debating which threat was the most imminent: Nigel or the Corp Police. The boss lowered his cane, leaned on it, and motioned for his goons to lower their guns.

The Police Corp agents exited their vans and checked the perimeter of Brit's house. Once satisfied, they confronted Nigel, Mr. Thompson, and his entourage.

One of the agents asked, "Are you Nigel Blakesley?"

Thompson spoke first, preventing Nigel's response. "Why do you ask?"

The volatile confrontation was becoming more interesting. London's dark side of life was as dangerous as America's, and yet it maintained a higher degree of elegance. A certain classic sparkle. What could the Corp Police want with him?

The agent said, "Mr. Blakesley needs to come with us, and answer some questions."

Nigel maintained his smile, even though what had momentarily looked like his opportunity to escape hadn't panned out. *Where's my window of opportunity?*

Thompson asked, "How is it, officer, that you chose *this moment* to hunt for Mr. Blakesley here?"

"When anyone intrudes on the offices of a BSX member, we're mobilized to investigate."

"I see." Thompson tapped at the handle of his cane. "I'm sorry, Agent Whatever-your-name-is, but Mr. Blakesley is currently under my…*supervision*. It is urgent that he answer some of Lord Wright's questions."

"Sir, no one's authority supersedes the Corp Police."

"I must respectfully disagree, Agent. Mr. Blakesley is my employer's employee, and according to the contract between them, Mr. Blakesley has breached my employer's trust. This violation must be addressed personally. After Lord Wright finishes with Mr. Blakesley, I'll bring him to the nearest Corp Police Station. You have my word. Please, do call your superiors to confirm my authority on this matter."

These two men were measuring each other's pickles, and getting ready to piss the distance. *I could use a pickle right now.* He glanced at the house. Brit stood in the front room, watching out the window through a gap in the curtains, wearing the most obnoxious smirk. Nigel smiled back at Brit, turned back to the pissing contest, and slowly drew his gun.

"I'm sorry, sir," replied the agent, "but your request is unacceptable."

Nigel pointed his gun at the closest goon's waist, and then at his hand. When he pulled the trigger, the thug yelped in surprise and pain, his gun spun up in the air, and everyone turned their attention to him.

A moment later, everyone opened fire. Just as Nigel hoped.

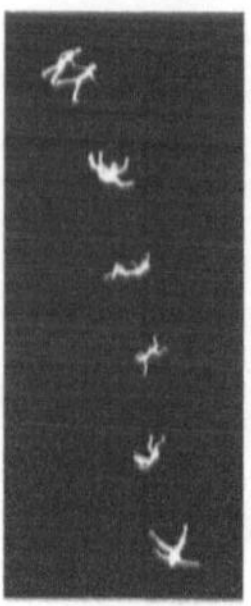

THE CIRCLE

Blake focused on driving, as the heavy rain soaked the windshield and turned the roads slick. His mind felt like a beehive, with angry and noisy thoughts swarming all over the place. He wanted to keep his feelings in check, but they refused to be tamed.

He'd never felt so helpless. So lost. He wanted to stop the car, open his notepad, and organize the pieces of his wife's case. Isa's kidnapping. He needed guidance, visual cues, and order. He also needed time, but Isa didn't have that luxury.

When he'd last worked on the plan, he'd written William Wilmot's name in the first circle of persons of interest. The name glistened in his mind, and he shook his head to regain focus. *One thing at a time.* Blake was on his way to speak to Wilmot, the slaver, human trader, organizer of the servitude black market in the States. He made a promise to himself: *I'll make the best of that meeting.*

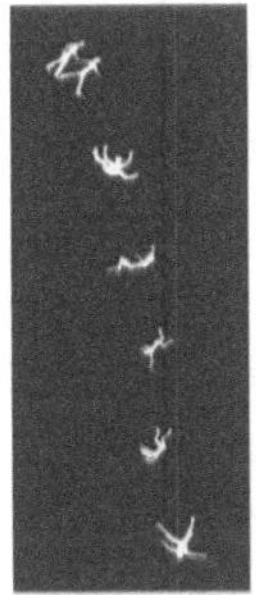

FOUR MONTHS EARLIER

The phone rang, but before Wilmot could answer, his door flew open and smashed against the wall. Gabriela was on fire, like a Valkyrie, her hair flowing behind her, eyes burning, her mouth like a grim line of vengeance.

Wilmot's assistant followed, looking terrified. He gestured at the assistant to leave, and added, "Close the door behind you."

With a nervous gesture, Gabriela selected a file from her wristband and threw it onto his desk. "What. Is. *This*?"

Wilmot opened the file. The video player activated and the *Debt Hunters* story began. He stopped it a few seconds in, frowned, and looked at his daughter. "Where did you get this?"

"It's all over the internet. Every major press organization is running with it."

"That's impossible." Wilmot opened an internet window and searched on "Debt Hunters." His screen filled with links, and the count at the bottom showed another hundred pages of hits. He could feel his blood pressure skyrocketing.

"Pa?"

"Give me a minute," he snapped. After taking a deep breath, he added, "Darling."

The accusation that he was in the business of servitude wasn't the worst claim. Practically every rival of equal financial status knew already. But they'd also accused him of murdering hundreds of his servitude subjects. If they had proof, his house could come crashing down around him before the Freedom Act passed through Congress and the Senate. The Act would redefine servitude subjects as objects, not persons. Once they were stripped of their rights as human beings and citizens, his crimes would change from murder to littering. Or illegal dumping.

Gabriela slammed into one of the guest chairs in front of his desk, and asked, "Why aren't you angrier?"

"I'm furious, I'm just handling it better than you are. This was supposed to be *contained*." Somebody's head was going to roll. He had the attorney general on his payroll, the NSA in his pocket, and half the police working as informants. How the fuck did the video get past them all?

"Contained by whom?" Gabriela taunted him. She was the only person who wasn't afraid of him.

"I settled it with the AG and the NSA. We arrested everyone involved."

"Clearly, Pa, you didn't get everyone. The internet is a free-for-all. Anyone with a copy of the story on a USB stick could've leaked it."

He ticked off the offenders in his mind. *We got the reporter, Taylor. We got the researcher girl. We fired the producer, leaving her career in ashes. Plus, we made her sign a nondisclosure agreement.*

He mumbled, "Could she be that stupid?"

Gabriela leaned forward. "Who?"

Wilmot dialed a number, then demanded, "Jeff, what happened?" As he listened, his face turned from red to purple.

"How could you let them go? They were supposed to be buried forever. You said you understood me, when I explained the threat they represent."

Gabriela huffed, and turned her head away, searching the internet on her wristband's holo-display.

"Well, it's all over the Web. Apparently someone broke the terms of the agreement you made with the network. Arrest them all. And for fuck's sake, wipe every digital copy of the video from existence."

Wilmot rose to his feet, trying to prevent his head from exploding. Sure, things went wrong in business all the time. But never twice. He'd personally instructed his connections to eradicate the story. If he couldn't rely on the Attorney General of the United States, then who could he trust?

"I don't care how you do it, Jeff! Bury every one of those bastards. And find out who's responsible for uploading the file."

Wilmot prowled along the glass wall behind his desk, taking in his extensive view of the Manhattan skyline. If anyone crossed him in the next five minutes, he'd rip their throat out with his bare hands. The AG was damned lucky he wasn't in the room.

"I'll force every site to take it down," he replied to the AG, "by the end of the week. You find out who performed the first upload, and gut them. Oh, and Jeff, I don't want them arrested by local law enforcement. I want the NSA on them. Agent Alvarez will be assigned to the case. He's to interrogate them like the terrorists they are."

Wilmot ended the call and slammed down into his chair.

"Think he'll do the right thing now?" Gabriela asked with a smirk.

"He will. Or else." Wilmot squeezed his hands open and closed, open and closed, trying to regain his composure. "We need a bill to take care of the internet content. I want it through Congress by two o'clock, and debated in the Senate by the end of the day. They will pass it by lunch tomorrow."

"Now there's my father." Gabriela chuckled.

Wilmot laughed, and raised his hands as if he'd just won a race. "I'm so lucky to have you by my side."

"Thanks, Chief!" Gabriela smiled and saluted like a soldier.

She really lights up my day, he thought. *My little soldier. My princess.*

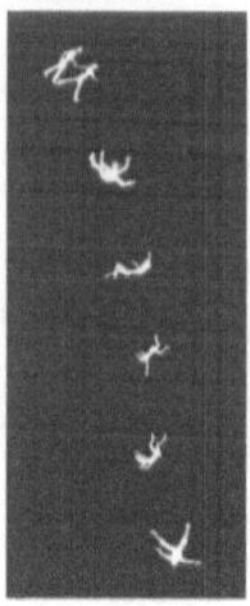

NIGEL AND THE LONDON BULLETS

Nigel dove behind his car for cover. The gun battle was all confetti and fireworks between the Corp Police and Thompson's goons for almost two full minutes. Then silence.

He could see Brit's face through the front window, going from satisfaction to confusion to complete puzzlement and anger. No panic. No fear. *Samuel Brit's a hard-nosed player*, thought Nigel. Going forward, he'd give the man his full attention.

Nigel rose slowly, checking every person that he had a clear view of, to see if any of them had survived. They were all motionless.

Then he heard one of them groan, so he moved around the car for a better vantage point. Thompson rose as well, but with some difficulty, sounding as though he was in significant pain. Nigel placed his gun's barrel on Mr. Thompson's nape and he froze.

Nigel said, "Stand, please."

Thompson nodded and pulled himself to standing, trembling with effort, groaning and leaning heavily on his cane. Nigel took one step back to allow the movement, taking the gun away from Thompson's nape. When he glanced at the house, Brit was nowhere to be seen.

As he returned his attention to Thompson's efforts, the old man slid down on his cane in a lightning move, twisted his body, and brought the cane up between Nigel's legs with a fierce whack.

Nigel grunted, bowed, and tried to remain focused on the battle. *Fierce whack's definitely an understatement.*

Thompson wielded his cane like a scythe, knocking Nigel's feet out from under him. He smashed into the road, the impact strong enough to restore some of his mental faculties and distract him from the pain in his nuts. Thompson kept lifting his cane in the air and then swinging it down, aiming for Nigel's head.

Dodging the blows, Nigel rolled left, right, and left again, as the old man continued his hockey stick-like assault with the cane. Nigel fired wildly at his target. The gunshots startled Thomson, forcing him to stop and step back.

By the time Nigel scrambled back to his feet and properly aimed his gun, Thompson's handgun was aiming at the center of Nigel's chest.

"What now, Mr. Blakesley?"

"Well, Mr. Thompson, I'm wondering if you're about to take the matter into your own hands." *For fuck's sake,* thought Nigel. *Why am I suddenly speaking like this asshole? Besides, more Corp Police are going to be here any minute.*

"All right," said Thompson. "What do you have in mind?"

"I hacked into Mr. Brit's computer system, and uncovered some nasty shit. I thought our employer would be interested in seeing the data. That is, before he started questioning my loyalty."

"Who gave you permission to hack into the system?"

"I did." Nigel scanned around them. "I don't have time for this bullshit debate. Are you interested in Brit's secrets, or not? Maybe want to earn yourself a raise?"

"For argument's sake, let's say I'm interested. Let's also say that Mr. Brit did indeed do some 'nasty shit.' The problem is, Mr. Blakesley, that regardless of his crimes, you and I have no power to take on a businessman of Mr. Brit's stature. And neither does my employer, I'm afraid."

Nigel considered Thompson's revelation. He hadn't expected an English racketeer to be so disciplined and politically inclined. He'd seen Thompson's catlike reflexes. If he shot him now, the chances of the old man returning fire were sky high. But he was bleeding, even though it wasn't bad enough to slow him down or finish him.

Nigel glanced at Brit's house again. Still no movement. *Time's up*, he thought. *Make a decision.*

Brit's meeting with Blake Frye was unsettling for Nigel's employer. The *previous* one, before the *English* one. The Frye meeting didn't concern his English employer or Thompson, but they needed to think it mattered. Once Thompson realized he'd been tricked, Nigel's true intentions would be all too clear. Until that happened, he had no choice but to take this chance with the old racketeer. So he shoved his gun into his waistband in the center of his back, hiding it from Thompson's view. Then he lifted his two empty hands in the air.

"Listen, Mr. Thompson, I put my gun away. Now we can talk. Like you said, as two civilized human beings."

Thompson kept his gun aimed at Nigel's chest. He was either thinking over the offer, or he'd already decided to bring Nigel back to his employer, alive. No raise, and no glory.

"Let me make it easy for you," said Nigel. "I'm onto something big for your employer, and more importantly for the BSX. I only need to finish up my investigation of Brit. And I hate to admit it, but I need your help for that part of the plan."

Thompson stood so still, he didn't even seem to be breathing.

"Mr. Brit is connected, and he's slippery. I need you to back me up, and discover the truth for yourself. If I'm in the wrong, you take me to your employer. If I'm right, we take Samuel fucking Brit to Lord Wright."

"I told you, we have no position to actually take on Mr. Brit."

"Maybe you don't, but I do. The moment you came after me, my employment with Lord Wright ceased. I'm a freelancer right now. An American one. I'm no longer loyal to anyone in England. Not to your employer and not to the BSX. I can do whatever the fuck I want. So, I'm very much permitted and able to take on Mr. Brit. I only need you to have my back. After, you can always claim that I forced you to help. That the plan was all on me. You simply stayed close to reap the rewards." He smiled. "What do you say?"

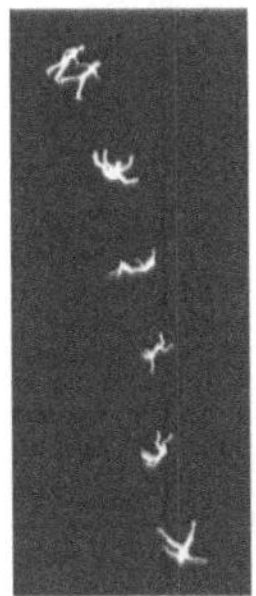

THE HEART OF THE BEAST

The Wilmot building was a fortress in the middle of Manhattan. The receptionist led Blake to a meeting room furnished with a long, dark metal table and overstuffed designer leather chairs. Even the air felt heavy. Blake imagined a room like this belonged in a private club, not a corporate headquarters. The shades on the windows had been lowered, making the room quite dark. A holo-video played above the table, in the middle of the room. A voice resounded in the background, like a recording.

He didn't see any security personnel on his way here, but he was certain they were close by. Not only that, but he was also sure that Agent Alvarez and his NSA minions were already on their way. Blake was early, but he already knew this meeting was a trap. His only play was to watch and wait for an opportunity or an advantage. The stalked animal looking for a way to reverse the hunter's trap.

Blake flung himself into one of the designer chairs and checked the time—10:06 in the morning. As he paid more attention to the video, he recognized John Taylor's voice. That's Isa's reportage.

The video flipped through a series of police mug shots of men, while Taylor narrated.

"So far, police have caught seventeen debt hunters in eight states. They've all been paid to make their victims disappear from accounts owned by companies that had nothing to do with the victims' debts."

The image changed to a spreadsheet containing a list of

companies. Lines were drawn with a red marker, linking one set of company names to another set. From that column, lines were drawn with a green marker from the second set of companies to the names of individuals. Taylor continued.

"The companies are owned by other companies, which are owned by businesspeople who are all William Wilmot's employees or associates."

A picture of a man, probably in his fifties, appeared on the left side of the screen. His name, *JAMES GUNNER*, was shown below. Another photo appeared on the right. Blake recognized Wilmot, and his name, *WILLIAM WILMOT*, appeared in the caption below. Once again, Taylor narrated.

"James Gunner, chief financial officer of Wilmot Enterprises, has run away from his master. He consented to our interview after he was granted asylum in a foreign country."

Immediately, Blake heard the voice of James Gunner. It was all too familiar, somehow bringing Isa back in a small way, and he had to fight the temptation to dive into her story and pay close attention to the dialogue. He needed to remain present in this meeting room, planning for his meeting with Wilmot.

Blake activated the recording app on his wristband and pressed Start. Then he activated his notepad and opened his sketch of the circles of interest. He added names: Agent Alvarez, Agent Saunders, and for the two unnamed NSA agents from the precinct, he wrote Agent X and Agent Y.

On Isa's story, James Gunner's revelations continued: *"When my objections to Wilmot's, uh, new businesses made me a 'persona non grata' in his entourage, William Wilmot himself gave the order to his henchmen to take me to his slave camp."*

"What do you mean by 'new businesses'?"

"They're servitude businesses. He's the number one servitude broker in the United States. He faked my financial situation, created fake debts for me, and intended to sell me into slavery—"

Suddenly, the video paused on the image of Gunner. Someone in the room cleared his throat. Blake stood and scanned his surroundings. As the video display vanished, he saw William Wilmot had already settled into a chair at the opposite end of the long table.

The man had no visible neck. His chin seemed to cover it completely, and somehow rest on his chest. He was dressed in such opulence that Blake had to blink to keep his eyes focused on him. Wilmot kept his fingers flexed above the desk, touching the surface lightly with only the tips of his fingers. His chest moved slowly with each breath, and his mouth was stretched into a rictus, spoiling the friendly expression he displayed.

"I'm glad you could make the appointment."

Blake folded his notepad, collapsed his holo-screen, and stood, presenting a dark and menacing face. He studied the room behind Wilmot. No obvious door. He turned and glanced at the only visible door in or out, the main one. "Where's my wife?"

"You should ask Agent Alvarez."

"Who works for you."

"He works for the NSA, and therefore for this country. But sometimes the country's interests coincide with my own."

"First you blamed this country's interests when you arranged to have my wife and her team fired. Next you blamed those same national interests when you arranged the closure of their television station. You continued to cite national security as you corrupted the NSA from within and turned the attorney general into your puppet. You're playing an awfully big game."

"Always." Wilmot tapped controls in the surface of the table that elevated his throne-like chair until he was higher than Blake and could look down at him, wearing a grandfatherly grin.

Wilmot was not the sort of man to forget. He would have his revenge, no matter how long it took. His goal was to eliminate every person involved in Isa's reportage. Considering Isa's current dilemma, Blake was the last one on that list. Reaching any sort of arrangement with Wilmot was unlikely. But he had to try, as a way to extract as much information as possible.

"You may think your wife's fiction is the main reason you're here." Wilmot brushed a finger along his hairline. "Combined with her decision to leak the reportage to the internet and damage my reputation, as payback for her sudden termination."

"When one gets invited to your office by an NSA agent, all sorts of ideas go through his head." Blake stared coldly at Wilmot, waiting for the first blow to fall.

"Neither incident is of any consequence. Journalists like your wife, and their misguided stories, are relics of the past." Wilmot spread his plump left palm across the table's surface. Then he placed his right palm over his heart. "I'm simply a patriot, Mr. Frye."

"You have a skewed definition of patriotism."

"Seeing as you work for a foreign power, which is scheming against your fellow citizens, your view of my definition might also be skewed."

"I suppose I am a traitor to your interests," said Blake. "The problem is that you're a traitor to this country, to its democracy, and its constitution." Blake remained calmer than he thought possible, in the presence of his wife's kidnapper.

"You know," said Wilmot, "my pa had a very wise saying: It is foolish to speak bad of others. If you're smart, you will keep quiet."

Blake smirked and inhaled deeply, giving Wilmot his most menacing glare. Wilmot continued to look slightly amused.

"The simple truth, Mr. Frye, is that traitors are simply those who find themselves on the losing side of history."

"The *truth* doesn't need a qualifier, Mr. Wilmot. Despite the way that politicians degrade truths, twisting them into lies that are seen as good for one party and bad for another. Truth is singular. It is only truth. It cannot be qualified."

"You're a detective *and* a philosopher. A rare combination. I'd heard you were a man of few words. A man of action, like your fellow policemen. But you're more. I'm impressed."

"Great." He exhaled loudly. "What do you want in exchange for my wife?"

"I didn't say that I *have* your wife. However, if she was within my grasp, I'd request a small token of your gratitude."

"Fine. I'm grateful. Now, where is she?"

"Well, seeing as we're both on each other's good side, I'd be interested to know more about your European adventure."

Blake hesitated for only a second. He'd recorded Wilmot's words on his wristband. He was, without question, the underground American slaver, and he had Isa. He would not give her up, not easily. The man still had the upper hand.

"I don't know anything about the European slavers," said Blake. "I can't help you."

"We can start small, you and I." Wilmot's tone dripped honey.

"Start by ordering your men to release my wife."

"Your lack of cooperation leads me to assume that your deal with the BSX and its directors is no longer valid. Have you become useless to them?"

"I never cooperated with them, so I suppose that I'm as useless now as I ever was."

"NSA has evidence to the contrary."

Blake bolted from his chair and rushed across the room. Wilmot tried to rise, but his bulk made a swift reaction difficult. Blake reached the man's chair, grabbed Wilmot's head in his hands, and fantasized about snapping it off. "We can start with me killing you."

"That would be a grave mistake."

Whose grave? thought Blake. He paused, his hands still pressing on Wilmot's head. When the man reached under the table to press a button, Blake kicked Wilmot's hand, crushing it under the sole of his shoe.

Wilmot groaned in pain.

"Now, that's a proper mistake," said Blake. "Men like you always think you can just take whatever you want. But men like me make sure you don't."

"Let's be rational here, Detective. I'm merely the NSA's voice. They want to know what the BSX asked of you. And before you deny your promise, let me explain. You met with them, talked to them, and then you returned home. Which means they want something from you here. They asked you to perform a task on their behalf in our backyard. I'm also aware of your large debt. A sum you're unlikely to ever repay. Your cooperation might encourage me to assist you with that loan. So, what is it the BSX wants from you?"

"I *want* my *wife.*"

"Agent Alvarez explained to me that the NSA doesn't negotiate with traitors. But he's willing to make a concession for me. Please, let me help you."

Blake made a sudden gesture, like the move he'd use to snap Wilmot's neck.

The fat man cried out in horror, begging, "Please, please, Detective! You'll lose your wife forever if you kill me."

Blake paused to think. Then he pulled his foot from Wilmot's hand and let go of the man's head. To ease his nerves, he arranged all the objects in front of Wilmot. Wilmot watched his movements with frightened eyes. Satisfied, Blake stepped slowly back to his chair at the other end of the table. As soon as he looked comfortable, Wilmot used his good hand to press the panic button.

"The Freedom Act is already before Congress. Why do you and the attorney general feel so threatened by a simple New York cop?"

Agents Alvarez and Saunders entered the room through a hidden door behind Wilmot's elevated throne.

Blake smirked, activated his notepad, and opened the sketch of the circles of interest. He wrote *William Wilmot?* in the second one. Wilmot watched him with interest. Blake wrote under all the circles: *WW afraid of something. No total control. Servitude in US uncertain. Opposition?*

"You mentioned truth earlier, Detective. Allow me to remind you of the truth in this room, right now. You don't have a single bargaining chip. I, on the other hand, have a stack of them. Beggars can't be choosers, Frye. So, the smallest token of goodwill on your part would be to tell me what the BSX asked of you."

Blake checked his buttons, then straightened his collar. *Time to end this meeting,* he thought. Once Wilmot learned that Blake's dealings with the BSX were so insignificant, the arrogant man would order him killed and sell Isa. *Best to remain silent about the meeting with Brit.*

Blake inhaled deeply and leaned forward on the table, inching closer to Wilmot. "I'll ask again, what could a simple New York detective do to threaten the servitude debate?"

"I'm not afraid. But I need to know the answer."

"Why?" Blake tapped his index finger on the table as though he was writing and arranging a list. He'd figured out a valuable piece of information, but he couldn't write it down. Not yet. Not while there still was a chance, a fat chance, of being taken down by Wilmot's men. "Perhaps you think the BSX is already infiltrated, and is trying to control the vote." He drew an X in the air. "Not possible, because you already arranged for Congress to pass the Freedom Act."

Wilmot chuckled and wiggled the fingers on his good hand, mimicking puppet strings.

"Besides, the BSX probably also wants servitude to be legal in the US. They're on your side. Thus, you can't be worried about my interference with the servitude vote. And that means your worry is fueled by something else."

"There are plenty of patriots in Congress. And everyone knows that birds of a feather flock together."

"You made sure of that, didn't you? It's not just the NSA. Somehow, you got to most of the Congressmen."

Wilmot made a modest face and raised his hands in self-defense. "I'm not that powerful, Mr. Frye. But I'm not alone, either."

Wilmot nodded at Alvarez and Saunders. They walked casually to Blake's end of the table. Obviously, Wilmot assumed their meeting was nearly done.

Neil would know exactly what to do, thought Blake. He had perfect instincts. *I really miss you, partner.*

"I've enjoyed our meeting, Detective. I could use a man like you in my employ. Please think carefully, and don't let your rigid attitude get the best of you when you answer me. What does the BSX want?"

Blake shook his head. "My question, first, Mr. Wilmot. What did you do with Detective Neil Grissom?"

For a brief moment, Wilmot looked surprised by the question. Then his eyes twinkled, as though he'd just remembered a joke. He rubbed his chin and smiled the same grandfatherly smile. "Was he your partner?"

"You know he was."

"I heard he ran off to Europe. It seems the New York Police Department churns out traitors like grommets."

"Did you kill him, or was he sold as a slave?"

"It doesn't make any difference. Not for you." Wilmot trailed a bit, narrowed his eyes, and stared at Blake with a bigger smile. "Would it ease your worry to know that he played his cards right, and now he serves the good side?" He paused then added, "The *winning* side."

Blake shook his head. "That's impossible. Neil would never—"

"*Never say never*, Mr. Frye."

"Neil was an honest cop."

"Well, keep an open mind. But enough about your former partner. You should focus on your wife's fate. She's still in your grasp. Only if you want her back."

Blake felt a genuine smile, for the first time in the last eight hours. "I will not stand idle while a mob of rich, greedy slavery lovers tries to sell out our democracy and freedom."

A hand pressed down on Blake's left shoulder. Instantly gripping the fingers, he twisted, and there was a loud cracking sound. Agent Alvarez howled in pain, gingerly holding his broken digits.

Agent Saunders pulled on Blake's chair, trying to topple it. Blake grabbed Saunders's hand, dragged him forward, and balanced the chair with the same movement. Then he twisted and the agent bent in the same direction. Blake grabbed his neck and forced his head down onto the table. Finally, in one swift countermove, Blake stood and smashed Saunders's head against the wall. Continuing his momentum, Blake swept the man's feet out from under him. Saunders landed at a bad angle, breaking his forearm with a loud crunch. The agent howled in pain, writhing on the floor.

Alvarez had his gun in his left hand and was trying to get his broken fingers around the trigger. Blake kicked his head several times until he dropped and lay still.

Blake took a few seconds to be certain that both men were

no longer a risk. When he looked across the room at Wilmot, his eyes were as wide as his neck was absent. He frantically pressed the panic button while lowering his chair to make a break for the exit.

Blake replayed the recording of Wilmot, cranking the volume to max. "I'm not that powerful, Mr. Frye. But I'm not alone, either."

Grim-faced and menacing, he leaned against the table and demanded, "You have six hours to give me back my wife. After that, I'll turn over my recording to the media. Probably upload it to the internet, as well. Finally, I'll come for you. I plan to kill you so slowly, you'll wish you'd died as an infant."

Several security guards rushed into the room through the hidden door. Blake turned and bolted out the main door.

He rushed down a short corridor and turned a corner into the floor's lobby. It was decorated in baroque hues. A massive reception desk stretched across one wall. Three sofas were arranged in a U, with a coffee table in front of each. Four huge abstract works of art adorned the dark walls. Blake finally saw the elevators and ran for them. The receptionist, a diminutive young woman, moved from behind her desk and followed him in confusion.

The employees were probably all trained to sound the alarm, so he flashed his badge at the receptionist. "Shush. I'm NYPD."

He heard the meeting room door fly open down the hall. He pressed the elevator button, then dashed for the stairs. The receptionist returned to her place behind the desk and watched him disappear into the stairwell. The elevator chimed and the doors slid open.

He heard the security guards rushing through the lobby at the same moment that the elevator doors slid closed. *That should give them something to do,* he thought as he pounded down the stairs, two risers at a time.

The elevator doors closed before the guards could see inside. As the elevator began its descent, one guard pressed the elevator button. Another took command of the situation, shouting, "You two wait for the elevator. You two take the stairs. You go to the security office and watch the cameras to tell us where he goes."

Meanwhile, the elevator panel showed the car's location: 86, 76, 66…

Blake was still jumping two steps at a time when he heard the door fly open two floors above, then loud, angry voices and footsteps. Using their commotion as cover, he slowed his pace and began to descend as noiselessly as possible.

He halted on the ninety-third floor, opened the door to the hallway, then resumed his descent, moving as quickly and silently as possible.

The elevator doors opened. A businessman and an elderly woman chatted as they entered the car and selected their floor. Security guards raced toward them, and a hand blocked the doors from closing. The couple stood silent, their mouths open, staring at the guards in confusion.

A gasping guard used his comm to send a breathless message: "Suspect is *not* in the elevator. Repeat, *not* in the elevator!"

The door to the stairway flew open and hit the wall. The receptionist on this floor raised her eyes and blinked at him, surprised. Blake rushed toward her desk. The receptionist reached out, no doubt aiming for the alarm button.

Panting from his sprint down the stairs, Blake managed to say, "You're safe, ma'am. I'm NYPD. Where's the InWay?"

The receptionist hesitated, then pointed. She kept her eyes on Blake as he ran to the indicated door. InWay access had been added to corporate buildings after the riots during the last financial crisis, when masses of people had squatted in corporate buildings, barricading themselves inside and refusing to leave for months on end. Employees were blocked from accessing their workplaces. The protesters crippled many financial corporations' abilities to perform daily tasks. The president at the time, the one whose fiscal policies had sparked the economic downturn in the first place, hadn't been interested in dialogue or peaceful solutions. He'd labeled the protesters as terrorists, declared a state of emergency, and ordered the army to engage the "insurgents." After many lives had been lost, the president's next decree was for every high-rise office building involved in the finance industry to install an exclusive access system for "first responders." He'd claimed this initiative would save lives, when its main purpose was to improve police and military access to protect the corporate world from any future threats.

Blake touched the door's ID pad to activate the system, then he pressed his index finger onto the scanner. Simultaneously, a retinal sensor scanned his right eye.

The pad's display beeped, then displayed: *DETECTIVE FRYE, BLAKE, IDENTIFIED. PLEASE SCAN YOUR BADGE.*

Blake whispered, "Shit!" and accessed his wristband. He didn't have his physical badge with him, having still not retrieved it from his confiscated luggage, so he had to use the digital badge he stored in his wristband. It usually worked on anyone skeptical enough to ask for proof of his authority.

As quickly as possible, he searched through the files. *Come on, where is it?* He tapped on the icon and nothing happened, so he tapped it again.

"Please scan your badge, Detective Frye." To his panicked mind, the ID pad sounded impatient.

Blake finally managed to open the right file to display the digital badge on his holo-screen. He twisted his arm and swiped the holo-screen over the ID pad.

"Scan failure. Please hold your badge over the ID pad."

Blake glanced over his shoulder. The stairway door was opening. Two guards burst onto the floor. "Shit, shit, *shit!*" He kept his holo-screen stationary above the ID pad.

The two guards yelled and ran toward him, drawing their

weapons. "Stop right there! Don't move!"

The receptionist's eyes grew wide.

The ID pad clinked acceptance and the InWay door slid open. Blake thrust himself through and shut the door behind him. Then he felt his way along the wall, looking for the touch sensors.

He heard the guards at the InWay ID pad on the other side of the door. Moments later, a red light began revolving above the InWay entrance, and a blaring alarm ripped the silence into bloody shreds.

Blake selected Underground Level as his destination and the elevator dropped free fall, leaving the guards screaming and pounding on the access door. Blake collapsed his holo-screen and leaned forward, resting his palms against the elevator wall, finally enjoying a moment of safety.

Martin Breckenwell, the Wilmot security chief, watched Wilmot Tower's CCTV screens with some amusement. His job at Wilmot Enterprises was well paid. *Fuck, beyond well paid*, he thought. *But boring as hell.* No one had ever dared go up against their security. He'd waited years for clever thieves to pull off an epic heist, or for covert assassins to kill the big boss-man. He'd even settle for insidious hackers sneaking through the firewalls to hack into their network.

Nothing. NOTHING. *Bor-ing!*

Until this morning's fateful events. When a fucking cop dared to resist. A man with the balls to stroll right into the bear's cave and fight his way out. Now that was an individual who appealed to Breckenwell's tastes. *I'd love to meet this customer face to face.*

In front of Breckenwell, several security personnel manipulated data on their screens. Everyone feigned looking busier than normal when he showed up to watch. He loved that feeling of power, fueled by other people's fear. Fear was musky and exhilarating, especially when weeping from a roomful of pores.

A guard rushed into the room and said, "He took the InWay

on floor 76, sir. He's on his way down."

Without being asked, one of the data security techs added, "There are two exits from the InWay. The lobby on the ground floor, and the Police Access Tunnel on the underground level.

Breckenwell grunted, and said, "Send a team to the lobby, and two more to the street." He turned to the skinny kid who always looked too young to have a full-time job, and ordered, "Call our contact at NYPD. Get them to authorize our access to that underground tunnel." When the kid just stood there with her mouth open, he added, "Now!"

Samuel Brit worked on a new lapfoil in business class. He felt tired and somehow disappointed with his team. They knew who Nigel Whatever was, and still they sent him the images. The plot had worked as planned, and yet it had also worked against him. *Against me, personally,* he thought. He'd pulled down the shades on the plane's windows as he worked relentlessly to recover some of the lost data.

His phone rang. He ignored it. It continued to ring, over and over. Clearly, the caller assumed that the call was so urgent it should not be ignored. "Fine," he said, and answered.

"Sir! I'm so glad I reached you. Frye's tracker indicates that he's in Wilmot's Manhattan tower, and that he may be in trouble. Should we intervene?"

Brit grinned, exhaled with satisfaction, and said, "No. Stand down. Let's see if we bet on the right horse."

He switched off the phone, rotated his chair left and right, and pondered the interaction with his eyes half closed. After half a minute, he checked his watch and whistled. "Quicker than I thought. What do you know—Mr. Let-Me-Think-Frye is a man of action after all. Good for you, Frye. Good for you."

The InWay door slid open and Blake cautiously emerged. He looked left and right. The exit was on a platform at the end of the Police Access Tunnel, underneath Wilmot Headquarters. The underground level was eerily quiet. The building's alarm was only a distant, muffled tone.

He spotted a door labeled *EXIT* in large red letters. He exhaled, jumped off the platform, and crossed the tunnel. When he opened the door, he heard heavy boots pounding on the stairs, and people shouting orders to one another. Security was on its way. Normally they shouldn't have access to the police tunnel, but given what he'd found out about Wilmot lately, the man probably had some cops in his pocket. He shut the door and jumped back into the tunnel.

Think, he told himself. *What are my options?* The elevator. But it might not be long before they disabled his access. The exit door, with the sounds of his enemies on the other side. The tunnel.

Since it posed the lowest risk, Blake ran down the tunnel.

A few paces in, the sound of a police train's whistle made him freeze. Damn, SWAT reacted fast. He'd hoped they might be more lenient in pursuit of one of their own, but their response time from the alarm to their arrival in the tunnel was astonishing.

He spun around, looking for options There was another door a few steps down the tunnel, labeled with a biohazard sign. The train's headlight loomed ahead.

He sprinted forward, toward both the train and the biohazard door. As the train cut the distance between them, he pressed his palm on the door's ID pad and quickly used his holo-screen to display his digital badge.

As the door slid open, the train's momentum whooshed him inside the room. Blake fell to the concrete floor, breathing hard. Once his head cleared, he peered into the tunnel before the door could close and lock.

The security guards overran the access tunnel, but halted and retreated in front of the train. The train came to a full stop and a SWAT team jumped out, at the ready. The security team leader was trying to see beyond the train. There was little space between the train and the tunnel walls, preventing anyone from slipping through.

Blake allowed the door to lock behind him. An emergency light switched on automatically. He held his left hand in front of him. His holo-screen still displayed his badge replica. He kissed it and whispered, "Thank you."

The room was small. On one side, several containment suits hung on a rack, enough to protect an entire intervention team. At the other end, there was another door. Blake approached it, and the door slid open to reveal another Police Access Tunnel, this one empty and silent.

Blake stepped out of the InWay elevator into the lobby of another building where people moved casually around. He crossed the lobby through the buzzing crowd, and approached the revolving door. A business woman arrived at the same moment, so he smiled and gave her priority, before he slipped into the next opening behind her.

The door expelled him into the street. Several patrol cars were parked on the other side of the road, farther down from where he'd left his car, also parked in the police lane. He looked around and joined the flow of pedestrians on the street. Those in the crowd were moving at different paces, so he slipped in and out of the stream until he reached his car.

The SWAT team emerged from the same revolving door. In diamond formation, they scanned each direction in their immediate vicinity, just as Blake reached his car and climbed in.

When he started the engine, he alerted a Wilmot security guard. The man approached the car with his right hand extended, signaling for Blake to stop. He rested his hands on the wheel, in plain view. The guard gestured at Blake to roll down the window.

"NYPD," said Blake. "I need to get to a call."

Several members of the SWAT team were approaching his car, checking every vehicle along the curb. The security guard squinted at Blake, bit his lip, then smiled and stepped back.

Blake tore down the police lane to get back onto the street. Glancing in the rearview mirror, he saw the SWAT team still checking parked cars. Blake entered the street, switched into the civilian lane, turned right, and disappeared into traffic.

Hopeful that he'd made a clean escape, he switched control to automatic pilot and bit his lip. *Time to cover my ass*, he thought. He loaded the recording from Wilmot's office. Then he selected Captain Moore's contact information and sent his boss a message: *Attached, find my discussion with Wilmot. Be sure to distribute to all interested parties, including the AG. Be ready to send to all news media outlets in case I don't make it. Corbin will* —Blake stopped typing, remembering.

They were visiting Corbin on a cold winter day. Blake sat on a couch, brooding over a glass of scotch. Corbin showed Isa his facts board, including his research and theories about Wilmot. He pointed to the tidbits he could share, if she wanted them. He hid the research that he couldn't share, if he still wanted to maintain his own career.

The entire media industry was in disarray, not only the magazines and the newspapers, but television as well. Flash news, which consisted of a title and a few teaser lines of text was the main staple in online news. As every outlet's target demographic became narrower and hyper-precise, media news focused on "alternative facts", a transformation that caused such polarized consumption of information that the television networks could no longer compete for eyeballs. When it came to content, the networks had to work under too many restrictions, giving digital companies the freedom to generate movies and shows with complex storylines and far more adult content. Enthralled by this innovative entertainment, the viewers migrated, and so did the money. Network budgets dropped and cable ones swelled. Hard-hitting, investigative journalism appealed to an increasingly smaller pool of customers. People were always working, always checking their phones and other electronic devices, and they wanted their news to be just as easy to digest. Well documented and researched reportages took too many minutes to watch, and didn't often line up with their social or political viewpoints.

Truth had become debatable. Everyone had *their* own, personalized version of the facts, easy to access on targeted media outlets. They no longer questioned the facts they consumed. Doubt took too much effort. Everyone was entitled to their own opinions, and considered them the definition of a political truth. That philosophy had been in effect since 2017, the year that practically everything that mattered in the world deteriorated.

Isa and her journalist colleagues were seen as dinosaurs. She wasn't scared or angry about this demotion, but Blake carried enough anger for them both. She did mourn the fact that the world was turning its back to the age of light and knowledge, truth and progress.

A ringing sound in the background dragged Blake back to reality. The vivid memory of Corbin and Isa sharing journalist notes faded into the dark regions of his thoughts.

After a cleansing breath, he finished typing his message to Captain Moore: *Corbin will help.*

He skimmed the message once for typos, then pressed Send. Then he dialed Corbin.

The call went straight to voicemail. "This is Simon. Leave—"

Blake ended the connection, and almost immediately took an incoming call. Captain Moore appeared on the car's onboard display. "Frye! What happened?"

"A lot, Captain. I just sent you a message."

"Where are you?"

"In my car. Why?"

"We're in full-blown red-alert mode at the precinct. Everyone is after you."

"I'm not surprised, after my meeting with Wilmot. I don't have much time, Captain. I need to keep moving."

"Where will you go?"

"To where it all started."

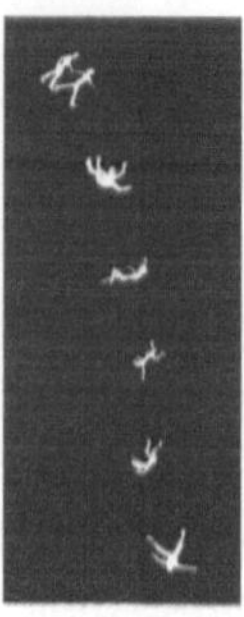

FOUR MONTHS EARLIER

The coffee that Blake had brewed for Isa was getting cold. So were the eggs and bacon he'd cooked. She'd dragged herself out of bed at Blake's insistence, changed into daytime clothes, and come down to the kitchen. The table had been set already, every piece in its precise place, from the silverware to the napkins. Blake's attention to detail could not be outmatched. When he'd plated the food, he'd arranged the plates on the table so the food would be presented color-wise. Only when the pattern had met his standards did he sit beside her and begin to eat. All she could do was sit in her place and watch him. Eventually she picked up her fork.

For the third day in a row, she wondered, *Why is picking up a fork so difficult for me?* They'd spoken about her mood, and she'd insisted that she wanted to pull herself out of this dark place, but she couldn't find the will. Or the strength. Or a good reason to try.

Ever since she'd been fired, they'd both wondered, What now? She'd insisted that once she found the answer, she'd be okay. Be herself again.

Blake had offered plenty of suggestions for this elusive "answer." None of them had struck the right cord. His comforting gestures didn't help. She needed *real* answers. She needed a reality check and a perspective on her life. She was aware that it might take some time to find a new direction. Any life's course, if it was worth pursuing, was too big and too complicated to find in a drawer next to the last one she'd been using.

The doorbell rang. She felt her eyes twitch, but the rest of her body couldn't react. She watched Blake as he answered the door, having a perfect view from her chair at the table. He opened the door partway, and braced it so it wouldn't open any farther. Outside, from her vantage point, she could see a cop and a guy in a dark suit.

The dark suit held up a paper for Blake to read, then said, "We have a warrant for your computers." He then tried to move past Blake into the house, but her husband didn't budge.

The cop placed his right hand on his gun and said, "Mr. Frye, I need—"

"I know what you need," snapped Blake. "First, I need to examine that warrant. Then I need to study your badges."

Isa's heart skipped a beat. *Will I feel threatened by anyone in authority for the rest of my life?* At least Blake was calm. She took solace in the thought that few bad things could happen to her in his presence.

The two men at the door stood in surprised silence as they cooperated with Blake's requests. She found their reactions amusing. Blake studied their badges long enough to memorize them. His considerable memory defied logic. Few people knew that about him. He preferred to keep most of his talents hidden from the world.

After the dark suit accepted his badge back, he slapped the warrant against Blake's chest and tried to push him back with the same move. Blake stood his ground, pushing back only enough to maintain the standoff and not hard enough to be misinterpreted as aggressive or dangerous. The dark suit tried to push back, but Blake squared his shoulders and filled the doorway in such a way that they would've needed to punch him to get through.

Blake calmly stated, "I need a moment to read your warrant, please."

"You can read it while we're taking your computers."

"No, I'll read it first, to ensure you're not breaching the limits of your warrant, DA Gibson."

"Are you kidding me?"

"No, sir. I'm only reminding you of the law. Now, please, would you give me a moment of silence so I can focus?"

The district attorney froze; obviously he didn't usually meet this kind of resistance. The cop looked with uncertainty from the DA to Blake. Isa felt something more than she'd felt in the last forty-eight hours. She suddenly didn't feel paralyzed. Tired, yes. Furious, absolutely. As exhausted as anyone might feel after a breakdown, but alive.

"DA Gibson, please wait here. I'll bring you our computers."

"Sorry, Mr. Blake, but we have to come in and take them ourselves."

"Your warrant, DA Gibson, doesn't give you the right to enter my home. Only to pick up our computers. If you'd like, you can recheck it yourself, to ensure that you understand its boundaries."

"Detective Frye, you're obstructing justice. For the last time, I'm asking you to move aside and let us in." The district attorney's voice sounded high pitched. The cop drew his gun.

Isa rose from the kitchen table and moved slowly toward the door. Blake activated his wristband: "Record. Send live to Captain Moore and Judge Barrystan."

"Hey, stop," said the DA, sounding more angry by the minute. "You're not allowed to record our interactions without my permission."

Blake kept his wristband up, and continued to record.

"DA Gibson, your warrant gives you the right to pick up my computers. It doesn't allow you or your police escort to enter my home. I offered to give you the warrant so that you could reread it, to confirm that those are the written terms. You rejected my offer and threatened me. Do you still insist on breaking and entering my house?"

The DA kept quiet for a few seconds. Then he signaled the cop to holster his gun. "How can I know for certain that you've handed over all of your computers?" The shrillness in his voice had dropped by a tone or two.

"You can't. What you *can* do is return to Judge Marlow and

ask him for a more comprehensive warrant. I'll be home for the remainder of the day."

The DA sighed. "Fine. Go get them for me."

Blake stepped back and closed the door.

"Hey, what are you doing?" Gibson screamed from outside.

Blake turned the lock, set the alarm, and answered, "I'm bringing you the computers. Please wait outside."

Blake turned and met Isa's eyes. She smiled at him and mouthed, *I love you.* Bewildered by her attentiveness, he hurried over and gently held her hand. She caressed his face, kissed his cheek, and said, "Let me help you get those computers."

He nodded, and said, "I'll get the tablets," before he hurried up the stairs. Isa trudged to her office, unplugged her main laptop, wrapped it in a blanket, and brought it to the front door.

When Blake arrived with the tablets, she asked, "What do you think happened?"

"I'll tell you after they're gone."

Her eyes grew big with surprise. He unlocked the door, opened it, and handed the two tablets to the district attorney. Then he reached down, picked up Isa's blanket-wrapped laptop, and handed it to the cop.

"I want receipts for all of them," said Blake. "And I'll need them back, intact, in twenty-four hours."

They drew up the receipts, handed them to Blake, and left without another word.

While they watched the men retreat, two other uniformed officers appeared along the side walkway. She asked, "Were they in our backyard?"

Blake nodded. "In case we ran."

"Why are they treating me like a criminal?" Isa could feel the heavy weight of depression falling back over her body.

Blake moved to the kitchen table, sipped his coffee, and motioned for her to join him.

She sat in her chair.

He said, "I need to show you something."

"Okay."

"It's big. Are you ready?"

"Sure, I guess."

He projected his holo-screen above the table, opened a web browser, and found a video on one of his favorite news sites.

She recognized it from the very first image. "That's my story." Her eyes began to water, and she realized she was crying. She felt as though all the anger, frustration, and pain had finally found a way out of her heart. "How is that possible?"

"Well, I was thinking about that "answer" you've been searching for, and I came up with this idea. I'm hoping it's close to an answer. Maybe a working premise?"

"You're kidding." Isa watched Blake's face for a hint that he was pulling a prank. That he'd faked the website. But her husband had never been good at humor. "Shit, you're not kidding."

"Your story's out."

"All right, HoneyB. I'm listening."

"Someone leaked your piece to the NSA, before it was scheduled to air. Even before the final edit was ready."

"Who would—"

"I don't know. Maybe someone on your team? Or one of the production people who worked on it during the final week? Maybe your boss, Kadesky?"

"They all knew about the nondisclosure agreement."

"This was *before* NDA was in play. The only thing I'm one hundred percent sure of is that you wouldn't leak it to the NSA. The rest of them are potential suspects."

"You mean, *traitors*?"

"Even though I doubt anyone would endure three months of intense work and then betray their own project, I think either John or Sam has a fifty-fifty chance of being the leaker."

"What about Senator Chadwick? Or your brother, Corbin? Even your partner, Neil, knew about the story."

"Corbin's off the list. No way would he betray us, or jeopardize his own project before completion. The NSA would've asked him how he knew about the story, and then he'd be compromised. As for Norman Chadwick, I really believe he's in love with my brother, so I don't see him risking his career, or his safety. Any leak would lead the authorities to his secret affair."

"What about Neil?"

Blake leaned on the chair. Isa could see that the thought of his partner's betrayal was painful to even consider. After a couple of minutes, he said, "Neil's a potential leaker, though he's less likely than Sam or John. What about the editors, or the production staff at the network?"

"I don't know about some of them, but Philip *definitely* didn't do it. He was in utter terror the other day, when the NSA descended on us." She took a bite of her cold bacon. "To maintain secrecy, only one woman was assigned to help with the edits. I stayed with her during the entire process, from the moment she watched the first rough edit, to the moment she delivered the final cut. She didn't have the time or opportunity."

"That narrows the suspect pool," said Blake. He collected his plate and placed it in the sink. "Do you want any more?"

"One more bite." She nibbled on the bacon again.

Blake grabbed her plate, dumped the uneaten food in the trash, and added it to the sink. For the next few minutes, they found their couple's rhythm, Isa helping collect items from the table and Blake straightening and adjusting what remained to ensure perfection.

When they were finished, Blake grasped Isa's shoulders and looked her in the eye. "One of three people leaked it to the authorities, and another one posted it on the internet. The district attorney and the police don't know which one. And since this story was your baby, you're at the top of their short list."

Isa sighed, her energy level still seriously depleted. Eventually she needed to learn the truth about what had happened. At that moment, she wasn't strong enough to try. "I heard you tell the DA you'd be home all day. What about work?"

"I told Moore I'll stay home today. I needed to be here if they showed up with a warrant. There's still a chance they'll return with a stronger warrant. I don't want you to face them alone."

She thought about what they might find on her computer, and said, "Oh, shit."

"What?"

"On my computer, I had files that weren't supposed to be

seen. By anyone."

"Anything incriminating?"

She shook her head. "Nothing illegal, just...*intimate*."

In a matter-of-fact voice, he said, "I scrubbed the dirty stuff from your computer last night. Don't worry." Then he left the kitchen.

She shouted after him, "B! You're my *hero*!" She found the energy to follow after him, and noticed he'd entered her office.

"How long have you known about the investigation?"

He slumped into one of the armchairs and said, "You better sit down."

The depression loomed again. *How can my feelings be so erratic?* Lately, she'd felt as though she was driving a race car from gravel roads to smooth racetrack and back again. The car was always a little out of control. And the steering wheel was malfunctioning.

"John Taylor was supposed to meet Philip Kadesky for coffee yesterday morning, to discuss John's employment prospects. Kadesky showed up at the precinct yesterday to report that John never showed up for the meeting. He hadn't been at home all night, either. So, theoretically, John's been missing for twenty-four hours. Tomorrow morning, at the forty-eight hour mark, we'll open an investigation."

Isa felt the world begin to spin, so she sat before she fell, fighting to breathe. "What does John's disappearance mean, B?"

"It means that either he leaked the story, and they eliminated him to make sure he never tells anyone, or he didn't leak it to the NSA, but he uploaded it to the internet, so they took him out as punishment."

"Either way, they took him out," said Isa. Fear replaced the depression, and she used its fury to fight back the darkness. "He couldn't have uploaded it to the net, not if he was meeting Kadesky about a job."

"Which means he was the traitor who leaked the story to the NSA. That's the only explanation that would keep him in the game, at the negotiating table with Kadesky."

"I can't believe John would go behind our backs like that, B.

He's an ass but he's not—"

"How well did you know him, love?"

"Before this project, I didn't know him at all. But we worked together, closely, for three months."

Blake sighed. "I'm sorry."

"How could I be *that* wrong about him?" Months of betrayals, witch hunts, and hide-and-seek with the government had left her vulnerable. She didn't know how to trust anyone anymore. Reading people and situations had always been a big part of her job. Reading intentions, and unearthing the motivations behind words.

"That means," said Blake, "that only Sam or Mr. Kadesky could have uploaded the story."

"Oh my god!" Isa felt the fear kick up another notch. "Sam!" She activated her wristband and dialed her researcher's number. It rang and rang. No answer. No voicemail.

"We need to find her," said Isa.

"I already asked the captain to inform all the New York precincts to watch for Sam. The moment they spot her, we'll arrange a meeting."

"Oh, B, you're an angel."

"No. I'm just furious. I don't know how to help you," he confessed.

"None of this is your fault, HoneyB."

"If my task force hadn't been assigned to those graves, I wouldn't have told you about the missing families. It's all my fault."

"Oh, B. No. You gave me a *purpose*. I can't thank you enough. While I've been wallowing in my own misery, you've kept everything organized."

He nodded, then studied Isa's wall of pictures and documents, where her team kept track of every lead.

He asked, "Remember that documentary about the last communist dictatorships?"

"That's kind of out of the blue, B. What about it?"

"Every day, more and more, it feels like our world is turning into that world."

She covered her mouth as tears welled up in her eyes.

He said, "People lived with persecution for generations. They were terrified, and paranoid, living in constant fear and suspicion of their neighbors, their friends, and even their families."

"And every act could be taken out of context and interpreted as treason," said Isa. "That's what they're going to do to me, isn't it?"

"Or worse," he said. "I can't let them take you, love. I'd die if they disappeared you."

She looked away, feeling shame for her depression. For wallowing over a job, when so much more was at stake.

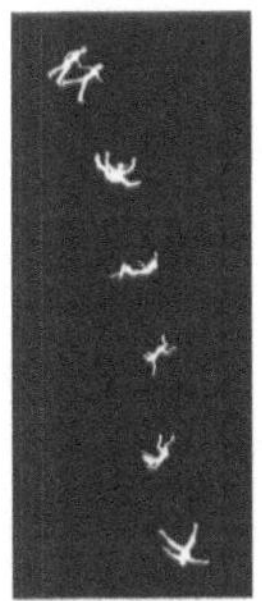

NIGEL AND THE RACKETEER

Nigel walked up the street toward Brit's house with Mr. Thompson following behind, cane in hand. Two civilized men, visiting a third. Apparently appearances were important in the new slavery-loving England, and Nigel was happy to oblige. He rang the bell once, twice, thrice. No answer, even though Brit owned an automatic answering system.

Nigel looked over at Mr. Thompson. "I'd like to break and enter. Do you mind?"

"Go ahead, Mr. Blakesley. I'll wait here for you to open the door. I can't afford to break and enter with you."

Nigel nodded. He took out his gun, aimed it at the lock, and shot it. A good shove didn't open the door. He looked left and right, checking through the window for an option. *I guess it's the noisy way.* He smashed the window with his gun barrel and used the stock to clean the shards of glass from the frame. Then he crept through the opening and dropped to the fancy carpet.

He listened for any sounds within the home. No alarm, no movement, and no shouts of condemnation. Satisfied that the house was empty, he hurried to the door, unlocked it, and invited Mr. Thompson to join him.

The old man had his gun drawn and at the ready. Nigel smiled. *I guess he doesn't trust me after all. Let hunting season commence.* He wondered which one of them would have the first clear shot, and which one would die.

As they moved through the house, Thompson stowed his

gun. They strolled into Brit's office. The BSX man was gone, the desk completely clear. A fire roared in the fireplace, fueled by what had earlier been on the desk.

"There's the proof," said Nigel.

"Concerning what, Mr. Blakesley?"

"That Mr. Samuel Brit was a rich and powerful BSX broker, and something darker." Nigel didn't know exactly what that meant yet. He would when he had the opportunity to read the recovered files.

"Or," said Thompson, "perhaps Br. Brit was frightened by all our shooting, and he decided to move to a safer location before he got hit by a stray bullet."

Nigel looked at him and lifted an eyebrow.

"I have a knack for thinking through multiple scenarios."

"Ha," said Nigel. "I didn't figure you for an amateur sleuth. Or maybe a cop."

"I was a fucking pig a long, long time ago. When they still mattered."

Well, wasn't that a revelation? Mr. Thompson, the racketeer, was now a colleague of sorts. Nigel smirked as he continued to check the house. His mind was racing, his fingers twitching on the trigger. He'd never had the patience to enter psychological battles. Luckily for him, he hadn't crossed paths with many psychologically-inclined criminals. Ha, speaking of criminals, *What would Jack the Ripper do now?* The infamous killer had always been in control, according to Nigel's research. Never had the Ripper allowed another man to dictate his next step. *Good advice, Jack my friend.*

Nigel walked to the back of the house. Wall against wall, no backyard, no fucking passage, no basement. How did Brit disappear? He tiptoed upstairs, Mr. Thompson an annoying shadow behind him.

This floor was silent, and all the rooms were empty. He concluded the house was too damn quiet for anyone to still be hiding somewhere.

To be thorough, he dashed up to the third floor, again finding only silence, until…

A faint screeching sound drew him to a wardrobe door that was not completely shut. Nigel advanced slowly toward the wardrobe from the left, gun at the ready.

Mr. Thompson paused outside the room and peeked around the corner, making eye contact with Nigel. *You first,* he mouthed.

Nigel placed his left hand on the wardrobe doorknob and pulled it open. The wardrobe was empty, and the rear panels had been removed to provide access to a door in the wall. An entrance into the neighbor's house.

Fucking Brit!

Nigel quashed the urge to open the door and run into the other house, chasing after Brit. He didn't like the feeling of Thompson's gun against his skin, so he needed to end this game, one way or another.

Thompson said, "I'd like to see that proof now that you mentioned earlier."

Nigel tucked his gun in his belt and activated his holo-display, then searched through his folders, buying time while he devised a strategy. *Do I show him the files? Or bluff?*

Mr. Thompson stood straight and patient next to Nigel, despite his wound. "How did you acquire this proof?"

Nigel wished he could see the wound, to get a better idea of how much time he had before Thompson collapsed, or succumbed in some way to the injury. He looked at Mr. Thompson's posture and mimicked it, to make himself look as strong while he glanced around the room.

The bedroom had a double bed, two nightstands, and a wardrobe without a back panel. "When he complained about the 'attack on his house' to your employer, he wasn't talking about a physical breach. I hacked into his data system."

Thompson didn't respond.

Nigel opened the recovered folder and found only a few files. He double-tapped one document. It was encrypted, scrambled beyond recognition. Even after he ran it through a cleaning, he only had a fifty-fifty chance of recovering any coherent data. He glanced at Thompson, who waited like a statue. *Snake reflexes on this one,* Nigel reminded himself.

Next he opened one of the JPEG files. It was one of the same images he'd received from an anonymous source that morning, showing Brit's meeting with Blake Frye. Nigel froze. That...that was...

"What?" Thompson leaned closer.

"I just...I need—"

Mr. Thompson shushed him.

Nigel scratched his head, thinking. He had to stall before he opened another JPEG, and Thompson realized that Nigel had no proof against Mr. Brit with respect to Thompson's employer.

Listening carefully, Thompson snarled, "It's a bomb!" Then he dove for cover.

Nigel threw himself on the bed just as the bomb exploded.

He felt the percussive wave jolting his innards in uncomfortable directions, and his ears felt as though they'd been packed with mud. His head pounded. One of the wardrobe's doors had landed on top of him. He pushed it away and it fell with a distant, unusual thud. He pressed his palms over his ears and curled into a ball, trying to take an inventory of all the places his body had been damaged.

After a time, he climbed from the bed on uncertain legs. Splinters from the wardrobe lay all around, and most of the wall between the houses was gone. Under some of the debris, Mr. Thompson groaned and moved a leg.

Nigel pulled out his gun, aimed, and fired. Thompson's head burst, decorating the wardrobe splinters with his gray matter.

One danger eliminated, thought Nigel. *Fucking Brit!* He wished the dick was in the room so he could disembowel the asshole with his bare hands.

He moved slowly into the hallway, where the air was less thick with dust and smoke, and tried to draw a deep breath despite his painful ribs. Why were the pictures of the Frye meet stored in Brit's data system? Had he been contacted by the same source? Or was he the unknown contact?

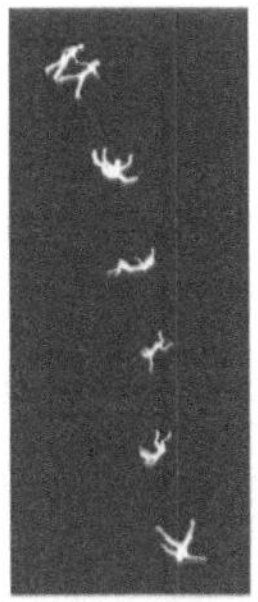

SIMON WITNESSES THE FUTURE

Gabriela led Simon through a very long and narrow corridor with hundreds of transparent doors on either side. She stopped in front of the last one. "This is a cryogenic chamber." She pointed out the half glass, half steel coffin on the other side.

Simon gazed at the sleeping woman whose skin had a pale blue tinge. She looked to be in her mid-thirties and wore only orange plastic panties and a bra. Cables snaked from the coffin into the wall, some winding toward a control display at eye level next to the coffin. A matching panel had been built into the door.

"Well?" asked Gabriela, sounding as though she expected to be praised for her prize.

"I'm *impressed*." Simon hoped his enthusiasm would appease her. On one hand, he was terrified to imagine what it must feel like to be stored in a freezer like a side of beef. On the other hand, he was impressed by the complexity of the technology. Cryogenics had always been more fiction than fact. He'd had no idea that anyone had designed a workable solution, especially on this massive scale. In this one area of science, the Wilmots had accomplished something good for humanity.

"We found a viable solution for cryogenics a couple of years ago," she boasted.

Simon asked, "Why haven't I heard about this?"

"We haven't patented the technology yet. We're still working out long-term safety."

"Darling." Simon pressed his hand gently on the glass.

"This. Is. *Revolutionary!*"

Gabriela stepped back, smiling icily.

"What did you mean about long-term safety, exactly?"

"Nothing you need to concern yourself with, for now."

Simon stared at the woman in the coffin. "Who is she? Some billionaire's wife who wants to live forever?"

Gabriela activated the door's control panel and displayed the woman's identification chart.

SERVITUDE SUBJECT: Gutierrez, Luciana J.
FILE NUMBER: P3G462044L

An active link, presumably to the woman's digital file, had been embedded with the file number.

"Oh," said Simon. "Interesting solution. Using servitude subjects during the beta trials."

"It solves many of the legal issues," said Gabriela. "You can search the file number in our database, and quickly retrieve an exact map of the subject's location."

"So, are your ultra-rich pals lining up for a spot in one of these? When it's safe, of course."

Gabriela grimaced.

Simon walked down the corridor and looked through many of the glass doors, seeing coffin after coffin filled with a frozen slave. Blue skin wrapped in orange plastic. He asked, "How many do you have?"

"Around fifty in the cryogenic chambers." Gabriela's voice sounded really sexy. Simon frowned at his impulse, looked away from her, and said, "That's a good-sized sample for the experiment."

"They've been put to sleep under different conditions. We continue to observe and improve."

In front of the next chamber, Simon faltered. The coffin held a sleeping girl with curly red hair. "What's she doing here?"

"Oh, her parents carried such an overwhelming debt that we had to take the entire family."

"Wait." Simon tried to calm his outrage. "Is the Freedom Act allowing children to be taken into servitude?"

"It doesn't forbid it, per se. And in cases where there's no other choice, I think the wording will make the practice feasible. Right now, the option hangs in a bit of a no-man's land."

Simon looked down the fifty yards of corridor visible before it turned beyond his view. "Feasible…"

"Papa's expecting us for the big event." Gabriela walked to the end of the corridor. Simon followed. She turned at the end of the cryogenics hallway and stopped at a bank of elevators.

He asked, "Is the big event in this building?"

"No, but this is the shortest route to the events room." She smiled at him, looking clever and hungry at the same time. "I also wanted to show off the lab. Now that you've witnessed our tech, you're either with us, or you're dead."

He grinned wider than he wanted, to give her the impression that he understood she might be joking, and said, "I'm with you. One hundred percent."

She offered her eye for a retinal scanner, and one of the elevators opened. They got in, and Simon took a quick look around for cameras. None visible.

Gabriela smirked. "Smile. You're always on cameras here."

Simon snorted. "Obviously. But, are they listening, too?"

"Not everywhere. You're safe here."

Simon kept his head down, hiding his face from the hidden cameras. "Does your father know about…"

"What?" Gabriela grinned a little.

"Us?"

"There's no *us*, Mr. White."

Simon raised his head and stared at her incredulously. "In my books, the wild sex we've been having usually counts toward an *us*."

The elevator dinged, and the door slid open directly into a meeting room decorated in a luxurious outer-space theme, with a huge oval table and one long glass wall. On the other side of the room, planters had been installed at various heights along the wall, each filled with a different tropical fern or flower. Hidden lights mimicked sunlight to nourish the garden.

At the farthest end of the table, William Wilmot watched a video on a large flat screen. As the footage unfolded, Simon realized they were watching Wilmot hurrying down the steps of the New York Courthouse, followed by Gabriela and an entourage of other people dressed like lawyers and security guards. Reporters preyed on William and his daughter

One reporter shouted, "Mr. Wilmot, is it true that you own slaves?"

Another demanded, "Mr. Wilmot, is your daughter also involved in the slave trade?"

Gabriela led Simon to her father and stopped a couple of steps away, waiting for the old man to acknowledge their arrival. Wilmot switched off the screen, turned, and stared at Simon as though he were a cockroach—afraid to touch him, yet curious about how he'd scurried into the room.

"Papa, this is Mr. White, the reporter I mentioned."

"It's such an honor to meet you, sir," said Simon. He took a step forward, but Gabriela placed a hand on his arm to stop him before he could extend his hand in greeting.

Wilmot didn't hide the disgust on his face at Simon's hovering hand, but he spoke in a neutral tone. "Are you here to prey on me and my family, like all the other vultures of your trade, Mr. White?" He definitely didn't sound as cold as his daughter, but he was just as menacing.

"No, sir," said Simon. "I'm at the far right of the 'pro' side of the Freedom Act debate, and I'm one hundred percent supportive of both you and your endeavor."

Still studying him, Wilmot proclaimed, "God helps those who help themselves."

"Very true, sir," Simon said, though he didn't see the connection to their discussion.

"My daughter speaks highly of your skills. She believes your reporting will *right* all the wrongs that the whore and her minions have done to us."

"The whore?" Simon knew who Wilmot meant, but pretended ignorance. Better that they introduced him to their world and its secrets.

Wilmot's voice was devoid of passion of any kind, as though he were stating facts that didn't concern him. "The television producer, Isabella Frye."

"Oh, right." Simon imagined the sounds of frost painting the glass and Wilmot's breath condensing in thick puffs, from the sudden chill in the room. "I will right every wrong, and then some, sir. I promise. I won't let you down." He glanced at the empty room and added, "Are we waiting for others to arrive?"

Wilmot's demeanor instantly did an about-face. For the first time since they'd arrived, the old man smiled at Simon. It felt like a seal of approval. As if on cue, the sun entered the room through the glass wall, warming the space.

Wilmot said in a warm, low voice that inspired trust and opened the door for anyone to confide in him, "The meeting with the Russian representatives of their servitude organization, uh…" Wilmot looked a query at Gabriela.

Disgusted, she snapped, "Does it matter what they call themselves?"

Wilmot chuckled at his daughter's contempt. "My pa used to say, 'Don't put all your eggs in one basket.' In this case, the Russian market is one of the good baskets for our eggs—"

Agent Alvarez burst into the room, his expression hard. Everyone turned to him as he demanded, "You need to see this, sir."

As he showed Wilmot the pictures on his holo-display, Agent Saunders slipped in behind him. Simon stepped forward to get a better look, watching over Gabriela's shoulder. Alvarez slid through three images of five dead people in a hotel room. Their eyes had been gouged out, and their mouths stretched from ear to ear.

Wilmot banged his fist on the table and growled, "Who did this?"

"Based on the MO, I'd venture to say the English slavers are responsible."

"They have their own MO?" Simon wasn't sure whether he was allowed to speak, but he needed to learn as many facts as possible if he was going to survive the weekend. Agent Alvarez glared suspiciously at him.

Wilmot nodded his approval. "He's one of us."

Alvarez shrugged, and explained, "That's a Chelsea smile." He indicated the dead mouths, cut at the corners and stretched.

Wilmot looked back at his daughter and asked, "What do they say, Gabriela?"

She crossed her arms over her chest, and answered, "Do unto others as you would have them do unto you."

Simon said, "I don't—" Gabriela shook her head, immediately ending his question in mid-sentence.

Wilmot turned to his daughter and asked, "How's the whore?"

"Good. She's in solitary."

"Wonderful." He smiled at his daughter and added, "She'll pay dearly, in time."

Gabriela turned to Alvarez, and ordered, "Go find the son of a bitch who did this to our people!"

"And if he resists?"

"My best advice." She regarded him with her icy glare. "If at first you don't succeed, try, try again."

Alvarez cocked his head as if processing her quip.

Wilmot added, "I need him alive. To make a last appeal to his patriotism. If these images and the sight of his imprisoned wife won't help, then we'll sell him."

Alvarez left, followed by Agent Saunders.

After the door closed behind them, Wilmot rose from his chair and began to pace the room.

In a low voice, Simon asked Gabriela, "What just happened?"

"Apparently, the Russians lost their eyes and their lips. So it looks as though our big history-making meeting has now been canceled." Gabriela's voice was back to its usual iciness.

Wilmot stared at Simon, suddenly smiled, and said, "I want you to write about this new development. Use all the glorious words."

"Report that the Russians were carved up before your meeting?" Simon's voice reflected his confusion.

"Of course not. Don't be *crude*. I want you to chronicle our milestones. Write about the rise of the new era we launched."

"Great; thank you, sir," said Simon. "I'm to be the king's chronicler. I appreciate—"

"No, Mr. White. Not the *king*. Someday you might meet the real monarch. Until then, I'm asking you to write about us. About our movement."

"Of course. Like I said, I appreciate the opportunity."

"Come, Mr. White." Gabriela took Simon by his elbow. "Let me introduce you to the rest of management. You'll get your own pass, which will give you access to the compound and everyone in it."

Raising a glass of bourbon, William Wilmot theatrically declared, "A toast, to our glorious southern revival."

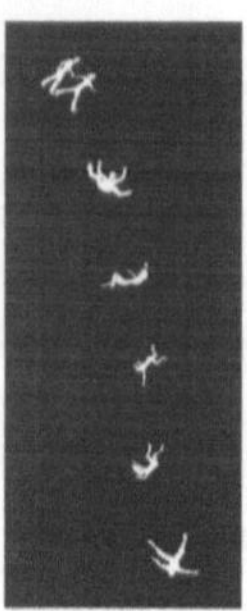

FOUR MONTHS EARLIER

The door to Sam's apartment had been kicked in, and stood half open. Blake pulled Isa behind him, drew his gun, and signaled Isa to wait in the hallway. Without waiting for her confirmation, he nudged the door all the way open and stepped into the entranceway.

Silence, except for the noises of the city, drifting through an open window.

He turned a corner and checked the living room. Sam's few pieces of furniture had been shredded, splintered, and thrown around. Blake moved into the kitchen, which was small and empty. Then he made his way to the bedroom. Again, all the furniture had been damaged, and her clothes scattered all over the place, no drawer or closet left unturned.

When he returned to the living room, Isa had stepped inside. She was holding her arms pressed close to her chest while she studied the apartment, looking shocked. She said, "We need to call the police."

"I *am* the police, love." Blake placed a hand gently on her shoulder, trying to help calm her nerves. Normally, his wife was very physical, sharing touches, hugs, and kisses. She expressed all sentiments physically. He wasn't a touchy-feely person, even though she kissed and hugged him a lot. Sometimes he'd return the gesture, though most of the time he'd merely accept them, content in knowing her actions made her happy.

He called in his position and the state of the apartment to

dispatch. Once they confirmed that a cruiser had been assigned to the call, he returned his attention to his wife, who was frantically searching through the mess.

She asked, "What happened here, B?"

He sighed, unable to meet her eyes. What could he tell her that wouldn't shatter what little remained of her strength?

"You think someone broke in and took her, don't you?"

He grabbed both of her hands to stop her frenzied hunt. "Look at me, please." Her pained stare nearly made him look away, but he had to admit the truth. "Yes. I think they took her."

"Do you think they ra—" she bit her lip, and managed, "*hurt* her?"

"This type of destruction isn't from a struggle. They probably arrested her, and then they searched the place. Thoroughly."

"Who's *they*, Blake?"

"No idea. The government? One of the agencies?"

"Because my story..."

"Yes. Because it was uploaded onto the internet. Government agencies thrive on control, and now your story is out there, beyond their reach. From the look of the place, they're sure she leaked the video."

"How could they be sure?"

"I don't know. But that's probably why they only took your computers this morning, and didn't arrest you. They're covering all the bases. Confirming they have the right culprit."

"We need to find her."

"Based on the mess, the police will investigate. But the DA will probably shut them down. Especially since the NSA were the ones at the house this morning. They probably have Sam in custody, and don't want the uniforms sniffing around where they don't belong."

"What can they charge her with?"

"Anything from slander to espionage."

"She'll need a good lawyer. Norman might know somebody."

Blake pointed at the mess and asked, "What were you searching for?"

"Her research," said Isa. "I guess they took it all."

Two uniformed officers arrived at the scene. Blake identified himself, flashed his badge, shared what little he knew about the break-in, and led Isa out of the apartment.

"Listen, I have to go to the precinct. Why don't you visit a friend? Or go to a museum? Make sure you choose a public place, with lots of witnesses."

She shook her head. "No way. I'm coming with you."

"I have some boring, tedious police work to follow up on. A museum, or maybe the library, would help keep your mind off…" He pointed to the apartment and added, "The state of things."

"Can we meet for lunch?"

He looked at her nervous, hurt-filled features, and nodded. "Definitely. I'll drop you wherever you want to spend the morning. And I'll pick you up at the same place, at 12:30. Deal?"

"Deal."

Once they were in Blake's car, he could feel the danger escalating. Sam's apartment had been a wake-up call. He placed his hands on the steering wheel, then turned to Isa. "I want you to open a live recording, and link me to the feed."

"B!" Isa started to tremble.

"Just as a precaution. I want to know your location, every minute, for the next forty-eight hours. Can you do that for me?"

Blake climbed out of his car, locked it, and checked the time—11:46. He wanted to surprise Isa by arriving early. Maybe take her for a walk in Central Park. As he approached the Natural History Museum, Isa's feed played in his earbuds app. Every half hour or so, he'd checked the visual feed to see where she was, and then he'd been able to focus on work, reassured that she was safe.

The last time he'd visited this museum had been five years earlier. They'd purchased tickets for a special exhibition on extraterrestrial life that included every sample and artifact the scientific community had accumulated that held traces of life from the solar system's planets and hundreds of meteorites. The exhibition had been impressive, even though it didn't include any press-worthy items. No alien contact, no Rosetta Stone for undiscovered languages or the like. As far as Blake was concerned, it was proof enough that life existed in the universe in places other than Earth. Too bad the universe was so damned vast.

"Take your hands off me!" Isa's angry voice blasted in his left ear like an ice-cold shower. He shivered, unable to move for a brief second.

Other voices in the background sounded like the distant buzzing of insects.

"Hey," shouted Isa again. "Hey, help! Someone, help me!" Isa's labored breathing, her grunts, her calls for assistance continued, as if the assault was happening in a secluded place, far away from friendly bystanders.

Blake broke into a sprint, up the stairs, through crowds of people, and past the museum gate. An alarm sounded, blaring at him for rushing through the metal detectors. He flashed his badge and continued running.

In his earbud, he heard Isa shout, "Get away from me." The feed dropped out for a few seconds, and then, "…third floor. Who are you? What do you want?" Another drop, and then, "Outside the Mars Hall."

Blake was proud of her for smartly finding a way to share information about her location.

A thick voice snapped, "Disable her wristband! She's *transmitting*."

He slowed down so he could activate the video feed. For less than a second, he could see the Mars Hall, and then the connection cut out.

Almost there, he thought as he raced up the stairs.

He reached the correct floor, and saw two men dragging Isa through a door toward an administrative area. Onlookers watched the scene unfolding, but no one rushed over to intervene, or to defend her from the men. The Mars Hall was full of visitors, yet no one seemed to care. Blake gnashed his teeth in frustration and bolted across the open area. When he reached the door, he pulled but it was locked. The control panel was probably activated with a museum ID.

He scanned left and right, hunting for anyone dressed in the museum uniform, or a security guard. None of them were close enough to make a difference. With no other option, he pulled out his weapon, aimed at the door, and fired.

People panicked at the sound of the gunshot, running in every direction.

Blake kicked the door in and entered with his gun at the ready. The two men were almost at the end of the corridor, dragging a kicking and screaming Isa. As Blake hurried to close the distance, he aimed his gun and ordered, "Stand down! Move away from her!"

The two men wore museum security uniforms. They stopped, surprised that someone was interrupting them. Blake flashed his badge and repeated, "Step away from the woman! NYPD."

"Hey man," said the taller one. "This is museum business. She tried to steal an artifact."

The shorter of the men raised his hands peacefully, to show Blake that he wasn't armed. "We deal with this kind of thing all the time. No need to interfere."

"Look." The taller guard slowly brought something out of his pocket. Isa struggled to free herself, but the shorter man held her close.

Blake fired a warning shot. "Last warning. Let. Her. Go."

The tall guard waved a small stuffed animal from the museum's store. "We caught her with this. I watched her sneak it into her purse, without paying."

Blake slowed his pace, stopping one foot from the guards, his weapon pointed at the tall one's chest. When they didn't react, he cocked the gun.

"Okay," they said in unison. Both raised their hands in the air.

Isa ran to him and hid behind him. He slowly began to retreat, keeping his gun aimed at them, nudging her away from her captors. Before he reached the shot-out door, he heard steps behind him.

A firm voice demanded, "Drop your gun!"

Blake raised both hands in the air, frustrated, but still gripping his gun in an unaggressive hold. With his back to the new man, he clearly stated, "I'm NYPD."

A second voice insisted, "Drop. Your. *Gun!*"

Before he could follow the order, Isa's two museum security assailants fled through the nearest exit. Blake found himself alone with the real museum security at his back, and his two suspects out of reach. He turned slowly, gun relaxed on his fingers, then slowly placed it on the tile floor. "Can I show you my badge now?

"Slowly. We're watching you."

Blake displayed his detective's badge.

The official guards put away their Tasers. The closest one took a deep breath and exhaled slowly. After shaking out his hands, he asked, "What happened, Detective?"

"Long story," said Blake. "I'll explain it all, if you show me your security video for this area, from the last half hour."

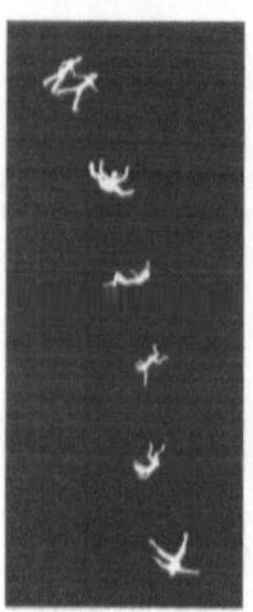

THE CHAMBER OF SECRETS

Blake knocked, then listened with his ear against the door. No noise from inside. He used his key to unlock Corbin's condo, and opened the door. Still no movement.

Blake moved farther inside, looked around, and shouted, "Corbin?"

Nothing.

In the kitchen, he switched on the coffee maker and started a large pot. One of the cupboards had been left open, so he closed it.

Back in the living room, he hung his jacket on the coat rack. Then he noticed one of the paintings was slightly askew, so he straightened it.

My anxiety is in overdrive, he thought. Corbin would be furious when he found out that Blake had snooped around his condo. How many times had he tried to please his little brother? Part of the reason he became a police officer was because when they were growing up, he'd had a deep need to protect Corbin. He also wished he could give his little brother all that Blake had missed during their childhood. All the love and attention, all the chances no one had offered to Blake. He wanted Corbin to have a better life, a more accomplished one. And Corbin had accepted every bit of help. But instead of the warm, cozy life Blake had wished for his brother, the man had chosen a difficult path. A life on the edge, full of risks, hazards, and chaos.

Blake paced back and forth in front of the sofa, glancing at the closed door to Corbin's office. To lessen the temptation, he returned to the kitchen, grabbed a mug, added sugar, and poured himself a freshly brewed coffee. He noticed a forgotten croissant in a plastic container. It was stale, but he didn't care. He hadn't eaten since the previous night, so he wolfed down the pastry in two bites and shook his head. *Everything tastes fantastic when you're starving*, he thought.

One lonely apple sat in the fruit bowl. He picked it up and took a deep, satisfying bite, munching slower this time. Retrieving a napkin from the drawer, he placed the apple on it so the juice wouldn't leave a sticky mark. When he'd chewed through the mouthful, he picked up the apple in his right hand, shoved the napkin in his pocket, and picked up the coffee in his left hand. Out of patience, he strolled over to the office door and stood in front of it while he slowly finished the apple.

You know you need to look in there.

He wrapped up the apple core in the napkin and placed the package on the coffee table. *Remember to bring it with you*, he told himself. It might be rotting for a long time in Corbin's trash before he returned home.

Taking a deep breath, he opened the office door.

The room looked almost the same as it had on the night when he and Isa had last been here. This time, the scribbled notes and stacks of research looked busier and more chaotic. I hate chaos. His need to tidy the room, to give it a proper sense of order, made him ache. The compulsion felt like a toothache: not painful, but so annoying that it drove him crazy and destroyed his concentration.

Coffee in hand, Blake approached an empty white wall near the desk. When he pressed his palm in the center, the wall came to life.

In a baritone voice, the wall asked, "Who do you call?"

"Raven and Noir," said Blake.

"Raven and Noir" had been the name of their secret detective agency, back when they were children and still played together. He would never forget the name. That secret agency had been one of the most amazing, important things they'd created together. The pretend cases they solved had helped them survive their difficult and bloody home life.

The wall's surface switched from plain white to a digital investigation board. Hundreds of pictures, notes, and documents had been attached using virtual pins.

In the center, Corbin had attached Wilmot's photo. Blake followed a thread from Wilmot's face to another headshot, this one of a young woman. The label below identified her as Gabriela Wilmot. *The daughter.*

He cleared every object from Corbin's desk, then flicked Gabriela Wilmot's image onto the desk's digital surface.

He activated his wristband and brought forward one of the airport images—the one showing the partial face of one of Isa's kidnappers. Blake flicked a copy onto the investigation board. "Identify," he commanded.

Corbin's board began to link Blake's photo to different items on the board. Following one of the threads that landed close to Wilmot's central headshot, he studied the image of a black man who resembled the one from Blake's holo-display. The board labeled the man as Martin Breckenwell, Wilmot Enterprises Chief of Security.

"Just like Margaret discovered," said Blake. Corbin's board showed more details on the security chief, including a brief bio. Blake read the details aloud. "Martin Breckenwell, former Black Ops, CIA operative, contractor for five years with Higgins Security in the Philippines and Indonesia." He digested the information. "Whoa."

Stepping back, he tried to view the entire board all at once, hoping some crucial detail would stand out.

"Where is…" His need for order forced him to shuffle some of the details around. Pointing to one section, he said, "Everything begins from here…"

He moved to the right edge of the board and scratched his nape. "Sorry, bro." He couldn't stop smiling, knowing he wasn't sorry at all. Disrupting Corbin's work and putting it in the correct order, Blake's order, was not only the smart move, it was an improvement.

He began moving photos around; some he even flicked onto the desk. There were hundreds of images, labels, notes, and questions. Luckily, the board filled the large wall.

A knock at the door made Blake raise his head from his work. The board was mostly empty, except for a few dozen photos and documents, arranged in a spiral that began at the center of the board.

Blake activated his wristband and checked the time—a bit more than an hour had passed. *I'm nowhere near finished.*

Another knock. *Who the hell?*

Blake moved away from the board, picked up a paperweight, and held it ready. He tiptoed out of the office, crossed the living room, and activated the condo's security screen. Captain Moore stood in the hall.

Blake opened the door for his boss. Moore hurried inside and without any preamble, said, "Frye, I don't know what you did, but the DA is frantic. Everyone is looking for you."

"Coffee, Captain?"

"Shit, Frye!" The captain planted his feet in front of Blake, his hands on his hips, and stared at him like a father staring at his misbehaving child.

"You have to hear me out, Cap. I have Wilmot on record as he's spewing a lot of sensitive information that could possibly influence the servitude debates in Congress."

"Seriously?" Moore relaxed his stance. "That's fantastic. We can…" He paused, scratched his head, and said, "We should…"

"Exactly," said Blake. "What can we possibly do? The district attorney is involved with the slavers, the NSA works for Wilmot, and the only FBI agent who could've made a difference has vanished without a trace. Makes you wonder who to trust, and who to avoid. What's left? The CIA?"

"We're obligated to do something. To share what we know with someone in authority. Someone with enough power, and enough distance from the rest of them, to make a difference."

"Until I get Isa back, we can't approach anyone." He pointed over his shoulder toward Corbin's office and added, "I have a lot of ground to cover."

Moore shook his head and sighed. "And I'm old and tired."

"You've already done so much for me—for us, Captain."

"I'm still here. To the bitter end. But once your wife is safe, I'm out. My wife's been nagging me for a long time, and she's right. I should retire while I still can."

"Your wife's a smart woman." He smiled, and added, "Thank you so much. I couldn't do this without you."

Moore nodded, then looked around and raised his hand as though he was a kid in grade school. "So, what exactly are we doing here?"

"I called you here because Corbin has a ton of intel on the servitude movement in the States. He's gathered more on Wilmot than anyone else. I'm certain we'll find some small detail in his office that can help us find Isa. So we can finish this shit." Without waiting for a response, Blake hurried back to the office, picked up his coffee, and sipped while he admired his work. As he lost himself in the details, he added, "There's fresh coffee in the kitchen."

Moore followed Blake into the office, and stared in amazement at the large investigation board. He studied the images and papers spread on the desk and glanced up at the ones hanging as holograms in the air, all over the room. "Bloody hell, Frye, please tell me you didn't do all this."

"I have a system. I'm almost there."

"Frye..."

"It'd really help if you'd just keep quiet for a few moments." He added, "*Please.*"

The captain gave Blake a sad stare, then he sighed and scanned the images on the board. Blake returned to frantically arranging photos on the board.

After a while, Moore placed himself in front of Blake and blocked his hands. "Okay, Frye. We'll do it your way. Explain what you've got so far, and we can split the job."

When Blake dropped his hands to his sides, the captain moved away. Blake bit his lip, thinking over Moore's proposal.

Then he said, "I appreciate the offer. But I'm afraid you'll make a mess of it. I need to do this. It's my process. It's my wife. But you should watch and listen. Be my sounding board."

He pointed to several photos on the board, and said, "That's Wilmot's daughter, Gabriela. According to Corbin, she's in charge of the company's research."

"What kind of research?"

"Officially, they have a dozen research projects on the go. Once a year, they unveil them to the press, at a big event at Wilmot Research Center."

Blake detached a printed press release from the board, and showed it to Moore. It was clipped from one of the last three printed newspapers. Wilmot had taken out a sizable ad.

WILMOT SCIENCE FESTIVAL—LIVE AT THE WILMOT SCIENCE RESEARCH FACILITY, NEW YORK STATE

Below the headline was a map and the street address of the facility. Following that were a few details about the day's schedule. Finally, there was a Web link for more information.

"Look at the date," said Blake. "Their press event is happening right now, as we speak."

"So?"

"The facility is roughly an hour's drive from the airport."

"Still don't get it." Moore smiled encouragingly.

The captain knew how to fuel the detectives under his command, including how to pull Blake out of his own head and get him to express his thoughts and communicate verbally. Three years earlier, he'd broken through to Blake when he'd been knee deep inside a serial murder case, and hadn't gone home in a week or spoken to anyone in the precinct during that time. He'd been behaving like a solitary cave man, not allowing anyone else into his lair where he was studying the case. Even Blake's partner, Neil, couldn't get past the barrier. Moore had been the one to pull Blake out of that dark place and bring him back into the human fold.

Blake smiled at his boss. "Roughly an hour after Isa was taken hostage, a woman called to tell me they'd kidnapped my wife. A woman called me."

"Since we know that Wilmot has Isa, you believe his daughter called you. From the Wilmot Science Research Facility."

"Yes," said Blake. "Gabriela Wilmot is in charge of the research facility. Considering that today is this big press event," he held up the newspaper clipping, "she should be there right now."

Before Moore could reply, Blake raised his index finger to silence him. "I just had a revelation." He retrieved the memory, trying to play it back in his mind as precisely as possible.

They were back in Corbin's condo. Isa had just offered to include his name in the credits. His rejection of the idea had been almost cruel. His hands up in the air in a defensive posture, Corbin had said, "I don't want my name anywhere on your story. Not even on internal documents at the station."

Isa asked, "Why? Your information is sound and reliable."

From the doorway, Norman added, "This could be good exposure for your career."

"Stop," said Corbin. "I'm in the middle of an undercover investigation. I need anonymity. Corbin Frye must keep a low profile for now."

"Still doing your cape and sword thing, bro? Which alias is in play? Roger Black?"

"No," said Corbin, "Black's compromised. I'm Simon White now."

Isa had exhaled with ease and smiled. Blake had known that she was on the same page at that moment. "Blake appreciates you protecting the family name," she said. "Cops generally prefer to fly under the radar."

Blake took the beer Norman was offering, twisted off the cap, and asked, "What's Simon White up to?"

"Playing Casanova," said Corbin, "with the daughter of an important player in the American slavery business."

Blake returned from his recollection, turned to Moore, and exhaled noisily. "I know how to get to Wilmot." He activated his wristband, selected Corbin's name from his contacts, and wrote, *I'LL BE IN WILMOT'S FACILITY IN MAXIMUM 2 H—*

Before he could finish, a thunderous crash stopped him. Blake quickly collapsed his display. Both men looked through the open office door. Blake could hear loud voices, and footsteps moving through the living room.

He turned to Moore. "Were you followed?"

"I doubt it. I was careful."

Before hearing the answer, Blake turned to the board wall and shouted, "Shut and lock!" The wall turned plain white, appearing to be nothing more than a normal wall. All the holograms, the ones hanging in the air and floating on the desk's surface, vanished.

Moore pushed the door closed, but a kick shoved it open again, knocking the captain to the floor. He drew his weapon.

A gunshot deafened Blake in the small space. Moore shuddered, rolled onto his side, and lay still. A red spot spread across his chest.

Several NSA agents led by Alvarez burst into the room, their guns in their hands. They aimed at Blake, who was staring in disbelief at Moore. Suddenly, the gravity of the situation slammed through the barrier in his mind, and he collapsed next to Moore, taking his boss's head in his hands.

The NSA agents yelled something, but the words didn't sink in. Blake only had ears for his captain.

"I'm sorry…" said Moore. Moore's head slumped to one side, and he exhaled his last breath.

The agents tried to grab Blake, but he screamed and pushed them back. He twisted one of the agents' arms and threw the man's head against the wall. The second agent punched him in the back. Blake turned and hit the man with the back of his fist.

Alvarez shot Blake in the arm. He shook from the impact, and turned to face the NSA agent who had kept adding misery to his life. The second agent scrambled to his feet and tried to kick Blake. The detective caught the foot in midair and twisted it.

The agent twirled in the air and landed on his face.

The next thing he knew, Blake's body jolted and shook as he was Tasered with not one but three guns. He continued to shake for a long time, until he finally fell to the floor, and the world turned black.

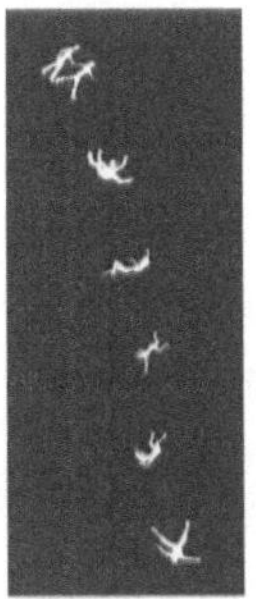

THE BIG DECISION

Gabriela brought Simon to a studio. It looked and felt like any normal recording studio, except cameras had been installed on several of the walls. They could be operated remotely, to professionally film whatever or whoever was working inside.

Simon stood behind Gabriela. She sat in front of the sound board, beside the engineer. The glass wall in front of them separated the control booth from the studio.

Two men dressed in blue dragged Isa into the studio. Simon moved to the corner chair, being careful to stay out of Isa's line of sight. *What can I do?* He wanted to help his sister-in-law, but had to watch and wait for the right moment. Until then, he needed to prevent her from recognizing him and blowing his cover.

Isa was pushed onto a chair in the center of the room, all lights on her. The engineer remotely adjusted one of the cameras, shooting Isa from the front. Simon watched the monitor, controlling his face so it remained as neutral as humanly possible. No reaction, no feeling, nothing a hidden CCTV might catch. He was certain that every move he made in this camp was being observed. Hell, he was sure that every single person in the facility was always being watched, down to the last janitors and dishwasher. He also figured that the employees monitoring the cameras were also being watched in turn.

Gabriela's voice startled him, after the long the silence in the soundproof booth. "Good," she told the engineer. "Keep the shot in close." After a pause she added, "Now pan slowly, and make sure you get a close-up of her barcode."

Simon winced at the sight of the burn on Isa's arm. It was red and inflamed, her flesh raw. Isa's face was unreadable. It was clear that earlier she'd been crying. In the studio, she looked determined to give them nothing, aiming her gaze straight ahead, unflinching.

"Back to her face," Gabriela directed. "Widen the shot."

The camera zoomed out, showing Isa from head to toe, dressed in the orange clothes of a slave. Her face was defiant, despite her puffy red eyes. Simon realized he'd never seen her cry before. He'd always assumed she was completely happy. Not any longer.

Gabriela said, "Add some over-text, that says, 'The auction begins in one hour. We already have 337 potential buyers. You have one hour to come to us, before she's lost forever.'"

As Gabriela dictated the words, they appeared on top of Isa's image. Simon watched, fascinated, not only by the situation, but also by the cruelty of the people in the room. The world was changing faster than he could've possibly imagined. Everyone needed to adapt or die. Ride the wave of change or get crushed by the surf. There was no middle ground anymore.

"Let's go, Mr. White." Gabriela was suddenly next to him, ready to move on. He wondered what his expression had looked like, at that moment. He'd let his guard down. A dangerous mistake. His heart skipped a beat at the idea of being on the other side of that glass wall.

Simon stood, keeping his back to Isa, and followed Gabriela. Trying to sound casual, he asked, "Why did you show me this?"

"You need to witness how we treat traitors."

Simon gazed out the window. He was naked. The shower was running in the bathroom, and Gabriela's clothes were thrown over a chair.

I need to do something. Now, or...

He activated his wristband, selected the messaging app, and double-checked the bathroom door. It was still closed, and he could still hear the water flowing.

He typed quickly.

THESE ARE THE COORDINATES WHERE ISA IS BEING HELD CAPTIVE. HURRY. SHE'LL BE SOLD IN LESS THAN AN HOUR.

He reread the message, then nodded, satisfied. Then he hesitated over the Send button, rubbing his fingers together, thinking. *I need to do something. Is this the right move?* So much depended on him doing the right thing.

He cringed, rubbing his face in frustration. The water shut off. Simon's finger closed in on the Send button. He hesitated once more, at the last moment. I need more time.

Behind him, the bathroom door opened. He pressed the Delete button, deactivated the cell, and rolled over, exposing himself on the bed.

"Unfortunately," said Gabriela, standing naked before him and dripping onto the carpet, "we have to reschedule."

"You want to reschedule love?" Simon gazed at her innocently.

"Simon, I told you…"

He grinned from ear to ear. He enjoyed their verbal sparring. And the sex. The sex was great. Gabriela was a bit stiff for his taste, but she had a fabulous body, a beautiful face, and…

And what? He loved the power game the most. She definitely held a position of real power. With one gesture, she could have him killed, imprisoned, or sold to the highest bidder. Whatever she wished. But instead, she was sharing his bed. Returning for more, every time.

Simon pointed, laughed, and said, "Got you."

"Ha." Her laugh sounded incredibly insincere. "Once I deal with this issue, I'll slot our sex into the schedule as soon as possible." She was at her most sexy when she spoke of their affair. Somehow the promise of sex was more arousing than the act itself.

He said, "Can't wait to get that memo." Sarcasm was his only leverage.

Gabriela began to dress, unaware of the effect she had on

him. In her mind, she was probably already two steps ahead on her to-do list.

Her cell beeped and she answered. "Yes." A pause. "I know they got him." Another pause. "He's *shot*? Well, take him to medical."

She switched off, then dialed another number. "Isa Frye, that subject I told you to sell? Prepare the contract. I'll be there in five minutes."

Simon hurried over to zip Gabriela's dress. She wore nothing underneath. He pictured her moving through the facility, working with her employees, speaking with security guards, making life and death decisions while covered only in that flimsy piece of material. A single tug on the zipper, and she'd be naked in front of them all. He felt excited by the image.

Then he processed what he'd heard her say. *He's shot? Well, take him to medical.*

As he climbed back under the covers, he said, "I overheard you mention that someone was shot. What happened?"

"Just got news about that cop. They're en route with him. Our problems are over."

"You're going to sell his wife in front of him."

"If he doesn't cooperate, yes."

"Can I tag along?"

"If you like. Use your new pass. Come to the ranch in thirty minutes." She kissed him and left.

Simon rested on the bed, wearing a rigid smile as he stared at the wall. *Holly shit, they have my brother.* The Wilmots had both Blake and Isa, and they'd both be sold, unless... *Unless what?* He was missing a vital piece of information. What was so important, that Wilmot needed from Blake? How could Blake possibly hurt Wilmot so badly that it was worth the effort of kidnapping Isa, and using her as leverage?

Simon hurried down the road in time to see Gabriela's vehicle braking in front of the slave camp. She jumped down from the vehicle and entered the camp. He walked fast, trying to keep a casual appearance for the watchful guards. When they'd approached him, he flashed his new pass, and they let him through. Gabriela was only minutes ahead of him.

In the lobby, Gabriela was chatting with the receptionist. Simon took a sudden right, ducking into a nearby corridor so she wouldn't notice him. He didn't have time to check the signs, to figure out where he was headed. *It doesn't matter,* he told himself. As long as he could buy himself some time.

Simon strolled down the corridor, trying to appear as though he knew exactly where he was headed. When he reached the first intersection, he had to make a quick decision. Left or right? Without hesitating, he turned right, then faltered as the double doors in front of him opened. A group of men in black suits were carrying an unconscious Blake inside the building. *Holy shit!*

Simon stared in fascination for a brief second, then reversed direction and took the left corridor. Slowing his pace, he activated his holo-display, mumbled, and nodded as though he was speaking to someone on his cell. All the while, he tried to listen to the black-suited men. Their voices and steps melted into the distance.

Simon collapsed his holo-display and turned around again. As he reached the intersection, the group carrying Blake were entering the lobby. He watched them from a distance. The agent he'd seen with Wilmot was among them. He seemed to be the leader. *So, they're NSA.* He tried to remember the agent's name. *It's Alvarez.*

Alvarez spoke to the receptionist, nodded, and spoke to his agents. Two men dressed in blue coveralls arrived with a stretcher. The agents placed Blake on it, and the blue guys took him away. Alvarez and his agents walked in the opposite direction, their job apparently done.

As soon as the agents exited through the same door Gabriela had used, Simon turned and followed his brother's stretcher.

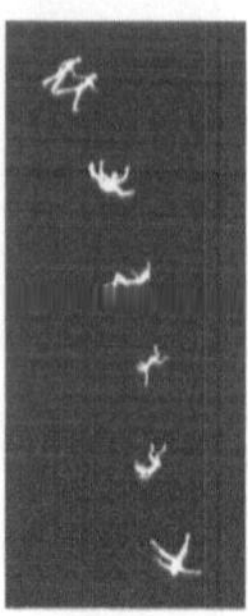

FOUR MONTHS EARLIER

Blake and Moore tapped their beer bottles together, then guzzled them down.

Moore's wife slipped up next to Isa, offered her a glass of red, settled gingerly next to her, and asked, "How are you, dear?" As if to confirm her concern, she brushed Isa's hand.

Isa took the glass, but didn't drink any. "I've never been so scared, truth to be told." She paused, trying to sort her emotions, and blurted, "I'm mostly angry." Her confession felt surprisingly accurate, so she added, "I'm furious all the time now. Which makes me tired, which in turn makes me more offended." She checked to see if Blake was paying attention, but he seemed to be busy with his boss. "I don't have the patience to focus on anything for more than ten minutes before my thoughts slide back into reliving the last forty-eight hours." Her foot began to tap a frantic rhythm. "Even now, I feel the need to walk around, and try to find something to *do*."

Moore's wife looked over at her husband. He must've recognized the signal, because he sighed and set down his bottle. "I got orders today," he said, loud enough for everyone to hear, "to drop both the John Taylor and Samantha Cruise disappearance investigations."

Blake jumped to his feet, staring at his boss and then at Isa. "I predicted this, didn't I?"

"We dug deep and far, looking to ID the two museum assholes." He scratched his temple, and added, "They're ghosts."

Isa leaned forward. "What do you mean, ghosts?"

"We ran facial recognition, fingerprints, and shook all the usual trees. We didn't find so much as a driver's license for a search history, which is almost impossible for anyone in our high-tech world. Everyone leaves a data trail."

Moore licked his lips, as if he had more to add. Isa wondered what he was hiding. She glanced at Blake, and got her answer. He didn't want her to know about some horrible detail, and he'd probably ordered his boss to keep it from her.

She turned to her husband. "Blake?"

He huffed, and crossed his arms over his chest.

"Be straight with me, HoneyB."

"Ghosts usually turn out to be covert operatives who've had their background traces erased, giving them the freedom to move unhindered by security cameras. Even if we added them to the system today, their entries would be erased by tomorrow."

"Operatives," Isa drew quote signs with her fingers.

Blake nodded.

"So, let me get this straight." She raised her glass, at the ready. "They only failed because you arrived an hour early. What about next time?" Without waiting for the answer, she drank the wine as though the world was ending.

"Assuming the system works like I think it does," Moore said, "they've already disappeared John Taylor, the public face of the scandal." He held up one finger. "And they eliminated Samantha Cruise, the fool who probably uploaded the video." He held up a second finger. "When they failed to grab you, people noticed. There's security footage and probably a few social media images. They'll stop tailing you for now, to avoid any more exposure, unless you provoke them." He held up a third finger. "Chadwick's a goddamn senator, so they won't touch him." Waving his four fingers in the air, he said, "That's the list, right? Or did I miss another threat?"

Isa tapped her empty glass with her nail. "Do you think failing once is enough for them to leave me alone?" Isa couldn't believe how calm everyone seemed to be. Those "lost" people were her friends and colleagues. If this was their way to make her feel better, they sucked at it.

Blake took her hand in his. "They'll back off because *official-ly*, they don't have grounds to arrest you. Sam's been arrested, not kidnapped. For breaking the NDA. John's probably been charged with slander. In your case, they tried to kidnap you, because they have no legal reason to drag you away. Someone down the chain of command was overly zealous. That mistake, combined with the failure, will make them stop. That's the difference."

Isa pulled back her hand, bit her lip, then sipped the last drop of wine. She glanced at Moore's wife, who was keeping her eyes averted, as if somehow, if she couldn't see anyone, they wouldn't see her. *We all want to be ghosts,* thought Isa. *Welcome to the new world order.*

Mustering up a calm tone, Isa asked, "Do any of you feel like the facts don't sit right with you?"

Blake sighed and looked away.

Moore stared at her, looking a bit confused. He looked at his wife, but refused to make eye contact with anyone. He shrugged. "You're probably safe for now. Isn't that enough?"

"So I should be relieved, even though they've arrested John and Sam. I was spared, so I should be—what? *Grateful*? As long as I keep my head down, I'd *probably* be safe?"

Moore scratched his head and grabbed his empty beer bottle.

Blake shook his head, staring at her as if to say *stop stirring up trouble.*

"Even you now?" She shook her head. "I'm a *journalist*." She jumped to her feet. "No, we are journalists, John, Sam, and I. *We* did our job, staying well within the law. *We* served the people of America by telling the truth and exposing a monstrous cover-up. *They* arrested John and Sam for sharing the truth. A truth that doesn't endanger, in *any* way, our national security, as they claim. It only affects horrible people committing heinous crimes. Except those criminals also happen to be well connected. And powerful."

She stomped in a circle, trying to find calm, and gave up. "To protect those mass murderers, the people in power arrested Sam and John. And I should be thankful, because I'm still free." She shrugged and added, "Hell, they can continue to arrest anyone they want, right? When did all of you decide to accept living in a fascist dictatorship?"

Silence followed her outburst. Moore finally seemed to understand why she was so furious. He headed to the kitchen and returned with two new beers, and another bottle of wine. He twisted off a cap, tossed it across the room, and drank several long pulls.

Blake slumped in his armchair and stared at the beer Moore placed beside him on the wooden floor.

Moore's wife twisted open the wine, filled her glass, and said, "As long as I can protect my nephew, make sure he grows up safe in my care, then I'm okay. My primary concerns are him and us." She pointed at her chest, and then at her husband. "So, do us a favor. If you continue to oppose these people, please, don't come back. You'll no longer be welcome in our home." She headed for the back of the house.

Moore rose, tried to go after her, and gave up. He turned to Isa. "Don't mind her. She's just upset right now."

Blake threw his jacket on a chair and slumped into their rocking recliner. He pushed the button, closed his eyes, and the chair slowly tilted backward. He lost himself in the rocking motion, enjoying the quiet and the chill in the air. *Just how I like it,* he thought. The day that Isa lost her job, he and Neil were reassigned from homicide to domestic investigations. Neil hadn't complained about the demotion. He was a good partner.

William Wilmot had proved to be a heavyweight adversary, connected directly to the attorney general, the New York chief of police, the NSA, and a few senators and congressmen. He waved his baton and powerful people played his tunes. Taylor and Sam had practically vanished from existence—no trial, no counter motions filed, nothing. Every time he'd made inquiries through police channels, he received the same response: enemies of the state were kept in undisclosed locations. They were also quick to remind him to be grateful they'd spared his wife.

How safe was she, actually? Or Neil, for helping her? The list of possible traitors had grown smaller, leaving Senator Chadwick, Corbin, and Neil.

Blake rocked faster and harder, without realizing. The motion helped him think. That, and the darkness, which seemed to cut down so many distractions.

Corbin had his problems, and their brotherly bonds felt strained more often than not. But he wouldn't intentionally harm his brother or sister-in-law, or betray them. Family was family. A sacred connection. Corbin would remain dedicated to his kin. Plus, it wouldn't make sense to draw attention to himself, since his journalist nose was poking around the same story.

That leaves Norman and Neil, he thought.

"Honey?"

Blake sighed, soothed by her love. She didn't have a particularly calming tone or an overly gentle voice. It was simply the knowledge that she was by his side, and had his back. Isa was the one person who loved him unconditionally. He probably didn't deserve her. And yet, here she remained. He blinked, deactivated the rocking, and looked up at his wife.

"Are you all right?" She bent over, caressed his hair, then kissed his temple.

"I am now." He stood and stretched.

"A penny for your thoughts."

He shook his head. "That's a bad investment, love." Moving past her, he climbed the stairs toward their bedroom.

Isa followed behind. "Did you hear?"

"About what?"

"The Internet Safety Act."

He entered the bedroom and carefully unbuttoned his shirt from the bottom button up. She remained in the doorway, watching.

"After the week we've had, do I want to hear the rest?"

"They…" She started again, mimicking his cop voice. "*They* prepared a law in secret, and passed it this morning. The media is understandably shocked."

"And?" He waved his hand, encouraging her to continue. He knew his wife, understood that she needed him to occasionally react, or she'd stop talking and get angry, thinking he wasn't paying attention.

"They named it The Internet Safety Act, and they claim its main purpose is to protect us from cyber terrorism." She smiled with a crazy face, as though she were agreeing. Her way of being sarcastic. A childish way, he'd told her several times, but a sweet way nonetheless. It was as though she was incapable of malice, so she had to act out to show her disagreement.

Using his kindergarten-teacher tone, he asked, "And what do we think of that, love?"

"Well, if you study the act, you'll learn that there's no more unlimited access to the internet. The government has divided the Web into Domestic Internet and International Internet. While they've made it seem as though Americans will have unlimited access to the domestic version, the international one is censored and it costs significantly more to connect to it. They're debating the new rulebook, which will outline what information US citizens will be permitted to access beyond our border." She stopped and waited for his reaction.

While everything she'd explained had sounded serious, another indication of the dictatorship regime taking over their country, his thoughts kept returning to their personal safety.

Moore's wife had the right idea, he thought. He and Isa had to take care of each other first. Only if, and when, they were safe should they get involved with outside forces.

He struggled to properly arrange his shirt on a hanger. "Sounds awful."

"Don't hold back," she said, her eyes wide. "Today was that bad, huh?"

"No more than usual." He pulled off his pants, and arranged them carefully on a hanger.

"I see." She crossed her arms over her chest. "Care to share some of the *usual* stuff?"

He hung the pants on the correct side of the closet, and turned to face her. *We need to be cautious,* he thought. *Keep away from trouble.* He didn't want to scare her, but she'd barely survived the attempted abduction. He could protect her, even without her cooperation. But he had to tell her one important detail, or he'd have hell in their house.

She waved her palm in front of his eyes and said, "Hon-ney? You in there?"

"Yeah, sorry." He pressed his hand against his gut, and lied. "I'll tell you, later, okay? I'm hungry."

"Fine!" She threw her hands in the air, no longer hiding her frustration. "Dinner's ready, Detective Frye. Duck on cabbage, just the way you like it."

He pulled on his home pants and grabbed a t-shirt. "Duck sounds good."

"I'm sure," she snapped. "Except we only have grilled cheese and radishes. Ready in ten minutes." She ran down the stairs.

He retreated to the bathroom to freshen up. The man in the mirror didn't have any suggestions. *We can't live like this,* he thought. She needed to get past her anger, and he needed to keep her safe.

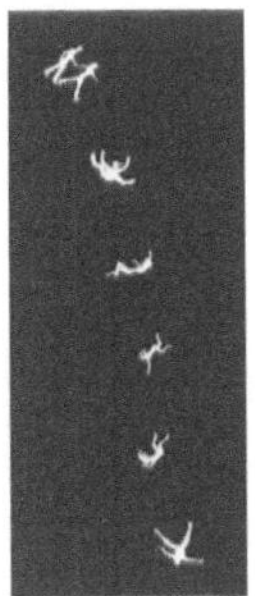

THE GOOD DOCTOR

The medical facility consisted of a large room filled with machines like defibrillators, IV pumps, portable X-rays, and the like. Several exam tables lined one wall, with surgical lights arranged above them. *Not a doctor or nurse in sight*, thought Blake. His eyes worked, but his arms and legs didn't seem to remember how they worked.

The two men moved him from the stretcher to a table, tied his right hand to the table's leg, and left him alone.

A man dressed in a doctor-like lab coat entered through a door Blake couldn't see. He didn't identify himself, and wasn't wearing a doctor's ID tag, but he examined Blake's gunshot wound, looking rather bored.

Still silent, he disinfected the arm and began to pull at the skin around Blake's wound. No anesthesia, no pain meds.

This guy's an animal, thought Blake. Like a lion, he was the king of the medical department. *Breathe through the pain*, he told himself. At least they were trying to keep him alive.

The doctor grabbed a pair of what looked like medical-grade pliers and drove them deep into the wound.

Blake's body remembered how to function, and he bolted upright, screaming and looking around frantically.

"Welcome to the servitude camp, Detective. Please try to keep still or you'll end up worse than you are now."

Worse? The closer he got to Isa, the better he would feel, despite the mad doctor's cruel treatment. He was inside the Wilmot compound. He'd find Isa.

The doctor dug a piece of the bullet out, and Blake bit at the inside of his mouth, struggling not to scream again.

"I met your wife," said the doc. "While she's rather beautiful, she's not a very nice lady."

Blake tried to raise his left arm to punch the asshole, but the doctor pushed back with his scalpel. Blake groaned in pain. *Take the pain*, he told himself. *I need to stay conscious.*

"The Wilmots asked me to barcode her, so of course I did my job. But I'll tell you a secret. I did something else to her. Something that I'll do to you, as well. Something that will stay with you both for the rest of your lives."

This maniac couldn't possibly be a doctor. They were supposed to help, not harm. But anyone who worked in a slave camp, and apparently this man did so freely, spoke volumes about his character.

The two men in blue coveralls closed the door behind them. Simon stepped away from the door, trying to remain undetected. After five paces, he looked over his shoulder and noticed that the men had moved in another direction. He returned to the door, just in time to hear Blake scream.

Simon slowly pushed the door partway open, and peeked through the gap. The doctor was tending to a wound on Blake's arm. *Without anesthesia, the fucker.* Blake was clearly awake and in tremendous pain.

Simon backed away and closed the door silently. He needed to give the doctor—*more like the butcher*—time to finish the surgery.

Needing more information, Simon walked around the corner, found a map of the building on a wall, and studied his location, familiarizing himself with this section of the facility.

After checking all directions to be sure no one would soon walk past, he dialed a number on his cell. "Where are you?" A pause. "I'm almost there, yeah." He listened, and said, "Selling Center, preparing Isa Frye." Finally he nodded and said, "I'm on my way. Be there in ten."

He switched off the cell, returned to the map, and pinpointed the location where he was supposed to be in ten minutes. After taking two cleansing breaths, he walked back to the door to medical, hoping the doctor was finished.

Simon slowly opened the door again. The doctor was sewing Blake's arm while he made small talk. His tray-table was littered with several bloody instruments, including a scalpel.

"I've got a friend in the IT department," the doctor explained to Blake. "He's a bright hacker. And he created sort of... phew...I'd have to call them *bugs*. Code bugs, to be more precise. I added them to your wife's official barcode information. They're currently broadcasting that your wife is the property of Wilmot, no-return class, blah, blah, that sort of thing."

Blake grunted, and managed to ask, "What's a no-return class?"

"You're an example, Detective. That designation means that you'll never earn your freedom. You're a permanent subject of servitude."

Blake hissed and struggled against the restraints.

"I added this bug to your code, as well. You're no longer human. The code defines you as an object. A thing. Forever."

Blake lay on the table, groaning, while the doctor yanked the thread through his flesh. Eventually he snipped the last suture and applied a bandage to Blake's arm.

Crouching, Simon crept slowly toward the table. He pulled his press pass over Wilmot's pass to hide his name. When he reached the tray-table, he picked up the bloody scalpel, rose, and pressed the blade against the doctor's nape.

The man raised his head. "Yes, hello?"

Simon palmed the scalpel in his left hand, activated his holo-display, and selected the recording app.

The doctor turned the stool to face Simon, and his eyes opened wide. "What are you doing here?"

Simon moved over to Blake's side, holding the recording app between the doctor and his left hand. Blake raised his head and stared at Simon.

"Detective, tell everyone how you ended up in the servitude pen."

Blake mumbled, confused, as he looked from the doctor to Simon.

"Leave, before I summon security," said the doctor, outraged. "No press is allowed in my lab!"

Simon handed the scalpel to Blake. "Detective, do you have a comment concerning Congress's debate on the servitude laws?"

The doctor shoved Simon toward the door and shouted, "Security! I need security in here!"

Blake cut the plastic tie that was holding him to the table's leg. He slid off the table, picked up the tray of bloodied tools, and tossed the metal instruments all over the floor. When the doctor turned toward the noise, Blake beat him repeatedly over the head with the tray until the man lay still on the floor, blood covering his face. Then Blake sagged against the surgical table to stay standing.

Simon approached him, angered by his brother's stupidity. "What the hell, Blake?"

"Thanks, brother. I wasn't sure you'd be here, but I—"

"How the *fuck* did you and Isa get sucked into this insanity? I mean, Isa, man!"

"Long story, Corbin. But I need to find her. Please, tell me you know where she is."

"She'll be," Simon checked the time, grimaced at Blake, and yelled, "Fuck!" as he hurried for the door.

"Take me with you."

"I can't."

"Yes, you fucking well can."

"I'm neck-deep in this shit, and I have to see it through. I can't compromise my position here." He pointed at his chest, and added, "Besides, I don't have an ID card for you." Simon was calming down, regaining his composure. He forced his cocky expression onto his face once more, before he dared enter a hallway.

"You found their camp. You have proof they keep slaves

here. You linked both Wilmot and his daughter to this operation. What more could you possibly need?"

Simon hesitated, bit his lips and hugged his brother.

"I'm glad to save you, bro. But this isn't over. Wilmot's just another puppet. I need to find the master puppeteer."

Blake stared at Simon. "Are you fucking serious?"

WILLIAM WILMOT

William Wilmot stared through the glass wall at Isabella Frye. She stood on a podium, dressed in an orange jumpsuit. The podium next to her remained empty.

The huge holographic display on the adjacent wall showed her name: *ISABELLA FRYE*. Below that was the number 113. Farther down, *113* small windows displayed the faces of the registered bidders, mostly men, all waiting for the auction to commence.

Beside Mrs. Frye's details, another name was displayed: *BLAKE FRYE*. His bidder count remained at one.

"Where are we, regarding Detective Frye?" Wilmot addressed no one in particular.

"He should arrive momentarily," said Agent Alvarez with an air of self-importance. "The doctor's removing his bullet."

What a child, thought Wilmot. *He catches the annoying detective, and now expects to be petted.*

"Good," said Wilmot. "You reap what you sow, Detective Frye! A good day, after all." Wilmot hoped this display would satisfy Alvarez's needs. The agent wouldn't soon forget the failed meeting with the Russians. *As I said, you reap what you sow.*

Next to her father, Gabriela grinned victoriously.

Simon silently entered, nodded to the few men who glanced over at him, and sat at the back of the room. *That journalist had better serve us well, or he'll be next in the selling pen.*

No, thought Wilmot. *I won't sell White through civilized*

channels. Reporters deserved a more gruesome fate. Perhaps a high-risk experiment that could go wrong at any stage. If he played his cards well, Wilmot would send White to endure some torture, and he'd make his daughter watch. *She needs to learn her lesson.*

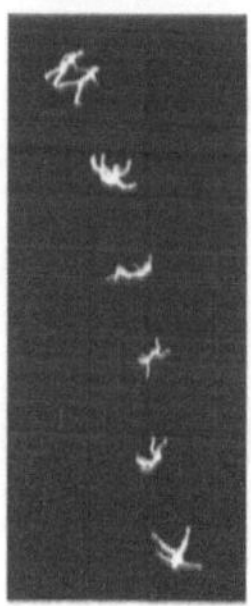

THREE MONTHS EARLIER

The cargo plane was full of glass coffins. Each one contained a human in cryogenic sleep, dressed in orange, and carefully labeled. Robotic pickup vehicles unloaded the cargo into a warehouse. On the warehouse's east wall, huge red letters proclaimed the facility was the *HAMBURG CENTER FOR DISTRIBUTION OF SERVITUDE SUBJECTS.*

Warehouse administration was a two-man job. The *Knechtschaft Distribuzion Meister,* or the Servitude Distribution Supervisor, sat in front of a computer, ensuring that every detail of the operation ran smoothly and efficiently. He was three years from retirement, and needed the pension to remain free, and to keep a roof over his wife's head.

At the beginning of his job posting, he'd thought long and hard about the demands of his new assignment. Who wouldn't struggle with the ethics of helping his employers unload and distribute slave bodies? But then his wife had lost her job, only four years before she would have qualified for a pension. If they were to stay ahead of debt payments, one of them needed to work. To stay ahead of the *Bundes Corp Polizei.* He'd never been so ashamed of a decision in his entire life.

In those first few months, he used to look at each and every one of the sleeping slaves, and imagine where they were coming from, and what bad turn in their lives had sent them to this warehouse. Then self-preservation took over. Those serene faces haunted him in the dark of night. Now he remained behind the computer, doing his job from a safe distance. For his own salvation.

His assistant, the young man with silver tattoos, scanned the labels with his data-foil and pressed a command. Every command sent a robot for another glass coffin. At more than fifty loading docks, special trucks arrived every day to pick up their precious cargo. Most of the trucks were refrigerated, designed originally to carry meat. The corporation had refitted the vehicles to safely transport the maximum number of coffins.

The *meister* noticed that sometimes the young tattooed man lingered over one coffin or another. The *meister* wondered what his young assistant might be thinking. But after more careful observation, he noticed that the young man's face maintained a constant, focused grin. After that, the *meister* had been afraid to ask.

Sam felt cold air against her face. Her mouth was dry and she felt profoundly exhausted. *Did I party too hard last night?*

She opened her eyes, inhaled in surprise, and choked when the cold air dried her throat even more. She tried to sit up, coughing and gasping for air.

Someone, a woman, stood over her, and then said a phrase in what sounded like German. Others behind the strange woman laughed.

The stranger helped Sam sit up and offered her a bottle of water to drink. Sam gulped down half the bottle, panted to catch her breath, and studied the woman's features. She was old, and her face was painted garishly.

Sam looked down and realized she was lying in a glass coffin, in a large room with a terrible paint job, next to several other coffins. Other young women and men were also waking up, from however long they'd been sleeping, like a bad version of a fairy tale. Except there was no one to wake them with a kiss.

The attendants who were moving around, offering water, looked like bad actors from the porn industry. *No,* she thought, *they look like sex workers.*

Then she remembered the moment she'd been kidnapped. "Fuck me," she said aloud. "I'm a goddamned slave."

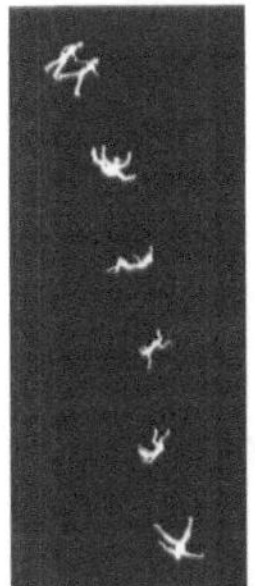

THE WAKE-UP CALL

"Sorry, bro. But this assignment is more important than any-thing I've ever done. Leave the camp, while you still can." Simon turned and hurried away.

Blake watched the door for a couple of seconds after it closed, feeling confused, tortured, and betrayed. "Corbin!" he shouted, knowing he was probably too far away to hear. More quietly, he asked, "What about Isa, Corbin? What about Isa?"

Blake paced past the surgical beds, trying to decide how to proceed, lost in his thoughts. He stepped on one of the tools on the floor, and felt the need to pick them up, one by one, arrang-ing them neatly on the tray. Then he returned the tray to its stand.

As he adjusted the tools so that they were in the best order, the doctor groaned behind him. Startled by the noise, Blake turned and looked down. His face hardened and he grabbed the tray, sending all the ordered tools flying. He bashed the doctor on the head.

Bastard. This time he shoved a bloody cloth into the doctor's mouth, and tied him to the examination table.

The doctor's cell rang.

Blake considered ignoring it, then he answered. On the other end of the line, he heard that woman's voice. The cruel woman who'd called to tell him that they had Isa. He had no doubt now that it was the same person. It was Gabriela Wilmot, William's daughter.

"Doctor? Hello?" Gabriela sounded cold and angry. "We're all waiting in the Sell Center. We need the detective, *now*. I don't care if you're halfway through stapling his chest together. We need him now!" After a pause, she repeated, "Hello?"

Blake ended the call and scanned the room. He remembered the earlier events, before Corbin appeared. Blake had tried to raise his left arm to punch the doctor, but the doctor had pushed back with his scalpel, and Blake had ended up groaning in pain, with no strength to fight back. The doctor was gloating about something he'd done to Isa.

"The Wilmots asked me to barcode her, so of course I did my job," the doctor had said. *"But I'll tell you a secret. I did something else to her. Something that I'll do to you, as well."*

That was the key, thought Blake. The barcode. As with any merchandise for sale, the slavers were barcoding their property, to assist with tracking and accounting.

The room had several displays mounted on the walls, and one of them was on. Blake activated the keyboard and typed *ISABELLA FRYE.*

A barcode and a file popped up on the screen. Blake clicked on *LOCATION.*

The screen displayed *SELL CENTER.*

Then then the display changed, showing the feed from the Sell Center. The ongoing bids for Isa and—*shit*—for Blake were shown below their headshots. He felt a chill race down his spine. One day ago, he'd watched news coverage about these…sales in England. Now it was happening here, in the land of the free, and strangers were bidding on the value of his beautiful wife. One hundred and thirteen people were registered to bid for Isa, and only one was registered for his upcoming sale. *Oh, Isa, what did I do?* He caressed the screen over Isa's face. She was in pain. She was suffering and he wasn't there to protect her.

The door to the room opened. A security guard stopped on the threshold, staring at him. Blake gripped the scalpel and rose to his feet, ready for a fight.

The security guard spoke into his comm. "The prisoner's escaped! I repeat, the prisoner's escaped! I need backup, in the medical facility, now."

The guard stepped all the way into the room, reaching for his gun. But while he'd been calling for assistance, Blake had crossed the room. As the guard drew his gun, Blake grabbed his arm and thrust the scalpel deep into the man's armpit—one of the soft places that bulletproof vests didn't protect.

The man staggered backward, looking shocked. Blake slashed across the man's neck. A gush of blood sprayed them both. Blake caught the man and lowered him to the floor, spat to clear the blood that had entered his mouth, and wiped his face.

A beep sounded from the display. *SOLD* appeared across Isa's face. Blake exhaled, staring at his blood-covered hands. *I murdered this man,* he thought. *They pushed me to the brink, and I killed this man. And they just sold my wife.*

He grabbed the security guard's gun and communication device and started toward the exit, then stopped and looked back.

He rushed over to the fridges and read the labels on the drug bottles. He located the painkillers, grabbed one bottle, popped the cap, and tipped two pills into his palm. He washed them down with some water. As he took another long gulp, his eyes fell on some empty test tubes, the kind typically used to collect blood, scattered across the counter. He blinked in distress, turned for the door, stood for several seconds, then turned back, unable to stop himself. He wasted precious time arranging all the tubes by color and size.

When he finished, he exhaled, feeling significantly stronger. Only then could he make his legs work again, and he rushed through the nearest exit as he heard voices nearby, and boots pounding on a tile floor.

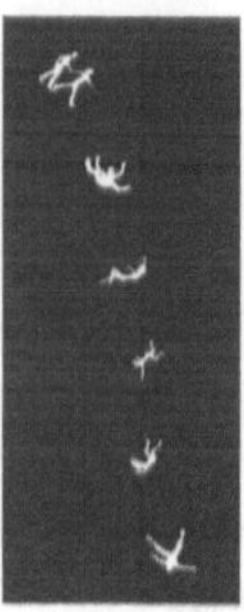

GABRIELA ON THE RISE

Gabriela monitored the bids on the screens as they pushed higher. Isabella Frye's price continued to climb as hundreds of interested buyers tried to outdo their competitors. Her detective husband, Blake Frye, had stalled at one lone offer. But one low-ball bid for the husband provided enough motivation to make the detective feel threatened and defeated. To bring him to heel, like a cowed dog. Her father had said that their main objective concerning the slave auction was to convince Detective Frye to cooperate by threatening to sell his wife. Her father recognized the benefits and nuances of presenting Isa as a bargaining chip.

Gabriela had a different endgame. She planned to reveal the details to her father once the detective conceded. People like Blake Frye need not be subdued. They needed to be vanquished. Showcased as imposing examples designed to deter future dissidence.

Gabriela had expected the Freedom Act to be passed through the Senate and made into law by now. Her father had so many supporters in the Senate. More than half were in his pocket. How could the vote take so long? She was tired of operating the business under the radar. She longed to parade her servitude trade acumen and elevate her reputation, sitting in a new chair at the table in the inner circles where those in power conferred. She had established the preeminent servitude business in North America. Soon, the elite would recognize Gabriela Wilmot as the second Lady of the United States. Her future could evolve into a historic life, fueled by such an impressive beginning.

Another buyer raised the price for Isa.

That impudent news producer was the dumb little stone in Gabriela's shoe. Soon the young Wilmot would pull the stone from her shoe and throw it onto a road, to be driven over by thousands of cars, until only dust remained of Isa's bones.

At the sound of her father's puffing, she turned her attention back to the room, and watched him check the time. Agent Alvarez appeared worried as he checked his wristband and the comm channels for a reply from Frye's doctor. The agent noticed her watching, turned his back, and whispered into his comm device.

You call yourself an agent? Gabriela thought. *You can't seem to control one annoying detective!* She wondered why she continued to be the only person able to take care of business in this facility.

William Wilmot turned to Alvarez and demanded, "Well?"

Alvarez turned to face the Wilmots.

"We'll hear from security, any moment now. Isn't that so, Agent Alvarez?" Gabriela sneered.

The old man addressed Alvarez again. "Wasn't he secured?"

"He was, sir." Alvarez smiled as if he were as trustworthy as a puppy.

At that moment, a voice broadcast at full volume over Breckenwell's comm device. "The prisoner's escaped! I repeat, the prisoner's escaped! I need backup in the medical facility, now."

The old man turned to Alvarez, and in a cold voice asked, "You were saying?"

He seemed calmer than Gabriela expected. Her father knew how to be a great leader in a crisis. She still had so much to learn from him. He'd turned NSA agents into his lapdogs, with almost no effort at all. *He could easily become the next president of this great nation.*

Chief of Security Martin Breckenwell stood emotionless in his corner, a step behind Wilmot. He maintained order and discipline across the entire facility. His team patrolled its corridors, and yet one of them was now sounding the alarm. Clearly, they'd arrived too late to medical. Breckenwell should've anticipated the need, and sent some men earlier, before the situation got out of hand.

Alvarez glared at Breckenwell. "How the fuck did you let this happen?"

This should be fun, thought Gabriela.

Ignoring the NSA Agent, Breckenwell murmured something in his comm.

Alvarez pressed. "Why didn't you assign extra guards to medical?"

Breckenwell stood up straighter, towering over Alvarez, and demanded, "Why didn't your agents stay with the prisoner, especially since they were the ones who brought the detective to medical in the first place? Did they duck out for coffee?"

Alvarez faced him, nose to nose. "Security is *your* fucking job!"

"And I'm handling it," said Breckenwell. "Cleaning up the mess *your* agents made."

Alvarez placed his hand on his gun.

Breckenwell quickly pressed a hand against the agent's arm and said, nodding wisely at Alvarez, "You can't make an omelet without breaking a few eggs."

Gabriela flashed her coldest glare at Breckenwell to get him to stand down. The security chief seemed oblivious to Alvarez's threatening gesture.

One of the other NSA agents in the room cleared his throat and stepped closer to Alvarez. "Sir, I could take one man and go after him."

Gabriela tried to remember the agent's name. *Smith? Sanford?*

As if he'd read her mind, Alvarez said, "Stand down, Saunders." He paused, glared at Breckenwell, and added, "Escort the slave to her new master."

Alvarez gestured to his men and said, "Some of you need to stay here, and protect the Wilmots." The NSA agents regrouped around Gabriela and her father. Alvarez turned to her father and asked, "Mr. Wilmot, where will the winning bidder pick up their merchandise?"

"In the meeting room," said her father. "Normally we would just ship them off. But in this case—"

"I understand, sir," said Alvarez, all business and ready for action. To his agents, he said, "Let's move the subject to the meeting room."

Gabriela disliked how Alvarez had cut off her father in the middle of a sentence. She considered disciplining him, but the old man seemed to be untroubled.

Or was he? Her father's secret weapon was the ability to show you one face and be thinking or operating on an opposing level. When you woke up, it was always too late to apologize. The man was merciless.

Two of the NSA agents entered the adjacent room and grabbed Isa.

Breckenwell turned to her father and said, "I'm going to the security center to coordinate my men from there." He grinned and added, "If you need me, just buzz."

The old man nodded his approval.

Isa was escorted into the bidding room. The NSA agents regrouped around the prisoner, maintaining a barrier between Isa and the Wilmots.

Gabriela said, "Shall we go?"

Saunders led the way, followed by four agents flanking Isa in a diamond formation. Then Alvarez followed, keeping William Wilmot on his right side.

As she followed, Gabriela looked over her shoulder and said, "Come on, you."

Simon followed at the end of the column.

Gabriela cycled through the approaching dangers in her mind. Their group would be walking along too many corridors with too many corners. They could be ambushed at nearly every intersection. Then they'd need to cross the lobby, a huge expanse where they'd have almost no cover. *We'll be safe once we're through the lobby.*

She'd been listening to too many of Breckenwell's briefings. Detective Frye was one man. A desperate, wounded, lightly-armed man, who wasn't familiar with the camp's layout. They had the home team advantage, more manpower, and more weapons.

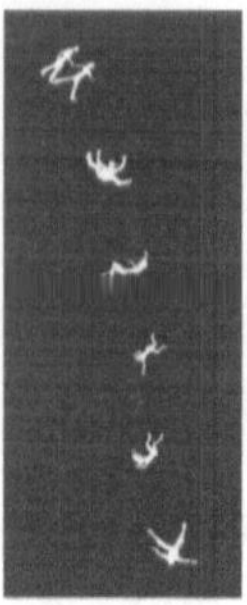

THREE MONTHS EARLIER

Gabriela stepped through the door and into the street, speaking on her cell. Like a pack of rabid dogs, dozens of reporters swarmed around her, their microphones extended toward her face, shouting their invasive questions all at once.

She hesitated for a second, switched off the cell, and studied their faces. Her father was inside, sitting through the preliminary hearings for the case brought against them by that damned news story.

The old man had no doubt whatsoever that he'd fly through the hearings and eliminate this nuisance once and for all. Until then, the vultures circled around the Wilmot family, eager to sip from the blood fountain.

Pa sees this as an opportunity as much as a nuisance. She grinned, imagining how proud he would be if she handled the crowd well. *Time for a surprise, Pa.*

"Good day," she said, trying to speak as loudly and clearly as possible. "Please, one at a time. Or I won't be able to hear your questions properly."

The reporters' clamor died down, and they tightened the circle. She fought her claustrophobia. *I can handle them. A couple of questions, a couple of smart answers, a joke or two, and I'll be on my way. Pa can handle the court, and I'll handle the press. Then we'll all go home happy.*

In a shrill voice, a woman quickly asked, "Are the allegations from Debt Hunters true?"

"No. Next question?"

Close to her, a man jumped in with his question. "Why, then, did your father have the news journalists arrested?"

"William Wilmot is a businessman. He cannot *have* anyone arrested, as you implied. We'll probably press charges for slander. But that's the extent of our legal plan, moving forward."

"Then why did the NYPD arrest John Taylor, the news anchor?"

"You'll have to approach the department for that information. I can't speak to their actions."

Before they asked more questions, she raised her hands for silence, and elaborated further. "I'm told the news journalists weren't arrested for slander. They've been accused of something more *insidious*."

"What's that, Miss Wilmot?" another reporter snapped before Gabriela could finish.

"Terrorism." Gabriela said the word as clearly and simply as possible, then flashed a charming smile. During the brief pause, she thought the silence represented her triumph. But the victory didn't taste as sweet as she'd hoped. It had no taste whatsoever. Her achievement felt more like a drug slamming into her gut.

An old gentleman held his recorder close to her face and shouted, "What's the connection between terrorism and Debt Hunters?"

The other reporters nodded as though he'd asked the most important question. The silence stretched as they waited for her answer.

Couldn't they see the connection? Gabriela wanted to answer, but she needed to form her response with precision. *What's the connection between the two?* When Pa had explained the link, his words had made sense.

She frowned and smiled at the same time. Instantly, she realized that displaying her unhappiness had been a mistake. In addition, frowning and smiling never mixed well. She breathed in and out, trying to remember the specifics. *National security…* Her father had said something about national security.

"A news piece, like the one known as the Debt Hunters story, is not only irresponsible journalism, it's a criminal fabrication. It makes assumptions, *unfounded* assumptions, and then extrapolates from false data, which leads to erroneous conclusions."

"How is that terrorism?" the old reporter pressed.

"The false conclusions can threaten national security, particularly if they involve a criminal element, or instigate panic in the population."

The shrill-voiced woman clawed her way back into the debate. "Miss Wilmot, can you answer the question honestly? Or are you just going to make unfounded assumptions and extrapolate?"

The crowd of reporters laughed.

No one laughs at me. Or mocks the Wilmot name! "If false accusations are made about the biggest business in America, the business responsible for 35 percent of the gross national product and 60 percent of our collective financial prosperity, and fuels 45 percent of the daily market gains, then you'll destabilize our financial market. If you lower the American investment market, then foreign buyers will capitalize on the cheap prices, causing a more profound downturn in the economy. That's why, if any journalist decides to smear the reputation of the biggest business in America, that reporter should clear their facts with the attorney general. The only way to avoid a negative impact on our collective futures is to confirm their facts from multiple sources."

There was a brief pause as the reporters processed her speech. *Straight to the point,* she thought. Gabriela stepped back, trying to make a hole in the pack so she could withdraw back into the building.

In a deep, somber voice, the old man stated, "Unless the attorney general is William Wilmot's puppet."

Who the fuck is this guy? "Well, sir, if you are one hundred percent sure of your accusations, then I suppose I have nothing more to say."

She glanced around at the other reporters, reading the tension, and cleared her throat. "Look, everyone. I'm here to cooperate with all of you. Please wait here while I bring your concerns to my father. When I return, I'll have an official statement on behalf of Wilmot Enterprises."

Gabriela shoved her way through the throng of reporters and ducked into the building. As soon as the door closed, she felt safe. Despite the building's stuffy interior, she gulped down what felt like the freshest air. *I'm safe.*

Except she wasn't. The miserable vultures lurked outside and Pa expected her to handle them. Not wobble inside with her tail between her legs, begging her father to write her speeches for her.

Gabriela waved over the nearest member of the Wilmot security team and whispered in his ear for some time. He nodded his assent and hurried away.

She glanced through the door at the reporters, smiled, and turned her back on them to dial a number on her cell.

Simon's voice answered in her earbud. "Hey, honey. What's up?"

"Not much. I'm in a bit of a conundrum." She paused. "But I think I worked it out."

"Care to share?"

"It's too complicated." After another deep breath, she asked, "Have you heard of the Gordian Knot?'"

"Did you cut through," he asked, "or pull the pin?"

"There's no *pin.*"

"As a matter of fact, there are two versions of the story. In one, Alexander the Great cuts the knot with his sword. But in the second version, he removes the pin that secures the yolk to the pole."

"You're so full of shit."

"I'm guessing you cut through it, then."

"Of course I did. That's the whole goddamned point of the story."

"Unless, you're looking for a nonviolent solution."

"Are you calling me *weak*?"

"Absolutely not. I'm glad you solved your problem."

Gabriela noticed that her security men had taken up their positions outside. To Simon, she said, "Give me a second." With a quick nod, she signaled the leader of her security men.

They pulled masks over their faces, drew their Tasers, and

attacked the reporters.

That concludes my official statement on behalf of Wilmot Enterprises. Gabriela smiled happily and returned her attention to the call with Simon.

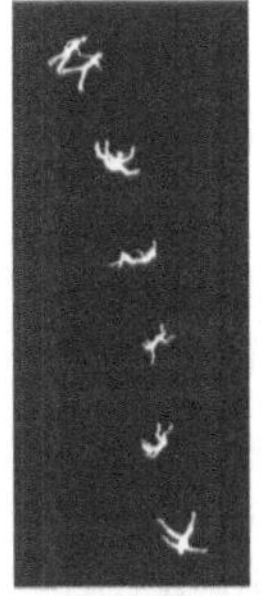

BLAKE

Blake ran down the corridors, his right arm extended with his holo-screen active. The map of the camp guided him to the Sell Center. To Isa. If she was already sold, would they ship her immediately? Or was the buyer available to take immediate possession?

They might ignore protocol, now that they knew he was on the loose. Get Isa out as quickly as possible.

According to the map, the Sell Center was close to the Business Tower. Blake assumed that if they wanted to close the deal, or whatever, the exchange would likely happen in the Business Tower. In the back of his mind, a small voice whispered that his assumptions were bullshit, a shield to prevent him from losing hope. So many variables and unknown elements were at play now. Blake knew almost nothing about the servitude camp, or its security force.

No more negativity, he told himself. *Think. Be rational and deliberate.* But he didn't have time to stop and think. He had to act *while* he was thinking, and that was *difficult*. And dangerous. So many D-words. *Deliberate, difficult, dangerous…*

"Focus!" The sound of his own voice helped. He continued to run, breathing hard, and forcing his fear into the background so he could concentrate.

Where am I?

He checked the map. *Take the next right, then straight ahead.*

Wilmot's plan continued to unfold. Blake was a puppet, acting in the slavers' play. *I'm focusing on the wrong team, he thought.*

Captain Moore had been right about focusing on the most important team: *family.* Isa and the baby. *Focus on them!*

Blake rounded a corner and skidded to a halt. The Wilmot security team stood just ahead, their weapons raised. He shot wildly at his adversaries, hoping to make them turn back.

The lights switched off, plunging the corridor into darkness. Blake disabled his holo-vid. Everyone was silent, waiting for the lights to blink back on. When the blackness continued, the men whispered orders to one another, arguing about how to proceed.

Blake backed away in the direction he'd come, touching the wall to keep moving in a straight line. When he reached a corner, he turned right.

Someone from the security team fired at him. The shot sounded loud, close. More shots, and Blake heard the bullets biting into the walls and scratching door frames. His emotions spun up, warning him that one of those bullets would soon drill through his skull. His rational mind kicked in, reminding him that he'd already turned a corner, and was no longer in security's direct line of fire.

The lights came back on.

Someone shouted, "Cease fire. He's gone."

Blake reactivated the map and hurried ahead as silently as possible, trying to keep his breathing under control. He was approaching the red dot on the map. *My destination.* The voices moved away, then seemed to turn closer again. Blake rushed down the corridor and pushed through a set of double doors into the lobby.

Across the huge room, Wilmot and Alvarez turned their heads, staring in disbelief at Blake. As he skidded to a halt, he heard her voice. His hope, in the form of her sweet, loving voice discharged a thousand volts into his chest, waking him from the fear-cloud.

"Blaaaake!"

Isa was surrounded by agents. She wore an orange jumpsuit, as if she were an inmate.

Agent Alvarez, whose name was now carved in Blake's heart

forever for murdering Moore, yelled, "You two, take position here." Two NSA agents turned to confront Blake, their guns up and aimed at his head. Alvarez pushed everyone in their group away from the reception area, toward the exit.

Blake fired a shot without thinking. One of the agents fell, his face a red flower. The second agent returned fire, forcing Blake to run for cover. He dashed left, hoping to reach the exit they'd taken Isa through.

The Wilmot security team pushed into the lobby, reacting immediately with covering fire, unaware that the shots were coming from their own team.

The NSA agent fired back while shouting, "Check your fire! Watch your targets."

Seizing the opportunity, Blake acted without analyzing his options. While they were busy shooting one another, he sprinted for the exit. Once, he shot over his shoulder, to keep everyone guessing.

The security team took cover. The surviving NSA agent fell behind the reception desk.

In Blake's experience, confusion during a gunfight never lasted for long. He burst through the doors, a rain of bullets at his back.

He found himself in a hallway. The people around him shrieked in fear, ducking low. Blake aimed the gun ahead as he sized up the risk. No guns in sight. *They're civilians.* They looked like office workers, not security. He yelled, "Did you see the boss and the prisoner? Which way did they go?"

A woman pointed down the corridor at another door. Blake glanced over, but from the look of the security pad, he'd need an ID pass to get through. As the civilians scattered in every direction, Blake grabbed the arm of the helpful woman and demanded, "What's down there?"

"The Business Tower," she managed. "Please don't kill me."

Blake snatched her badge, released her arm, and bolted down the corridor.

Her card wouldn't unlock the door.

He kicked at the door, then aimed his gun at the lock pad.

Before he could fire, he heard the pounding of boots coming from the lobby, and turned to defend himself. Two security guards turned the corner, and Blake shot the first one in the neck. The other man drew on him, and Blake shot his hand, knocking the gun aside.

As the man leaned down to retrieve the gun, Blake ran over and kicked him in the head. Then he pressed his gun barrel against the man's temple and said, "Give me your access ID."

"Go fuck yourself."

Blake shot the wall, inches from the man's face.

"Fuck you!" screamed the guard.

Don't analyze, he told himself. *Isa needs you.* "The card. Now!"

"It won't open that door." The guard sounded genuine. "I don't have clearance for the tower."

Blake relaxed his posture and said, "Stay down, or the next one won't hit the wall."

The security guard sighed with relief, pressed his good hand onto his head, and cradled the shot one against his chest. "Please," he whined. "I hate the Wilmots."

"How do I get into the tower?"

"There's no other entrance." The security guard's smirk told Blake he'd been wrong about the man. He fired another bullet into the wall, on the other side of the man's head, grazing his ear.

"Fuck!" He cupped his hand. "I told you, my pass won't work." Blood trickled from where a piece of his ear used to be.

"The other entrance."

"You're fucking crazy!"

Blake pressed the gun's barrel into the center of the man's forehead. His skin sizzled against the hot metal.

As the asshole grunted and writhed under the gun, he extended his good hand and said, "It's…it's that way. Exit the building and head for the landing pad. There's a door into the Business Tower from there."

Blake pistol-whipped the guard, smashing his gun across the man's nose, temple, and mouth. After the third blow, the guy fell, unconscious.

This isn't me, thought Blake. He never would've believed

himself capable of such violence.

Keep moving, he reminded himself. *For Isa.*

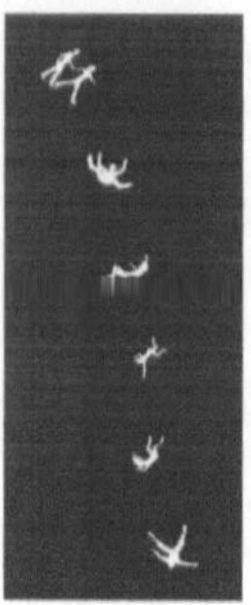

NIGEL

Nigel parked his car on a side road under a towering pine tree. The woods were dense and dark for the long walk to the gate. Any minute now, the police would swarm the camp. He prayed he could warn Wilmot in time.

As he jogged toward the main gate, he heard the sound of tires biting into gravel. He quickly dropped to the ground and rolled past the ditch into the woods. Crouching behind some low-growing bushes, he risked a peek at the road, just in time to watch a SWAT van followed by more than a dozen police cars race past. No lights or sirens. A few moments later, he counted four two-ton trucks, each marked with the Red Cross logo. Every vehicle headed straight into the slave camp, not the Wilmot Science Research Center.

Someone did their homework, thought Nigel. "Fuck," he whispered. "I'm too fucking late." He rolled away, turning his back to the road, and clenched his jaws in anger. His escape plan had dropped through a sewer grate, into a river of shit.

In an instant, he'd morphed from a man on a mission into a fugitive without an all-powerful master. All because of one man.

Actually, two, he thought. He'd lost everything because of the two fuckers.

Right next to him, Nigel heard a twig snap. He froze, just as a cop bent over him to get a better look.

Nigel smiled.

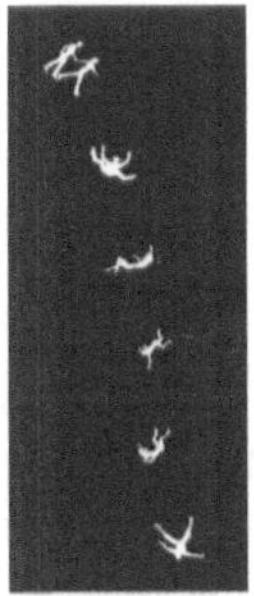

TWO MONTHS EARLIER

William Wilmot surveyed the huge, two-storey office. It looked abandoned, as though a tornado had swept through, leaving everything in disarray.

Ahead of him, the security detail scoured the vicinity to ensure the boss's safety. Above where he stood, the top ring was dotted with the senior executives' offices. A vast spiral staircase led down to the main floor, separating the elite employees from the dozens and dozens of unimportant cubicle-monkeys. The architecture reminded Wilmot of an observation balcony designed to witness the fights in the pit below.

Wilmot climbed the stairs to the upper level, and ambled along executive row, passing glass door after glass door. Inside each oversized office, only the furniture remained. None of them compared to the opulence of his offices in every building he owned. He preferred to occupy one-quarter of the highest floors, turning them into luxurious spaces where he could work, exercise, meet friends and associates, or simply relax after a difficult day. Every building he built had no fewer than fifty stories.

He'd acquired this building fully furnished, including the entire NWN TV network's facilities. With only forty-five floors, he would not be able to design an office suite here that could meet his requirements. It could serve as a starter-building for his daughter. She might enjoy building a media division. She'd always had a knack for public relations.

Once security finished securing the floor, they positioned

themselves at strategic locations. Martin Breckenwell approached, displaying his usual frown. The guy seemed to live only to scare the shit out of his underlings. Wilmot loved his style.

"No problems in the vicinity, boss. Miss G is arriving as we speak."

"Thanks, Martin. Please ensure that no one uses our elevator."

Wilmot's security chief nodded and left. Every one of his men and women snapped to attention when Breckenwell passed by. *They're like his own personal army,* thought Wilmot.

He stopped outside a door with John Taylor's nameplate. *So, this is the little shit's office.* He'd hoped the celebrity would've been a stronger, more intelligent human being. As it turned out, Taylor had been just another fearful man. No grandeur. No vision.

Gabriela had set the minimum bid rather high for Taylor. Some tycoon from Malaysia wanted him, to narrate some very private shows. But that would've been too comfortable a fate for Taylor. Wilmot wanted him to suffer. To really pay for what he'd done.

The elevator dinged, and opened to the network's main lobby. Wilmot turned and watched Gabriela surveying what remained of NWN TV. He smiled, warmed by her presence. She was truly his daughter. Pity she hadn't been born a boy. *What does it matter, these days?* Women held positions of true power. Not as many as their male counterparts, but enough to give Gabriela room to dominate. As she made her way up the staircase, he thought, *She'll always hover a notch below the most powerful men, but in my domain, she shines.*

"Papa!" She kissed him lightly on the cheek. Scanning the mess with a look of disgust, she asked, "What are we doing here?"

"Celebrating." Wilmot leaned over the railing, looking down on the lower area.

Gabriela grimaced. "It's a mess and it's ugly."

"But it's ours." Wilmot's smile widened.

"We have nicer properties."

"Puppy, you must always take the good with the bad. This is our building now. And this area is where the former news channel for NWN TV used to operate. I acquired it last week, and closed it down. Fired every employee. We'll clean up the offices, and make a fresh start. I wiped out every last trace of that shameful, traitorous investigative news story."

Gabriela's eyes grew larger with understanding and then glee.

Wilmot turned to his butler and demanded, "Champagne."

From his satchel, the butler produced two glasses and a five thousand dollar bottle of Moët & Chandon Dom Perignon White Gold. He gently nudged the cork free as quietly as possible. A small stream of foam overflowed, and he wiped it carefully with a pretentious gesture.

It wasn't the most expensive champagne available at that time, but it was close to the best. Wilmot had stashed one of the most expensive, exclusive bottles of bubbly for a different celebration: when the Freedom Act became law. That milestone would mark the beginning of a new fortune for the Wilmot family, as they entered into a new sphere of power.

Gabriela accepted the glass of Dom Perignon, waited for her father to receive his, and clinked hers against his. "To great accomplishments!"

"To my sweet daughter, the future queen of America!" Wilmot held his glass aloft, and then drank.

Gabriela chuckled when she noticed the name on the door. "John Taylor, huh? So, this is where the snake worked."

"Yes." He waved his glass in an arc and said, "I thought you could take over this building, and have these two floors turned into your personal office suite. You can have your cake and eat it too."

"What would I do with this, Pa?"

"Take control of NWN TV. Make sure the network delivers only appropriate news. If it pleases you, feel free to sketch out a few ideas for episodic shows. You could transform the entire building into your own personal playground. Experiment. Embrace your youth. Enjoy yourself. Channel your brilliance and build an amazing future."

"The Wilmot Camp is my playground, Pa."

"Add this one to your collection. Don't limit yourself."

She weighed the idea, keeping her eyes half closed. Wilmot grinned. *That's my daughter. Enterprising. Eager.*

The elevator dinged again. Agent Alvarez stepped out. When one of the security men approached to check the agent for weapons, Breckenwell made a sign to let him through.

Wilmot chuckled. Obviously, some of their security staff possessed more muscles than brains. *The nerve of the man, asking an NSA agent to relinquish his gun.* Alvarez climbed the stairs to the upper level.

Gabriela stopped her introspection and focused on the NSA agent. She'd been briefed about Alvarez's recruitment, and understood the opportunities it opened up.

Alvarez nodded to Gabriela, and without preamble, asked, "Can I have a word, sir?"

"You can speak freely in front of my daughter, agent."

"This is a matter of a certain sensitivity."

"Freely," Wilmot repeated.

Alvarez narrowed his eyes, looking uncomfortable about speaking in front of Gabriela. "Sir," he began, "Do you remember Senator Chadwick?"

"The faggot that was arrested for homosexuality?"

"The case was dropped for lack of evidence, sir, but yes. That senator."

"What about him?"

"We have proof that he assisted Isa Frye with her research."

"Damn that woman," said Wilmot. "How far has her corruption spread?"

"At least as high as Senator Chadwick, sir."

"Isn't he the last Democrat in the Senate?"

"Yes, sir."

"Well, that makes sense. He represents the Democrats' last stand against the Republicans. The road to hell is paved with good intentions."

"What should the NSA do about it, sir?"

"What's your boss's take on the situation?"

"He thinks someone called in the homosexuality tip to smear Chadwick's reputation. It's the final nail in his political coffin. The director personally prefers the option of leaving the senator in place to finish his term. His *last* term, of course. Let the man retire."

The butler noticed Wilmot had finished his drink, and he offered the tray. Wilmot placed his glass directly in the center. Then he turned to pace along the circular railing, keeping his hands clasped behind his back. He believed he was accurately duplicating the pose he'd seen Napoleon using in old paintings.

I'm the Napoleon of the modern age, he thought. Instead of conquering the world using bloody warfare, he was conquering it through business acumen and market shares. Nobody knew it exactly, but he already owned one-third of the international servitude market, the most valuable market on the planet. The investor who owned the servitude market would eventually own every government worldwide. He'd soon decide who explored the solar system, and who colonized and exploited any new resources discovered out there. *I'll infinitely be better than Napoleon.*

Alvarez leaned forward and asked, "Sir?"

"Let me take care of the senator," said Wilmot.

"If you'd give me—"

"Listen to the director," said Wilmot. "Don't give him reason to doubt you. I'll take care of the senator in my own way. You know there's more than one way to skin a cat."

The agent nodded and walked away. Alvarez was straightforward, a man of action, and yet intelligent enough to understand the intricacies of politics. Wilmot decided to build a future for this Alvarez. He needed more men like him, in key government positions.

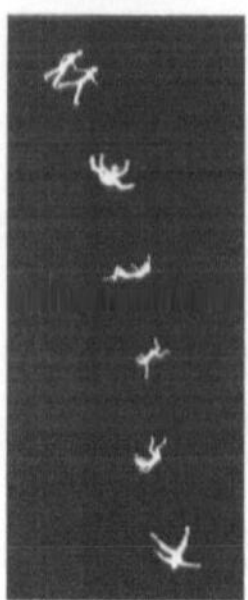

ISA

The NSA agents hadn't tied her wrists, leaving Isa a window to try and escape. Unfortunately, she was surrounded by trained agents with big guns, who were eager and authorized to inflict pain. Or death. She couldn't risk her life, not when it meant risking the baby. So, she cooperated, following their orders.

Blake was alive. He'd found a way to escape their shackles. And he'd seen her. Heard her call his name. If she kept her eyes and ears open, watching for a chance, she could help Blake when the time came.

They exited the elevator, and stopped briefly in front of a double wooden door. An agent pushed Isa forward through the doors into the meeting room. The opulent decorations had been overdone beyond good taste. The lurker—the man who'd been at the back of their entourage for the journey from the auction room to this meeting room—hurried into the darkest, most remote corner of the room.

William Wilmot had managed to arrive before them, taking a separate elevator. Wilmot spoke with an aristocratic-looking businessman via a large screen.

When Gabriela noticed Isa, she waved for the agent to bring the new slave right up to the screen, so that her new master could have a good look.

The agent squeezed her arm and dragged her over. Gabriela smirked, seeming over-satisfied with herself. Isa had never had the pleasure of meeting Wilmot's daughter until today. *Pleasure is the wrong word*, she thought. *What've I done to this woman, to make her hate me so much?* Considering what Isa had uncovered about Wilmot senior, she feared that the daughter was as damaged as her old man.

Wilmot turned, noticed Isa had arrived, and grinned. His face could switch so quickly, from a trustworthy, elderly man to a cold and calculating prick. Wilmot's eyes shone at Isa for a brief second, then his face turned all business when he spoke to the businessman on the screen. "Here she is," he said. "I sent you her information file, including her genetic makeup."

"Oh, she's lovely. Isn't she, doctor?" The businessman had a thick accent that Isa couldn't place. He wasn't alone.

On the screen, another man, this time dressed in a white lab coat, came into view and examined Isa, as though she was a specimen in a jar. He got bored quickly, and sarcastically mumbled, "She's a peach."

Wilmot addressed the businessman, "Do we have a deal?"

The man with the strong accent returned to the center of the screen. From behind him, the doctor said, "Definitely. How far along is she?"

"Only the second month of gestation," said Wilmot. "That's what makes her the perfect candidate. You must strike while the iron is hot."

Oh, my god, thought Isa. *Why is my pregnancy important?*

With a polite smile, the businessman said, "Good. Then it's settled. I'll transfer the money."

Wilmot nodded, and switched off the screen. He exhaled with satisfaction, and turned to stare at Isa.

She stared, bewildered, from the blank screen to Wilmot, and then to his daughter.

Wilmot took a seat at the big table and said, "Finally, a bit of a respite." He gestured to one of the agents, who poured scotch into a glass.

"On the rocks," said Gabriela.

The agent rushed to the fridge and dispensed several chunks of ice into the glass.

Isa scoffed.

Gabriela glared at her, looking as though she might slash Isa's throat in front of everyone. "Is something *funny*?"

"No." Isa shook her head. "Sorry." She couldn't believe the depths of the NSA agents' loyalty. They'd gone from puppets to pets. "I'm impressed by Mr. Wilmot's power. Finally, I know the truth. That it's been him, after all."

Wilmot's face switched into the concerned and loving "father of everyone" expression once more, as if he could change his mood as easily as changing his socks. He asked, "After all what?"

"My story was right about you. Now you're using me to get another serving of revenge."

"Revenge?" Wilmot smirked. "Why would a lion take revenge on the hyena that stole his meal?"

Slipping into her journalist skin, she demanded, "Why me, then?"

With a sad face, Wilmot said, "You really don't know, do you? That's very sad." He sipped at the scotch and smacked his lips. "You're a little late to the revelation, my dear."

"I'm not your dear."

"Let me explain what's happened." Another sip.

To Isa, the sound of the ice rattling sounded louder than thunder.

Wilmot tented his chubby fingers in front of his face. "I wanted to sell you in front of your husband. Unfortunately, he declined my invitation."

"Sounds like my Blake." Isa didn't know what else to say, but she wanted to stall, giving Blake time to find her again.

"My pa used to say, 'Nothing hurts like the truth.' Your husband cost me a treaty with the Russians. We're talking billions in annual revenue."

Isa opened her mouth to reply. Faster than she could've imagined the large man could move, Wilmot jumped to his feet and grabbed her by her throat.

"Don't *ever* interrupt me. You're a servitude subject. Speak only when I allow it."

Bright sparks clouded Isa's vision as she struggled to

breathe. Against his firm hand, she managed a weak nod.

Gabriela walked over to stand next to her father, grinning. "Can I have a turn, Pa? That looks like fun."

Wilmot released Isa. She fell to her knees, coughing and gasping. Wilmot waved his daughter away, and said, "Perhaps later, darling. It's rude to play with someone else's toy."

Gabriela made a show of stomping her foot, playing the child in her father's game.

"In any case," said the old man, "I will take my pound of flesh from you. More specifically, from your fetus. The embryo will be injected with new DNA. Your child will belong to science, since the child of a slave is the property of its owner. Welcome to our brave new world."

Against her better judgment Isa shouted, "Never!"

Wilmot turned to Gabriela, laughing. "She's rather slow."

Gabriela mimicked the doctor from the screen, and said, "But she's lovely. Isn't she?"

"Don't worry," said Wilmot. "If the experiment fails on the first fetus, they'll simply repeat it. They'll impregnate you with as many babies as it takes, until they get the results they require."

Isa collapsed into a ball, unable to process their words. *Impregnate?* Would they rape her? Inseminate her? Did it matter?

Wilmot downed the remainder of his scotch.

Gabriela watched Isa closely, savoring her misery. As if to fuel Isa's worst fear, she said, "It takes two to tango, Mrs. Frye."

As Isa struggled to stand, she noticed the mystery man leaving the conference room through the service door. *Hurry, Blake!* She sent the thought into the ether, hoping he would hear her plea.

Simon left the meeting room. He waited in the back hallway to be certain no one would follow, and then allowed his emotions to spill out. He felt like throwing up, and gulped air to try to stop himself.

I should've helped her, he told himself. Had he become as

uncaring as his fuck-buddy, Gabriela? *Isa's always been good to me.* Somewhere in the facility, his brother would find a way here. To rescue his beautiful wife. *I should've helped him, too.*

Blake will never get past Wilmot's security army. Or the NSA traitors. Isa's doomed.

He spat on the floor and activated his cell phone, but with his fingers ready to dial, he paused, trembling and uncertain. Then he felt something cold and round on his nape. He raised his hands, and said, "I have a fucking ID pass, asshole." He turned slowly, expecting to see one of the Wilmot security goons, and froze. The cop, dressed in the body armor of a SWAT member, patted down Simon for weapons. A team of four other masked cops controlled the service entrance corridors. As the cop pulled a zip tie out to cuff Simon, he whispered, "I'm undercover."

The cop hesitated. One of his teammates signaled for Simon to produce credentials.

Simon activated his holo-display and opened his reporter's identification. He pointed to the barcode at the bottom and whispered, "Scan it. It'll confirm I'm working with the CIA."

Another SWAT member approached, whispered, "Stand down," to the cop with the zip tie, and scanned Simon's barcode. After a few seconds, he grunted his approval, and whispered in Simon's ear, "How many are inside?"

"Four NSA agents, William Wilmot, his daughter Gabriela, and a female prisoner."

"We didn't bring NSA."

"These NSA agents are compromised. They work for Wilmot."

The team leader nodded, and signaled to his men to be ready to charge the meeting room. Realizing their operation would compromise his greater objective, Simon moved to block the SWAT team, and demanded, "Wait. You need to give me a minute."

The team leader said, "Step aside. Now."

Simon shook his head. "My mission is *vital*. I need to escape, with Wilmot's daughter in tow. It's the only way to catch the ringleader. Wilmot isn't the biggest fish in the underground slave trade."

The leader raised his hand to object.

"Look, this camp is only the tip of the iceberg. If you don't believe me, send a message to my CIA contact. He'll confirm my mission. I need to help Gabriela Wilmot escape. And I need her to think I did it on my own. You can't just let me go. She needs to believe I'm still working for them."

The team leader gave a quick nod, and said, "I'll give you three minutes to get her out. Not a second longer."

Before Simon could agree to the deal, the building's alarm sounded.

The team leader spoke softly into his comm, shook his head at his team, and said, "It's not ours."

Simon said, "Got it. Three minutes," and then he slipped back into the conference room. He needed to be sure that Isa didn't see his face, so he returned to his seat in the corner, acting as if he'd only left to relieve himself.

Seated in his presidential chair at the large table, Wilmot activated his display.

Alvarez approached him and said, "I need an update."

Breckenwell appeared on Wilmot's display, standing in front of the main bank of security feeds in his command center, looking frazzled. "The camp's under attack, sir."

Alvarez snapped, "Look alive, agents."

Wilmot pounded his fist on the desk and demanded, "Give me answers, Chief."

"Sir," said Breckenwell, "SWAT teams breached the gates. They're inside the Science Research Facility and the servitude camp.

"Countermeasures?"

"At this point, evacuation's our only option."

Wilmot glared at his security chief. "Unacceptable. You have two minutes to devise a plan." He switched off the display.

Alvarez exhaled and stated matter-of-factly, "I agree with Breckenwell. We should leave."

Simon checked his holo display—two more minutes. Time to

make his move, but he needed to get Gabriela alone.

Wilmot's anger boiled over. "This is my property. They have no right—"

"Save your indignation for later," said Alvarez. "We need to *evacuate*." The agent didn't seem intimidated by Wilmot's anger.

"No." Wilmot pounded his fist on the table. "I won't leave."

"We will," said Alvarez. "My agents can't be seen helping you." He nodded to his men, and walked toward an exit. One of the agents dragged Isa after him.

Wilmot insisted, "The slave stays with me."

Gabriela bit her lip, glancing back and forth between her father and Agent Alvarez.

Alvarez shook his head. "Mrs. Frye could blow the whistle on the NSA's involvement."

"As can any of the servitude subjects here. That's why I cannot allow the authorities to win. She stays."

"No fucking way." Alvarez drew his gun and pressed the barrel against Isa's temple.

Rushing the agent from behind, Simon smashed a large vase down on Alvarez's arm. The gun fell to the floor, and Alvarez spun around in shock. The three other agents aimed their weapons at Simon.

"Son," said Alvarez, "that's a federal offense. We're talking *life* in prison."

"Nope," said Simon. "I'm negotiating with Wilmot's *man* in Wilmot's *office*. There's no federal jurisdiction for puppets."

Gabriela mumbled, "Simon?" For the first time since he'd instigated this undercover affair, the woman looked lost.

He smiled at her, hoping to convince her to trust him for just a little longer. "Your father has one plan. His man of action has another. And it seems to me that Agent Alvarez has stopped taking orders from your organization. Cut him loose."

Gabriela smiled and nodded to her father. "Simon's right."

Wilmot asked, "Do we have your loyalty, Agent Alvarez?"

"Always, sir."

A loud slam from behind Wilmot's chair caught everyone's attention.

"The bitch escaped!" Alvarez snapped.

"Go after her, goddamn it!" Wilmot shouted, his face bright red.

Alvarez and his agents ran through the door after Isa.

Gabriela moved in the same direction, but Simon grabbed her elbow and whispered, "Come with me."

"They're heading for the helipad."

"They won't get away." He stared urgently into her eyes. "Breckenwell's right. We need to evacuate. Think about it. The SWAT's bound to have already secured the helipad. Come with me. I'll get you out."

Gabriela stared at him for a brief second, then she nodded. Simon led her toward the service door.

Back to his calm self, Wilmot said, "Get her to safety, Simon."

"You can count on me, sir."

Gabriela turned toward her father, smiled, and blew him a kiss.

That was too close, thought Simon as he rushed Gabriela through the service door. *Blake and Isa have a fighting chance.*

Simon and Gabriela dashed through corridors. He activated his holo-display and checked the facility map. A red light marked the nearest exit to the car park. Simon always planned for the fasted way out of any emergency. Keeping Gabriela in front of him, he pushed her through a door into the next corridor, then risked a quick look behind them.

Several cops dressed in armor followed at a strategic distance, with their rifles aimed.

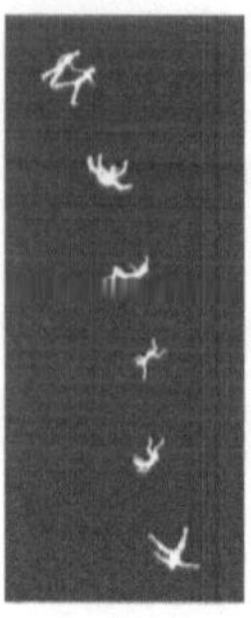

NIGEL

Nigel hid the cop's body in the bushes, covering her with leaves. Then he paused to listen carefully for any more intruders.

Only the rustling of leaves in the wind.

His jaw clenched. *Think*, he told himself. *Wilmot's finished. I need to find another player. Someone higher up the servitude chain.* But he'd need a gift to ingratiate himself.

He recalled a trail that led toward the slave camp, and risked a dash along the road to reach it. The cops weren't using much stealth beyond the gates. Every few minutes, the pop-pop of shots rang out. Not the huge gun battle Nigel had expected from Wilmot's security force. Both sides were pathetic.

He finally reached the edge of the woods, a few yards from the compound's fence. All the lights had been tripped, making the entire area as bright as noon on a cloudless day.

He watched for activity while he memorized details, including the density of the forest, his proximity to exit points, and defensive strategies. From his hiding place, he could infiltrate the compound, and had a direct trail back to his car, hidden in the same woods half a mile down the road.

He circled back to the road, set down his rucksack, and readied himself.

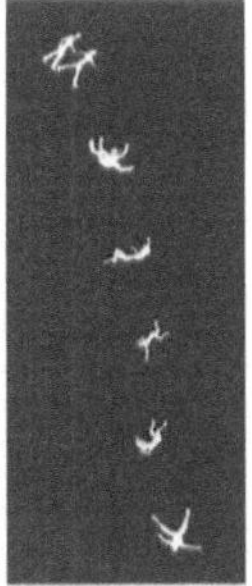

TWO MONTHS EARLIER

It was a warm spring evening, already dark. This far away from the city, the sky displayed so many more stars. Leaning against his car, Neil stretched, then checked his wristband. *It's time.* He heard a vehicle approaching, and watched a car turn the corner and park near him.

Norman stepped out of the driver's side, looking a bit confused. When he spotted Neil, he smiled, walked over, and said, "So, what's the big secret, Detective?"

"I'll take you to it."

"Can't I follow you?"

"Trust me, Senator." Neil stuffed his hands in his pockets. "I'm about to gift you a once in a lifetime opportunity."

Neil returned to the driver's seat and waited for Norman to join him in his car.

"I dug deeper than Isa asked me to," Neil said, "and I found some extraordinary things. There's enough here for you to stop the Republicans."

Norman huffed, confused. "From doing what, exactly?"

"Kick them out of office. It's been—what?—ten, twenty years since they took over every branch of government."

"Don't remind me." The senator stared at the road ahead. "History will refer to their dominance as the counterrevolution."

"I thought we'd just call them assholes."

Norman laughed. "I'm talking textbooks, not social media." He sat up straight, and began to speak in a smooth professor's voice, as though he were addressing a lecture hall full of university students. "After the Second World War, the democratic revolution began in the Western World. Its last victory was the overthrow of the Communist regimes in Eastern Europe. Fast forward a few decades, to the uprisings known as the Arab Spring. That was the beginning of the counterrevolution. Conservative forces moved against all the democratic advances and freedoms, focusing the battle against the globalization phenomenon. In a very short time, they managed to overthrow all democratic forces and reinstate a sort of a new medievalism. Republicans live for that shit."

"Right, professor." Neil chuckled.

Norman looked away, as if lost in history as it unfolded. The senator had become a fossil of sorts, from an era soon to pass out of memory. "My party," he said, "have become the enemy, like the way the aristocracy were persecuted after the industrial era. Easily overthrown and forgotten."

"This is going to sound offensive," said Neil, "but aren't you kind of behaving like an aristocrat right now? With your tirade—"

"It's a *reminder*."

"All I'm saying is, if you keep acting like you're smarter than everyone, then someone might try to teach you a lesson, to put you in your place."

Neil pulled the car to the side of the road, and he and Norman stepped out in front of a tall metal gate. Beyond the bars, the country road led into a field. In the middle of the field there was a hangar, lit just enough that they could make out the edges. Neil pointed at it. "Do you see that building down there?"

"Sure," said Norman.

Leaning against his car, Neil lit a cigarette, took a long drag, and blew the smoke high over his head. "That, Senator, is the slave camp of the American servitude underground movement. The facility that everyone's been hunting."

Norman gaped at Neil. Then he stared at the hangar. "Doesn't look like much, does it?"

"Did I deliver, or what?" said Neil. "D'ya want a smoke?"

"No thanks." Norman raised his hands to touch the gate, then dropped his hands to his sides. "Why bring me? You're a detective. Why not call in the troops to shut it down?"

"He's following my orders." The man's voice came from the darkness beyond Neil's car.

William Wilmot leaned into Neil's car and flipped on the headlights, forcing Norman to shield his eyes. As the old man stepped in front of the headlights, another man appeared, from the other side of the road.

"Martin Breckenwell," said Neil, by way of introduction. As more men stepped out of the woods, he added, "And four of his security force."

The senator glared at Neil, looking both angry and disappointed. Then he turned to the old man and said, "I should've smelled your finger in this pie, Wilmot."

"I'm more of a cake man," said Wilmot. He nodded to Breckenwell, who waved his men into position.

"Grab him," said Breckenwell. Two of them advanced and seized Norman's wrists.

"You won't get away with this, Wilmot! I'm a *senator*."

"I'll take my chances. Since you're a senator, as you're so eager to remind me, I wonder what I should do with you. The open market isn't likely to risk bidding for you." The old man gazed at Norman from head to toe. "You don't look as though you've done any manual labor for a decade or more."

"My disappearance will be headline news. They'll expose all of you." Norman tried to pull free of the guards, but they were too strong.

"Wait," said Wilmot. "I have a brilliant idea." He tapped a finger against his lip, and said, "I'll donate you to science. My researchers are always in need of additional subjects for their experiments."

The guards dragged away the struggling senator, ignoring his shouts and demands to be released.

Neil watched, smoking his cigarette.

Wilmot stepped closer to him and said, "Thank you, Detective. You're smoother than I expected."

Neil nodded and smiled.

"I have another mission for you, Detective."

"I'm listening." He dragged on the cigarette, making the tip glow a bright orange.

Wilmot waved Breckenwell over. The security chief handed Neil a folder, and waited while he studied the contents.

Confused, Neil stared at Wilmot. "What's this?"

"Your new identity," said the old man. "And the specifications of your new assignment."

"Nigel Blakesley? In London? The NYPD doesn't take too kindly to cops not showing up for work."

"You'll be dead for them. Or disappeared." Wilmot smiled. "Like the good senator."

Breckenwell said, "My guys will take you to a private airport. We'll ditch your car somewhere obvious. You'll be another MIA linked to Frye and his bitch wife."

Neil looked from Breckenwell to Wilmot and back. "Why not use someone local? I'm an American. I'll stick out."

"Your detective position is compromised," Wilmot explained. "Time to move on."

Neil shook his head. "My wife hates Europe."

"Your widow won't be joining you," Breckenwell sneered.

"Be patient." Wilmot spoke softly. "Our need to remain underground won't last for more than a year. Once we legitimately seize power, you'll return to a position in my top ranks. You and your wife will have a tearful reunion. She'll welcome the money, and the prestige, if what you've said is true about her."

Neil stared at the new passport, his photo and his new name. Nigel Blakesley didn't sound very American. But he didn't do accents.

Wilmot placed a hand on his shoulder and added, "First, you must deliver on this mission. Soon after, you will reap what you sow."

"You can count on me," said Neil. "I won't let you down."

"Study your assignment details on the plane," said Wilmot. "Report directly to Mr. Breckenwell. He'll give you any additional orders as your mission unfolds."

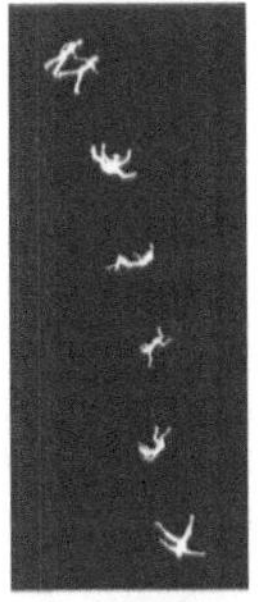

BLAKE

Blake raced out of the building, and found the metal ladder that led to the low rooftop for the helipad, about six stories above ground level. Even though no security staff stopped him during the climb, he knew they had to be watching him on surveillance cameras. He wondered whether he'd hear them coming from below, or find a team waiting for him at the top. Out of options, speed and decisiveness had become his only allies.

He missed his partner, Neil. As a cop, he'd spent most of his career knowing someone had his back. During his partnership with Neil, they'd chased a few cars, had fist-fights with a few perps after foot pursuits, and even experienced three shootouts. Neil had always been the one to jump headfirst into the fray. Blake had always paused to calculate the risks and outcomes. He generally didn't rush until he had a solid plan. And a backup one. He tried not to think about how scary it felt to dash without thinking. Thoughts only slowed him down. Isa didn't have time to wait for him to see the next possibility.

He stopped to catch his breath and look down. A SWAT team was making its way across the lawn, closing in on the slave camp. Blake hoped they'd arrive in time, hope being the magic word.

Another alarm filled the open area with shrill bleating. Other alarms sounded from the adjacent buildings.

Time for all-out war, he thought. *SWAT versus security. Wilmot versus NYPD. NSA versus who? The FBI?*

He heard the helicopter rotor, and climbed faster, two rungs at a time. *I won't let that chopper take off.*

As he climbed over the lip and onto the wide helipad, the pilot was strapping herself into her seat. No other passengers were visible inside. Crouching, Blake dashed across the landing pad. When he reached the glass door, he shouted, "Hey!"

The pilot wore a helmet with built-in ear protectors. She shook her head in a friendly way, as if to say, "Can't hear you."

I'm not wearing slave-orange, thought Blake. No reason to worry about me. Blake reached up, opened the glass door, and smiled as he drew his weapon. "Shut it down. Now!"

The pilot's expression changed to one of surprise more than fear. She shrugged, implying she still couldn't hear him.

Blake drew his finger across his throat.

She flipped a few switches and the blades' rotation slowed. Then the pilot removed her helmet and raised her hands in the air.

"Get out!" Blake took a few steps back to give her room to step down. After a quick scan, he couldn't see anything he could use to secure the pilot to the roof. So as soon as she reached the ground, he clocked her over the head with the butt of his weapon.

Needing her ID to get past the door's lock, he dragged the woman toward his objective. With a grunt, he lifted the pilot up and opened one of her eyes to be scanned by the pad. Then he pressed the pilot's hand on the palm-pad. The door clicked open.

Using the pilot's body to prop the door open, Blake stepped inside and listened carefully, both up and down the stairwell. He heard a door opening one floor up. The stairwell offered no cover, and he needed the element of surprise.

Out of options again, he dragged the pilot free of the doorway, and allowed the door to close, trapping the two of them on the roof.

Isa ran as fast as she could. Alvarez and his agents climbed down after her, faster. When she reached the exit door, she found it locked. From outside she could hear helicopter blades, but they seemed to be slowing down, not speeding up.

She turned just as Alvarez caught up to her. He wrapped his arms tight around her shoulders, and motioned for his agents to move ahead of him and exit through the door. The agent on point unlocked the door and opened it wide.

The instant the suited man stepped through the door, Blake took aim and fired two shots. *Cold and calculated.* The man dropped, blood dripping from his leg and arm. His buddies stopped in confusion. With their weapons drawn, they checked on their buddy.

Blake stepped closer, and with precision, he shot each of them. *First one in the kneecap. Second in the shoulder. Third, ankle and thigh.* The agents fell and their weapons scattered.

Alvarez pressed his gun to Isa's temple and demanded, "Drop it, Frye!"

Blake shot the wall next to Alvarez's head, sending concrete splinters flying, nicking Alvarez's ear.

"Don't fuck with me!" snapped the agent. "I'll kill her, I swear!"

Blake shot Alvarez's left thigh. The agent toppled back onto the ascending stairs, dragging Isa with him. Blake rushed closer, but Alvarez shot several times in Blake's direction.

Inches from one of the other agents, Blake watched the man reach for his gun. He shot the man in his palm, and the man shrieked.

Alvarez staggered to his feet, brutally grabbed Isa by the hair, and retreated up the stairs. Isa struggled to free herself, stepping on his toes and elbowing him to little effect. Alvarez twisted and punched her in her kidneys from behind. She groaned, and stopped fighting back.

Blake shot again above their heads, spraying more concrete chips at Alvarez's head. The agent groaned and climbed up the last few steps to another door. Using his badge, he unlocked the door and shoved Isa through ahead of him.

Blake sprinted up the stairs, stopped on the third step before the landing, and shot the lock three times. *I'm almost out of ammo,* he thought. Running forward, he kicked the door open, dropped, and rolled through the opening as shots nicked the wall above his head.

He scanned with his weapon aimed. Alvarez had his gun trained at Blake's head. Wilmot held Isa to the agent's left. Without hesitation, Blake emptied his clip into Alvarez. The agent slumped as three red flowers blossomed on his white shirt.

Blake took in the room.

With Isa in his arms, William Wilmot retreated, grabbed a letter opener from the table, and pressed the blade against her throat.

Above the table, an active holo-vid showed Wilmot's security office. The man in the center of a bank of surveillance feeds said, "Mr. Wilmot, you're out of time. Follow the NSA bastards to the chopper, and get the fuck gone."

With his eyes fixed on Blake, Wilmot asked, "Breckenwell, how many people do we still have?" Where his letter opener pressed against Isa, a trickle of blood painted her neck. She bit her lip, but didn't struggle.

Breckenwell answered, "Too few."

"Bring them to me. We'll make our stand here. Plan our strategy to retake my camp."

"You're delusional. There's not going to be a fucking stand."

"Bring. The. Men. Here." Wilmot's face turned crimson with fury.

"Enjoy your one-man stand. We're out of here."

Wilmot continued to watch the holo-vid, even after Breckenwell moved beyond the feed's range.

They're abandoning you, thought Blake. *Like rats off a sinking ship.*

Isa stared at Blake, her face looking more angry than afraid.

Wilmot shouted, "Drop your weapon!"

"Don't do it, Blake." Isa's voice was surreally cool.

"Drop it, or I swear to God I will open her throat!"

"Shoot the bastard," screamed Isa. "Kill him, Blake!"

Wilmot slid the blade, increasing the size of her wound.

It's not critical yet, thought Blake. *And he doesn't know I'm out of ammo.* Blake bent down and placed his gun on the carpeted floor. Both Wilmot and Isa watched his every move. Blake looked around the room, noticing papers that had been scattered below the table. He picked up the nearest sheet of paper and placed it on the table. Reaching down for another one, he retrieved a stack of pages stapled together, and arranged them perfectly on top of the first page, all corners meeting.

"Oh, Blake. No…" Isa began to sob.

"What's he doing?" Wilmot's hand changed position, not pressing as firmly against her throat.

"Honey, no. Blake, listen to my voice. Now is *not* the time. Please, honey." The tears were streaming down her face now. Blake watched her press one hand on her belly.

On the baby, thought Blake. He collected several more sheets of paper, straightened them, tapped them against the table, and added them to the perfect pile.

Wilmot's hands dropped to his sides, the letter opener no longer pressed to her throat. "What's he doing?"

"It's a compulsion," Isa managed between sobs. "In times of stress…" She choked, coughed, and tried to finish. "…he arranges things. He can't stop."

Wilmot released Isa and she collapsed to the floor, one hand pressed to her neck and the other around her waist. "Please, HoneyB. Come back to me."

Blake picked up a gold pen holder, surveyed the table, and placed it on the dust mark where it belonged.

"Are you fucking kidding me?" Wilmot walked around the table toward Blake, holding the letter opener in front of him. "He's a goddamned mental case?" In a cold, angry voice, he said, "Good things come in small packages. When I'm finished with you, you'll wish you were never born!"

As Blake leaned below the table to pick up the gold pen with the steel tip, Wilmot rushed him and backhanded him across the face with the letter opener.

Isa rose to her hands and knees, feeling around for something to use as a weapon.

As Wilmot raised his left hand to slap Blake again, the cop snatched the pen and rammed it through Wilmot's palm.

Wilmot howled in pain.

Blake yanked the letter opener from Wilmot's other hand, grabbed the old man's wrist, pressed his palm against the tabletop, and thrust the blade so hard it stuck straight through Wilmot's flesh and deep into the wood. Wilmot screamed in pain and terror, struggling to pull the knife free, using the left hand with the pen still sticking out of it.

Blake grabbed the pen and tugged it free. Wilmot was crying and moaning, unable to contain his misery. Grabbing the hand with the pen-hole, Blake forced Wilmot's palm onto the table next to the impaled hand, and thrust the pen through both hand and table.

Isa stood and stared at Blake with a mixture of relief and fear. "My Blake," she mumbled, her voice trembling.

Blake ran over, pulled her close, and hugged her tightly. As they stood there, hugging and weeping, he kept repeating, "I've got you. I've got you."

He leaned back to get a better look at her. As gently as he could manage, fighting back the adrenaline racing through his body, he touched her face, and then stroked her hair.

"We need to hurry," he said.

"Which way?" she asked.

From beyond one of the doors, Blake heard one clank, and then another. A muffled voice yelled, "Clear."

"Shit. Get down." He pulled her behind the oversized table. "They're blowing the—"

The explosion forced his breath from his lungs. The door flew into the room like a huge metal shield. It hit Wilmot with such force that his body smashed into the wall, leaving pieces of his hands still stuck to the table.

Men in full tactical gear swarmed inside, yelling, "Freeze! Drop your weapons."

Blake stayed under the table, covering Isa's body with his own.

One of the men pulled Blake off the floor and screamed, "William Wilmot! You're under arrest!"

Blake raised his hands in the air and said, "I'm not Wilmot!"

The tactical unit poured into the room, all rifles aimed at Blake and Isa. The one who seemed in charge said to Blake, "Prove it."

"My ID badge is stored on my wristband. I'm Detective Blake Frye, with NYPD." He pointed at his wristband and asked, "May I?"

"Slowly."

Blake activated his holo-display and showed his badge. The team leader examined the details, then ordered, "Stand down. He checks out."

Blake hurried to help Isa to her feet. "This is my wife, Isabella Frye. She was kidnapped by William Wilmot, with the assistance of several rogue NSA agents under his control."

Isa straightened, and said, "They sold me as a slave."

The team leader asked, "Where's Wilmot?"

Isa pointed to the blown door, but instead of speaking, she choked out a giggle. A second grunt-giggle. Then she began to laugh hysterically, seemingly unable to stop.

Blake was drawn into the contagious laughter. Through it, he managed to say, "The asshole got squished behind that door." Pointing to the hand pieces, he added, "and that's the rest of him, here." He stared at the gold pen, still stuck into the table, and choking back his own hysterics, he said, "Apparently, the pen is mightier than the door."

Two members of the tactical team pulled the door aside. Wilmot's deformed body dropped to the floor, his blood staining the carpet in a growing wave of red.

The team leader asked, "Are there any other hostiles?"

Blake managed to catch his breath and stop laughing. He pointed at Alvarez, and said, "That dead man is Agent Alvarez from the NSA, a traitor and Wilmot's puppet. There's a hidden door in that wall that leads to a stairwell that'll take you to the helipad. I left three wounded NSA agents on the stairs, all of them Alvarez's minions and traitors to their organization. I also subdued the chopper pilot. She's outside."

"Uh, okay." The team leader waved his team to investigate the stairwell and the helipad. Then he shouldered his rifle, looking pleased, and added, "Anything else we should know?"

Using his detective's voice, Blake said, "If you go through the main doors, second corridor from here, you'll find two Wilmot security staff. One's probably dead, the other one is cuffed, and has a gunshot wound."

"Are you finished?"

"After that corridor," said Blake, "you'll reach the reception area. Multiple wounded there."

"I understand," said the team leader. "If they'd taken my wife, none of them would still be breathing."

"Take me in, question me, or arrest me," said Blake. "Do your jobs. But please, safely escort my wife to a hospital. She's pregnant and she's been through a lot." He nodded at her arm, looking raw and weeping, and kissed her cheek.

"Take her yourself," said the team leader. "I'll vouch for you with chain of command."

"Thank you." Isa sounded shaky. The tears started again, but this time they sounded like tears of joy.

"My pleasure, ma'am. I'm sorry about your ordeal. Follow my man. He'll escort you out of here."

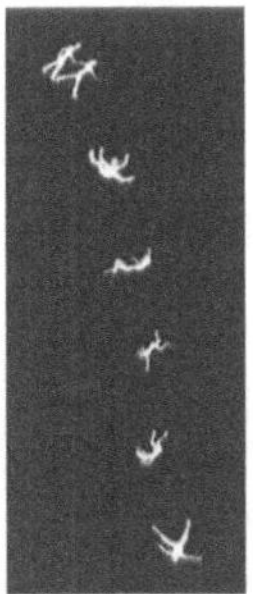

TWO MONTHS EARLIER

Blake knocked on Moore's door, and the captain wave him in. Ducking his head through the open door, Blake asked, "Have you got a minute to grab a coffee with me, Captain?"

Moore stared at him for several seconds. Just as Blake expected a rejection, Moore stood, grabbed his blazer from the back of his chair, and followed Blake out of the precinct. They crossed the street to the Greek sweet shop, a precinct favorite for the last few years. Blake ordered two sweet Greek coffees and loukoumades. When the order was ready, the two cops strolled to the nearby park and settled onto one of the benches. Sweet coffee—Greek style—and honey-sweetened pastries were a sin Blake and Moore shared. The shop had appeared like a refugee, a lonely Greek island in a sea of Chinese grocers and dim sum spots. Neither Blake nor his captain had had a clue what made a coffee "Greek" until one fated afternoon when their neighborhood coffee shop had been closed due to a health code violation, and the only available coffee had been at the new Greek shop. After that, Greek coffee became their go-to afternoon pick-me-up. Blake had even purchased a tiny brass pot, and he and Isa had learned to prepare a similar treat at home.

The park was small, with only a couple of benches, but it was enough for Blake to eat his loukoumades, and spill his secrets to the captain without being overheard.

"We need to talk, sir. I have some ideas—"

"Before you start, I have to tell you something confidential."

Blake looked at Moore in surprise, and popped another loukoumades ball into his mouth. He bit down, and the honey felt ridiculously cool and sweet as it squirted onto his tongue. "I can keep a secret."

"Senator Chadwick is missing."

"The pattern continues," said Blake. The previous night, he and Moore had discussed Neil's disappearance. "They're getting bold, taking a senator." *And Isa and Corbin are the only ones left*, he thought.

"Someone should be shadowing your wife. Especially after the incident at the museum."

Blake let out a long sigh. *Either Corbin's the traitor, or "they" got everyone. Except for Isa.* "I brought you here to tell you my plan," said Blake.

"Shoot." Moore looked grim.

"I want to take down Wilmot, before he gets to my wife."

"I agree."

"Are you serious?"

Moore smiled. "I spoke to one of my guys in the FBI. He has some inside information, if you're willing to enlist in their war."

"They're at war with William Wilmot?"

"Not exactly. They're battling illegal slavery in America."

"Captain…" Blake shook his head, disappointed.

"Listen to me, Frye. And think about it. I can't believe I'm saying that to you, because you always think too much."

Blake stared at him. "I'm listening."

"Isa investigated the underground slavery industry." Moore spoke slowly, as if explaining the details to a child. "In the course of her research, she discovered that Wilmot is *the*—or *one of the*—main players. That's why the story focused on him."

Blake watched the domino pieces fall into place in his mind. "If I join the fight against American underground slavery, I'll inevitably confront Wilmot."

"Exactly."

"My problem though, Captain, is time."

"Let me buy you some time."

"In one month, they took Taylor, Sam, Chadwick, and Neil.

Isa won't be safe for long."

"I could arrange FBI protection. That could buy some time."

"Wouldn't it be easier to assign a couple of uniforms from the precinct?"

"Maybe not, if you factor in the attorney general's witch hunt."

"If the FBI can protect my Isa, then I'm in."

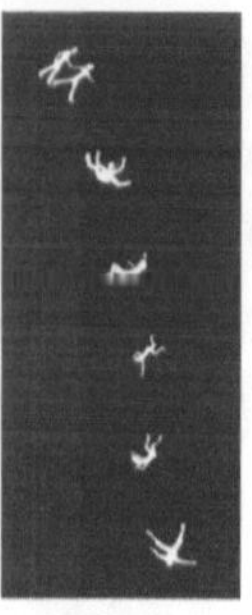

BLAKE

Several armored SWAT vehicles were parked in front of the slave camp. Cops in uniform and some in tactical gear were rounding up civilians as they streamed out of the building. Behind the armored vehicles, several Red Cross trucks and ambulances stood at the ready to provide medical assistance.

Adrenaline continued to course through Blake's bloodstream, keeping him in a heightened state, ready for action. Part of him wanted to hug Isa forever, to ensure she would never be in danger again. But deep down, he feared the worst was not yet over.

The cop from the tactical team led Blake and Isa to the ambulances. A paramedic approached them and led the two Fryes to his rig.

"I'm fine," said Blake. "Focus on my wife. She's pregnant."

The cop tapped Blake on the shoulder, pointed to the trailer next to the ambulance, and said, "My boss needs to debrief you, sir."

While the EMS guy checked Isa's vitals, Blake kissed her forehead. He tried to smile, but couldn't manage. "I'll be right here, love."

Isa nodded and smiled.

Please, thought Blake, *let her recover from this ordeal.* He wondered if she could ever forgive him for everything he'd put her through. His thoughts remained on his wife as he followed the cop into the trailer.

The trailer had been set up as a command station. Two police detectives, a senior supervisor from the SWAT unit, and three civilians in suits were busy entering data into their wristbands, speaking into their cells, or watching the live feeds from officers' body cams.

One of the civilians turned, noticed Blake, and hurried over with his hand outstretched.

Blake froze. The approaching civilian was Samuel Brit, the Englishman. Blake remembered the conversation in that hotel lobby with the British rich guy, less than two days ago, and yet it felt like a lifetime.

Everyone turned to face Blake, remaining silent. They were all American law enforcement, except for Brit. Why was the British slaver involved? Had every branch of Blake's government been compromised?

Speaking with a southern American accent, with no sign of his British lilt, Brit said, "I think we need a proper introduction, Detective Frye."

Normally Blake could place the subtle origin of an American accent without effort, but right now, he was rushing to analyze his options, trying desperately to find a way out of this madness.

Brit kept his hand out, waiting for Blake to shake it. When he refused, Brit grinned. "Okay, then. My name is Samuel Pierce. I'm a CIA operative, assigned to take down William Wilmot. I've been keeping a careful watch on you."

Another civilian approached Blake. "Detective Frye, my name is Luciana Cortez. I'm your FBI handler. I heard about Captain Moore. I'm sorry for your loss."

Without warning, Blake unleashed his rage against Brit—Pierce, or whatever the fuck his real name might be. He sucker-punched the asshole, right across the jaw. Pure instinct. No forethought.

Startled, Luciana Cortez tried to catch Pierce before he fell.

Blake punched the FBI handler, too. Cortez flew across the trailer and Pierce crashed into stack of communication units, scattering them in every direction. The cops all drew their weapons on Blake.

From the floor, Pierce said, "Stand down. All of you. From Detective Frye's perspective, we had that coming." He carefully felt the edges of his swelling chin, laughed, then winced in pain.

The mood lightened for everyone except Blake. *I can't let this go*, he thought. For the first time in his life, instead of abandoning his thoughts and pushing himself to act, he was struggling to rein in his instincts, and slow down enough to process his thoughts.

One of the detectives grinned and said, "Don't we know it."

Don't we know what? Blake tried to think back, and realized that they meant they deserved to be punished. *Punched*, he corrected himself. The adrenaline must've been leaving his system, because his mind began to slow down. To focus. He continued to see red, but here and there patches of white shone through.

Blake stepped closer to Pierce and said, "What happened to your British accent?"

"I'm sorry, Frye. Our orders were to keep you in the dark."

"I insisted that you to keep my wife out of trouble. You failed."

"I know. And I'm truly sorry for what she's been through."

The answer turned up Blake's rage. He took some deep breaths and clenched his fists. The CIA bastard was one level of ugliness, but the FBI shit-pile was something else. He pointed at Cortez. "And *you*, Agent Cortez. You're responsible for Captain Moore's murder. He trusted you."

"We had no intel on the NSA's involvement. If we'd known, we would've acted differently. You're a hero, Detective. Thank you for all you've done."

"A true hero!" Pierce took over. "From what I hear, you practically took down Wilmot Industries by yourself. You single-handedly neutralized more than fifteen hostiles. That's—"

"That proves you put your trust in the right man." One of the detectives stepped in front of Blake and extended his hand. "Detective Frye, I'm Captain Ballard. I know I can't replace Captain Moore in your heart, but trust me, I'll make every necessary effort to fill his shoes. It will be my greatest challenge."

Blake shook his new boss's hand. "Captain Ballard, the

attorney general works for Wilmot. That's probably where you should begin."

"We already have the attorney general in custody."

"Fantastic," said Blake. "Now, Captain, I need to go back to my wife."

"Of course."

Pierce held the trailer's door open, then followed Blake outside. "Detective, I want to personally apologize for everything you've been through. I take full responsibility."

Blake shook his finger at Pierce, holding back his anger. Without another word, he turned and walked away.

Pierce grabbed his shoulder, stopping Blake. "I'm so, so sorry. I… we all owe you a lot…"

"You leaked the photos, and all my information to Wilmot. You set me up!"

"If we'd had another option, a better way, trust me—"

Blake caught up to his wife. She lay on a stretcher, inside an ambulance. When she caught sight of her husband, she smiled and stretched her hand to him.

"How can I trust you? You gave Wilmot the time, the leads, and the desire to kidnap my wife!"

"These are the risks involved, with undercover missions."

"My wife's a civilian. Not your undercover pawn. Walk away, right now, or I swear to God—"

Pierce nodded, raised his hands in surrender, and turned back.

A shot rang out. It sounded loud, like a small explosion. Blake startled, dropped to the ground, and scanned around for the shooter.

The SWAT teams trained their guns at every roof, toward the fences, and the trees. The silence stretched as they all waited for the second shot.

Blake looked at Isa, in the Red Cross truck. She stared at him with wide eyes, her hands covering her mouth. *She's okay,* he thought. *There's no blood. She's safe.*

From a crouch, he continued to scan the scene for the shooter.

Pierce lay on the ground, a red hole in the center of his

forehead, his eyes staring blindly at the sky, a blood pool, mixed with gray matter, spreading behind his head. Blake crawled to the CIA agent to check his pulse, but he knew what he'd find. Staying low, he rolled closer to Isa's location, making signs to the paramedics to close the doors.

The officers from the command trailer scanned the scene and then ran for shelter. Everyone seemed to come to life at that moment, screaming orders and taking cover against the sniper.

Blake scooted under one of the Red Cross truck's tires. From his hiding place, he could hear heavy boots stomping in the grass, and orders shouted to nearby personnel. Beyond the staging ground, an eerie silence spread across the facility. Blake inhaled and felt a sharp pain in his chest. Two paramedics crouched next to him, telling him something, but he was having trouble understanding their words. He looked down at his chest, and saw the blood flower spreading like an abstract painting on his shirt.

Isa crawled up next to him and squeezed his hand, her eyes filled with terror and tears.

"I'm okay," he reassured her. "I'll be fine."

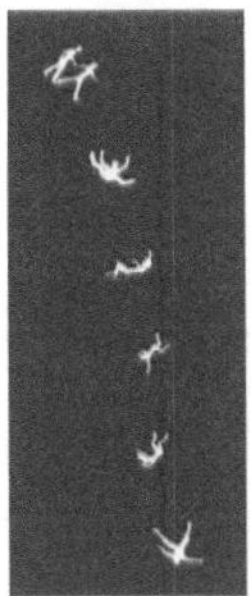

NIGEL

Nigel retraced his steps, checked over his shoulder, and nodded, satisfied. He climbed the tree, found a comfortable branch, and slowly spread out, lying chest-down, with his rifle set up. *Lucky I remembered you*, he told the weapon. *It would've been fun to take down the SWAT team, one by one, from the Business Tower.* He felt out of the loop here, so far away from the action in the camp. The SWAT guys were all probably congratulating one another on a job well done. The camp was theirs now.

Breckenwell, the tough son-of-a-bitch chief of Wilmot security, should've had his men trained and ready to stop something as predictable as a SWAT take-down. *I would've done better.*

Nigel used his scope to spy on the camp, and located the temporary command center. The guards had been deployed haphazardly, making the command zone an easy target. Obviously, the fools believed the only enemy was inside the camp. They'd even left the door open.

"Motherfucker!" he whispered when he saw Samuel Brit leave the trailer with that fucker, Frye. *I was right about him. Brit's a spy, probably CIA.*

Holding his breath, Nigel followed his target, allowing for wind and distance. He had a clear shot of the two fuckers who'd ruined his life. They seemed to be arguing.

Then it happened—the moment of perfect alignment. He aimed, exhaled, and squeezed. *Hell yeah. Two fuckers with one stone.*

He slung his rifle, dropped from the tree, and ran through

the woods to his car. As he neared his parking spot, he heard the engine of an armored SWAT vehicle rumbling out of the camp.

A few seconds later… BOOM! A big explosion.

Nigel grinned as he unlocked his car. Time to find out who William Wilmot answered to.

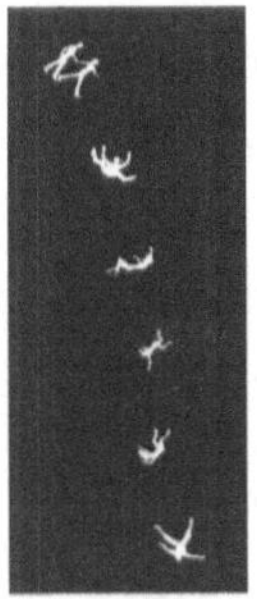

THREE WEEKS EARLIER

The man on top of Sam stank of beer and something rotting and metallic at the same time, like the sweat of someone who hadn't washed in days and worked a job involving hard physical labor. He had a beastly smirk on his face, and was grumbling continuously in German. Obviously addressing her, although he'd been told she didn't understand the language. From his mannerisms, she guessed he spoke of his prowess, and expected her to confirm. They'd all been taught to fake it. At that moment, not only did she refuse to fake it, but she was struggling to stop from losing her fucking mind. Her first two clients had demanded refunds, after she'd puked all over them.

They'd doped her up with an anti-nausea drug before her third client. *The third try's lucky*, they'd claimed. She didn't feel lucky. If she focused on averting her eyes from his sweaty face, she could finish, but...

She needed to build a wall, a safe distance between herself and the act taking place inside her body. She wondered, *How many times before I'm done for the day? Before I kill myself?*

She'd once researched material for a story on the sex trade. She'd learned that people are far more resilient than they thought they were. That anyone could survive harsh conditions indefinitely, if they focused on surviving. If any chance of rescue existed, people could endure extreme pain and prejudice. Hope, even faint hope, kept them alive.

She'd loved all her assignments as a journalist. Some she

loved unconditionally, and others had felt more like love-hate relationships at times. The uglier the truth she uncovered, the more she hated the subject. And yet, she was most proud of those horrid stories.

The sex trade story had fallen in between the extremes. The uncovered truths were not that ugly, so she disliked some of them, but the final result had been fantastic. Her team had even earned a few awards for it. Although, what good were those awards now?

Do I have any hope at all?

The client finished with a round of fierce grunts, then lay on top of her for a minute. His weight crushed her chest, and she struggled to breathe. When she felt on the brink of passing out, he rolled off, pulled on his pants, and grumbled.

On his way out, he turned to her, spoke a harsh word—probably a crude insult— and then he spat on her face. She wiped the spittle away after he left the room.

She lay still, feeling groggy and filthy, listening to his angry voice melt along the corridors. After several minutes, her co-workers entered, picked her up, and guided her to the bathroom. *They're watching me,* she thought. *To score my moves, so they can coach me to do better for the next one.*

Sam's next client was a young man with blond hair and a face so red, he was obviously terrified. For the first time, she didn't feel disgusted. She even felt a bit of pity for him. Her body began the learned motions, while her mind took her far away, to a place where she remembered freedom.

The story she'd hated researching the most had been the one on Henri Gunt, the serial killer. When the police had caught him, they gave Isa Frye special access to interview him for a story on NWN TV, in collaboration with the Discovery Channel. Sam had to verify all the information that Gunt shared with Isa during the interviews. Sam had worked at the speed of light, since Isa needed to check every word spoken, from one interview to the next. Ten interviews in all, over a two-week span. His trial had been accelerated, and they only had two weeks and two days before he'd be executed by lethal injection.

The research had given her nightmares. Sam had to check everything he'd said about how he'd killed his victims, and why each kill was slow, drawn out to maximize suffering and please him. Gunt had amassed extensive knowledge of the human body, and recorded a thousand ways to kill a person in his diaries. He'd studied both Roman and medieval torture, focusing on keeping the subjects alive for at least a month. The work had been both fascinating and gruesome. Sam couldn't sleep for months afterwards.

The young client had obviously found his courage, having dropped his bag against the wall and removed his jacket. He'd loosened his tie, and now wore a reassuring smile.

Sam returned the smile. It was the first one she'd managed since being sold into slavery. She pushed him down onto the bed, and climbed on top of him.

Eagerness and pleasure painted his features. At his age, imagination alone could result in a happy ending. So, she undid his belt and slowly pulled it free of his pants. She breathed in his musk, and bent over him. When she found his neck, she punctured his carotid artery with the buckle's needle, and jumped off the bed. He gurgled, trying to speak through his shock. Best-case, the young man had a few minutes to live. She probably had even less time before they punished her.

She made a knot with the belt, passed it over her head, and climbed onto the window sill. She opened the window, hooked the buckle into the window's locking bar, and glanced down at the street, bustling with people.

For a moment, Sam hesitated. Again, she asked, *Do I have any hope?* The answer had already come from the nightly news. All of Europe had accepted the Freedom Act. No one would ever free the slaves.

Sam smiled, and let herself fall.

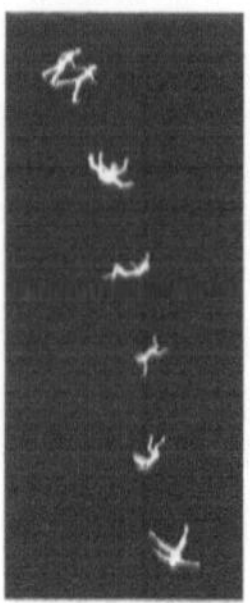

SIMON

Simon accelerated along the forest road. He checked the mirror again, to see if they were being followed. One more task, and he'd reach the home stretch. He needed to learn whether Gabriela still trusted him, and if she would still need him after their escape.

She used men, plain and simple. Even if he was to marry her—an absurd thought—she'd still use him up and throw him away once he'd finished being useful.

He relaxed a little, and flashed his most charming smile. The one that always got to her. "Where to now?"

"Time's running out. We need to report this to…" She hesitated, and looked at him.

He frowned and suggested, "To the king?"

"Don't bite off more than you can chew."

"Don't bite the hand that feeds you."

They both laughed.

"So," said Simon, "to the king, then?"

"What king?"

"Your father called him that."

Gabriela chuckled and stared out the windshield. She nodded. "Yeah, okay, to the king. Only she's more like the queen."

Simon felt a heavy burden lifting. *Almost done,* he thought. *Everything was worth it.*

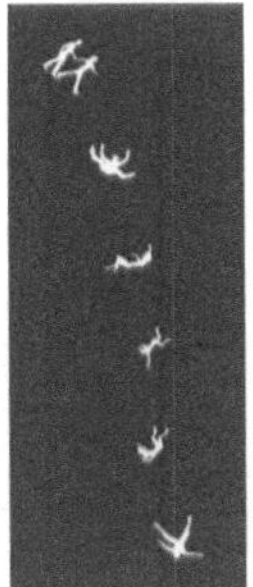

ISA

The paramedics lifted Blake into the ambulance. Isa followed. Two paramedics climbed into the cramped space, and another one closed the doors, then headed to the driver's seat. Isa sat on the bench next to her husband, sandwiched between the two paramedics. A young, solid woman took his vitals. A man who looked more like a boy added another bag to Blake's IV.

Isa felt beyond exhausted. Neither of them had slept properly in more than twenty-four hours. She couldn't remember when she'd last eaten, and wondered if Blake had made the time.

He was shot, she thought. *More than once.* She stared at the ugly mess on her arm, and thought, *I'll have this barcode for the rest of my life.*

The paramedic asked, "Ma'am? Would you please lie on this bench? I'd like to hook you up with some fortifiers."

The noise of the explosion was deafening. The ambulance braked suddenly, causing every loose item in the back to fly forward. Isa screamed and fell over the female paramedic, who knocked the needle out of Blake's vein.

Blake tried to rise. "What happened?"

The man-boy pushed him back. "Sir, you're gravely wounded. Please try not to move."

"Isa? Are you hurt?"

Isa climbed back onto the bench and pressed her fingers over the hole in his arm, to stop the bleeding. The man-boy pushed her gently aside, and applied a bandage over his arm. Then he checked the pressure bandage on Blake's chest. It was already red and damp.

Next, the young man checked on his colleague. She'd bumped her head, and was staring blankly at her surroundings. Blood trickled down her face.

The driver slid open the window between his cabin and the back of the ambulance. "Everybody still breathing?"

"What happened?" Blake asked again, his voice sounding weaker.

"A bomb took out the SWAT vehicle ahead of us. We may have to wait while they check the road for IEDs. I'm sorry."

"Oh, God. Please, can you do something?" Isa asked the man-boy.

"What's wrong, ma'am? Are you hurt?"

"Not me, my husband. He needs surgery. Please!"

"We'll keep him stable, ma'am. But we can't operate in here. I'm sure they'll clear us as quickly as possible."

"It's okay, Isa," said Blake.

"Can't we take another road? They brought me here on a different road. I'm sure we can find it. Please!"

"I'm okay, Isa," said Blake.

Isa caressed Blake's hair.

He kissed her hand, and said, "I'm so sorry you got mixed up in all this."

She stared at him, and started crying. She lowered her eyes. Blake recognized that look. She was ashamed of something. Whatever it was, he was sure she'd tell him. He couldn't possibly be angry with her now. "What is it, love?"

"When I asked Wilmot if he kidnapped me, and sold me, because of my story, he said, 'You really don't know.' I didn't. I still don't know, Blake. And then I saw that English guy…"

"I'll tell you everything about it when we get home."

"When we get *home*." She smiled. Tears rolled down her face and landed on Blake as she kissed his forehead.

"Yes, love."

"Did you get them?"

Blake nodded.

"So, is it over now?"

Blake smiled, then sighed and looked away. When he looked back at Isa, it was hard to hold his smile.

"Don't lie to me."

"It's not over, love. I'm afraid this is only the beginning."

Born in Tomis, **Costi Gurgu** grew up in Bucurcity. He is the author of many acclaimed science fiction short stories and the award winning novel *RecipeArium*.